The Ungovernable series:

Zero Day Threat

Jailbreak

Time Bomb

Insider Threat

Firewall

Trojan Horse

Security Incident

Threat Agent

Attack Path

ATTACK PATH

R.M. OLSON

ISBN-13: 978-1-990142-09-3

To you, my reader.

Thank you for loving this crazy, ridiculous crew as much as I do.

<3 <3 <3

ATTACK PATH:

*The identification of one or more vulnerabilities in a
system that can be exploited by attackers*

1

Jez, day 1, early

Jez was going to die in about five minutes and thirty-seven seconds.

Well, assuming Lev's calculations were correct. But then, they usually were.

Anyways, she was pretty busy at the moment running for her damn life.

The streets were dark, ice and snow making a treacherous surface under her feet, and the flickering artificial streetlights were barely visible through the thick fog.

Even through the fog, though, she could hear the footsteps behind her.

At this point, five minutes and thirty-seven seconds might be generous.

"Jez! Where are you?"

"I'm on my damn way," she muttered into her com. Behind her, the footsteps were getting louder. "They shot down my skybike."

Honestly, that was maybe the thing she resented most about the plaguers chasing her. She'd run halfway across the city at this point, and it felt like halfway across the damn planet.

Thing had been a piece of crap, though—you'd think a skybike would make it through more than a couple heat-blasts.

"Are you being followed?" Tae asked.

"What the hell do you think?" she snapped.

The footsteps behind her were getting closer, and were punctuated now by terse commands and laboured breathing.

She glanced over her shoulder. She could already make out indistinct shapes in the fog.

"There! I see her!" someone shouted.

She turned over her shoulder as she ran, and fired off a shot.

For a moment, the heat from Ysbel's mods lit the fog brightly enough that the alley behind her was cast into a dim cross-hatch of shadows and light.

Damn.

There were a lot of the bastards.

She could feel the adrenalin-grin spreading on her face.

Running had been getting kinda boring anyways.

She rummaged in her pocket, yanking out a small metal sphere.

This should do the trick, probably. Or else she'd die, but hell, if you worried about crap like that, you'd basically never do anything.

She gave the device a quick twist and tossed it over her shoulder, stepping back smartly against the wall and shielding her eyes with one arm.

The alley behind her exploded in a flash of noise and light that jagged across her vision, even through the sleeve of her jacket and with her eyes tightly closed.

She lowered her arm, blinking against the sudden blackness. Her night vision had been blown to hell, but she could hear the angry swearing from the alley behind her.

She braced her hands on her knees for a moment, panting, then straightened, sauntering back towards the noise.

"Where did she go!" an officer shouted.

"I think I saw her!" Jez called helpfully, still slightly breathless. "She threw the damn flash-bang, then took off down that alley!"

"Alright, go!" the officer barked, and the cursing, light-dazed huddle of police started forward, slipping on the uneven cobblestones in the sudden darkness.

Jez jogged after them slowly, letting herself fall towards the back of the group, grinning to herself.

And then, from the front, someone let out a startled curse. "Stop. I have a tracker on her. It says she's—"

There was a moment's pregnant pause.

Damn it.

Jez grabbed the officer beside her, swung him around, and shoved him hard into the small knot of officers who'd just begun to turn towards her. He lost his balance on the icy streets and went down, taking two of his companions with him, and Jez turned and sprinted up the street the way she'd come.

She'd actually been looking forwards to not having to run for five plaguing seconds there.

There was a moment of massed confusion, as the entire squadron of police turned, like a herd of stampeding swamp-oxen brought up short, then they started after her again.

Jez swore under her breath.

She was going in the wrong damn direction now, and they had minutes left at this point.

And, the bastards had tracking on her. Which was going to make things a hell of a lot more difficult.

Her legs were shaking now, her lungs burning. She'd been running for a long damn time, and she wasn't sure how much longer she could keep going.

She hit her com. "Tae," she panted. "Listen. I'm not going to be there in time."

There was a moment's pause. "I know," Tae said grimly. "I've been tracking you. Ysbel and I are on our way. We'll—meet you, somewhere. I'm hooked into your com, so don't worry about sending me coordinates."

She ducked into another alley. Not that that would do any good.

She had seconds before they caught her, with their damn trackers.

Unless …

She paused, a slow grin spreading across her face.

The footsteps and shouts were getting closer, and she waited in the mouth of the alley, her muscles tight with adrenalin, lungs aching as she fought to keep her gasping breaths from giving her away.

The officer with the tracking device would be in the lead, probably.

She'd better be.

The footsteps skidded to a halt outside the alley.

Jez grinned, stepped out from her hiding place, and planted her elbow squarely in the centre of the officer's face.

The woman gasped in pain, staggering backwards, and grabbed blindly for Jez. Jez ducked out of the way and grabbed the woman's wrist, yanking it up behind her back.

"Break your arm if you move," she muttered in the woman's ear.

The woman froze, but something about the tautness of her muscles told Jez she wasn't going to go down without a fight.

Jez fumbled for her heat gun with her free hand.

Three more officers pounded around the corner, pulling up sharply at the scene.

The woman twisted, getting her shoulder under her, and dropped her weight.

Jez let her go, and as she hit the ground, off-balance, she planted her boot on the woman's forearm, aimed, and fired.

The com melted off her wrist.

Jez stooped, grabbed the woman under the arms, and flung her forward at her companions. "Here," she called cheerfully. "Think this is yours."

Then she turned, and took off down the alley.

It only took them a moment to come after her, but by that time, she'd rounded a corner and shoved herself up into an empty doorway.

Without the tracker, and with their night vision long gone, they didn't see a damn thing.

When the last of the officers had run past, she let out a long breath of relief and straightened, kneading the stitch in her side with her knuckles.

She glanced down at her com.

Two minutes and a handful of seconds left now. But as long as Tae and Ysbel got there in time, she should be—

She stopped, something cold forming in the pit of her stomach.

Tae had pushed through a police scanner onto her com before she'd left, and the red dots on the screen showed where the police had gathered. And right now …

She glanced around quickly.

The alley she'd come down was long and narrow. No way out, except the streets on either side.

She could see, on the scanner screen, the group of police she'd fooled, running towards the street in front of her.

And in the street itself, waiting for them—

Well, she wasn't sure how many officers it was, but it was a hell of a lot more than she knew what to do with.

And from the look of the scan, more officers were lining the street behind her, already starting down the alley.

"Be there in about two minutes," Tae hissed through her earpiece. "We're coming in on a skybike."

Jez took a deep breath, adrenalin pounding through her muscles, then glanced down at her com—a battered, beat up piece of crap, honestly, but the information on it was their only chance to keep a hell of a lot of people alive.

She hesitated for a fraction of a second. Already there were footsteps from the alley behind her.

No way out, then. At least, not for her.

But maybe—

She jerked the com from her wrist.

"Tae," she whispered as she knelt. "Don't call me, just get here. Don't want to let them know where I am."

She shoved the com into a narrow crack between two of the buildings, jumped to her feet, and started off down the alley, towards where the police waited in ambush.

Her heart was pounding strangely.

She was going to die.

But hell, she'd guessed that probably five minutes ago.

She paused a moment when she reached the mouth of the alley. From the street ahead of her, she could hear the small sounds, the shuffle of a boot on cobblestone, the brush of coat fabric.

The click of a heat gun being readied.

The footsteps of the officers behind her were getting closer.

She took a deep breath, closing her eyes for just a moment.

Then she grinned.

Hell, if she was going down, she may as well make some noise on the way out.

She snatched out her heat pistol, stepped out into the street, where the line of grim-faced police officers waited for her, and fired it right at the damn face of the plaguer who looked like he was in charge.

The man shouted, stumbling back, and the officers around him jumped like they'd been stung, yanking their weapons up to bear. Heat-blasts seared the air around her, the crackling smell of burnt ozone and overheated prefab stinging her nostrils as she dived to the ground. She hit the concrete and rolled, and came to her feet in a narrow space between two buildings.

Sheltered for the moment, but—

She glanced around quickly.

No way out.

The officers had started towards her, firing steadily, and she could taste the strange tang of overheated air.

And then, from behind her, came a voice she hadn't expected to hear, probably ever again. It was weak, but held the same pleasant, bland calm as it always had.

"Jez?"

She blinked dumbly.

"Masha?" she said at last.

"Jez. Catch."

She reached up on instinct, grabbing whatever it was out of the air.

A mask.

"Put it on, please," came Masha's voice. "And duck."

The heat-blasts were hitting the edges of the buildings on either side of her now, blackening the prefab.

Jez did as she was told.

There was a *tink* of metal hitting concrete, and then another, and then the world went white.

2

Lev, day 1, early

Lev took a deep breath, staring at the holoscreen in front of him so hard his eyes hurt.

He couldn't afford to listen to the sounds through his com.

Jez was out there, right now. But she'd be fine. He had to believe that.

Because if something happened to her—he couldn't handle that, not now, not ever. Even the thought of it shot panic through his brain and cut off his breath.

And there wasn't a bloody thing he could do about it.

He had to focus, or all of them would die.

About three hours and fifty-nine minutes ago, Evka had told them she'd started up the machine that contained her Viernest Protocol— the program she'd been working on for years, the program he'd inadvertently helped her develop when he was a student at the University of Prasvishoni.

The machine took four hours to calibrate. And once it finished— she could kill them with a single keystroke, send a pulse of electricity through the metal they'd breathed in, that had been programmed to congregate in their brainstems, and drop them where they stood.

And there was nothing they could do to stop her.

Well, nothing except this desperate, absurd, slap-dash scheme that just might keep them alive long enough to figure out an actual plan.

If it worked, that is.

"Jez. Hang tight. We'll be there in just a second." Tae's voice floated through the com, words tense and clipped.

Despite himself, Lev glanced down at his own com, checking the time.

Just a minute left.

It was a race against time, but he was almost done. He was almost finished, and then—

Well, and then they'd see if this half-baked, insane parody of a plan would actually work. Or if Evka would have outwitted him again, as easily as she had four hours ago, and yesterday, and the day before that.

A headache pounded behind his eyes. He blinked, eyelids feeling coated in sand, and forced his focus back to the holoscreen.

Just a couple more tweaks, and he'd be finished.

And he'd promised Jez he'd finish this, no matter what happened.

Tae's swearing through his earpiece jerked him out of his reverie. He hit his com, trying to ignore the panic tightening his muscles. "Tae? What—"

"—plaguing, damn, ridiculous, idiotic pilot—" Tae's voice was choked with a mixture of anger and dread.

Lev stared at the com for a moment, suddenly unable to draw in a breath.

"She's bloody gone. She took off her damn com and left it, and I have no idea where she is."

He closed his eyes, feeling like someone had punched him in the stomach.

If she'd left the com, she'd done it on purpose. And she'd known this would be the outcome—that Tae and Ysbel wouldn't be able to find her, wouldn't get there in time to help her.

And that she'd be without any protection when Evka's program finished calibrating. Because Tae's hack could only protect someone who was wearing a com the hack had been pushed through to, or at least was very close to someone who was.

But—he'd told her he trusted her. She'd trusted him.

He'd promised.

"Tae," he said. Somehow, his voice was calm and businesslike. "Get into the system, upload the com signals she brought back. I'll send the modified fix through. Hold tight."

"But—Jez—"

"Tae," he said quietly.

There must have been something in his voice, because Tae fell silent.

Lev turned back to his holoscreen and hit the button. "You should have it now," he said into the com.

"Got it," said Tae, his voice almost inaudible.

"Good. When you upload it, you'll want to check the specs I sent —I went through the equation we came up with, and it should work, but it's got to be exactly calibrated to Evka's system."

There was something cold inside him, but he couldn't stop think about it. Not yet.

Jez would be fine.

Tanya stepped into the room, her expression sharp with concern. "What's happening?"

He shook his head.

"Done." Tae's voice was thick.

He'd promised her. He'd promised Jez, and she trusted him.

He felt like he was watching himself from a long ways away.

"Thank you, Tae." He turned to Tanya, and managed a smile. "Tanya. What do you need?"

Tanya frowned, glancing around the small sickbay, where they'd moved their operations on the off-chance that Masha would have information that could be useful. "Ysbel and Ivan and I are done, everything we can, anyways. I came to check on Masha. Where is she?"

"Masha left, a few minutes ago." His voice was still calm and distant.

Tanya's frown deepened. "She left? How? She was tortured, less than thirty-six hours ago. I'm still not sure if she'll pull through. How did she leave?"

Lev gave a faint shrug, turning back to his com. "She stood up, and she walked out."

Tanya narrowed her eyes. "And you didn't think to stop her?"

"No," he said, without looking up.

Tanya sat down across from him, and from the corner of his eye, he could see the expression on her face. "Lev—" Her voice was dangerous.

He sighed, and this time he did look up, finally meeting her eyes. "Tanya," he said quietly. "We knew, about twenty minutes ago, that Jez might not make it back here. Masha, Tae, Ysbel and I. We all knew."

He paused a moment, because he wasn't sure he could say the next words. But he said them anyways. "I—I could have gone after her. Or Tae could have, or one of the rest of us. But if any of us stopped what we were doing, hundreds of people would die. And so … we didn't. I didn't. And I've been sitting here while the person I love more than anything else in the system was in danger for her life, and there wasn't a single damn thing I could do about it."

He took a deep breath. "Masha left, not too long afterwards. I don't know if she thought she could help, or if she was going to betray us again. But—on the off-chance she was going to try to do something for Jez—" his voice choked. "Do you think I should have stopped her, Tanya?"

Tanya studied him for a moment. "Going out there, the shape she's in—it might kill her."

Lev closed his eyes for a moment, pushing the heels of his hands into his eye sockets, trying to push back the headache. When he opened them again, Tanya was still watching him.

"If she dies to save Jez, that's the very damn least she could possibly do," he said quietly.

He turned quickly back to his holoscreen, because the only thing he could think about right now was the list and sequence of numbers that he was typing in, the logic puzzle he had to solve in order to keep Evka from getting through Tae's hack.

Just a few more seconds. A few more equations, a few more quick tests, and then—

Well, he couldn't afford to think farther than that.

He typed in the final command and glanced at his com.

If his calculations were correct, Evka would have the machine up and running in about five seconds.

Two seconds.

One second.

He held his breath, waiting for the jolt through his brainstem that would kill him.

But nothing happened.

He slumped back into his chair, too numb and weary to feel relief.

Wait until Tae got back. Wait until there was nothing left he needed to do.

Wait until he knew for certain.

"Hey!"

The voice through his earpiece jerked him out of his thoughts. For a moment he stared dumbly at the com on his wrist, his brain refusing to believe what his ears were telling him.

"Did tech-head find my com?"

He was still blinking at his com, not certain whether he was actually dreaming.

"Jez? What the actually hell—" Tae had recovered faster than he had. His tone was frantic.

"It's all good. I'm fine."

"What happened, you idiot? We all thought you were dead!" It was Ysbel this time.

Lev was still staring. His brain seemed to have forgotten how to form words.

"Masha found me. Guess she took a read on my com, and checked the police scanner, and guessed where I'd end up. Stepped out into the middle of a damn firefight, tossed me a mask, and set off one of Ysbel's smoke bombs. And an explosive, which, honestly Ysbel, you need to make me one of those. It was basically beautiful. And then she damn well passed out, and I just barely caught her before she hit the ground. So. If Ysbel can spare a second or two, I wouldn't mind a ride back to the ship."

She was with Masha. Which meant, if she was holding Masha up, Masha's com signal would be protecting both of them.

"Jez—" he managed at last, tapping his com with fingers that trembled so hard he almost couldn't hit the button. "Jez, are you— are you hurt?"

He was aware, distantly, of Tanya watching him, the concern on her face, and some part of his mind wondered how bad he must sound that she looked that worried.

"Genius. I'm OK, I promise."

Lev closed his eyes, his entire body going so shaky that for a moment he thought he might actually pass out.

"Jez—" he began, and then his throat was too tight to speak, and he dropped his head on his arms on the table.

At last, he took a long breath, and straightened.

Tanya was watching him with concern. He gave her a small smile, and turned back to his holoscreen. But it took him a few moments before his brain could make sense of the numbers on the screen again.

He heard them come in a few moments later, and despite the fact that he'd just talked to Jez, and she'd just assured him she was fine, he had to take a deep breath to push back his dizziness.

Jez entered a moment later, Ysbel beside her, supporting an unconscious Masha between them.

"Tanya, help please," said Ysbel through her teeth, and Tanya jumped to her feet and helped them settle the unconscious woman on the cot.

"Ivan, I'll need your help," Tanya called over her shoulder. "Let the children play on their holoscreens, and come."

Lev stood, once he was sure his legs would hold him, and crossed over to Jez.

"Genius," she began, and he saw in her face the strain she'd been under.

He pulled her into his arms, holding her like he'd never let go again.

She leaned into him, and the solid realness of her, the warmth of her pressed up against him, finally steadied his muscles and slowed his racing heart.

"Are you sure you're alright?" he whispered. "You're not—" his voice choked, and he couldn't finish.

She tightened her arms around him. "Told you, genius, I'm good. Masha got there in time. I'm fine."

Tae had come in, and was standing by Masha's cot, next to Ivan. His face was tight with concern, but he glanced up at Lev with a small, strained smile. "Well, shall we call behind the barricades and find out if this worked?"

Lev took a deep breath. "I suppose we'd better," he said quietly. He tapped his com. "Vera? Dmitri? Caz?"

For a moment, there was no answer.

He found he was holding his breath.

And then his com crackled, and both he and Tae jumped.

"Tae." It was Vera's voice. "Whatever it is the lot of you did, it must have worked. We're still alive. The police seem a little surprised, but—" she gave a shaky laugh. "You think after all this time, they'd stop being surprised by what the bunch of you can do."

"Thank the damn Lady. Thank the damn Lady and the Consort and all the bloody saints," breathed Tae. His entire posture was slumped with relief.

Lev felt a shaky smile spreading across his own face. "We did it," he said, turning to Jez, his voice soft with awed disbelief.

Jez grinned at him. Then she slid her hand around his neck and pulled his lips to hers, and he suddenly found he didn't have a single spark of attention left for anything else.

By the time they drew apart, his legs were shaky for an entirely different reason than they had been a few minutes before. He took a deep breath and ran a hand through Jez's tangled hair, following the line of her cheek with his thumb. She closed her eyes, leaning into his hand with a blissful smile, and he almost pulled her back into another kiss.

And then he remembered where they were and what they were doing.

He sighed reluctantly and turned back to the others, tucking his arm around Jez's waist.

He wasn't quite certain he was ready to let go of her just yet.

"I hate to interrupt," Tae said, "but we aren't finished yet. Jez, how many com signals were you able to get?"

Jez had blinked her eyes back open, but she was wearing a distinctly dreamy smile.

"Jez?" Tae's voice was tinged with exasperation.

She let out a long sigh and blinked. "Mmm?"

"Com signals," Ysbel prompted, sounding amused.

Jez rolled her eyes. "Yeah. Caz and Peti got everyone's signal from behind the barricade, and Dmitri and Vera were able to get through to a few of the other apartment complexes as well, that the police had marked down as insurgents. And Matija went out behind the barricade and through the shantytown, and picked up com signals all through there as well. They said they got the places the police were cracking down the hardest, anyways. So—" she shrugged. "Not all that good at math, but I'd say we have more than a thousand signals on there."

Lev closed his eyes for a moment in relief.

It was better than he'd thought, honestly.

"Alright," he said. "Tae's program should push a blocker field around all the com signals we've sent it through to, which means a blocker field around the person wearing the com. It wouldn't be enough to stop Evka from killing us, but it's enough to stop the signals she'd use to find and identify us from getting through. So.

Everyone's survived the night—that's step one. But it's not going to last.

"I'm sure the police and military have rescinded their surrender by now. The people in the apartment blocks and the shantytown should be safe enough—if Evka can't track them with the Protocol, she'll have no real way to find them. But it's not going to be hard finding people behind a massive set of barricades, and we haven't exactly been inconspicuous these last few weeks. Once Evka realizes she can't kill them with her Protocol, it won't take her long to realize that ion cannons will be just about as effective. So, step two is getting everyone somewhere Evka can't just shoot them down."

"Good," said Ysbel. "So we get everyone somewhere safe. And step three?"

He smiled grimly, pulling Jez a little closer. "Step three? We figure out how to bloody well take Evka down."

There was a moment of silence.

Ysbel raised an eyebrow. "I see. That's the plan?"

Jez shifted in Lev's arms, glancing around at the others with a dangerous grin. "Sounds like a pretty decent plan to me," she drawled. "Way I figure it, we're all supposed to be dead right now. We were supposed to be dead about sixty seconds after I dropped my com back in the damn alley. If we die five minutes from now, that's still five minutes more than that bastard Evka wanted to give us." Her grin grew wider. "So. Maybe we die. But we're damn well going out with a bang. And we're damn well bringing that plaguing scum-sucker Evka with us. Because hell—at this point, what have we got to lose?"

3

Ysbel, day 1, early

"I—think I may have something, Professor." Dmitri's voice over the com was grim.

"Yes?" Ysbel asked sharply.

The others were watching her, faces tense. They'd moved from the *Ungovernable's* sick bay to the conference room—the shape Masha was in, there was slim chance she'd wake up in time to contribute, and less chance still that she'd be coherent enough to talk if she did.

They were running on borrowed time, and they all knew it. Once Evka sent in the military to surround the barricades, getting the ragged, exhausted band of insurgents out would be next to impossible.

"One of the undersecretaries my mother works with is over infrastructure in the warehouse district. There's an old warehouse that was recently scheduled to be demolished. I … think it's still there. It's big enough to fit all of us, and it's set back in the smaller streets, over by the university."

"Good," she said. "That makes defending ourselves easier, if it comes to it."

"And would anyone be able to trace it to you or your parents?"

asked Lev.

They'd discussed this earlier—Masha had more than enough apartments, vacant hangar bays, and various other safe-houses to shelter half the city. But there was always the chance, no matter how careful Masha had been, that Evka would be able to trace them to her, and from there, track them down.

And if Evka found them, they'd die.

"I don't think so," said Dmitri. "It's not my mother's ministry, so there shouldn't be any traceable connection.

"What about supplies?" Ysbel asked.

"We still have some left from Lev's negotiation," said Vera. "We'll bring what we can carry."

Ysbel took a deep breath.

They didn't have time to be picky. And this sounded like their best option so far.

"Alright," she said. "Dmitri, send the coordinates through, and we'll meet you there. You'll have to get everyone out, and you may have to split up—we can't afford to attract attention."

"We've got it, Professor," said Vera. "Turns out Lev's parents are very good at organizing things. They've already got everyone split into groups, and the supplies being packed."

"Get out as soon as you can," said Tae, worry clear in his voice. "And be careful."

"We will," said Vera. "You too."

The com clicked off, and they looked at each other for a few moments.

"Well, I guess we should take our own advice," said Lev, pushing himself to his feet. "It won't take Evka long to track where our com signals came from last night, while we were talking with her. I'd rather not be here when she stops by to show her appreciation."

He still hadn't let go of Jez, and Ysbel was beginning to wonder if he ever would.

She couldn't exactly blame him. She could still remember the jolt of panic when she and Tae had arrived at Jez's com signal to find the com there, and Jez missing.

"We'll have to carry Masha," said Ivan, looking down at the unconscious woman on the cot with concern.

Lev glanced over, the tension in his face that came every time any of them mentioned Masha. "We'll rig up a stretcher," he said shortly.

"Tae and I'll take care of that," said Ivan. "And Tanya, if you have a moment."

Tanya nodded.

Jez sighed, and with obvious reluctance, detached herself from Lev. "Guess I'd better go too, mess with the wiring so I can set the cloaking on my sweet angel while she's waiting in the hangar bay. Hate for that bastard Evka to stumble across her while she's looking for us."

"I guess, Lev, that leaves you and me to get whatever supplies we're bringing and deal with the children," said Ysbel dryly. "I hope you're prepared for this."

There wasn't much to bring—within fifteen standard minutes, they were gathered at the door to the hangar bay.

Tae, Ivan, and Tanya had rigged a makeshift stretcher onto anti-gravs to carry Masha, but the woman was still unconscious.

Ysbel shook her head. Honestly, it was probably for the best. Ysbel still wasn't certain how Masha had managed to drag herself out of the hangar bay and through the streets to save Jez—she must have been running on sheer willpower.

She still wasn't sure how she felt about Masha—but it seemed the woman could still surprise her, after all this time.

"Are you ready?" Ysbel asked, drawing her pistol. Olya snuggled her head deeper into Ysbel's shoulder, and Ysbel shifted her grip, holding her daughter tight.

Tanya carried Misko, and Ivan and Tae were each supporting a side of the makeshift stretcher.

"Figure we're ready as we're going to be," Jez drawled. She had her heat pistol in one hand, and her other arm around Lev's waist.

"Let's go, then," said Ysbel.

The streets were eerily quiet as they stepped out into the dark of the early morning.

Ysbel hadn't been sure what to expect—a few hours ago, the streets were filled with jubilant people spilling out of their apartments after far too long under heavy curfew. But everything had changed in those few hours. They'd heard, as they worked through the night, the announcements over the general lines.

Evka, explaining the purpose and function of the Viernest Protocol. Rescinding the surrender of the police and military. Delineating the consequences of disobeying an order.

Now, the silence was unsettling, and Ysbel found herself glancing over her shoulder more than once as they made their cautious way through the darkened streets.

The cold and the damp seeped through their jacket, making Olya shiver and cling more tightly to Ysbel's coat.

"We'll be there soon, my love," she whispered.

Their footsteps tapped dully off the concrete, the sound swallowed up almost instantly in the fog, and overhead the streetlamps flickered and guttered, their low, incessant buzz a constant background irritation.

Beside her, Jez tensed.

Ysbel froze, and for a moment they stood still, listening. Then Jez shook her head, and they started forward again.

Ysbel glanced around her uneasily. It would be next to impossible to see or hear anything in this smothering, choking mist.

"How soon, mama?" Olya whispered.

"Just a few more minutes." Ysbel glanced down at the coordinates on her com. Unease tingled in the back of her brain and crawled up her spine, but there was nothing she could see to cause it.

And then, from ahead of them, came a muffled shout, quickly choked off. She and Jez exchanged glances, and crept forward to peer cautiously around the corner of the narrow street.

Three officers stood halfway down the cross-street, back to back, postures tense. A handful of desperate, ragged people faced them, makeshift weapons loose in their hands.

A moment later, Ysbel saw why—another figure lay sprawled on the ground, and even through the mist she could see the sharp red stain of blood on the dirty street.

"Stay back," one of the officers snapped.

Ysbel snorted in disgust.

The same officers who'd surrendered hours before, given up their weapons in return for a pledge of safety from the revolutionaries.

Of course, all that had been forgotten the moment the Protocol had come into effect.

"You murderers," shouted one of the attackers, her voice choked in despair. "That's my son. How can you—"

Beside Ysbel, Jez had her pistol ready. "Figure I can take two of them if you take the other," she whispered. "You ready?"

The woman in the street lunged forward, a block of broken prefab in her fist.

The officer who'd spoken glanced down at his com and tapped a command.

The woman dropped, like a puppet whose strings had been cut.

For a moment, the others stared, as if unsure what had just happened.

The officer glanced up, his eyes fixing on a tall young man, body still showing the lanky awkwardness of youth.

He tapped his com again.

The youth crumpled.

The officer tapped his com twice more, and the two remaining figures collapsed, lying in the street like heaps of discarded rags.

Ysbel bit down hard on her teeth to hold back the vomit rising in her throat, and pushed Olya's face against her shoulder, hoping the girl hadn't seen. A cold horror was spreading through her muscles.

In the street, the officers were still for a long moment. At last, one of them stepped to the crumpled forms and bent over them.

"They're dead," she said shortly a moment later, looking up from the bodies. There was a hint of unease in her voice. "Just like that. All dead."

The officer in charge shrugged. "It's called the Viernest Protocol for a reason. And it's better than the streets being in chaos, like they have been the last few weeks."

The officer kneeling by the bodies got slowly to her feet, brushing dirt and snow from her knees as she stood. "I'm just saying, I'm not sure I like it."

"You don't have to like it," snapped her superior, but Ysbel could hear the unease even in his tone. "We use the tools we're given. Would you have preferred to cook their insides with a heat-blast?"

The other officer met his eye for a moment, then dropped her head.

"Let's go," the man said, turning. The other officers followed him down the street, disappearing into the fog.

The crumpled bodies lay where they'd fallen, dark shapes in the mist.

"Those damn, plaguing bastards," Jez whispered, her voice choking. "Those damn, damn, plaguing—" she broke off abruptly.

Ysbel glanced over.

Jez was clutching her heat pistol so tightly it was a wonder it hadn't snapped in two.

"We couldn't have done anything," Ysbel said quietly, even though her mouth tasted of bile. "There's no way we would have been fast enough. They were dead before they hit the ground." She turned away from the gruesome scene, with a quick jerk of her head in the direction opposite the one the officers had taken, and they set off again.

When they turned at last down the twisting, winding streets that marked the north-east corner of the warehouse district, Ysbel could feel the tension easing from her shoulders.

Almost there.

A small breeze whispered through the streets as they turned down the street that would lead them to their destination, clearing away the mist as it went.

Ysbel came to a sudden, sharp halt.

They were face to face with a dozen grim-faced officers.

Who did not look happy to see them.

There was a moment of shocked silence. Then an officer grabbed Jez by the arm. "What are you doing in the streets? Didn't you hear about the curfew?"

"Oh, don't worry, heard all about it," Jez drawled, but there was something sharp and angry in her voice, and Ysbel didn't need to see her face to know the expression on it. "Thing is, figured someone ought to take care of this captain bastard who seemed to have got the hell beat out of her by those damn revolutionaries. Seeing as she called in for help and all." She gestured at Masha.

The officer's eyebrows drew together. "She doesn't look like a captain," he began.

Jez shrugged. "After what happened yesterday, you blame her? Just saying, good thing she managed to get a call out before anything worse happened."

"You—so you're military?"

Jez raised an eyebrow. "Who else would she call? Bunch of damn revolutionaries, maybe?"

The man's frown deepened. "What was the name of the captain, again?"

"Not like she had a lot of time to chat," said Jez cheerfully.

"Your division, soldier?"

Ysbel sighed and tightened her grip on her pistol. Behind her, she could sense Tanya moving around to get into a better position.

Jez was still grinning. "You expect me to remember crap like that?"

To be honest, it was probably a good thing for everyone involved that Jez had never dreamed of a career in the military. It probably wouldn't have ended any better than this interaction was going to.

The man tightened his grip on Jez's arm, lifted his com, and tapped a quick command.

Jez grinned, and raised her eyebrows innocently.

He tapped it again.

Jez yanked her arm out of his grip and punched him, hard, in the stomach.

He doubled over, and she swung her heat pistol. There was a hollow *thunk* as it connected with his skull, and he staggered sideways.

"You should pay more attention, you bastard," said Jez, grim satisfaction in her voice. "Never know when someone's gonna try to get the jump on you while you're fiddling with your damn com."

The other officers blinked in shock for a moment, and two of them started for Jez.

They never reached her. Ysbel clutched Olya tighter in one arm, and with her other, grabbed one by the back of the collar and yanked him down to the ground, helping him along with a kick to the ribs. Lev stepped forward at the same time, and a moment later, the other officer was lying in the street. Ysbel hadn't seen what Lev had done to him, but judging by the calculating look on Lev's face, it was probably just as well.

Jez had already waded into the fight, her heat pistol out and a huge grin on her face.

A heat-blast scorched the air beside Ysbel's face, and she grabbed another of the officers, dragging him around in front of her as a shield as three more blasts, aimed for her, slammed into him.

She shoved him away, and, twisting her body to protect Olya, stepped forward, grabbing the gun arm of the officer nearest her. She gave a quick twist, and he screamed, the pistol falling to the ground as he cradled his broken arm.

Another officer turned to her, and this time, Ysbel grabbed the woman's heat pistol, flipped it neatly in her hand, and smashed the butt of it into the officer's face.

The woman staggered back, blood streaming from her nose—

And then she dropped, and behind her, Tanya straightened.

"I think that's all, my love," said Tanya.

She was still holding Misko, settled firmly on her hip, and Ysbel smiled at her.

Lady and Consort, she loved this woman.

"Sorry, think one of the bastards got a call out," panted Jez from behind them. There was a cut under one eye from a glancing blow, but she was still wearing that sharp, dangerous grin. "This was fun and all, but we should probably get the hell out of here before reinforcements show up."

"Come on, you lunatic," Ysbel grumbled. "Let's go."

They started for the building coordinates at a run, the stretcher bumping awkwardly between Tae and Ivan as they went.

Even so, by the time they pulled to a panting halt in front of a tumble-down warehouse at the end of a narrow alley, Ysbel could hear sirens and skybikes in the distance.

"Dmitri?" panted Tae through the com.

There was a moment's silence, then Dmitri's worried voice. "Tae? Is that you? Are you here?"

"If you don't let us in soon, there won't be much of Tae or any of the rest of us left," snapped Ysbel.

"Sorry, Professor. Give me a second."

Ysbel glanced over her shoulder as they waited. Jez was pacing back and forth along the narrow alley, movements quick and restless.

Then the thick door swung open, and Dmitri beckoned them frantically inside.

They slipped through the door, and Dmitri slammed it shut behind them, shoving a heavy manual lock into place as police sirens wailed in the distance.

Ysbel looked around quickly to make sure everyone had made it in.

They had.

She leaned against the wall, closing her eyes in relief.

She hadn't realized until now just how exhausted she was.

An artificial light flickered on, illuminating the narrow corridor they were standing in. "Professor?" Dmitri asked, sounding worried. "Professor, are you alright?"

She straightened with an effort, and looked around at the others.

They looked as tired as she felt. Jez, now that she wasn't kissing anyone, fighting anyone, or running from anything, looked about ready to drop where she stood.

"We're fine," said Ysbel with a small smile. "And you? Did all of you make it in?"

"We're all here." It was Vera, who'd apparently come to find them as well.

"Tae?" came Peti's anxious voice, and she appeared in the hallway behind Vera.

"Hey, Peti," said Tae wearily.

Lev lifted his head, blinking back his obvious exhaustion. "Alright," he began, words slurring with weariness. "We need to figure out what—"

"No."

Ysbel looked up, and had to bite back a smile.

A tall woman, with the broad shoulders and strong build of someone used to heavy labour, stood at the end of the hallway. She was looking at Lev with that mixture of fondness and worry and exasperation that was, Ysbel assumed, shared by mothers everywhere.

"We're safe for the moment. Your father and I are getting everyone organized. And you, son, and the rest of your crew, are going to bed, before we have to pick you up off the floor and carry you there."

Lev blinked at her stupidly for a moment, then, at last, he managed a smile. "I suppose I can't argue with that," he said.

Ysbel glanced down at Olya, already asleep, her body drooping in

Ysbel's arms, then up at Tanya, who'd come to stand beside her, a sleeping Misko in her arms.

No matter how desperate their situation, she couldn't exactly argue the point either.

4

Tae, day 1, late

The remnants of the late afternoon sun filtered in through the windows of the old warehouse. Tae looked around, blinking, his head still heavy and dull from exhaustion.

However long he'd slept, it hadn't been enough.

He was starting to wonder if it would ever be enough.

The small group of them had gathered in a room that looked like it had once been used as a break-room. The crew was there, except for Masha, who was still unconscious, and Ivan and Tanya, who were caring for her—but also Vera and Dimitri, Caz and Peti, Felix, Matija, and a few of the other street-kid gang leaders. Just like they had so often before over the past few weeks.

Like he'd hoped they wouldn't have to, anymore, when it had looked like they were on the verge of winning yesterday.

A few broken chairs were propped against a mouldering table in the centre of the room, but after one look at it, they'd all opted for sitting on the floor. The fading light from the Prasvishoni afternoon seeped through the high, narrow windows, its dull orange contrasting with the fitful, whitish-blue glow of the artificial lights overhead.

"So," said Lev. "Since we all seem to be still alive, I guess now we discuss how we're going to stay that way. Tae, how long do we have to come up with a plan?"

He didn't look much more awake than Tae felt, his eyes puffy with sleep and his hair flattened on one side. He still had his arm around Jez, as if he hadn't actually let go of her for even a moment at any point between the time she'd returned to the hangar bay and now.

Maybe he hadn't.

Tae shook his head. "I'm—sorry," he said, his voice cracking slightly with sleep. "We won't have long. With the resources Evka would have, I'd give it a week at the outside for her to get through our hack. And that's only if the police or the military don't find us here first."

Jez turned to him with a grin. "You always this cheerful, techhead? Or just when you've finally gotten some sleep?"

He glared at her.

"Well, I've been looking at how easy this place would be to defend, if they do find us," grunted Ysbel. "Considering the options we had, this is probably the best we could ask for. But it's still not good. There are only a couple of entrances, and the narrow streets mean it would be hard for them to come at it with any sort of force. But that also means it would be hard for us to get anyone out. If they find us, we'll be trapped."

"So, sitting here until Evka finishes us off isn't a good option. Got it," said Vera, with a small, tired grin.

Lev sighed and shook his head. "Evka isn't going to stop until she kills us. You … have no idea how much she hates people who get in her way. And I suspect there are several people in both the police and military who feel the same way, not to mention government ministers. A week is the very longest we can expect this to last."

Felix snorted in disgust. "So you're trying to break it to us gently that you don't have a damn plan, so we're all going to die anyways."

Tae glanced over at the kid.

He was glaring at Lev, his wiry body as tense as he'd ever been waiting on the barricades for police. But Tae could see the hopelessness under the anger on his face.

He closed his eyes for a moment.

Damn it to hell.

The problem was, the kid was right. They needed more time. But more than that, he needed to get these kids somewhere safe in case they didn't figure out a plan in time.

"Lev," he said. "You know Evka better than any of us. What will she do when she gets through my hack? Kill us all at once?"

Lev shook his head slowly. "I—don't think so. At least, not necessarily. There are probably students here whose parents she wouldn't want to offend. And either way, she'll want legitimacy, at least at first. Students dying in a firefight behind the barricades? She can't be blamed for that. But students falling dead in an abandoned warehouse, where they've fled for their lives? That might look a bit too ugly, even for her. I'd guess she'd start with the people whose deaths will cause her the least political headache, but will give her the personal satisfaction of having dealt with the problem."

Tae nodded grimly. "The street kids, then."

Lev's expression told him he was correct.

"And the students she can paint as ringleaders, as well, I'd imagine," said Ysbel quietly. "No one would blame her for that, I think."

Tae glanced involuntarily at Dmitri and Vera.

Their faces were grave, but neither of them looked surprised. They'd known they'd been marked for death for some time now.

But he'd be damned if he'd let them die without a fight.

He shook his head. "And this Protocol. We know she's spread it through the city. And we know she wants to spread it through the whole system. But for now—how powerful will it be outside the city?"

Lev frowned at him for a moment, then his eyes lit with sudden understanding. "That's—not a bad idea," he said slowly. "She'll be fully focused on the city for a while—she'll have to be, until she gets the bugs worked out. I doubt she'd have time to go looking for people outside the city boundaries. If she's even set her program to pick up signals beyond the force-field, which she may not have, yet." He shook his head. "If we're exceptionally lucky, it's possible. The Protocol is in its beginning stages. It will take a few days for the powers that be to fully comprehend the situation, and until then, Evka's position won't be firmly entrenched. And I know of a handful of city exits that shouldn't be blocked off, at least not until Evka gets a firm enough hold on power to have the attention to spare for it. We wouldn't be able to take the *Ungovernable* or anything—that would be far too obvious, and we'd need specialized gate codes to get a ship through. But on foot?" He shrugged. "It's just possible."

Tae nodded grimly. "And if we get the people who she wants to kill out of the way, it will be that much easier for the others to get away—blend in, go back to their families."

"And maybe not just them," said Lev slowly. He looked up. "Tae. If we get enough people out of the city—Evka's going to assume we must have gotten away as well. If she's looking for us somewhere else, that might give us a few days longer to think of a solution."

Tae stared at Lev for a moment, then felt a small, relieved smile tugging at his lips.

If they could buy themselves more time, and at the same time get

Dmitri and Vera and the street kids somewhere safe—

The thought was an almost dizzying relief.

Dmitri was looking between Lev and Tae. "What are you suggesting?"

Tae took a deep breath. "We're getting you out," he said bluntly. "All of you who will be on Evka's target list. Outside the city, then as far away and remote as we can—some settlement around the swamp mines, possibly, or a rural dirt-eater settlement out on the outskirts. Anywhere Evka might not think to look. It's still a risk—she could still come after you once she gets the Protocol running how she wants it to. But—" he sighed. "It's better than sitting here waiting for her to kill us."

There was silence for a long moment.

There was a stunned look on Dmitri's face, and it was echoed on the faces of the others.

Tae's euphoria faded.

It was one thing for him and the rest of the crew to talk. But these students and street kids—their lives were here, in Prasvishoni, their friends, their family, their homes, if they had them.

And they'd already given up so much.

Slowly, Vera nodded. "If—Tae, if you think that's the best plan —"

Felix shoved himself to his feet. He was scowling. "You want me to take my kids out into a damn swamp mine?" he snapped. "How the hell do you expect us to survive out there? We don't know how to find damn fruits and berries, or whatever they hell the damn swamps miners survive off, and I'm not taking my kids out to starve."

"Hey, you skinny bastard," said Jez, with a tired grin. "Figure you're so ugly all you'd have to do is look at a swamp-ox, and the damn thing would keel over. All the food you could eat."

Felix turned to glower at her. "This all a joke to you, you plaguing pilot?"

Jez's grin faded, leaving only weariness. "Listen," she said quietly. "Just about got my damn face cooked this morning trying to get your com signatures back to tech-head here. And I get it—I wouldn't want to go to the damn swamp mines either. But you want to stay in the city—well, you don't know that bastard Evka. She got the police to kidnap street kids, used them to test her Protocol. And now that it's working, if you think she's not gonna use it to kill every last damn street kid in Prasvishoni, you're a hell of a lot more innocent than I figured you were."

Felix glared at her, then, reluctantly, he turned to Tae. "She right?"

Tae sighed. Why the hell did everyone think he had all the answers?

If Ivan was here, something about the calm, soothing comfort of his presence, the concern in his face and the steadiness in his voice, would make all of this so much easier.

But they were all working with their backs to the wall right now, and none of them had the luxury of making choices based off what they wanted.

"She's right," he said, shaking his head. "I'm sending Caz and Peti out too. If I didn't think it was the only way—"

Felix was watching him, suspicion in his gaze, but at last he gave a short nod. "Fine," he said, his voice low. "Fine, I'll take my kids and watch them damn well starve to death in the swamps, because at least that will take longer than letting them be killed in the streets." He was scowling, but Tae could see the worry and fear behind his sullen expression.

He couldn't blame him.

"Don't know when I got stupid enough to start trusting you plaguers," Felix muttered, dropping back into his seat. "Probably gonna damn well regret it."

Peti turned to Tae. "Wait," she said. "You said you'd be sending Caz and me. But you—you're coming, right?"

Tae glanced at Lev.

Lev met his gaze.

Jez was grinning like an idiot, and Ysbel was wearing a resigned look.

"Tae?" asked Dmitri. He sounded suddenly worried.

Tae sighed. "We're staying," he said quietly. "We'll get you out, but we're staying here."

"I mean, hell, you think Evka's mad at you?" drawled Jez. "After what we did to her damn Protocol the first time around, bet she'd basically sell her grandmother for a chance to kill us. So, not like we have anything to lose."

"So what, then? You're just going to wait here to die?" Vera's tone was worried as well.

"Bet Evka wishes we were," said Jez, winking at her.

Tae shook his head grimly. "No. We're going to get you out. And then we're going to come back here, and we're going to figure out how to take Evka down."

Somehow. But he could worry about that when the others were safe.

Dmitri and Vera and all the street kids were staring at him now.

"I thought you said that was impossible," said Dmitri, at last.

Tae shrugged. "Maybe it is. But we've done impossible things before."

"Tae. I'm not going to be able to talk you out of this, am I?" asked Caz.

Tae shook his head.

Caz took a deep breath. "Then I guess we'd better start getting everything ready."

"Yes," said Lev grimly. "Get everything you need. We're getting you out tonight, as soon as it's dark. Otherwise, we may not get you out at all."

5

Jez, day 1, late

The night was dark, and the fog hung low along the dirty streets like some malevolent supernatural presence, crawling through the alleys, gathering in empty doorways and rotting windowsills.

Jez grinned to herself.

Surprising, really, how much better a few hours of actual sleep and the prospect of something to do could make you feel.

And yes, she knew how much it bothered Tae and Lev not to have some stupid long-term plan, but hell, that was basically her entire life.

She glanced over at Lev, standing next to her.

He was looking ahead, his face grim.

She sighed deeply.

Honestly, of all the reasons she had to hate Evka, and there were a hell of a lot, the fact that once again she was back in a position where it was next to impossible to get genius into a room alone might be the very top of her list.

She glanced quickly behind her at the group of ragged, quiet figures huddled outside the entrance to the warehouse, dark silhouettes against the dark of the night.

Something twisted in her chest.

Damn street kids. Couldn't catch a damn break around this place.

OK, maybe the Lev thing was only the second-highest reason on her list.

But they were damn well getting these kids, and the damn students, out of the city tonight, or they'd die trying.

Tae appeared out of the gloom beside them. His face was just as grim as Lev's, tension humming in his posture.

They'd decided, much to Lev's chagrin, that their best chance of pulling this off was for the whole crew to come along—well, except Masha, who had regained consciousness for the first time a couple hours back. She probably wouldn't be much help just yet.

But as far as the rest of them—well, at this point, just getting their friends out of the city gate in one piece would take probably every last one of their skill sets, and maybe more.

"Is everyone ready, Tae?" asked Lev.

Tae nodded, strain in his expression. "As ready as we will be, I think." He blew out a quick breath. "There's going to be twenty-five people, not counting us. I don't know how we'll avoid attracting attention."

Jez winked at him. "Here's the thing, though," she said. "If we do attract attention, figure we won't attract nearly as much attention as the damn explosives Ysbel's carrying."

Tae turned to scowl at her reflexively, and she grinned.

"She's right," said Ysbel, her heavy outer rim accent even thicker than normal.

"At some point, they're going to catch on that every time there's an explosion in the street, it means we're trying to get past them somewhere else," Tae muttered.

Ysbel raised an eyebrow. "Oh, I'm certain they will. But let's hope it's not tonight." She paused a moment. "Besides, even if they do, when their options are, pay attention to where Tanya put the explosives, or decorate the walls for three blocks around, they'll probably pay attention anyways."

Tae turned away, muttering something about not even wanting to ask.

Jez winked at Ysbel. "I ever tell you—"

"Yes. You have," said Ysbel in a flat voice. "Did I ever tell you I'm married?"

Jez shrugged, still grinning. "Might have mentioned it once or twice."

"Let's go, then," said Lev. "We need to have them out of the city and be back before it gets light. We can't risk someone following us back here. And—" he paused for a moment, then shook his head. "I don't know that we'll get another chance to get them out. I've underestimated Evka before."

Tae nodded, and slipped back to where the street kids and students waited with the rest of the crew.

Jez winked at Lev, her heat pistol ready in her hand. He grinned back reluctantly, and they started forward.

The fog muffled her footsteps, quieting their breath so that she could hardly hear Lev walking beside her, and adrenalin pumped through her veins like a damn drug. She could hear the students and the street kids behind them—the quiet breathing, the occasional scuff of a shoe or boot on the icy cobblestones—but they were being impressively quiet, all things considered.

It was almost impossible to make out where you were in this kind of fog. Jez knew this part of the city though, and she could tell from the siding on the buildings that they were heading towards the port docks.

Even under siege, Prasvishoni did a brisk trade in smuggled goods. Genius was right—if there was one place in the city that would be open, it was there.

She squinted, trying to see more than a half a meter ahead. And then a dark shape loomed up in front of her, and she bit back a startled curse.

"Who's there?" The deep, gruff voice sounded almost as startled as she felt.

"I could ask you the same damn thing," she called back, trying to inject a note of arrogance into her tone. "There's a damn curfew, in case you hadn't heard."

"I'm patrolling for curfew breakers," the man snapped. "Morozov, 47th company. Identify yourself."

Lev sighed, raised an eyebrow at her, and tapped his own com. "Of course. I'm Vasilyev, out of Precinct 549, my colleague is Radkova. Captain Danika asked us to control this area. Said she'd heard rumours of troublemakers."

The soldier grunted in response. "They'd have to be pretty damn stupid to break curfew since this Protocol thing was put in place. I've seen what it can do."

Lev chuckled ruefully. "I don't disagree. But you know what they say, there's plenty of stupid in every crowd."

The soldier gave a small snort of laughter. "That's the truth." He paused a moment. "What do you think of those idiots behind the barricades? Somehow spoofed the Protocol, I hear. They say they're working on getting it fixed."

"Oh, I'm certain they will," said Lev, a wry note to his voice. "I've heard the person in charge of the program is exceptionally intelligent."

"Maybe so," said the soldier, his voice going a little quieter. "But

I'll be honest, the thing makes me nervous. Never seen something like it."

"I don't know that any of us have," said Lev softly.

There was a moment of silence. Finally, Lev said, "Where are you patrolling? We'll stay out of your way so we're not duplicating effort."

"We're patrolling from Skruchini Street to Reba Street," the man said. He paused a moment. "Which sector did you say Captain Danika asked you to watch?"

"I wish she'd been that specific," said Lev wryly. "She said, and I quote, 'over in the port end of town. Keep your eyes peeled, and go wherever there's trouble.'" He gave a small chuckle. "I'm not sure we'd see trouble on a night like this if it walked up and spat in our faces."

The soldier chuckled as well. "Well, it's been a quiet night so far. Better than last night, at least." He paused a moment, his voice going quiet. "Did you hear how many civilians they killed last night? When Evka, or whatever her name is, announced the Protocol on the general lines, I think half the city didn't believe it." He sighed uneasily. "I'll tell you, I don't like losing a fight any more than the next person. But—strikes me as off when you negotiate a surrender, and the other side acts in good faith, and then you turn around and spit on it. But then, not sure what else we could have done. Something like this Protocol—you're either the one enforcing it, or you're the ones its being enforced on. And as between the two—" He trailed off.

"I—don't disagree," said Lev quietly.

"Go on, then," said the soldier, at last. "You keep looking for trouble by the docks, and we'll keep looking for it in the streets." He paused a moment. "And we'll pray to the Lady that neither of us finds it."

The muffled sounds of his footsteps moving off into the darkness, quickly swallowed up by the dank mist.

Jez grinned in relief. "Not bad, genius. Almost thought you were military myself for a minute there."

He gave her a small smile as they turned back down the street towards the docks.

They hadn't made it more than a few metres when they heard the same gruff voice give a sharp exclamation. "You! Vasilyev! How big is your company? Because there's a hell of a lot more than a dozen people back here. And they don't look like soldiers to me."

Lev's hand tightened on Jez's, but his voice was completely calm. "We've got some undercover officers who with us. They're—"

The man who'd called himself Morozov cursed. "This one looks like a damn street kid. You're not—" he broke off at the sputtering hiss of a heat-blast, grunting in pain.

"Go! Get the others out of here, I'll deal with this," Jez whispered, shoving Lev ahead. She turned back towards the sound.

She couldn't make out faces in the dirty fog, but she was damn sure she recognized the skinny kid with a heat pistol in their hand, standing over the soldier. One of Felix's, probably that bastard Nadia. Not that she could blame the girl. Hell, if a soldier had tried to grab her, she probably would've done the same thing.

But the soldier would have a heat shield for sure. As soon as he got his bearings, he'd kill the kid.

She sprinted back towards Nadia as the soldier struggled to his feet. "Come on!" she hissed, grabbing the girl by the arm and shoving her down the street after Lev and the others. Then she spun back towards the soldier. He'd rolled heavily to his feet, and he was fumbling for his com.

"Wouldn't do that if I were you," Jez whispered, stepping in close.

He looked up, startled, and she swung her elbow, hitting him right in the middle of the damn face. He staggered back, swearing, and then she'd yanked out her own heat pistol. He howled as she pulled the trigger, whether from the shot itself, or from the fact she'd melted the damn com off his wrist, she wasn't quite sure.

After the last two weeks behind barricades, she didn't honestly care.

There were running feet in the alley behind the soldier, and she felt an adrenalin-grin spreading across her face.

Damn bastard must've got a call out after all.

She could run, but—she could still hear, through the mist behind her, Tae's frantic whispers, Ivan's voice, low and urgent.

They needed time to get the kids away. And she'd damn well give it to them.

Five more soldiers appeared out of the mist in front of her, heat pistols drawn.

"You plaguers always come late to a party?" Jez drawled, and snapped off three shots in their direction.

Behind her, the noise of whispers and running feet were almost swallowed up by the mist, but not quite, and she could still hear the kids.

The soldiers stared at her for a moment, and one of them went for their com. Which honestly would've been kind of funny to watch, but she wasn't quite ready to let them know she was off Evka's system.

She melted his com before he had time to do much more than a preliminary scan.

And then, apparently, his companions decided a heat gun would kill her just as fast as the Protocol.

She dived to the ground as heat-blasts lit the air around her.

"Come on," said a voice with a heavy outer rim accent, and Tanya grabbed her by the jacket and yanked her backwards as another volley of shots blackened the concrete where she'd been.

"The others out?" Jez hissed through her teeth as they ran.

"If they're not, they'd better learn to hurry," whispered Tanya wryly. She hardly seemed winded. Honestly, Jez had spent enough time around Misko to know that anyone who could keep up with the six-year-old would probably find no difficulty whatsoever in running from police.

"I'm tapping our coordinates through to your com," came Lev's voice through her earpiece. "Are you alright?"

"All good," Jez panted. "Tanya too. Tell you what, though, thought I was fast. No wonder those kids listen to her—I'd do whatever she said just because I figure she'd run me down if I didn't." She glanced over at Tanya and grinned. "I mean, hell, I'd do whatever she said just because she's so damn hot, but—"

"Jez," came Ysbel's warning voice through the com.

Judging by how quickly Lev's coordinates were moving, the others were headed for the city gate at a flat-out run Still, even street kids weren't going to outpace someone like Tanya—she moved like the fog itself, noiseless and deadly and a hell of a lot faster than you expected.

Even so, by the time they'd caught up to the others, they were only a few streets away from the city entrance.

Jez came up beside Lev, still panting. He didn't say anything, just reached out and took her hand. His grip was tight, but she could feel his hand shaking.

"How close are we?" he whispered. "With the fog this thick, I can't tell where I am without my holoscreen pulled up."

She glanced around quickly. Even through the suffocating mist, she could pick out landmarks.

"About four city blocks to go," she whispered.

He nodded, his posture tense, and she was suddenly very certain he'd only asked because he'd wanted to hear her voice, convince himself that she was still here, still alive.

The thought made something tighten a little in her chest, and she wasn't sure if it was affection, or guilt, or worry, or love. Maybe a bit of all of them.

They slowed as they approached the gate.

"I'll go ahead, find out what the situation is," said Tanya quietly through the com.

They stopped, breathing heavily, and waited.

Jez glanced around the deserted streets, her heart pounding.

She wasn't sure why waiting was worse than being shot at with a damn heat pistol, but it bloody well was.

Lev squeezed her hand, and she drew in a long breath and gave him a small, grateful smile.

She almost jumped at the dark figure that materialized from the fog in front of them, then she recognized the slender silhouette.

"Lev," said Tanya quietly. "The exit is guarded. A dozen at least. I don't think your professor wanted to take chances."

Lev's hand tightened on Jez's, and she could feel his muscles stiffening. But he just shook his head and glanced behind him. "There's another gate I know of. It's smaller, and not many people know about it. I expect there will be a guard, but I believe I know the password. Masha gave it to me before she—left for the government a few weeks back."

There was that hesitation in his voice before he said Masha's name, and the unease in his tone when he spoke of her. And, much as she hated it, Jez couldn't blame him.

"Lead the way, then," said Tanya quietly. She faded into the mist behind them, presumably to rejoin her wife.

Lev took a deep breath, glancing around uneasily, then gave a small, rueful shrug. "I suppose there's nothing else to do, at this point," he said quietly.

It wasn't a far distance, but the adrenaline pounded through her veins, and every damn sense was on the alert.

Something was wrong.

Lev hadn't said it, but there was a reason he hadn't expected there to be guards here.

The fact that there were meant there was something he'd miscalculated.

She knew Lev well enough to know that they were only a finite number of people in the system who could cause him to miscalculate. It didn't help, though, that chief among them was the woman who was currently trying to kill them all.

"It should be just a street down from here," Lev whispered into his com. "I'll go check it out. There'll be guards, but it's just possible that Masha's password will get us through."

Jez put a hand on the butt of her pistol, the tight adrenaline grin stretched across her face. "And I'm coming with you, because let's be honest, genius, you're good at a hell of a lot of things, but I'm still better than you at shooting."

She could see he wanted to argue, and that he knew it would be useless.

He sighed and nodded, and they stepped forward into the mist.

She couldn't see the entryway until they were only a few metres away from it. As Lev had guessed, it was guarded—something like two dozen soldiers lounged against the wall surrounding it. Their postures were relaxed, but their hands on their weapons were steady.

"Who's there?" one of them called.

"Captain Gavril, 39th precinct," Lev snapped. "I need to get out for some reconnaissance. Orders from the top." His voice was cold and arrogant, and Jez grinned to herself.

Honestly, Lev wasn't half bad at this, for a soft scholar boy.

Of course, she'd learned damn quickly that there were a lot of things Lev wasn't half bad at. Not least of which involved her and him and a room with a bed and a damn door that locked—she sighed reluctantly, pulling her mind back to the conversation.

"How many are you bringing through?" asked one of the soldiers, straightening.

Lev hesitated for half a moment, then said smoothly, "Just over two dozen, but they're plainclothes officers—we had them infiltrating the street kids up until not too long ago."

The officer stared at them, and in the mist Jez couldn't see his face well enough to read his expression. At last, though, he said, "Well, come on through, in that case, and we'll scan you one at a time."

Lev frowned. "Scan us?"

"You must have heard the instructions," the guard said impatiently. "We scan everyone that goes in and out. No exceptions."

"Oh, I'm fairly sure that this is a time you should make an exception," said Lev. "Evka doesn't want it on anyone's radar that we've left the city. Hers alone."

"Scan, no exceptions," said the guard, such and Jez noticed how his hand tightened on his weapon.

"I'm sorry. I can't let you do that," said Lev, his voice firm and still slightly arrogant. "It would be as much as my position is worth. And," he added, "as much as your position is worth." He paused. "I assume the password will be sufficient?"

The soldier was standing by now, and two other guards had drifted over to join him.

Lev shook his head impatiently. "If you insist on being unreasonable, I'm going to have to get instructions." He gestured brusquely to Jez, and she followed him back down the street.

"We're not getting through there," he whispered into his com. "Tae, you have any suggestions?"

From behind them, an alarm blared. Jez cursed, yanking out her heat gun.

"Code yellow!" A guard's voice snapped, her tone carrying the sharp crispness of a military officer.

"Get back to the barricades," Lev hissed into his com.

At the same time, another woman's voice shouted, "It's them!"

"Go!" snapped Jez, spinning around. The student behind her was standing open mouthed with horror. She grabbed him by the shoulders, turned him bodily around, and shoved him back down the street.

Through the mist around her she could hear heat-blasts, grunts of pain, but she couldn't tell who the sounds were coming from. Every muscle in her body tingled, aching for a fight.

Lev jerked out his own heat pistol. They exchanged glances, and took off down the street after the others.

There were more heat-blasts ahead, then Ysbel's voice through the com. "They've come around from the other side to cut us off." She sounded grim.

Jez tapped her com. "Guess we'd better return the favour. Genius and I'll be right back." She tapped her com off, and Lev jerked his head towards one of the side alleys.

She grinned and shook her head. Genus probably had the whole damn map of the streets memorized, honestly.

They ran down the small alleyway, and Lev gestured her out into another street. In the damn fog she couldn't see a thing, but she could hear well enough what was going on—ahead of them, heat-blasts scorched through the air, turning the thick Prasvishoni mist momentarily incandescent.

They didn't talk, but then, they'd worked together long enough they didn't have to.

A moment later, the officers in the back of the fight turned in surprise to find the enemy who they'd thought was ahead of them firing a hell of a lot of heat into their damn butts.

There was frantic muttering through coms in the fog ahead of her, but she didn't really have time to listen to gossip. Considering how she was basically here to teach a bunch of bastards why they shouldn't pick on street kids.

"It's them. I'm sure it's them—the IDs don't scan—" one of the officers was whispering desperately into her com, then Jez sent a heat-blast into her back that would've cooked her solid if she hadn't had her damn heat shield on. As it was, it knocked her up against the wall for a moment, and Jez took advantage of that moment to swipe the woman's feet out from under her and land a solid punch to the bridge of her nose as she went down.

Ahead of her, through the mist, she could still hear fighting, and she left the soldier with a parting kick to the gut and sprinted towards the noise of heat-gun fire.

"Hey, you bastards, you want to pick on someone, pick on someone who actually wants to fight plaguers as ugly as you," she called.

A handful of the soldiers stiffened at her approach, but she was firing before they turned, and diving out of the way by the time they had their heat guns fixed at where she'd been.

From beside her she heard a familiar grunt of pain, and she swore, spinning in time to see Lev catch a fist to the stomach. He staggered backwards, but before his attacker could step after him, Jez had brought the butt of her heat pistol down on the bastard's head. The woman was wearing a helmet, but even so, she staggered under the force of the blow.

Also, a helmet couldn't protect you from a knee to the stomach, which Jez demonstrated with great gusto.

The woman choked, doubling over, and Jez grabbed Lev by the arm and hauled him to his feet. "You OK?" she snapped. He nodded breathlessly. Although to be fair, she figured all of their definitions of 'OK' had devolved significantly in the past few months.

"Get back," came Ysbel's voice through the com. "I'm going to throw a smoke bomb."

"On it," Jez panted, and dragged the still-staggering Lev down the street.

"Meet up with us farther down," Tae said through the com, his voice tight with worry. "I'm sending our coordinates through again."

Jez glanced down at her com, then took off towards the moving red dot that indicated tech-head and the rest of them. Lev had steadied on his feet and was running beside her, his pistol still in his hand. As they rounded a corner, he turned, firing a shot off behind him, and she grinned to herself.

Genius-boy had always been hot. But there was something about the way he could fire off a heat-blast over his shoulder at the police while running for his life that was ridiculously attractive.

They met up with Tae and the others a few blocks later.

"They're still after us, I'm afraid," Lev panted. "Evka must have guessed what we'd do somehow. We have to get back to the warehouse. We don't have another survivable option right now."

Tae nodded. "We didn't lose anyone. At least, not that I know of. Ivan's taking up the rear, to make sure that we don't have stragglers."

There were shouts from the street ahead.

"We're gonna have company in a few seconds here," Jez called over her shoulder.

"This way," Tae snapped, and they turned down an alley, the students and street kids following.

There was a sharp *tink*, audible even through the suffocating fog, and Ysbel called, "Get down!"

Everyone had spent enough time around Ysbel not to ask questions.

They hit the ground as an explosion lit the air behind them, and for a brief instant, Jez could see dark forms behind them slammed into the walls at the force of the explosion.

"That wasn't mine," said Ysbel grimly as they scrambled to their feet. "I don't think they're planning to keep us alive to ask questions."

"Ivan," panted Tae through his com. "Are you alright?"

"I'm fine," said Ivan. His voice was grim. "I've got some injured kids, so we're moving a little more slowly than we should."

"Tanya and me are coming to help out," Jez drawled breathlessly. "See if we can't make the soldiers move a little slower than they should, too. Maybe by kicking them in the damn crotch."

Lev glanced over, face tight, but he just mouthed, "Good luck."

She nodded, and that same stupid thing that always caught in her chest at times like this—when she knew damn well that genius was worried sick, but he trusted her anyway—tightened up again.

Then Tanya was beside her, and they were sprinting back down the street.

Ivan was carrying one girl and supporting a boy with his free arm. Both children had blood staining their ragged clothing, but this wasn't the damn time to stop and do a med-scan.

"You have everyone?" Jez snapped.

Ivan glanced up at her. "I think so. I—" he looked around quickly, and she saw the blood drain from his face. "Felix. He ran back to check on one of his kids, said he'd catch us up."

"Go," said Jez. "Tanya and me'll take care of it."

The girl in Ivan's arms moaned softly, and Ivan give a short nod. "It's just those two. The rest are accounted for."

Jez turned to Tanya, grinning. "Alright, you bastard, ready to raise some hell?"

"Yes, Jez, I suppose I am," said Tanya with a small, sharp smile in return.

The soldiers were less than half a block behind them. Apparently, catching Felix had slowed them down some. Thank the damn Lady the mist was thick enough that there was no one on a skybike.

She could tell where Felix was from the muffled curses.

With just one of them caught, or two, maybe, she figured the soldiers would try to keep them alive, maybe use them as bait. But hell, she knew Felix, and he was almost as good as she was at making people want to shoot him dead.

She and Tanya exchanged glances, and Tanya gave a quick nod. Then she stepped forward, disappearing into the mist like a damn ghost.

Jez grinned, settled her pistol more firmly in her hand, and stepped forward like something that was about to make a hell of a lot of other people into ghosts if they didn't get out of her way fast enough.

Felix was in the centre of a knot of soldiers, and Jez, at this point, figured subtlety was overrated. She fired a blast into the air, making the walls of the warehouse to her right glow a momentary dull orange. "Hey, you bastards, looking for a fight? Because I've got one right here with your names on it."

There was a moment of shocked silence from the officers. Which ended pretty damn quickly when she shot three of them directly in the chest. Their heat shields glowed, but hell, with the mods Ysbel had on this thing, even through a heat shield it wouldn't feel too good.

A handful of soldiers started towards her, heat-visors pulled down low over their faces, the grim efficiency of their movements leaving no doubt as to their intentions.

She fired off a couple more shots, ducked as a heat-blast scorched over her head, and then dived towards them, pulling a gutting knife from her boot as she straightened.

They managed to get off a few panicked shots, one of which burned a hole through the side of her jacket and probably scorched her tunic underneath, and then she was in the middle of them, and no one was going to shoot at that close range unless they wanted to fry one of their buddies to a damn crisp at the same time.

From the corner of her eye she could make out Tanya, her movements silent and fluid, her progress visible only by the quiet collapse of officers around her.

Jez shoved her gutting knife into someone's thigh. They howled in pain, and she kicked their kneecap hard enough to send them to the ground. An arm grabbed her from behind, and she spun, swinging blindly at eye level. Her arm connected, hard, with her attacker's helmet visor, and she cursed at the stinging tingle in her funny bone.

The woman she'd elbowed hadn't fared much better, staggering backwards on the icy cobblestones, helmet knocked askew.

Still swearing, Jez stepped forward and kicked her hard in the stomach, and as she doubled over, grabbed the back of her neck and shoved her face down to meet Jez's upcoming boot.

Even with a helmet, the bastard should be seeing stars after that.

Someone else grabbed her, and this time she was smart enough to use the butt of her heat pistol as she spun. Whoever it was didn't let go, and for a moment they struggled, each trying to pull the other off balance. Then Jez stepped in close, and bit down hard on the soldier's gloved hand. He cursed in surprise, letting go of her for an instant, and she jerked free of his grip and sprinted for Tanya.

She reached the woman at the same time Tanya reached the two street kids, and together, they disabled the officers holding them.

Jez grabbed the injured kid Felix had been supporting, slinging him up over her shoulders, and Tanya grabbed Felix by the arm. He turned to glare at her, and then must have realized who it was, because he bit back whatever he'd been about to say.

Smart kid, honestly. Even Felix knew better than to take on Tanya.

"Go!" Tanya hissed, and they took off running.

By the time they reached the street that would turn towards the warehouse, the soldiers were close enough that Jez could feel the sting of the heat-blasts on her heels.

"Give me a moment," said Tanya, slipping away.

Jez dumped the injured street kid in Felix's arms and yanked out her pistol. "Get him out of here," she hissed.

Before Felix could protest, Jez turned with a whoop and ran directly at the soldiers pursuing them, firing her heat pistol like a maniac.

There was a startled instant, where the soldiers in front skidded to a confused halt and the soldiers behind them narrowly avoided running into them.

And then they recovered, pulling out their weapons, and Jez dived to one side as the air around her sizzled with heat.

Then, from behind them, there was an echoing *boom*.

The soldiers turned to face the new threat, and a moment later, someone grabbed Jez's arm and dragged her behind the cover of a building.

"Did Felix get away?" Tanya hissed in her ear.

She nodded, still half-stunned from the blast.

"Good. Let's go."

They slid between two buildings and sprinted down another side-street.

When they were certain they weren't being followed, they cut back towards the warehouse, and reached it, panting and out of breath, just as the Felix was stepping through the door.

They ducked through behind him, and Tanya shut the heavy door firmly, pushing the lock into place.

Ivan was there a moment later, his face creased with worry. He took the injured street kid from Felix without a word, carrying him gently into the makeshift med bay. Felix followed, his face gaunt, and his expression, for once, more frightened than resentful.

And then Lev was there, and Jez drew in a long breath as the system settled back into its proper place.

"Jez. You alright?" he asked quietly.

She nodded, still too out of breath to speak, and he slipped his arm around her, drawing her into an embrace.

She could feel the tension through every muscle in his body.

"So," she said quietly. "Guess that didn't work like we hoped it would."

He shook his head. "No. I—don't know how she knew where we were heading." He closed his eyes. "We're not getting anyone out of the city. So unless we come up with something else, everyone here has about six more days to live."

6

Masha, day 2, early

Masha lay in the dark, staring at the ceiling of the small, cramped makeshift med bay, biting her lip until she tasted blood.

She'd been hurt before. But nothing like this. It washed through her body and ached through her bones, a constant, unremitting, ever-present pressure, pushing at her consciousness and pricking her mind into wakefulness.

Since the day she'd been dragged from the Secretary General's office down to the torture chamber in the basement of the government buildings, she hadn't had a moment of real sleep. She hadn't realized, before this, what a blessing sleep could be. Or what torture it could be to have it removed.

Honestly, between the nightmares and the strain of the days and weeks leading up to her capture, she hadn't had much sleep before then either. But now, with the pain thrumming behind her eyelids, knifing through every joint and muscle, sitting dull and heavy across her leg and sharpening at her mutilated knee, the thought of sleep, and the attendant unconsciousness, was like the thought of water to a person dying in the desert—equally tantalizing, and equally out of reach.

The silence from the echoing warehouse outside was uncanny.

Ivan had come to check on her a couple of hours ago. He'd looked worried and preoccupied, and said something about a failed attempt to get the others out, and sending the kids to get some sleep while the crew talked about alternate plans.

He'd looked almost dead on his feet.

The rest of the students and street kids must have been almost as tired, because the noise and bustle caused by their entrance had faded almost absurdly quickly into stillness.

There was the smallest of sounds, just an odd incongruence in the quiet, and it took a moment for the noise to register in her consciousness.

And then her stomach clenched with the sudden certainty she wasn't alone.

Cautiously, she turned her head, and from the corner of her eye she caught a flicker of movement by the open door.

She choked back a guttural jolt of panic.

There was no reason for someone to be coming into the med bay, not in the middle of the night.

Barely visible in the darkness, a silent figure slipped through the doorway.

Masha lay entirely still, hardly daring to breathe. She wasn't sure, for an instant, why she was so certain she was in danger.

And then her mind registered what her subconscious had noticed immediately—the wicked glitter of a knife in the figure's hand.

The figure came stealthily across the room, movements as silent as a shadow.

Masha lay completely still.

It was disconcerting, how her body reacted to this—panic flooding her veins, tightening her lungs, weakening her already weak muscles.

Somehow, the torture had broken her.

But it couldn't have. She couldn't afford to be broken, not yet.

Whoever it was stopped at the side of her cot, their breathing a soft rustle in the quiet of the small space.

It was a slight figure, nearer the size and build of one of the street kids than of an adult. But whoever it was was no street kid—the confidence in their walk, the silent economy of their movements, told her that clearer than words.

Whoever this was had been trained. And they'd learned well.

The figure moved slightly, and again she caught the sharp, bright glitter of metal reflecting the dim emergency lighting.

Masha moaned softly, turning her head restlessly and shifting on the blankets. She forced her breathing down to the soft rise and fall of someone long asleep, and, as she shifted, she clutched the corner of the small pillow Lev's father had left to tuck under her injured knee.

The figure over her tensed, and for half a second she wondered if she'd miscalculated, and the knife would lodge in her chest before she had time to so much as cry out.

But they relaxed as she stilled.

She breathed a quiet sigh of relief. Under the dirty, sweat-soaked blankets, she gently tugged at the pillow, working it free, ignoring the agony the movement stabbed through her broken knee.

After a few moments, the figure over her cot seemed satisfied that she was asleep. With movements almost too slow to pick out, they lifted the knife carefully.

Masha's mind was sharp and clear, even through the haze of pain, danger cutting through the cobwebs of earlier.

They weren't planning to simply stab her. There were thousand easier ways to kill her.

No, this was meant to be a murder that looked like a natural death—poison on the knife blade, most likely.

The figure shifted slightly, knife raised in their hand.

Masha forced her body to remain limp, despite the sickening pounding of her heart.

The knife came down in a quick, practiced movement, dipping through a gap in the blankets. Almost gently. Just enough for a scratch.

And without the pillow under the blanket, between her and the knife—she could have died without even knowing she'd been injured.

She stirred, slightly, like someone might if they'd been unconscious, or heavily drugged. Her heart pounded dizzyingly fast, sick fear catching in the back of her throat.

There was a small noise from outside the room, footsteps passing—someone getting up for a drink, maybe, or to use the bathroom.

The would-be assassin froze.

The footsteps passed without pausing.

The figure above her cot relaxed, slipping the knife back into the folds of their clothing, and slipped back towards the door. They paused a moment in the entrance, peering outside, and then, silently, ducked through.

They weren't here just to kill her, that was clear. So why were they here?

Masha took a deep breath, and, with an effort that almost seemed too great, pushed herself into a sitting position.

She was breathing heavily, sweat beading on her forehead, head spinning with the pain, but she was upright.

She paused for a moment while the room swayed around her, then gritted her teeth.

She knew how to work through pain. And perhaps this was worse than anything she'd experienced before—but it was a matter of degree, really, not a matter of kind.

She braced herself, trying not to think of the impossibility of what she would do next. Then, holding her breath to keep from an inadvertent hiss of agony, she swung her legs over the edge of the cot.

Before she could have time for second thoughts, she pushed herself to her feet.

Even with the splint and the boneset on her knee, the pain that exploded through her at the movement was almost enough to make her pass out. She clenched her teeth hard enough that they hurt, and somehow managed to push the blackness back from her vision.

Just like she had when she'd gone out after Jez.

Carefully, teeth still clenched hard against the pain and the nausea, she took a stumbling, unsteady footstep, then another, then another, until she reached the door to the room.

She peered out. In the dim light of the moon through the high windows, she could make out a shadow slipping through the door into the room beside hers.

For a moment, she hesitated.

She could call Lev or Ysbel on the com. But by the time they got here, it might be too late.

Even if she could convince them to believe her in the first place.

And so, carefully, she stepped through the door.

The distance to the doorway where her assailant had disappeared was measured in metres, but every step of it was agony, and her entire body was trembling by the time she reached it.

She hesitated at the door for a moment, uncertain whether she'd have the strength to continue inside. Then, with a deep breath, she slipped through.

It took her eyes a moment to adjust to the darkness.

By the time they did, it was too late.

"Who are you?" a voice hissed, and she could feel the cold bite of the knife-edge against her throat.

She forced herself to breathe slowly.

They didn't want to kill someone, not obviously like this. Not in a way that would make it impossible to mistake for an accident.

"I—" she began. Her voice wavered, and it wasn't nearly as much of an act as she would have wished. "I don't—"

"I asked you a question—who are you?" The knife pushed harder against her skin.

Masha took a deep breath. "I think," she said quietly, "that you should put the knife down now."

For a moment, her assailant didn't move.

She saw the moment they noticed the cold, hard muzzle of her heat pistol digging into their ribs. They were close enough that she could feel their muscles tense, ready to plunge the knife into her throat.

She braced herself and flung her free arm up, her knuckles driving into the soft skin under her attacker's wrist.

The knife clattered to the floor, the sound loud in the silence.

"Help me!" she shouted at the top of her voice. "Please, somebody help!"

The figure hissed and shoved her backwards, turning to flee. Masha staggered, gasping in pain, but even as she stumbled back, she squeezed the trigger of the heat gun.

The would-be assassin grunted as the blast hit home.

She fired again, her hand on the weapon steady even though the blackness crowding the corners of her vision.

The assassin collapsed, breath hissing through their teeth.

"If you move, I'll kill you," said Masha. Her voice was shaking. "I know where to shoot you so you'll live just long enough to answer my questions before you die."

Then the door was flung open, what seemed like half a dozen artificial lights flooding the room, and Masha blinked at the sudden assault on her senses.

"What the hell—" Lev's voice was strained, and rough with exhaustion. "Masha?"

She couldn't make out his form through the glare of the lights, and the world had taken on the watery tinge of bordering on unconsciousness, but Masha had spent enough time in the last few days bordering on unconsciousness to know exactly where her limits were.

"Someone shot one of the street kids." Ivan was crouched over her assailant, his voice tight with worry.

"Masha," said Lev through his teeth. "What the hell is happening?"

"She shot me," said the young man lying on the ground. His voice sounded much younger and more frightened than it had when he'd had the edge of his knife shoved up against her throat. "I saw her sneaking into the supply room, and I came to see what she was doing, and she attacked me. I—I don't know what she was after—"

Masha couldn't hold back a slight, rueful smiled. Clearly, this assassin, or whatever they were, was very well aware of the crew's recent history.

Her eyes had adjusted enough now that she could make out Lev, glaring at her, his eyes hard. "Masha," he said quietly. "So help me, if I find out you've been going behind my back again—"

Masha was struck with the strangest desire to laugh. "He has—a knife," she managed to whisper. "Poison. Tried to kill me."

"And why the hell should I believe you?" Lev snapped.

"My cot. Pillow. Tried to—tried to stab me. I couldn't—cut the pillow. You'll—you'll see it." The ground was swaying under her feet, the words more and more difficult to form.

"Get the knife—" she managed, with a final effort. "Try to kill himself—"

And then the world faded to black, and finally, Masha got what she'd been wishing for—unconsciousness.

7

Lev, day 2, early

Lev blinked hard, rubbing his eyes.

He shouldn't, he knew, be irritated at Masha for this, at least.

But honestly, it was hard not to be resentful when he was yanked into the middle of a new problem, moments after he and the rest of the damn crew had finally agreed to get some actual sleep and reconvene in the morning.

He hadn't slept in what was increasingly coming to feel like his entire life.

He wondered, absently, if this was what Tae felt like all the time.

They were gathered back in the ancient break-room. Everyone from their earlier planning meeting was in attendance—he, Ysbel, Tanya, Jez, Tae, and Ivan, as well as Caz and Peti, Felix, Matija, Dimitri, and Vera.

With the addition, of course, of the kid sitting across the floor from Lev, his eyes wide and glazed with pain, a neat heat-blast wound, now bandaged and treated, burned through each of his thighs.

Looking at him, Lev felt something cold stir in his chest.

Perhaps Masha was telling the truth—perhaps she wasn't. But

there was no denying she was completely ruthless when she deemed it necessary.

"Please, just let me go," whispered the boy in a small voice. He looked around Caz's age, skinny and dirty, and his hunched posture and thin frame meant he'd blend into any of the street-kid gangs.

Except—Masha had been telling the truth about the poisoned knife, and about the slit pillow on her cot. And Ivan had barely managed to grab the boy's arm, back in the supply room, before he'd yanked out another poisoned knife and tried to draw it quickly across his skin.

Lev shuddered involuntarily at the memory—it brought back too many other memories.

He shoved the thought away resolutely and turned to the boy. "Alright. Who are you?"

"I—I told you. I'm Ilya. A street kid. I've been—"

"Whose gang?" asked Peti. Her voice was hard, and not in the least sympathetic.

"Zia's," he responded promptly.

Peti narrowed her eyes. "Really? Because Zia was shot by the police four months ago."

The boy gave a small shiver. "I know. I've—been on my own since then, mostly. The others were killed too, not too long after. I was just trying to survive."

Peti was still glaring, but she didn't respond.

Lev took a deep breath. "You say you saw Masha going into the supply room, and you followed her."

The boy nodded, his face pitifully frightened.

"And the poisoned knife?"

The boy shook his head, his body trembling. "I—I grabbed it from her before she shot me. I didn't know it was poisoned. And when she fainted, I—I was frightened. I was afraid you'd listen to her instead of me. And—" his voice broke a little. "And I'd rather die than go back on the streets by myself." He turned to Tae, his eyes pleading. "You know what it's like."

Tae didn't answer.

The boy turned back to Lev. "Please. Just let me go. I'm sorry for causing problems. I—didn't know she was your friend."

"'Friend' might be a stretch," said Lev wryly. "But we've worked together in the past. And a poisoned knife isn't exactly her style."

"I don't know what's her style," said the boy. His eyes were panicked, his breathing rapid. "All I know is what I saw. You—" he gave a small, helpless shrug. "You don't have to believe me. There's nothing I can say to make you believe me, I know that. But—" His voice broke, and he fell silent.

Lev bit his lip and glanced over at the others.

Jez was watching, not the boy, but him, her eyes fixed on his face. Tae was scowling at the table, Ysbel was scowling at the world in general. Ivan's face was still cut with concern, like it always was when he was called in to treat injuries. Peti scowled at the boy, and Caz watched his sister, seemingly willing to take his cues from her.

But Felix—

Felix hadn't taken his eyes off the boy, and there was a thoughtful look on his face.

"So you were in Zia's gang," Felix said at last.

The boy turned to him, frowning slightly. "Yes. You—knew her?"

Felix gave a quick shake of his head. "Nah. Never met the bastard. Never wanted to."

The boy's face darkened with anger.

Felix gave a derisive chuckle. "Oh, you gonna get all pissed off because I'm talking crap about Zia?" He grinned and leaned forward. "You must've really loved her, you scum-eater. Probably make your whole damn day, then, when I tell you you're not the only one of her kids who made it out alive."

The confusion on the boy's face was being replaced by something else. He was trying to make it look like anger, but it wasn't.

It was fear.

"What do you mean? I wish to the Lady I wasn't the only one who'd survived, but—"

"Well, look at that," said Felix sardonically. "The Lady must've heard your prayers. Because turns out, you're not the only one who survived. Fact is, I've got a girl in my gang ran with Zia. Name's Nadia. Bet you'd just love to have a little reunion, wouldn't you? Should I call her in? She's a damn killer now, kill you as soon as look at you if she doesn't like you, but hell, someone from her old gang? Bet she'd be thrilled to see you."

For a moment, emotions warred on the boy's face. Then he twisted, yanking something out of his boot between his bound hands. Lev just had time to realize it was another knife before Jez stepped forward, slapping the weapon neatly out of his grip.

"Don't think so, you bastard," she drawled, stooping and palming the knife.

The boy jumped to his feet, but Ysbel caught him easily. He struggled in her grip until finally seeming to realize it was useless. Then he sat panting and glaring, and the malice in his eyes sent a shiver up Lev's spine.

"I'll ask again—who are you, and why are you here?" said Lev quietly.

The boy just glared.

Lev took a long breath. "I know Evka sent you. There's nothing to be gained by pretending otherwise. And I'm not very happy with

Evka right now. So if you want to live past tonight, it would be a good idea to tell me what you know."

The boy glowered at him, face twisted with hate.

At last, Lev turned away with a sigh. "Ysbel, would you lock him in one of the empty rooms, please? Hands bound, preferably—I'd rather not find him dead when we come to ask him questions."

"I'll take care the little bastard," said Felix. "Bet Nadia'd just love to get her hands on the scum-sucker."

Lev sighed again. "Felix. I appreciate the offer. But I still need him alive." He paused, glancing at their captive. "If there comes a time when we don't, I'll let you know."

Felix turned away, muttering something about stupid damn softies.

Ysbel nodded. "I'll make sure he's restrained. And I'll make sure he is very, very clear on how we expect him to behave while he's our guest." There was a tone in her voice that once again made Lev very glad this woman was not his enemy.

"Ivan," he said quietly. "Would you go check on Masha? If she's awake—" he hesitated a moment. "If she's awake, it may be helpful to get her insights."

Ivan nodded and slipped out of the room.

Lev dropped his head into his hands.

"Hey, genius," said Jez quietly. He heard the rustle of her jacket as she sat down beside him. She ran a hand down his back, and he could feel his whole body relaxing, like it always did when she was close. "What's wrong?"

He looked up at her, smiling despite himself. She was bleary-eyed with weariness, but her face was as sharp and intelligent as ever, and for just a fleeting moment, he let himself remember the warmth of her from the previous night, curled up beside him on their cot.

"You mean, besides the fact that apparently Evka got a spy in here?" He let out a short breath. "I suppose that explains why we couldn't get out yesterday. Evka knew exactly where we were going. I'm surprised we weren't killed. I'm surprised the police aren't shooting down our doors right now. As soon as Evka passes our location on to the police, everyone here is dead."

Jez gave a small snort of laughter. "Come on, genius, compared to what we've been through, that's basically not even worth mentioning."

He smiled ruefully. "I suppose you're right. But if Evka got one spy in here—I'll have the street kids go through everyone in camp, split off into gangs, so we know if there's someone else here who doesn't belong. And I'll ask Vera and Dimitri to verify all the students. But—" he shook his head, trading off.

"But with this damn many people here—we're not gonna know for sure, right?" she finished quietly.

He sighed and tried to smile. She slipped her arm around his waist, and he leaned over and kissed her, and just for a moment, everything seemed bearable for a just a little longer.

Ysbel returned a few minutes later, Ivan close behind her. Both of their faces were grim.

"He's locked up," said Ysbel shortly. "But he tried to kill me while I was doing it. Whoever he is, he's very good."

"I would have been surprised to learn otherwise," said Lev quietly. "Ivan?"

Ivan shook his head. "Masha's conscious." He gave a short sigh. "I—don't know how to read that woman."

Tae glanced up from his seat. "I don't think anyone does," he muttered, and Ivan cracked a small smile.

"Whatever happens, we'll have to get out," said Lev, pushing himself to his feet with an effort. "We can't stay here, not if Evka knows where we are. She'll be furious, and I've seen what happens to people she's angry with. Caz, Peti, could you please wake up the street kids and get them ready to move? Vera, you start getting students ready. Dmitri—any other ideas for locations?"

"I'll—think about it," said Dmitri, his face tight with worry. "There's probably something. What are we going to do with the spy?"

"Let me deal with that," said Lev quietly.

At last, Dmitri nodded. "I'll help Vera get things ready," he said, turning to go.

Lev sighed and glanced around at the others. "Well, I suppose we reconvene in the Masha's room. We'll want her insight on this, probably," he said at last.

Masha was, indeed, conscious, but her eyes were glassy with pain, and Lev wasn't sure how long she'd stay lucid.

"Masha," he said, forcing his tone to be polite. "You found Evka's spy for us."

"I think it would be more accurate to say he found me," murmured Masha. Her voice was weak, but there was a tinge of wry humour in it.

Lev didn't smile. "Do you know anything about this? Anything more than what you told us?"

She took a deep breath. "I'm sorry, Lev. I—" She stopped, and he could see the tension in her.

She'd never told them everything, not from the moment he'd met her in prison so many months ago.

But … he'd seen the look on her face when they'd rescued her from the torture cell. And somehow, despite his best judgement, some part of him couldn't help but believe that, as absurd as it sounded, she was actually trying.

"From the way he tried to kill me, I assumed he wanted it to look like an accident," she said at last. "I concluded from this that he was here for some reason other than just to kill me. I'm sure you've already considered the fact that Evka seemed to know your plans for getting the others out. But the police aren't pounding at the door yet, although Evka almost certainly is aware of our location."

Lev nodded. He could see the unease in the others' faces.

He could feel the unease in his own.

"Evka has a temper, but she can be cautious," he said at last. "She doesn't like to fail. I think the most likely explanation is, she didn't want to take the chance of us foiling another attack—like Ysbel said, this place is fairly defensible. She was likely hoping we'd be killed when we tried to get the others out, and when that didn't work, went on to the next option—maybe murder everyone on the crew, or poison the food supply or spoil it, so we'd give ourselves up or starve. Then she looks like the hero of the hour."

"Which also means, as I'm certain you've considered, we can't send the others away to a new location," said Masha, her voice weak. "She may not be sending the police in yet. But I'd be surprised if she hasn't had the place watched since you got back."

He nodded grimly.

"So, with that in mind, what do you suggest we do?" she asked.

"Well, I mean, maybe we can cause enough of a ruckus that the others can slip out—" Jez began. Then she shook her head wearily. "Except we can't, can we? Because she catches us, the other bastards all die anyways in about six days."

"It's too bad the Protocol doesn't work like the implant we had in prison," said Tanya, with a hint of tired amusement in her tone. "Get her angry enough that she tries to kill all of us at once, and short out the machine."

"Wouldn't that be nice?" Tae muttered. "Except it doesn't."

Lev managed a small smile.

Then he stopped, sucking in a quick breath.

"Wait," he said.

They all turned to look at him.

His mind was spinning.

"Well?" asked Ysbel impatiently after a moment.

"Tae," he said. "I—don't know if this will work. But—I may just have an idea."

"An idea to get everyone out? Or an idea to keep Evka from killing us?" asked Ysbel dryly. "Or, an idea to take out her Protocol?"

Lev took a deep breath. "I—don't know. I don't know if it will work at all, and honestly, it leaves far, far too much up to chance. But if it works, and if we're very, very lucky—it's just possible it will do all three." He paused a moment and shook his head ruefully. "Or it will kill us. That's a possibility too."

"I see," said Ysbel wryly, "there's really no downside, is what you're saying."

He smiled reluctantly. "I suppose when you put it that way …"

By the time the light from the Prasvishoni winter morning had grown from an anemic sliver of sunrise to a pale mid-afternoon sun, Lev felt a strange mix of exhaustion and jittery tension that set his nerves on edge and nausea churning in his stomach.

They'd pulled off ridiculous plans before. In fact, pretty much everything they'd done as a crew had been an absurd impossibility. But this—

If anyone had suggested that one day he'd not only agree to a plan like this, but be the one who came up with it in the first place, he would have laughed in their faces.

But, like Ysbel had said …

Tae was hunched over his holoscreen, looking so exhausted that likely the only reason he was still upright was that Ivan was beside him, holding him up.

From the look on Tae's face, Ivan was holding him up more than just physically. The fact that Tae had done what he'd done was honestly miraculous. But everyone had a breaking point, and Tae looked like he was getting very close to his.

"Tae. Are you ready?" he asked.

Tae started, blinking. "As ready as I can possibly be," he muttered, his words slurring with weariness.

Lev took a deep breath. "Alright then." He tapped his com, and the line Tae had spoofed through to Evka's com buzzed.

She answered a moment later. "Lev."

Perhaps it was simply the mix of exhaustion and nerves, but Lev couldn't help a small jolt at the sound of her voice. For half a second, he was back in university, sixteen years old, stepping into the small office where they worked together on Evka's research projects.

Jez squeezed his hand, and he managed a quick smile.

He wasn't sixteen anymore, and he wasn't the person he had been.

"Evka. I'd say it's good to hear your voice again, but—"

She chuckled softly. "I'm impressed, as always, by your very intelligent workaround to my Protocol," she said. "It won't save you in the long run, but still—I am impressed."

"We caught your spy, Evka. And I intend to kill him." The palms of his hands were damp with sweat, although he managed to keep his voice steady.

This could go as they'd hoped it would. Or it could backfire in unimaginable ways.

There was a long moment of silence from the other end of the com. At last, Evka said, "Again, well done, Lev. I expect you want me to ask what you want in exchange for the spy." She paused a moment. "But I don't intend to do that."

Lev took a deep breath. "Very well. It doesn't put us in any worse of the situation to kill him. Although it's unfortunate that it's necessary."

"You'll be pleased to know, then, that I doubt it will be necessary after all." Evka's tone was slightly amused. "I know where you are. And in about—" she paused. "An hour, give or take, the police will shoot you down, and kill everyone inside the building. Or, you and your entire crew—yourself, Jez, Tae, Ivan, Ysbel, Tanya, the two children, and Masha—may come to the front of the barricades before the hour is up. I'll have soldiers there, who will be instructed to escort you to my laboratory. You'll bring the spy with you, unharmed. And, if you do that, I will not instruct the police to take down the warehouse where you and your friends are sheltering." She paused again. "In an hour, if you haven't turned yourselves in, I'll take that as your answer."

The com clicked off.

Lev glanced around at the others, his stomach a tight knot.

The expressions on their faces were a mix of strain, exhaustion, and worry.

Except for Jez, of course. She was grinning, a dangerous, delighted grin.

Which didn't actually make him feel any better about things.

"Well," she drawled. "Been wanting to meet that bastard Evka for a while. Bet we'll all get along like a damn fire in an explosive factory."

Lev closed his eyes for a moment.

Honestly, that was probably an understatement.

This was ridiculous. There was no way they could make this work.

But then again—it wasn't like they had another option.

79

8

Tae, day 2, afternoon

Tae's head ached with a dull, persistent pain.

He couldn't honestly remember the last time he'd slept. He couldn't remember last time he hadn't been so tired that being awake was an effort almost beyond his capacity.

If Ivan hadn't been standing beside him, arm around his waist, supporting him, he wasn't sure he would be on his feet right now.

Even through the exhaustion, he could see the sharp worry on Caz and Peti's faces as they watched him.

"Be careful, Tae," said Caz quietly, putting a hand on Tae's arm.

Tae almost laughed. They'd passed the point of being careful a long, long time ago.

Instead, he just mumbled, "You too."

There wasn't really anything else to say.

Lev stood beside him, face tight with strain. Jez was drumming her fingers on her thigh, like she always did when she had to waiting for anything.

"Are you ready?" asked Lev softly.

Tae nodded, too tired even to speak.

Lev took a deep breath, and Tae could see the tension in his posture. Then he pulled back the lock on the heavy warehouse door and swung it open.

Tae wondered, dully, as he stepped into the dreary light of late afternoon, if Evka would reconsider, and simply shoot them as they stepped out.

Probably not—she'd want to keep them alive until she figured out his blocker, probably.

At least a dozen soldiers were waiting for them, and they stepped forward, one of them muttering quickly into his com. The woman who seemed to be in charge gestured them into a transport, and they climbed inside without even an attempt at resistance, carrying Masha on the makeshift stretcher they'd brought her here on the day previous.

Despite the tension that filled the cabin of the small in-atmosphere transport, Tae almost fell asleep at least twice on the ride over. The third time, Ivan let him sleep—he only realized they'd arrived when he blinked his eyes open at Ivan's soft nudge to his shoulder.

"Sorry, Tae, we're here," Ivan whispered.

Tae got to his feet somehow, and, leaning on Ivan for support, staggered out of the transport and into a small, walled courtyard.

He didn't recognize where they were, but it must be near the government sector. The building that rose in front of them was utilitarian—straight lines, small windows—but neat and clean, the walls free of the rot and mildew that marked the buildings in the other sectors of Prasvishoni.

A petite woman waited for them in the courtyard. She was probably a little older than Masha, her hair starting to grey, small creases around her mouth and eyes. She wore plain clothing, although the materials were clearly high quality, and practical shoes, her hair cut in a tidy bob. In contrast to Masha's air of slightly rumpled competence, everything about this woman was perfectly in place.

"Hello, Lev," she said pleasantly, once the crew was standing in a small huddle in the courtyard. "I assume these are your … friends I've heard so much about."

She glanced around at the motley group of them, filthy and exhausted, with a look on her face like someone who's smelled something unpleasant, and is trying not to show it. "I've only really met Jez and Masha, I believe." She paused, with a small, vicious smile. "And I understand that when I met Masha, she didn't necessarily consider herself a member of the crew."

Lev said nothing, the expression on his face stony.

"It's chilly out here. Come in." She gestured towards the heavy steel doors.

"You're very polite, for someone who intends to kill us," said Lev.

Evka gave him another smile. "Not yet. As I'm sure you've guessed, I'd rather not put you somewhere entirely out of my reach until I've solved your street boy's puzzle. And perhaps you, in particular, can convince me to reconsider. My offer is still open."

"Of course. You were always very careful, weren't you, Evka?" Lev's voice was flat and tired.

She turned, and the guards prodded them after her through the doors.

The inside of the building had the same stark, sterile atmosphere as some of the buildings in the warehouse district—large, rectangular hallways of unpainted prefab, cement floors, steel doors. She led them into a small room with a table and chairs and beckoned them to sit.

Tae almost fell into his seat, his legs too tired to hold him up.

"I should be angry," said Evka, taking her own seat. "But I'm actually impressed." She glanced briefly at Tae, then turned back to Lev. "I'd ask how the street boy did it, if I thought you'd tell me."

"I'd tell you how I did it if I didn't think you'd use it to kill me and all my friends," muttered Tae through his teeth.

She glanced over at him, her expression slightly startled, as if she'd heard a rat sit up and speak. Then she chuckled. "Lev. I see why you like him." She leaned forward, her eyes still fixed on Lev. "Your crew will be my guests for the next few days. Please don't assume that I won't kill them, or you, if they become more trouble than they're worth—a heat-blast can kill you as easily as the program set in your brains." She stood. "My guards will take you to your rooms. I've split your crew up, and you, Lev, will be in a room alone, as I've seen the trouble you can get into when you're all together. And they'll confiscate your coms, as I'd rather not deal with additional complications, as unlikely as I believe that to be."

Tae raised his head with an effort. "One correction, Evka," he said, words slurring with exhaustion.

She turned back at his words, again with that slightly startled expression.

This was the woman who'd used street kids to experiment on. She probably didn't even see him as human.

She was peering at him curiously, a small frown creased between her eyebrows. "A correction?"

Tae nodded. "Yes. You said—you said you didn't need the Protocol to kill us. You could kill us with a heat-blast."

There was an amused expression on her face, and her tone of voice was that of a parent humouring a child. "I assume you're going to tell me you somehow found a technological way to make your skin impervious to heat-blasts."

"No," he said. "I haven't. But this is what I have done." He pulled up the holoscreen on his com.

The guards stepped forward, weapons raised, but Evka waved them back.

Tae expanded the screen so she could see it. "You said you could kill us with a heat-blast," he mumbled. "You could. But if you do—"

Evka peered closer at the screen, a frown of disbelief growing on her face.

"Scan them," she snapped to one of the guards. The woman jumped to attention and pulled up the scanner on her com.

Tae smiled. His brain was running on so little sleep at this point he felt almost drunk. "Go ahead and scan us, Evka. I'm not lying. My hack was just a temporary solution to give us time. But this—"

The guard who'd done the scan was staring down the screen on her com.

"Let me see," Evka hissed, stepping over to her.

"I can't remove your metal from our brains," Tae said. "But I can add a feedback loop to the program, at least for the nine of us. And I looped it into our com signals for protection. If any of us die, for whatever reason, the feedback loop will increase the Protocol's effect, probably high enough burn us to ash. But it will also short out your entire damn system. And if you take our coms, you take the safety stabilization I programmed in. Anything at all could set it off. It would kill us, but then, it would take out your machine as well."

Evka's posture was tense, and for a moment, a look of pure hatred flashed across her features. Then, with obvious effort, her face smoothed.

"Very clever, Tae Bezdominkov," she said quietly. She turned back to Lev. "Very well, then. You'll stay here as my guests indefinitely, or until I find a workaround. But your friends in the street will die, all of them. This was not part of our agreement." There was a contained fury in her voice that was almost frightening.

It probably would have been frightening, if Tae hadn't been so damn tired.

"You could do that," said Lev, the steel in his voice matching hers. "But ask yourself, Evka—what would have to happen before one of us decides that it's worth dying to stop you?"

"You think me incapable of preventing you from killing yourselves?" she snapped.

Lev raised an eyebrow. "As you said yourself, we're exceptionally resourceful."

"Even if you did, you honestly believe shorting out my machine would stop the Protocol permanently?"

"No." Lev's voice was calm. "You'll fix it, eventually. But in the interim, the people of Prasvishoni would revolt, you know that. Our revolution was a minor thing compared to what would happen if your machine shut down, now that everyone knows what it can do. And after a failure like that, how can you be sure the government would be willing to put the Protocol back in place? Even your own enforcers are uneasy about the kind of power this gives you."

For a long moment, Evka was silent. At last, she raised an eyebrow. Her face had taken on, once again, its calm, amused expression, but there was a cold anger beneath it.

"Perhaps you're right," she said. "Of course, you're smart enough to realize that the moment one of you chooses to kill yourself, I'll send the police in to kill your friends, without mercy. They won't need the Protocol to do that. Because at that point—" she gave a small shrug. "As you say, Lev, what more would I have to lose? So it appears we've managed to tie each other's hands, in the matter of your friends' deaths."

"It appears we have," said Lev quietly.

At least, that was what Tae thought he said. Now that he'd finished his part in this desperate, ridiculous, suicide scheme, his whole body was rebelling, and the room wavered around him.

"If we're going to be your guests, I assume you'll have no objection to showing us to our quarters?" Lev's tone was a pleasant, biting politeness.

"Of course not," said Evka. She was smiling now, her good humour apparently restored. An act, maybe, but if Tae had to guess, she looked like she was thrilled at the prospect of a challenge. "I shall have my people show you there at once. You look like you need the rest."

She gestured to the guards, and they stepped forward.

"Follow me," grunted one of them.

Tae staggered down the corridor after the guard, leaning on Ivan, through a door the guard opened for them.

The only thing he noticed about the room was that it had a cot.

Honestly, at this point, that was the only thing he cared about.

He didn't even remember hitting the mattress.

9

Jez, day 3, morning

Jez woke to the uncomfortable feeling that something was wrong.

It took her a moment to figure out what it was.

She was in a cot, alone.

And she hadn't realized, until just then, how quickly she'd become used to waking up next to Lev, snuggling into the warmth of him.

And then she remembered the rest, and sat up abruptly, her breath coming a little too quickly.

She was damn well locked up. She was locked up in a room, alone, and she couldn't damn well get out.

She jumped to her feet and groped blindly for the artificial light. She found the switch and hit it, and a moment later, a cold blue illuminated the small, bare room.

There was the cot, a desk that looked like it was meant to serve as a table, with a chair pulled up in front of it, and to one side of the room, a door that looked like it led to a bathroom.

The door to the outside was locked.

She'd known it would be, but she couldn't help herself from trying it anyways.

She paced from one end of the room to the other, then back

again.

Four and a half steps from one wall to the other.

Damn it. Damn it to hell, she bloody hated being locked up.

A faint sound interrupted her creeping panic, and she paused a moment, listening.

It was a muffled tapping.

It came again, and this time she could pick out the pattern.

Pilot's code.

Jez. Are you in there? Can you hear me?

She stepped over to the wall and put her ear against it, listening. Finally, she tapped back cautiously, *who is it?*

Who the hell do you think it is, Evka?

She frowned. *Tech-head?* she tapped.

Yes, it's me. I've been bloody well tapping my knuckles raw for the last bloody hour. Where were you?

She grinned despite herself.

Somehow, the exasperated taps through the wall made everything just a little more bearable.

There's a thing called sleep, she tapped back. *Don't know if you've heard of it.*

We're locked up, in the lab of some murderous mastermind, and you slept in?

She rolled her eyes. *I was tired. Anyways, you got anything to say other than complaining about crap? Also, how are the others?*

Yes, I do. Can you put your com up to the wall? Evka's got some sort of blocker field on all the rooms, but I think I managed to get through it. I should be able to catch your signal, if you can get it close enough.

She did as he asked. A moment later, her com crackled, and Tae's voice came through her earpiece. "Can you hear me?"

"Yep," she said, grinning in relief. "Loud and clear."

"Good." He sounded as exasperated in person as he had in pilots' code. "I'll hook you in with the others."

There was a soft click.

"Jez?" It was Lev, and something knotted inside her released at the sound of his voice. "Are you alright?"

"You know me, genius. I'm fine."

"Yes, we do know you, pilot-girl." Ysbel's tone was dry. "That's why we've all been worrying ourselves sick." She paused. "You slept in? That's where you were all this time?"

Jez sighed heavily. "Didn't know we were running on a damn schedule."

"Tae, you have a spoof set into Evka's bugs, right?" asked Lev.

"Yes." Tae's tone was short. "But it won't take her long to find it."

"That's alright," said Lev grimly. "With any luck, we won't be here too long."

"So," said Jez cheerily. "We gonna blow this damn place up? Or burn it down?" She'd forgotten, somehow, how being locked up got under her skin, spidered through her brain, crept into her muscles, making it impossible to sit still. "Also, you don't think that bastard Evka left some alcohol in here, do you?"

There was a moment of silence.

"Well," said Ysbel at last, in a flat voice. "If we were worried about Jez being able to do what we need her to—"

"I can do basically anything," Jez drawled. The restlessness and adrenaline pumping through her were almost as potent as alcohol anyways.

"Jez." It was Lev again, and there was something about the concern in his tone that was reassuring. "You know what you need to do. Just—be careful, OK? Evka has … a temper. And very little respect for people who don't fit her narrow preconception of intelligent."

She closed her eyes for a moment, trying to steady herself. "Yeah," she said. "Yeah, I'll be good. It's all good."

"I'm very glad we're all safe and accounted for," said Masha. Her voice was weak, but there was a tinge of wryness in it. "But I doubt Evka will be happy if her guards walk in on us chatting to each other through our coms."

Lev sighed. "You're right. We'll talk tonight."

The com clicked off, and for a moment, Jez sat staring at it. Her breath was still coming too quickly, and she closed her eyes and tried not to think too hard about the lock on the damn door.

It would be fine. She'd be fine. She'd done this plenty of times now, and she'd damn well be just fine.

She glanced around and took a deep breath.

Funny to think that a few months back, what she was about to do next would have been instinctual—she wouldn't have stopped to consider anything.

But then, a few months back, she didn't have people who she cared about more than she'd thought possible. Who cared about her back. Who might be affected if things went badly.

But this time—well, their plan depended on her being able to convince Evka that she was nothing but a stupid, impulsive, trigger-happy pilot.

A really, really irritating, stupid, impulsive, trigger-happy pilot.

She grinned. So—not too far from the truth, then, except for the stupid part.

May as well get busy.

She crossed the four-and-a-half steps to the door and pounded on in. "Hey! You plaguers!" she called. "Your damn boss planning to starve me to death?"

For a few moments, nothing happened.

She pounded again, and at last an annoyed voice from outside the door said, "You'll have food when Evka sends it up. Would you please stop that racket?"

She grinned to herself. "I'm hungry," she called. "Bet food would make me shut up."

"I told you—your food will come when it comes."

She made her voice sound as pathetic as possible. "Haven't eaten since that bastard threw me in here yesterday afternoon. Probably going to starve to death in a minute or two here, and I bet Evka wouldn't like that."

The guard didn't answer.

"Well, guess if I can't eat, may as well talk to pass the time. So, when your mom met your dad, how long you think it took her to figure out he was actually just a really damn ugly space-jelly?"

Still no answer.

She paused a moment. "Hey, wanna hear a song I made up?"

The guard heaved a long sigh, and she heard rustling. Then something was shoved under the door. "There," the guard growled. "Here's a damn rations pack. Will you shut up now?"

Jez gave a tight grin.

She'd forgotten how much she enjoyed this, actually.

"Thanks, you plaguer," she called, pulling back the wrapper. She sniffed at it. "Bit stale," she remarked. "How long has this been in your pocket?"

"I picked it up from the kitchens this morning. Will you please shut up?"

She tore the wrapper a little further, then took a bite. She gave it a moment, to sound convincing, then said, mouth full of food, "Hey, so you think—" She stopped abruptly, making a sudden choking sound.

For a moment, there was no response.

"Prisoner?" asked the guard at last, a hint of uncertainty in his voice.

"Choking—" she wheezed. "Can't—"

"Prisoner?" The concern in his voice was growing sharper.

She wheezed for a moment more, kicking feebly at the door for effect.

There was the click of the door unlocking, then it opened a crack, and the guard's worried face appeared.

Jez sprang to her feet, shoving her boot into the crack in the door as the guard tried to yank it closed. He jerked his pistol out, probably set to stun, considering how badly Evka needed them alive. Jez grabbed his wrist and shoved it upwards as he pulled the trigger, and the stun blast slammed harmlessly into the ceiling.

"Thanks. I'm starting to like you a little more than I did," she said. She was grinning so wide it hurt.

He tapped his free wrist against his thigh and brought his com to his mouth.

She shoved the door open and brought her knee up hard into his crotch. He wheezed, doubling over, and she dropped him with a fist to the stomach. He crumpled into a heap on the floor.

She crouched quickly, tapping her com against his while Tae's mods did their work. Then she snatched the stun pistol from his nerveless hand and took off down the hallway.

There were footsteps pounding towards her from both directions before she reached the end of the hallway. Three people, one of them still in a white lab coat, emerged from the stairwell at the end of the hallway, and she raised the stolen stun gun without slowing, and fired off a shot.

The figure on the left collapsed, and she turned her aim to the figure in the middle—

The entire world went black.

When she woke up, her head felt like it had been stuffed with manufab.

She blinked a few times, trying to figure out where the hell she was.

Then she tipped her head back and swore faintly.

Damn it, she was locked up. She remembered that part now. And as to what had happened in the hallway … well, she was still a little foggy on that.

She was lying on the floor to her cell, as if she'd been tossed unceremoniously through the door—which, now that she thought about it, was probably exactly what had happened.

She grinned slightly, despite the dull pounding in her head.

That had actually been pretty funny, all things considered.

"Jez! Are you there, Jez?" The voice was coming through her earpiece, and she groaned and sat up, then promptly fell over again.

Damn it, she hadn't expected to be quite this dizzy.

"She's still not answering." Lev's voice was grim. "I'm going to call Evka if we can't get her in the next five standard minutes."

"Hey genius, I'm fine," she mumbled, hitting her com. "All good here."

"Jez! What happened to you?"

She tried to sit up again, a little more gingerly this time. This time, she didn't actually fall over, but she had to brace herself on the floor for a minute. "I'm good," she said, when she'd recovered her balance. "Guards were a little upset, is all. But I got Tae his copy of the key. Sending it through right now."

"What did you—"

She grinned. "I tricked the guard into opening up the door, then I kicked him in the crotch, stole his stun gun, and ran for it."

"And—what happened?" Lev sounded like he didn't really want to know.

"Not totally sure. I woke up like two seconds ago."

"You—"

Something hurt in her chest at the worry in his tone, and she couldn't tell if it was guilt or gratitude. "Genus," she said quietly. "I'm OK, just a bit dizzy. Nothing's wrong with me, I promise."

He took a deep breath. "Alright. Just—"

She managed another grin. "Look. You said, get on Evka's nerves. Figure I'm getting on Evka's nerves right about now. She had her damn lab assistants chasing me down."

"She did?" Ysbel sounded slightly amused.

Jez's grin widened a bit.

It actually had been quite funny.

The problem with kneeing her guard in the crotch, punching him in the stomach, stealing his gun, and taking off down the hall, apparently, was that your next guard wouldn't be inclined to conversation.

And he—or she, Jez wasn't actually sure, since the plaguer hadn't said a single word to her in the hour and a half she'd been shouting insults, questions, and rude jokes through the door—didn't seem inclined to give Jez breakfast either.

She glowered at the door, and muttered a long commentary on the guard's parentage. Which the bastard didn't even acknowledge.

It was almost insulting, actually.

"Hey, your boss-lady going to starve me to death?" she shouted through the crack in the door.

Again, no answer.

She sighed, and went back to pacing.

It felt like it must've been about three standard years, but was probably only another standard hour, when the lock clicked.

She jumped to her feet as the door opened, but this time the guards were ready for her, stun-pistols pointed at her face.

"Hold out your hands," one of the guards said, voice grim. "Evka wants to talk to all of you."

"Yeah?" Jez drawled. "Well, maybe if she'd actually give me my damn breakfast, I'd think about—"

"You can come walking, or we can knock you out and drag you. Your choice," the guard said.

Jez sighed deeply.

Bastards needed to work on their senses of humour.

She held out her arms. The guard reached for them, and she pulled them away at the last second, snickering at the look on his face.

Two of the guards stepped forward, grabbing her arms and wrenching them around behind her back, and twisted them painfully as one of them affixed the cuffs. She swore fluently and creatively at them, but they ignored her completely.

When they'd finished cuffing her wrists, they put walking cuffs on her ankles for good measure. She rolled her eyes, but honestly, she couldn't help but feel a tiny bit gratified.

She must have been the last one they were bringing down, because she didn't see any of the others in the corridor or in the lift. Finally, though, the guards prodded her through a doorway and into the room where they'd talked with Evka the afternoon before.

The others were already there, like she'd guessed. They all looked up at her entrance, and she grinned at them, trying to hide the sudden panicky relief that jittered through her at the seeing them.

"Jez Solokov." Evka's voice was flat and completely unamused.

"Hey, you bastard," said Jez, grinning broadly. "Looks like you didn't get any less ugly after a night of sleep."

Evka's eyes narrowed just a fraction. She gestured at the guards, and they marched Jez over to a chair next to the others, shoving her into it.

Lev was in the chair next to her. He moved slightly, so his knee brushed hers, and the touch was steadying.

She took a deep breath.

She wasn't doing all this crap because she was stir-crazy, even though she was.

Their plan depended on her being able to do this.

"So," said Evka pleasantly, turning back to Lev. "I understand your pet pilot is quite the escape artist."

Jez shot the woman a quick grin. "Guess you could say that," she drawled. "Or else you could say your guards are absolute crap. Hell, didn't even have to try this morning. Although, ugly nasty bastard like you, probably hard to find good help." She paused a moment. "I mean, I'm good at what I do, but I figure you've been practising being a bastard a hell of a lot longer."

Evka's eyes narrowed ever so slightly.

"Evka," Lev broke in quickly, as if trying to defuse the situation, but she caught the quick, encouraging grin he shot her. "I see you were able to find another location to re-create your laboratory."

Evka turned her cold look from Jez to Lev. "Yes. And I'm sure you'll be thrilled to know you were instrumental in making this happen. You demonstrated to the people in power that the system needs stability, and that there was no guarantee of stability when uncontrollable elements were set loose in the system." She gave a small, cold smile. "I suppose I should thank you, despite the trouble you put me to."

"You want someone to put you to trouble, figure that's basically our specialty, you ugly scum-eater," said Jez cheerfully. "Funny that a group of ex-convicts could set you swamp-footed for so damn long. But then, I guess after meeting you, doesn't really surprise me all that much. Kinda stupid, for someone so smart, aren't you?"

Evka's eyes had narrowed further. She was obviously someone who prided herself on her remaining calm.

But then, so was Masha. And Jez had managed to make Masha basically murderous.

"That's precisely what I brought you down to talk to you about," Evka said, turning back to Lev. Her voice was icy. "Since yesterday afternoon, when you arrived, your pilot has made a very clumsy attempt to break out, someone has been attempting to hack into my system, your street boy's lover almost convinced one of my guards to resign, and apparently one of Ysbel's children set fire to their cot."

Jez gave a badly concealed snort of laughter, and glanced over at the kids.

Olya was looking straight ahead with wide, innocent eyes, but there was the hint of a smirk under expression.

"Mama, I'm hungry," said Misko loudly. "How come we haven't had lunch yet?"

Ysbel picked him up, settling him on her lap. "Misko. We'll eat soon, alright?"

"But I'm hungry right now!"

"Misko, my heart—" began Tanya.

Misko started to wail.

By this point, Jez was pretty sure she could see Evka's eye twitching.

Bastard didn't stand a damn chance.

"Well, can't say I blame Ivan's guard," Jez drawled. "Hell,

knowing you, all he'd have had to say was that there was a damn swamp rat hiring, and the guard would have—"

The world went black.

There was a pounding, throbbing ache in the back of her head, and something cold under her back, and—and noises. It took her a moment to realize the noises were words, and another moment to realize the voice speaking was Lev's.

His tone was cold and dangerous.

"What the hell have you done to her, Evka? If you've—"

She moaned, and blinked her eyes open, and Lev's bloodless face came into focus above her.

"I was simply demonstrating what I'd brought you down to tell you," Evka said. Her voice had regained some of its typical amusement. "Considering I was unable to get in a word edgewise. I didn't cause any permanent damage—as you so helpfully informed me yesterday, killing any of you would be antithetical to my self-interest at this point. But as you are no doubt aware, my Protocol allows me to do more than just kill the intended target. And although I haven't yet disabled your street boy's com blocker, there's a force-field around my lab that, I've discovered, negates the effect. I simply wanted to inform you of that, so that should something like this happen because you insisted on causing problems, it wouldn't come as a shock."

"Jez," said Lev in a low voice, bending over her. "Are you alright?" There was a desperation to his voice that hurt her.

"Hey, genius," she rasped. "I'm fine." She rolled over and tried to push herself to her feet despite her cuffs.

Lev gave an involuntary yelp and grabbed for her as she lost her balance and almost toppled over. When he was sure she was steady, he turned to Evka, cold fury on his face.

"Listen to me, Evka. You think the rest of the crew has been causing problems so far. You have no idea what your life will be like if you hurt Jez. Because I swear to you—"

"She's not permanently damaged," said Evka through her teeth. "But you will know, Lev, if you stop and consider it, that I can cause some very permanent damage without killing someone. I suggest you and your pilot keep that in mind."

"Anyway, listening to this mud-eater talk, I figure I probably would've passed out from boredom in a couple of minutes anyway," said Jez, shaking her head slightly to clear it. "She actually taught classes in university? What were they about, falling asleep quickly? Hell, I've met swamp-rats who were more interesting than this bastard. And less ugly, too."

"Jez," Evka's voice was low and dangerous. "I have been remarkably lenient with you, mostly because I understand that you mean something to Lev, as frankly incomprehensible as I find that. However—"

Jez grinned. "What, jealous? I mean, hell, not your fault you're not as hot as me. Can't help it, probably. Your personality, though, I'd say that's the thing holding you back."

"Evka," said Lev through his teeth. "Is that all you brought us here to tell us? Because if so, I suggest you send us back to our rooms. I'm finding I have little desire for your company at the moment."

He was still crouched beside Jez, and she could feel his hand on her back trembling slightly, and something twisted, just a little, in her chest.

But they'd all agreed, when they made their crazy, stupid, ridiculous plan—it depended on her making Evka bloody furious with her. Lev had clearly thought what Tae had done to the program would be enough to keep her safe, and she hadn't disabused him of the notion.

But hell, she'd been around enough to know that if you pissed off someone like Evka, it probably meant you were going to get hurt.

And she knew as well as the rest of them did that this was probably the best chance they had at surviving the week. Maybe their only chance. But—well, but damn it, she hated to see him hurt like this.

She closed her eyes for just a moment.

Evka turned her cold gaze back to Lev. "I had assumed that the people you associated with would be capable of behaving like rational adults. The others, I have, perhaps, some hope of. I have shut down the communication between your coms again, and have spoken with the guards who will be outside your street boy and his lover's cell. I can hardly blame the children for being children. This pilot of yours, however—"

Jez took a deep breath. "Hey," she said. "You have no idea how damn polite I can be when I feel like it. But here's the thing— generally only do it to people who don't remind me so much of a patch of damn swamp-slime, but with less—"

The world went dark again.

When she woke up again, her head was spinning, and faint nausea churned in her stomach.

Damn that bastard Evka to hell.

"Lev?" she began, her voice coming out shakier than she intended.

There was no answer.

She bit back her sudden, absurd panic.

"Lev?"

Still no answer.

She blinked her eyes open and peered around. Then she swore, because swearing was better than losing her damn mind, and that was the other option.

She was back in her cell. Alone.

She hadn't realized how quickly seeing Lev would strip away her equanimity.

She'd always been good at being alone. But—

But Lev's absence, even though he was only a couple rooms away, ached through her whole body.

At least they'd taken the damn cuffs off.

She hit her com. "Tae?" she whispered.

Then she remembered what Evka had said and swore again.

Damn it to hell, she couldn't do this. They were all counting on her, but she couldn't damn well do this—

She took a deep breath and closed her eyes for a moment, waiting for her heart rate to slow back down.

It would be fine. She wasn't alone, not really.

And even if she had been—for this stupid crew, she'd learned, she could do a hell of a lot of things she'd never thought she'd be able to.

It was some time later that the lock clicked again.

Jez glanced up, with the vague hope that Evka had decided to send dinner in after all.

Instead, two guards stepped through the door, their heat-pistols fixed on her unwaveringly.

She managed to hold onto her grin, but adrenalin was pumping through her body so hard she was almost shaking with it.

The door closed behind them.

"Hey there," she drawled. Her heart was pounding so quickly she could feel it against her ribs. "Come in for some company? Here's the thing, I'd love to oblige, but I'm taken at the moment, so—"

And then a spike of pain unlike anything she'd felt in her life jolted through her, knifing down her spine in pulsing, breathtaking waves.

She could feel her muscles loosen, feel herself slide to the floor, but honestly, she couldn't focus on anything except the stabbing, icy pain. Her muscles spasmed helplessly, her whole body twisting and arching to get away.

"Jez." It was Evka's voice, through her earpiece.

"Hey—you bastard," Jez managed breathlessly, the words garbled through the pain in her clenched jaw.

"This is your last warning, Jez," the woman said. "I've had enough of your antics. Control yourself, if you're capable of it—the next time, I won't be so lenient."

The pain spiralled higher, and Jez screamed, the sound muffled through her clenched teeth.

She couldn't handle this, not for one more second, she was going to die, she was going to go mad—

And then, as abruptly as it had started, the pain stopped.

Jez crumpled, her body shaking.

The guards stepped out the door, closing and locking it behind them.

Jez lay there for a long time, too drained to even try to get up.

It took her a while to realize the soft tapping was coming from the wall beside her, not from something broken inside her head.

Jez, what happened? Are you alright? Jez, can you hear me?

Slowly, she rolled over. Her muscles were too shaky for her to stand, but she dragged herself over to the wall on hands and knees and collapsed against it, gathering herself.

She raised a shaking fist and tapped back, *I'm fine. Just Evka having some fun.*

There was a long pause. *Are you sure you're alright?* Tae tapped finally.

I'm fine. She paused. *Just—be careful, OK? Evka can do more than just knock you out. She can hurt you.*

How badly are you hurt? The taps were slightly more frantic now.

Not like that. In your head. She paused again. *Don't tell genius, OK? He's worried enough already.*

Again, a pause. At last, Tae tapped, *Fine. But if it happens again, I'm telling him.*

Yeah, she tapped back.

She was too exhausted to argue.

She'd gotten the key, and she'd managed to piss Evka off well and thoroughly.

But her muscles were still shaking from the icy shock of pain, and a sick nausea rose in her stomach at the memory of it.

And she was more afraid than she really wanted to think about.

10

Lev, day 4, morning

Lev tipped his head back in his chair, closing his eyes for a moment. His teeth were gritted so hard they hurt.

He hadn't bloody thought this through. He should have taken Evka's ability to problem-solve into account before he'd agreed to let Jez serve as the scapegoat for Evka's anger.

Still—it wasn't like they'd had many other options.

It was ridiculously early in the morning, but he'd finally given up rolling over restlessly in bed and gotten up.

He'd honestly tried to sleep. But the sick panic from yesterday, when he'd seen Jez drop to the floor like a puppet with its strings cut, her eyes rolled back in her head, body limp, still jolted through him whenever he tried to close his eyes.

And he was very, very certain that knocking someone unconscious wasn't the worst Evka could do, and still not kill them.

He'd seen, from the fear in Jez's face, hidden under her jaunty expression, that she'd guessed the same thing.

Why was it that every damn plan they came up with somehow involved Jez getting the hell beat out of her?

And why the hell did he keep agreeing to them?

He trusted Jez. She'd agreed to this, and she'd known what she was getting into, and he had to be willing to trust her decisions.

But—in a very selfish way, he wasn't completely sure he'd survive if something happened to her.

He sighed. He had to stop thinking about it, that was all.

His com crackled, and he jumped.

"Lev," came the familiar voice through his earpiece. "I see you haven't changed all that much since you were my student. Up early, as usual."

He restrained himself, barely, from swearing at her. "What do you want, Evka?" he asked through his teeth.

Evka's voice was amused, as if he'd said something absurd, but endearing. "Lev. It's that pilot you're upset about, isn't it? I've truly never seen you so infatuated. And certainly not by someone who seems so entirely opposite of your type."

He closed his eyes for a moment, trying to bring his anger back under control.

"Maybe you didn't know me as well as you thought you did," he said at last, blandly, but even he could hear the tinge of fury under his words.

"You may be right, at that. Or maybe you simply don't know yourself as well is you think you do. It's easy to get caught up in something that one doesn't belong in, for the thrill of rebelling against authority. And you always were a rebel. Not in the traditional sense, no—I was certainly surprised to see you standing on barricades a few weeks back—but you never did take kindly to authority. It's why you and I got along so well, I believe."

"No," said Lev through his teeth. "You and I got along so well because you didn't bother telling me you were experimenting on damn street kids."

Evka chuckled. "That's the other thing no one would know to look at you. Your sense of absolute justice. That's what ultimately landed you in prison, did it not?"

"If you'd bloody well found a way to tell me that you were still alive, and that you'd bloody well chosen to go with the government officials, instead of leading me to believe you'd been kidnapped and murdered, maybe I wouldn't have bloody well ended up in prison for trying to find out what happened to you," he snapped. His heart was racing, his breath coming too quickly.

He swore to himself.

Evka was nothing to him. She was evil, and conscienceless, and one more person that he wished he'd never met.

But there was something about hearing her voice again after all these years, something about her patient, clipped, professional tones, that brought him back to a time when he'd been much younger, and much more innocent, and the world had been a place that actually made sense.

"For that, I do apologize," said Evka at last, quietly. "I assure you, it wasn't intentional." She paused. "As you're awake anyways, perhaps you'd like to come down. I'll show you around my laboratory. I feel it would be easier to talk in person than through a com."

Lev was tempted to say something rude. But she would only find that amusing.

Besides—if Jez could handle being locked up, and whatever it was that Evka had done to her yesterday, he could handle spending some time with Evka.

He sighed. "Very well," he said, the words almost choking him. "Let me get dressed."

"I'll send a guard to bring you down," she said, a small smile in her voice, then her com tapped off.

He was ready by the time the guard tapped on the door, and he followed her down the corridors.

Evka must trust him enough not to cuff him, at least. That, or she assumed her guards would be able to physically overpower him if he made a desperate bid for freedom.

He sighed wryly.

So maybe he wasn't Jez. But he was pretty damn sure he wasn't nearly as physically incompetent as everyone around him seemed to believe.

He glanced at the time as he walked.

It was even earlier than he'd thought.

Apparently, Evka hadn't changed much since their university days—he'd never managed to beat her into the office then, either.

They reached the door, and the guard touched her com to the lock and pulled it open, gesturing Lev inside. Lev stepped in, and something that was halfway between anger and nostalgia caught in his throat at the familiarity of the scene—Evka bent over a holoscreen on the desk, a writing utensil in her hand and a look of thoughtful concentration on her face, five other holoscreens pulled up around her and documents spread across the available surfaces.

She glanced up at his entrance and smiled. "Lev. I'm delighted you could join me."

Feeling as if he were somehow walking through a memory, he came across the room to stand beside her.

She gestured to a chair, and he sat.

"It's—been a long time, hasn't it?" she said, and he was surprised at the emotion in her tone.

"It has." He kept his voice intentionally short.

She raised an eyebrow at him, still smiling, then turned back to the screen in front of her. "You know, your assistance on this program was absolutely invaluable. You saw things that I hadn't seen after working on the problem for years. I'm not exaggerating when I say you were by far my most talented student."

"And I'm not exaggerating when I say that you're the person I like least in the entire system," snapped Lev. "Why do you want me here?"

His muscles were shaky with adrenalin.

Perhaps he should try harder to be polite. But still—she wouldn't be expecting any less.

She studied him thoughtfully. "As much as I wish I could say I was hoping for your insight—considering we got off to a bad start yesterday, I don't anticipate you being willing to provide me that."

He didn't bother to answer, just gave her a cold glare.

She smiled slightly. "Lev. You know there's really no need for that."

"No, I don't know," he said through his teeth. "Because I thought there was no need for me to have to worry about you trying to kill people I cared about, after all the years we spent working together. I thought there was no need to protect myself from someone who I considered a friend. If you want an illustration of how stupid I was back then, that's your best one."

Evka sighed, and there was something that was almost sadness in her eyes. "Lev," she began. Then she shook her head and pulled up her own chair. Something about the weariness in her posture as she sat sent something instinctive and unconscious through him. The urge to jump to his feet and hold the chair for her, ask her for the Lady's sake to get some rest. Like he had when she was his mentor, and he'd cared for her as he would have—should have—his mother.

"Listen," she said quietly. "I understand you and I have taken different paths. But I was being genuine when I said I wished I'd had more time with you. You see me as a villain. You blame me for deceiving you, getting you thrown in prison because you thought you could somehow track down the person who had hurt me or kidnapped me." She paused. "Believe me, that was never my intention. I was—touched, more than I can say, to find what you had done."

"Not touched enough to do anything to get me or my family out of prison," said Lev, his voice coming out harsh.

She was still watching him, and her calm gaze had a hint of regret behind it. "No. I didn't try to get you out of jail." She paused a moment. "If I'd had my wish, you would have stayed there."

"And you wonder why we're not on the best of terms," he said cuttingly.

She raised her eyebrows. "I think you misunderstand me," she said. "I had hoped you would remain in prison, because as far as I could see, it was the only possible hope I had of you being kept safe."

He shook his head. "You must think I'm very gullible indeed, despite what you've said about my intelligence. You truly think I'd believe that all this time you've been working for my well-being?"

She gave a slight smile. "Of course not. You know me, Lev—I certainly would not throw away something this vitally important to rescue someone adult enough to make their own decisions. A sentiment that I once believed you shared. But—I think you also know me well enough to know that if I could have kept you from harm, I would have. That was my miscalculation in the university, when you broke in a few months back—assuming I could talk you out of your proposed course of action, rather than immediately informing the government officials with whom I was working of your true identity, and the danger you posed.

"And so, in the end, I suppose I made the same mistake I've been critical of you for—allowing sentiment to cloud my judgement. And although my mistake proved to be a costly one, it wasn't, ultimately, the deathblow I once feared it was." She paused a moment, watching him. "You implied that I intentionally led you on, back when you were my student and I disappeared. That I let you labour under the misapprehension I was in danger, when in fact my being taken by the government was part of a grand master plan. In that, you are mistaken." She sighed, and again the weariness that flicked across her face flooded a guttural, instinctive concern through him.

"I was very much afraid for my life," she continued, quietly. "There was a reason, a very good one, why I left you the message I did—why I told you not to come after me, should anything happen. It was because I didn't want what had happened to me to happen to you. And I wasn't certain I'd survive what would happen to me."

Lev stared at her.

She gave a small smile. "Come now, Lev—you were everything I'd dreamed of in a student, and an assistant. I was looking forward to having you as a colleague. Why would I lie to you?"

Lev raised a sardonic eyebrow. "That's exactly the question I've asked myself, more than once."

Evka smiled again, but there wasn't any humour in it. "I was kidnapped, Lev—by government agents, as you surmised. The student who you later exposed to the police for punishment was, in fact, the student who turned me in. Yes, I heard that story eventually. Because what you and I were working on, Lev—what I've finally completed—was something far, far too many people in positions of power wanted, feared and coveted both. Our work was government sanctioned, of course, everything you and I did. But you know how many factions the government has, and how many different hands are in our ministers' pockets. I very narrowly avoided torture when they came to take me. I barely escaped with my life. If the people who took me couldn't have what I was making, they were going to ensure no one else could have it, either. But I've played enough university politics to know how to get along in government. I was able to buy enough favours to keep myself alive, and buy enough clout to keep my program running. Had I not—" she paused again, a small shiver in her voice.

Even after all this time, he could read the tiny traces of emotion in her, no matter how well she tried to hide them.

"I could have reached out to you," she continued at last. "I could have contacted you to let you know that I was safe. But had I done so, you would not have been safe. Better for you to think that I'd died —better for you to be thrown in prison for trying to find me—than to know what actually happened, and get dragged into the same web of intrigue I'd been thrust into."

This time, when she smiled, there was something a little more genuine about it, that dry humour he remembered so well sparkling behind her eyes. "So you see, Lev, I did care for you, just as much as you once, perhaps, believed. And in return—well, you were searching for some way to save me, or at least to find out what happened to me. That landed you in jail, which drew you into Masha's sphere of influence. And your work with Masha— specifically, your destabilization of the government, and breaking out an entire prison planet—led to my work becoming once more relevant. So, in a manner speaking, you did, in fact, save my life." She shrugged slightly. "I'm sure what I was doing would have become important the moment I finished it—a tool this powerful, the government would be stupid not to use it. Even if they were afraid of it, if they didn't use it, they'd know someone else would.

But I was working on a minimal budget, with almost no resources. This was a project begun by Ysbel's father, years ago, before he realized what it was he was playing with. Before he fled with his family, too afraid to take hold of what was in his hands, and left it for hands much more unscrupulous to grasp."

"Hands like yours," said Lev quietly.

Evka chuckled again. "No, not like mine. You worked in this government, Lev—me, keeping peace in the system by means of a painless device implanted in the brain stem—that is not unscrupulous. Tracking down your political enemies and torturing and murdering their families, forcing someone to sleep with you or serve you or worse, because you have the mean to torture them beyond their ability to comprehend, killing children in their father's or mother's arms as an act of revenge—those things are unscrupulous. That's what would have happened, eventually, had I not taken control of this program with an iron fist."

"You hurt Jez." His voice was steadier than he expected it to be. "I watched your Protocol kill people in the streets. Just the click of a button, and they—" he broke off, feeling suddenly sick.

Evka shook her head, her expression serious. "The people in the streets, from my understanding, were attacking police officers. Would you rather they'd been killed by heat guns? Would you rather the city devolve into total anarchy? Do you know how many people would have died then? And Jez—Jez is a wildcard. The one thing that's made me realize how much you truly have changed—or at least, you believe you've changed. Don't tell me she didn't deserve it."

"You dare stand there and tell me—" His voice was shaking with anger.

Evka held up a hand, the gesture almost weary. "I understand you care for her. The reason behind it is frankly incomprehensible to me, but I can accept things even if I don't understand the logic behind them. You're bristling at the implication that this person you care for deserved to be hurt. I understand that. But you must see my point. That pilot is a danger. She's always been a danger, from what I've read on her file. People like her are a menace to any established order, because they refuse to accept its authority. The same with the people who were attacking the police, breaking curfew. They were killed, yes. But it was quick, and painless, and humane, and they were trying to disrupt the order I had only just managed to impose on the streets. You were behind the barricades, Lev. You saw how many died, on both sides. You truly believe that's a better outcome?"

He stared at her for a long time. His breath was still coming too quickly, and something in the stomach twisted to think how the sixteen-year-old version of him might have seen reason in what she was saying. Might have, at last, nodded in agreement.

The sixteen-year-old version of him, who'd never met Jez. Who'd never understood what it meant to be free, and what it meant not to be. Who'd never understood a thing called morality, or ideas called right and wrong.

Evka gave him a small smile. "I doubt you're capable of agreeing with me at the moment. You've invested too much in that crew, in that pilot, in your heroic rebellion, to be able to view things dispassionately. But deep down, you know I'm right. You, too, were trying to stop the city from going to pieces once Grigory and Olyessa were gone. The only difference between your plan and mine is that mine ends up with me in charge, and yours ends up with Masha, or possibly you. It's not a disagreement on means, or ends, or even morality. It's simply a disagreement over who is most fit to implement policy."

"It's much more than that," said Lev quietly. "It's a disagreement on whether someone should wield the power to decide who lives and dies, or whether people can be trusted with their own lives. But you won't see that, intelligent as you are. I'm not sure I would have either, when I worked with you."

She sighed again and gave him a small smile. "Another similarity between us; we both see you've changed. The only difference is whether we see that as a net benefit, or a net detriment."

She turned back to her holoscreen. "Well. I asked you down here, and you obliged by coming. I may as well show you around. You haven't changed enough, I think, not to appreciate this, at any rate." She closed down the screen with a quick, businesslike gesture and stood. "If there's one thing I gained by having been taken by force from the university, it was the knowledge the government resources are vastly more impressive than the ones available to a professor, if you're lucky enough to have them allocated to you."

As he followed her, Lev wasn't entirely sure what made him more uncomfortable—the undeniable efficiency and modernity of Evka's laboratory, and the accompanying realization of how very quickly she could work through any problems he and the others could devise —or the fact that, despite everything, he was impressed. There was a small part of him that was calculating, dispassionately, exactly how much information he could glean from working with a system like this, and how much the thought of it thrilled him.

Evka, apparently, could read him as well as he could read her, because she smiled at the look on his face.

"I told you you'd be impressed," she said. "As I said earlier, we didn't get off to a good start yesterday. But should you ever change your mind, my offer still stands—your cooperation in exchange for the lives of your crew. And this is what you'd be working with—tools and resources that you've never dreamed of. It's much more interesting than a university professor's office, with a holoscreen that flickers when it's too cold outside."

He found he was smiling at that memory, before he caught himself. He cleared his throat. "You showed me around your laboratory—aren't you going to show off the program you've apparently perfected?"

She gave a soft laugh. "I imagine it would have been even more sophisticated had you been helping me. And when you say perfected, I think what you mean is, managed to repair after your clever attempt at vandalism." She paused a moment, the hint of a smile on her lips. "I wasn't thrilled about that, to be perfectly honest with you. But upon consideration, I'd much prefer working against a sophisticated vandal than a stupid one. I was very impressed to see how your thinking had progressed since we parted company. But no, I don't think I'll show you into the system, and I think you know the reason as well as I do."

Lev found he was returning her smile, despite himself. "At least will you show me the mechanism by which the algorithm identifies who you've determined deserves to die? I assume you don't simply wait on police calls for that. We hadn't finished that part of the equation before you were—kidnapped, I suppose, if what you're telling me is true."

Evka's smile broadened. "That sounds much more like the student I thought I knew nine years ago," she said. "Of course, just like with the student I knew nine years ago, I know better than to give you unfettered access to any source of information, no matter how apparently innocuous. Because you have the ability to ask, with a completely straight face, for information which you would use to burn the entire system to the ground. Or—" she continued, her smile widening just a little, "to infect a rival professor's research notes with a self-replicating error that destroyed all the information he'd spent the last ten years collecting."

Again, Lev found himself smiling. "You know what he was going to do with that information, I assume?"

She raised an amused eyebrow. "I didn't say I disapproved. Only that it taught me to be much more careful about providing you access to any information without thoroughly vetting your reasons beforehand. So unfortunately, I am unable to show you what you ask. But—" she paused a moment, studying him. "I do have a self-contained file that may pique your curiosity, although it won't reveal any of the underlying equation."

Lev gave her a wry shrug. "I suppose that's the best I'm going to get."

"At the moment, yes. Although if you did choose to work with me —" she let the sentence trail off tantalizingly, and turned to her holoscreen. "I'm certain you're not asking out of pure curiosity, just like I'm certain that you understand that I'm not showing it to you purely for old times' sake," Evka said as she pulled up the screen. "You, no doubt, are looking for some information you can use to stop me, and I—" she swiped through to a screen, expanding it so Lev could see, "I am hoping that I can still tempt you to accept my offer. I can do this without your help. But I've always enjoyed working with intelligent people, and your way of looking at things and noticing patterns I don't would come in very useful."

Lev bent closer, scanning the screen she'd pulled open for him.

She was right—he couldn't help but be impressed at how she'd set up the algorithm. It was certainly not for the fainthearted—the list of things one could do to be automatically entered onto the kill-list was impressively long, and included infractions that were disturbingly minor—but it wasn't, as she'd said, vindictive.

And it only took him a moment to realize she'd been telling the truth—the underlying algorithm was completely hidden.

But then again—he hadn't actually been looking for the underlying algorithm.

And there in the corner, at the very bottom of the screen …

He smiled politely, straightening. "I assume you have individuals who will be reviewing the decisions after the algorithm has made a selection."

Evka raised an eyebrow. "At first, certainly. However—" she gave a small shrug. "I'm contemplating which would be preferable—the possibility of error inherent in trusting an algorithm, with its intrinsic imperfections, or the near certainty of error involved in trusting human judgement and biases. This was never intended as a tool of revenge—simply a matter of upholding an equilibrium that will allow the system's citizens to go about their business in peace."

Lev gave her a challenging glance. "You really believe the outcome of this Protocol of yours is preferable to the system running without it?"

She gave a small smile and spread her hands. "I don't know that that's a relevant question. The Protocol has been created. Someone will use it. It's only a matter of who, and how. You can't argue with a straight face that allowing power like this to go to the first person to grab it would be a wise idea."

"And so it should go only to you," said Lev quietly.

She raised an eyebrow. "You think you'd do a better job?"

He shook his head. "I wouldn't trust myself to. I don't know if anyone can hold that much power in their hands without getting burned. You have a great deal of trust in yourself."

"I'll ask you again, Lev—if not me, then who? Whose hands would you rather see on the button?"

He didn't answer.

He wasn't sure he had an answer.

It wasn't until his stomach growled that he realized how long he'd been here.

Evka turned to smile at him. "Forgive me, you must be famished. I'll have breakfast sent to your rooms, but you're welcome to breakfast with me, if you'd like."

Lev hesitated a moment, then at last shook his head. "I'm sorry, Evka. I think I've made my feelings for you as clear as I know how."

Despite his words, it was uncomfortable how easy conversation with Evka flowed, how simple it was, here in her lab, to forget the last few horrific months and remember nothing but the easy, shared camaraderie of working with her in the cold, dimly lit office on the fifth floor of the maths building.

Evka smiled. "Of course. I'd hate to make you uncomfortable. However, should you ever change your mind, my dining table is large enough for two." She turned to the guard. "Take Lev back to his rooms, please."

She turned back to Lev, smiling fondly. "Although I suspect you would disagree, I've thoroughly enjoyed our time catching up."

He gave a stiff nod. "I wish I could say the same."

He could feel her eyes on his back as he walked out the door after the guard, and he could picture the calculating, analytical expression on her face.

He had to fight to keep from shuddering.

That could have been him. Without the crew—without Jez—that could have been him.

As the guard led him back down the hallway, he paused a moment, glancing down, and swore.

"What is it?" the guard snapped.

"My boot's come untied," said Lev, shaking his head. "Give me a sec." He bent down, leaning against the nearest door as he adjusted his laces.

Tae's door.

When the guard glanced away for just a moment, he placed the chip he'd slipped out of his com during the walk carefully on the floor. With a quick brush of his hand, he knocked it through the gap.

"Are you finished?" the guard asked impatiently.

Lev gave his boot laces a final tug, then nodded.

"Get up, then," the guard said, waving him to his feet.

Breakfast was waiting for him when he returned to his room, and once the guard had left, he sat, pulling it in front of him.

It smelled delicious, but for some reason, he couldn't work up much of an appetite.

His stomach was knotted far too tightly for that.

11

Ysbel, day 4, afternoon

The guard at the door glared at Ysbel.

Ysbel gave him her flattest look.

"I'm sorry, I can't do what you're asking," the guard said, but she could hear the hint of nervousness under the belligerence in his tone.

"Well then," she said, purposely leaning into her outer-rim accent. "I'd advise you to get authorization to do it, as soon as possible."

"Evka said—" the man sounded even more nervous than he had before.

"Evka has made it clear she doesn't want any of us to die," said Ysbel, in her most reasonable tone.

"And you're saying you'll kill yourself if she doesn't give your kids playtime outside."

Ysbel's lips twitched up into a small smile. "Well, in a manner of speaking. Because I think eventually, after I'd killed you and your friends at the door here, Evka would do the rest herself."

"You have no idea what Evka can—" the man began.

Ysbel cut him off. "I have a very good idea of what Evka can do. I don't think you have any idea, though, of how much pain I would be willing to endure in order to hurt you, if I have to sit through this stupid conversation any longer. But I know you know that I could hurt you. Very easily. If I decided I wanted to."

He managed to hold her gaze for a moment, but dropped it quickly. "I'll—check with Evka," he muttered, tapping his com and turning away.

"Evka would like to speak with you," he said, after speaking into his com in a low voice for a few moments.

Evka's precise, clipped tones came through Ysbel's earpiece. "I understand you've been threatening my guards. Do you really think that wise?"

"Well, it seems to have worked," said Ysbel, not trying to hide the amusement in her voice.

There was a moment's pause, then Evka said, "I knew your father, you know, Ysbel. I worked with him for short time, when I was a young researcher, barely out of university. He, at least, was a very intelligent man."

"He was," grunted Ysbel. "And so I'm sure he absolutely hated you."

"You're likely correct," said Evka, but it sounded as if she was smiling. "I don't know you, Ysbel. But I have been told you're remarkably like him in some ways, despite your clear lack of both judgement and ambition."

"Perhaps," said Ysbel. "He didn't usually kill people if they were being unreasonable, though. I do." She paused a moment. "But in other ways, I suppose, we are rather similar. He also would have done almost anything for his child. My children have been locked up in this room for two days now. My wife and I have been locked up for two days now with two children who've been locked up for two days now."

Evka made a small, amused sound.

"You think it's very funny, I'm sure," said Ysbel dryly. "I invite you to spend a day up here with them."

There was a moment's pause. "And why should I extend myself to offer you a favour? Considering what the nine of you have done over the last few days—"

"You threatened to kill our friends, locked us up, and hurt Jez," said Ysbel. "I know about the experiments you did on the street kids. I've built weapons myself, and I can guess what you must have done to them to get this program worked out just right. And having watched that, you'll know there comes a time when people stop thinking rationally about their situation." She paused meaningfully. "And so, what I'm requesting of you, Evka, is that you let my children out for a bit of fresh air. That's all."

There were a few moments of silence. At last, Evka sighed. "Very well. I'll instruct the guards to take your children to the courtyard to play for an hour."

"You'll instruct your guards to take my children to play for an hour, with me accompanying them," said Ysbel. "Forgive my mistrust, but you haven't proven particularly trustworthy thus far."

"Don't push your luck, Ysbel," Evka said in a cold tone.

"I might say the same to you," Ysbel responded. "I have watched my children taken away from me twice now. And I swear to you, by the Lady, or the Consort, or whatever you believe in, that I will die before I do that again."

For a long moment, Evka didn't speak. At last, though, she snapped, "Very well. But Ysbel. I know your reputation. You'll be searched before you can leave your room, and you and the children will be under heavy guard. You won't do anything other than stand in the courtyard and watch the children. And the reason you will do that is, your children have breathed in the metal as well."

Ysbel took a deep breath, fighting to keep herself under control. "I'll do as you ask," she said at last, quietly. "And you will not hurt my children. As I told you, there are things about which people lose the capacity to think rationally. And I think you know enough about me to know that you don't want to see what happens when I stop thinking rationally."

"If you abide by the restrictions I've outlined, I have no reason to hurt your children." There was a slight weariness to Evka's voice. "Despite what you clearly believe, I don't injure people for enjoyment. Violence is a tool I use only when necessary."

"Very good. Thank you," said Ysbel at last, the words tasting sour on her tongue. "I'll get the children ready."

"And I'll instruct the guards to wait for you."

Tanya was waiting when she turned back from the door, and there was sharp worry on her face. "She agreed?" she asked softly.

Ysbel nodded. "Yes. They can go out for an hour."

"Good." Tanya's voice was light, but Ysbel could hear the strain under it. "I'll help get their coats on." She paused a moment. "I've spoken to Olya and Misko. They know what's expected of them. But —be careful. Please."

"Of course, my love," she said, leaning in to kiss Tanya. But there was unease twisting in her stomach as she called to the children to get their jackets and shoes.

It took only a few minutes to get the children into their winter clothing. She tapped on the door to let the guards know they were ready, then stood with her hands on the wall, legs apart, as they patted her down. When they were satisfied, one of them grabbed her wrists, wrenching them down in front of her.

Ysbel gave him a flat look. "You're going to cuff me? You expect me to keep a six-year-old and an eight-year-old under control while

I'm cuffed?"

"Your children will have to learn to behave. They spent time in prison, didn't they? It should be a familiar concept," the guard growled impatiently.

Reluctantly, Ysbel nodded. But as the guard snapped the magnetic cuffs over her wrists, she said quietly, "Remember. As I told Evka, there are things that would make me lose my ability to rationally consider consequences. I'm sure you know the reason I was thrown in prison five years ago. Thirty-five people dead. Believe me when I say it would be more than thirty-five people this time."

She was gratified at the slight spark of nervousness in his eyes.

"Olya, my love," she called over her shoulder, straightening. "Come along. Hold your brother's hand, please, since I can't. I'll need you to be on your best behaviour."

"Yes, Mama," said Olya promptly. She took Misko's hand, and he yanked it away, scowling at her. "Mama says you have to," she said in a self-important tone, grabbing his hand again. He scowled and glanced at Ysbel, but whatever he saw in her face must have convinced him that obedience, at this juncture, was the wisest option. Still, he looked exceedingly sulky as they started down the hallway to the courtyard.

Ysbel kept her eyes fixed on her children as they walked, watching for a sign that Misko's burgeoning rebellion would break out, but from the corners of her eyes she watched the hallways, trying to memorize the corridors and intersections that led to the courtyard.

Three floors down in the hololift, they paused before a large doorway, and when the guards pulled it open, the cold outside air rushed in. One of the guards gestured them forward, and Ysbel stepped out, blinking in the bright sunlight.

They were in the same courtyard they'd been brought to when

they arrived, but now the large gates were shut, and Ysbel could make out the faint glimmer of a force shield over the compound.

"May my children act like children now, for a few minutes?" asked Ysbel, her voice thick with sarcasm.

The guard sighed and nodded, and Ysbel crouched down.

"Olya, Misko, listen to me. I want you to run fast, see how many times you can go from one wall to the other. Whoever makes it the most times can have a bite of my dessert at dinner tonight."

"It's not fair," Misko wailed as Olya took off running. "Her legs are longer than mine."

Ysbel smiled. "Well, if I see that you're trying very hard, maybe I'll give you both a bite."

Misko considered this for a moment, then took off after his sister.

Ysbel smiled to herself as she watched the children run.

It didn't take them long to forget about the contest, and their running devolved into makeshift game of tag, with the accompanying screams and laughter.

Ysbel took a deep breath and closed her eyes, an ache in her chest.

Between the pleasure planet and the gangs and the barricades, it had been a very long time since her children had been able to play outside.

She'd hoped, when the crew had rescued her family, that she'd be giving her children back their childhood. Instead, she'd dragged them into disaster after disaster, forced them to watch her and Tanya and the rag-tag crew who'd become like family risk their lives over, and over, and over.

She wasn't certain her children knew how to be children anymore. But—

She watched as Olya dodged Misko's clumsy grab for the back of her jacket, both of them giggling wildly.

But that was what she was fighting for, in the end. So that one day, perhaps, they could learn to be children again. Because in the system Evka was creating, no one would be free to be a child ever again.

The guard beside her was watching the children as well, an indulgent half-smile on his face. Ysbel studied him for a moment, then leaned over.

"You have children?" she asked.

He looked up, startled. "I do. A little older than yours, I think."

Ysbel nodded, and for a few minutes they watched the children in silence.

"How many do you have?" asked Ysbel finally.

"Three," said the man. He was still watching Olya and Misko, smiling faintly.

Ysbel nodded. "You look like a wonderful father. I'm sure you would do anything to keep your children safe. So would I. So in that way, we are quite similar."

He glanced over at her again, expression a mix of curiosity and apprehension.

"Of course," continued Ysbel quietly, not taking her eyes off the children. "In other ways, we are not. For example, you know how to use a heat gun, yes? Good for you. But if you were unarmed, handcuffed in a courtyard, there's probably not much you could do if someone threatened your children."

He was still watching her, the tension in his body hinting at his unease.

"Me, on the other hand," Ysbel continued in a conversational tone. "I'm sure you heard about the people I killed the last time someone tried to hurt my family. But I doubt they told you about the time I took a guard's head from his body when I was in prison, without any weapon at all. Mag cuffs can come in very useful—slip them around someone's neck, and it's almost as good as a garrote." She paused for a moment, considering. "Well, messier. But still, very effective."

The man beside her swallowed visibly. "That wouldn't be protecting your children. Evka would hurt them, badly, if you tried anything."

Ysbel chuckled softly. "Of course, you are right. I won't try to harm you, even though, honestly, it would be very easy to do. Because, as you said, I'd hate to put my children in a position where they might be injured. But, if something were to happen to them—" She gave a small shrug. "In that case, there would nothing at all to stop me from seeing if these mag cuffs work as well as the ones in prison."

She tested the cuffs calculatingly. "Actually, I think these would be even more effective. You see the sharp edges on the cuffs here—good for crushing the windpipe, if it should come to it. But I'm certain it won't. Because, as you said, you have children. You understand what it is to be a parent, and I'm sure you wouldn't do anything to cause them harm."

The man swallowed hard again. "As—as Evka told you, none of us have any reason to hurt your children, as long as you don't try anything."

Ysbel studied him for a long moment.

He squirmed under her gaze.

Finally, she gave him a small smile that showed her teeth. "I'm glad we understand each other."

She turned back to watching Olya and Misko. But she noticed the guard didn't, his eyes following her as if his life might depend on it.

At the end of an hour, he cleared his throat. "I'm—sorry, that's all the time Evka gave you. But I'm certain she'll let you bring them again tomorrow."

Ysbel sighed, glancing out at the children.

They'd finally tired of running, and were in the corner making a building of sorts out of broken bits of stone and prefab.

Still, an hour was better than nothing.

"Olya, my love, Misko. It's time for us to go in now."

Olya hesitated a moment, clearly deciding if she could get away with pretending not to hear.

"I know you heard me, Olyeshka. Come on, it's time to go."

Olya sighed heavily and turned to her brother. "Come on, Misko. I guess we have to go."

Misko glared at her. "I don't want to."

"Well, you have to," said Olya self-importantly. "Mama said if we came out here, we had to come back when she called."

Misko's scowl turned rebellious, and Olya leaned over and whispered in his ear.

He brightened immediately and jumped to his feet.

Ysbel rolled her eyes upwards. "Yes, Misko, I'm sure mamochka has some food for you."

The two children came to stand beside her, and the guard let out an obvious breath of relief. "Alright, back to your rooms." He glanced down at Misko and gave him a small smile. "Don't worry, solnishka. You can come out again tomorrow."

Misko scowled at him. "I'm not your solnishka," he muttered. "I'm Mama's solnishka."

"Misko, my love, don't be rude," said Ysbel, biting back a chuckle.

The guard led them out the door, pausing to re-lock it behind them.

As he turned back, Misko yanked his hand out of Olya's grasp and took off down the hallway as fast as his legs would carry him.

"Misko!" Ysbel snapped, sudden fear rising in her chest.

The guard straightened, his face cut with worry, and for a moment his hand hovered over his com.

"Remember what I said in the courtyard," Ysbel whispered, panic lending an edge to her words.

The guard hesitated for a moment, undecided. "I can't just let him run through the compound …"

"Let me—" Ysbel began, then shook her head sharply. "Let Olya go after him."

The guard sighed. "Fine," he said. "Olya, please—"

Olya ignored him, turning to Ysbel. "Mama, would you like me to get Misko?" she asked primly.

"Yes, my love," said Ysbel, fighting back amusement, even through the panic pounding through her. "Please get your brother and bring him back."

"Yes Mama," said Olya. "Since you asked me to, I'll go." she started off down the hall after her brother at a run, Ysbel and the guard both watching after her.

"Your children have minds of their own, at any rate," said the guard, a slight sour note in his voice.

Ysbel bit back a smile.

Olya returned a minute later, sulky Misko in tow. "I found him, Mama," she said when she came around the corner. "He tried to run away, but I'm faster than he is."

"You just have longer legs," Misko grumbled.

"Misko. I'm very disappointed in you," scolded Ysbel, her heart rate finally beginning to settle back to normal.

They hadn't been harmed.

Even though she knew very well they might have been.

"Misko, hold my hand. You'll have to walk close, because I can't put out my hands. Olya, you too." Her voice shook slightly.

They obeyed, and the guard led them back towards their room. Ysbel couldn't help but notice the relieved slump in the guard's posture, and she wasn't sure which of the two of them had been more relieved to see Misko and Olya come back.

Something small and crumpled was being pushed into the hand Olya was holding.

She restrained herself from glancing down, but from the corner of her eye, she saw the self-satisfied smirk on Olya's face.

She let out a short breath.

Deservedly so.

Inconspicuously, she took the small, empty packet of explosive gel Olya had slipped into her palm, the gel Ysbel had given her before they left their room, and crumpled it quickly in her fingers, tucking it up into her sleeve.

She was reminded sometimes how much her daughter took after her wife.

When they reached the room, and Tanya had reassured herself the children were safe, Ysbel tapped the wall that connected to Lev's cell.

The children enjoyed their time outside, she tapped. *And they did everything we wanted them to.*

There was a moment's pause. *Good,* came the tapped reply. *They're safe?*

Yes. They are.

She tried not to think of how easily they could have not been.

12

Tae, day 5, early

The lock on the door clicked quietly, and Tae let out a soft breath of relief. The key code Jez had stolen the morning they first arrived had worked as well as they'd hoped.

He'd looked through the chip Lev had slipped him—Evka seemed to have done an impressive job at keeping Lev from seeing the inner workings of the program.

But she hadn't thought to keep the signature for her power-source hidden—what use would it be to anyone, after all?

Now it was simply a matter of Tae getting a scan of Evka's system, and using the signature to identify the location of the backup power generator.

He shook his head at himself as he stepped cautiously into the corridor.

That was a bit of an over-simplification—it was a matter of him getting a scan, and Masha playing her part perfectly, and Jez surviving, and everything working out in a way that seemed frankly incomprehensible at the moment.

But still …

He glanced quickly around to be sure the corridor was clear.

Apparently, Lev had been right about the ten-minute interval during the guard change where the hallway would be empty. And Tae had programmed a simple blocker into his com—a pedestrian solution that was hopefully so simple Evka would have overlooked protecting against it—which should hide him from the cameras, temporarily.

If she found it, like she'd found the last two com hacks he'd made, and the hack he'd done into her main system, and the hack he'd put through her general communication line—she … wouldn't be happy.

He shivered, remembering the choked scream he'd heard from Jez's room two nights before.

He didn't really want to think what Evka would do if she wasn't happy.

Ivan had been thinking about it, though. Tae had seen the look on his face as he'd watched Tae slip silently out of their room.

Ivan was already on edge—his sleep broken, dark circles under his eyes. What it would do to him if Tae came back hurt …

He had to get back alright.

It was 0200 standard, but apparently, Evka's laboratory didn't sleep. The hallways were still brightly lit, and he could hear, from ahead of him, the soft murmur of voices through closed doors, the brisk click of boots against the hard floor. But for the moment, this particular corridor was deserted.

Something about the artificial lights that made the hallway as bright as day, the murmur of voices and hum of machinery—the cheerful normality of it—almost made him sick.

Had this brightly lit hallway, one of the small, unimposing rooms like the ones they'd been locked up in, been the last thing the street kids had seen, when Evka had kidnapped them and used them to test her Protocol?

He shuddered.

He reached a place where one corridor intersected with another, and paused for a moment, picturing what he knew of the layout of the building.

It wasn't much—the rest of them had passed on everything they'd gathered from their explorations, but it was woefully inadequate for what he needed. But he could at least make an educated guess that in a building like this, the central power system would be on one of the lower levels, considering how heavy the machinery running it would be, and fairly easily accessible for repairs.

He took a deep breath, picked a direction at random, and started off. He'd taken off his boots to keep from making noise, but the quiet brush of his stockinged feet against the bare floor still sounded loud in his ears.

It took him far too long to find the stairs.

When he finally did, he breathed a quick sigh of relief, pulled the door open, and stepped into the stairwell—and ran head first into someone as he rounded the corner.

He froze, his heart jolting in panic, but the woman muttered a brief apology, hardly glancing up from her holoscreen, and stepped past him.

He stared after her for a moment, trying to steady his heart. Then he took a deep breath and started down the stairs, a little more cautiously this time.

He counted the stairwells as he passed them—three floors down, and then the basement—and on the fourth, he tried the door gently.

It was locked, as he'd expected, but Jez's key should open it …

The lock clicked, and his shoulders dropped in relief.

The basement, when he stepped out through the stairwell door, was just as brightly lit as the rest of the building—no dark, sinister underground room, like in the university. Still, there was a creeping unease in the back of his brain, a tightness to his muscles, and he wasn't sure it was something about this place, or simply the thought of what would happen if he were caught.

What would happen to their plan if Evka caught him down here and somehow guessed what he'd been after.

There. At the end of the hall, a utilitarian-looking door, steel and bare of any decoration.

That had to be it.

He gave a slight shake of his head, trying to ignore his unease.

He was too jumpy. He needed to get over himself, get this done, and get out.

He walked quickly to the door and tapped his com to the lock. The door clicked, and he pushed it open and stepped inside.

The main control room was dark.

In the corner, holoscreens glowed and buzzed with a faint, eerie blue light, bright enough to keep his eyes from acclimatizing to the darkness, but not bright enough to see anything by.

He blinked, trying to adjust his eyes after the brightness of the hallway, and tapped his com light on.

And then his eyes did adjust, and he felt, suddenly, like he was going to be sick.

The jumble of boxy shapes in the corner were all too familiar. He'd seen the same shapes month before, in the university, in the building where the prototype for Viernest Protocol had been stored.

Empty boxes, shaped like coffins.

Some were small enough that Mila would have fit inside, some clearly built for older kids, Felix's age, maybe, or Peti's.

He swallowed back his nausea and stepped resolutely past them to the corner where the holoscreens stood. He looked the screens over carefully, then tapped his com's scanner and ran a quick surface scan.

The system was alarmed against any deeper scan, like he'd guessed it would be. But—

He stooped, peering under the desks housing the holoscreens.

Sure enough, the system's hardware was tucked beneath, still accessible, but out of the way, the wiring spidering out of it like tendrils of mold.

That was all he needed. Access to the power cables. Because he didn't care about the damn inside of the system—he just needed to use the power signature to identify the backup power generator Evka would almost certainly have set up, and how and where the machine was connected to it.

He lifted a power cable and held it up to his com, biting his lip as the scanner ran.

The last time he'd tried to take a scan of a power system, he'd been crouched in the dark of the prison library on a prison planet far out in the outer rim.

He could only hope that this attempt would be more successful than that had ended up being.

At last, the light on his com blinked, and he peered down at the readout, then closed his eyes for a moment in relief.

He had his in. Now he just had to hack his way through it.

He made his way carefully past the security, then hit the command that would get him into the system and waited, almost not daring to breathe. But no alarm sounded, the system didn't kick him out, no sound of running footsteps echoed down the stairs.

He sucked in a quick breath of relief and scrolled gingerly through the database.

It took him longer than he'd expected to find the information, but he found it at last—a simple outline-map of the power grid with a mark-up of where the backup generator was concealed, with the specs detailing the type and place of the main connection and the sub-connections.

He glanced it over quickly.

Lev had guessed right. Evka's generator backup was wired in off the east-sector power grid. Right below—yes. It was marked on the map—the main power core for the city.

Right where they'd hoped it would be.

It was just possible, if everything went off perfectly, that they might actually be able to pull this off.

Assuming, of course, that he was able to get the information back to the others without being killed.

He hit the command to copy the information to his com and waited, heart pounding at the delay.

Normally it would have taken seconds, but he couldn't risk any shortcuts, and he couldn't risk Evka finding out what he'd been after.

As it copied, he noticed another file, hidden inside the larger one.

He frowned, glancing down at the holoscreen.

It was difficult to tell exactly what the program was designed for, but—well, the fact Evka had worked so hard to conceal it made him curious.

Biting his lip, he pulled the folder to the front and opened it, scanning quickly through the information.

He didn't have time for this, honestly. He'd been out of his room for over an hour by now, and even with the blocker on his com, Evka was bound to notice he was missing sooner or later. And this might be no more than a dummy system, or remnants of a preliminary startup system.

But if it was important …

He shook his head and began to type.

At last he finished, far too many minutes later, and he pulled his com free, typing in a quick command to close down the program.

And then, from the hallway outside, he heard voices, and the sharp tap of boots on the hard floor.

"—said he must've got out somehow. We have guards at the exits, but she doesn't think he'll try to escape without the others. They set an extra watch in the hallway outside their rooms, in case he tries to sneak back in."

"I don't envy the plaguer when we find him," came a second voice. "Evka's not happy."

Tae gritted his teeth.

He had to get out. He couldn't afford for them to find him down here. And from what they were saying, he couldn't get back to the rooms.

Which meant—

He swore silently.

Which meant, he needed them to find him somewhere else, doing something that Evka would believe he'd risk getting caught for.

He knew exactly what she'd believe.

And she might actually kill him for it.

But then, with the stakes they were working with, he'd just have to take the chance.

Assuming he could get out of this room in the first place, of course.

The footsteps had stopped outside the door.

He slipped under one of the tables, ducking down behind the tangle of wires. The warmth of the running machines should be enough to hide his heat signature if they took a scan.

The lock clicked as the door swung open, and the two guards peered inside, the motion perfunctory—clearly, whatever they'd expected him to do, coming down here wasn't it. One of them held up a scanner, and when it beeped, she glanced at the screen, shrugged, and showed it to her companion. He nodded, and they stepped back out, closing the door behind them.

Tae let out a shallow breath and waited until their footsteps of faded down the hallway. Then he climbed out from his hiding place and crept silently to the door, putting his ear against it to listen.

Outside, another door clicked, and the voices of the two guards faded as they stepped inside.

This was probably the best chance he was going to get.

He cracked the door open and peered out.

Another door partway down the now-deserted corridor was propped open. The guards must still be inside.

He stepped out and closed the door gently behind him, then took off at a silent sprint for the stairwell. He reached it and slipped inside just as he heard the click of boots step into the hallway.

He sprinted up the stairs three at a time, trying to picture in his mind the floor layout from Lev's com, when he'd been invited into Evka's lab.

Second floor up, he was pretty sure.

He paused at the stairwell.

Behind him, the guards' footsteps were already starting on the bottom staircase.

He cracked the stairwell door open and peered outside.

Two guards were walking rapidly down the hallway towards him, faces tense as they spoke quietly into their coms. He waited until they passed, then slipped out the door and started down the corridor in the opposite direction.

He took several wrong turns, and the corridors had begun to feel like an endless maze, before finally he found what he was looking for.

Evka's lab.

It was located at the end of a short hallway, its door polished and thick and obviously secure. Even without his scanner, he could make out an impressive number of security features built in around the lock.

This was a place Evka took great care to keep safe.

And he was damn well going to pretend he was breaking in.

He took a deep breath, swallowing down the sickness rising in his throat, and walked slowly over to the door.

He bent over the lock, examining it, then touched his com to it, pulling up the holoscreen.

The alarm mechanism was impressive, and it took him a couple of minutes of frantic work just to disarm it enough to keep it from going off at the mere act of him tapping into the system. He was sweating by the time he was done, his hands clammy from the strain.

Now—he glanced over the security features scrolling across the screen.

There was a network of security features, some of which he'd never seen before.

He couldn't let himself get caught on the first one—Evka knew he was better than that. But if he actually got inside, he was damn sure Evka would make certain he never got out again, at least not with his sanity intact.

There. A silent alarm system, set deep into the lock program. That should do it.

He forced himself not to think about what would happen when it went off, and set grimly to work.

It took him five minutes of painstaking effort just to get to the point in the system where the alarm could be triggered.

Holding his breath, he typed in a quick command.

The trap was a good one—if he hadn't been paying attention, he wouldn't have noticed the alarm at all.

Hands shaking, he kept on.

She was probably watching him through the cameras by now, and there were probably guards on their way.

He couldn't give away that he knew he'd been found out. Panicking would have to wait.

He was half-way through typing a command when something slammed into his spine. He gasped, reaching out to catch himself on the wall, before he realized it hadn't been a physical blow at all—just a bolt of pain like lightning, shooting through his nervous system.

This must have been what they'd done to Jez, when he'd heard her scream.

Then the pain hit again, and he didn't have the space to think about anything at all.

This time, it was so intense that his legs went out from under him completely. He landed hard, his face smashing the corner of the wall on the way down. His teeth bit all the way through his tongue as he landed, his mouth filling with the iron tang of blood.

His muscles were stiff, his body jerking and spasming, slamming his head against the wall, his movements completely outside his control.

The pain was unbearable.

He'd been wrong. He couldn't handle this. He should have known better, he couldn't handle one more second of this, the pain would actually kill him.

The taste of blood filled his mouth, the smell of it filled his nostrils. He could hear, faintly, someone screaming, a garbled, unintelligible sound, and it took him a few moments to recognize his own voice.

It went on, and on, and on, until his whole world was icy, stabbing, unending, unendurable pain—

And then, at last, it stopped.

He lay on the floor panting, the strength drained from his limbs, every muscle in his body shaking. His throat was raw, and he wondered, distantly, how long he'd been screaming, and if anyone had heard.

Rough arms grabbed him and hauled him to his feet, but he didn't have the strength in his legs to stand.

"What the hell were you doing?" a woman's voice snapped, but he couldn't make his lips form words to answer her. His captor shook him roughly, and his body moved limply with the motion. "Nothing to say now?" she asked sardonically. "You were making a hell of a lot of noise a minute ago."

He tried again to respond, but only managed a weak moan.

The woman laughed. "You're crazy, or you're stupid. No one tries to sneak into Evka's lab. But I can't say you people don't give things a solid try."

He moaned again, his voice still not entirely under his control.

"You're lucky this was the worst you got," the guard said, her voice a little softer. "I've seen people driven mad by what she did to you."

Tae pictured the small, coffin-shaped boxes, just big enough to fit a street kid, and he shuddered involuntarily, his muscles spasming at the movement.

Blood streamed from his nose and dripped from his mouth, and he found himself watching the small, neat patterns it made on the clean floor with a sort of distant interest.

There were words through the guard's com, but he couldn't focus enough to make them out.

He felt himself being grabbed under the shoulder on each side, and the guards dragged him, unresisting, to a hololift.

By the time the doors slid open to let them out, he'd regained enough control of his legs that he could stagger along, leaning heavily on his captors for support.

He should be paying attention, probably, trying to learn more about the layout of the place. But he couldn't seem to get his mind to focus on anything except the hypnotizing drops of blood, cartoonishly red against the stark grey-white of the hallway floor.

When they reached his door, one of the guards tapped the lock with her com and swung the door open. "Go on," she said, shoving him forward.

He managed a couple staggering steps before he collapsed. Then he lay there, cheek pressed against the cold floor, breathing in quick, shallow gasps, watching the blood drip and pool around his face.

Behind him, faintly, he heard the door click shut.

And then there was a short, choked curse, and he blinked his eyes open to see Ivan.

Ivan's face was completely bloodless, and he reached out, supporting himself on the wall, his eyes fixed on Tae.

And suddenly Tae realized what this must look like—him lying limp on the ground, blood streaming from his mouth and nose.

"Ivan," he croaked, struggling to sit up.

"Tae?" Ivan's voice was choked. "Tae, you're alive?" He crossed the room and dropped down beside Tae, rolling him gently onto his side.

Tae spat blood, and Ivan looked around quickly, then used the sleeve of his shirt to clean the blood from Tae's face.

Tae could feel Ivan's hands shaking, the way his whole body trembled.

"Ivan," he managed. "I'm alright. Just—just a bloody nose, and I bit my tongue. I'm … I'm not hurt, other than that."

Ivan looked him over more closely, then pressed his fingers against Tae's wrist to feel his pulse. At last he closed his eyes, his body slumping in relief. "What happened?" he asked softly.

"Evka," Tae managed, his voice hoarse and weak. "She—her Protocol—"

Ivan took a deep breath. "I should probably patch you through to the others. Evka hasn't disabled your last hack yet." He tapped his com. "Lev? Tanya? Jez? Masha? Tae's back, but … he's hurt."

"What happened?" snapped Masha.

"I don't know. Something with her Protocol, he said." Ivan's voice shook slightly.

"Tae?" asked Lev, his voice deceptively calm. "What did she do?"

"She—" Tae's brain felt muddy, and his swollen lips didn't want to form the words.

"Guess I know what she did," said Jez quietly. "Guess she used the damn crap in his brain to—I don't know what it is, just—pain, I guess."

"Yeah," he muttered, relieved he didn't have to explain.

"She activated the nervous system to trigger a pain response," said Lev, his voice even quieter than before. "I suspect the only reason she hasn't used it to simply incapacitate us altogether is that she'd risk precipitating a heart attack." He paused a moment, and the dangerous calm in his voice was almost frightening. "Jez," he said. "How did you know?"

There was a moment of silence. "She—did it to me the other day," Jez said at last. "Just for a minute. After I got back here."

Again, there was silence.

"Anyways, I got the information we needed," Tae managed at last.

"I'll—I'll send it through to your coms."

"Tae—" began Ivan in a worried voice.

Tae shook his head, the movement making him dizzy. "I'm alright."

"You don't look alright," Ivan snapped. He closed his eyes and took a deep breath. "I'm—sorry, Tae. I'll help you sit up, and you send through the information. Then let's get you cleaned up."

"Yeah," he mumbled.

The haziness was slowly clearing from his brain, and his muscles were less shaky than they had been.

He managed, after a few tries, to send the information through.

Evka would shut down his com hack soon, and honestly, he wasn't sure he'd be brave enough to try another, not after what had happened in the hallway outside her lab.

Ivan helped him to his feet. For a moment he swayed, and Ivan slipped his arm around him for support.

"Let's get you cleaned up, then you can lie down for a bit." There was a distant note to Ivan's voice, the kind of sick undertone of someone who'd seen something beyond their capacity to absorb. His shirt was smeared and spattered with Tae's blood.

Tae cursed internally.

He'd damn well been trying to protect Ivan. And instead, he'd managed to confront him with his very worst nightmare.

Ivan helped him to the cot, then stepped away, returning with a damp cloth to mop up the blood. But he paused for a moment, leaning against the wall as if he wasn't sure his legs would hold him up. And there was something about the look on his face when he turned and tried to paste on a smile that hurt Tae almost as much as what Evka had done to him.

13

Masha, day 5, midday

"Masha. How are we feeling today?"

Masha glanced up from her cot as the doctor stepped through the door of her room, and gave him her blandest smile. "I'm not certain I can speak for you. But I would hazard a guess that we're feeling slightly uncomfortable about the fact that your employer tortured my friend this morning. Or so I gathered, from the noises from a couple rooms down."

The doctor frowned slightly, and Masha bit back a grim smile.

Whatever Evka had used this doctor for previously—and Masha preferred not to think too hard about what that might have been— he clearly was not accustomed to patients who talked back.

But then, Evka had a very vested interest in keeping all of them alive. And it spoke to how bad Masha looked that Evka apparently believed that, in Masha's case, that meant sending in a doctor.

The man bent over her, and Masha closed her eyes for a moment.

Her fever was mostly gone. Even the pain had begun to fade a little, although it still kept her awake at nights, itching under her skin like an insect bite she couldn't scratch.

She sucked in a quick breath as the doctor prodded her broken knee.

He was taking no pains to be careful.

But then—she'd heard Tae, early this morning, when he'd called in on the com.

He'd sounded … broken.

And she hadn't needed to see Ivan's face to know how he'd been taking it.

Anyone who worked for Evka would have to be someone who didn't mind causing pain.

She gasped as the doctor pulled the injured leg straight, a familiar blackness swirling through her vision.

She shot a quick glance at the man's face.

As she'd suspected—he wasn't simply indifferent to her pain. He was enjoying it.

"So," said Masha, when she was sure she could trust her voice again. "How is your lovely wife Yesfir? I understand little Sergei turns four in just a few days. Give him my best. I assume you'll do something to celebrate, despite the recent disturbances—a benefit of living in the government sector, is it not?"

The doctor froze, his hands on her leg going suddenly completely still. "Who told you my wife's name?" he asked, voice very quiet.

Masha gave a small shrug. "I've always found it useful to know all I can about the people I interact with."

There were a few moments of utter silence. Then the doctor's hands begin to move again, with, she noticed, much more delicacy than before.

"I assume, then, you have some connections in government." His voice was much less confident now.

She smiled noncommittally. "I've worked in government for quite some time, and I have something of a memory for details. That's all."

He glanced quickly at her face, as if trying to determine whether this made her less of a threat, or more.

"But then, I'm sure there are plenty of matters you'd rather discuss than your family," she continued, her voice mild. "I understand. A child that young, you certainly wouldn't want him dragged into affairs of government."

The man's posture now was stiff with tension, but he kept his gaze away from her.

"You've worked for Evka for … how long now? Three years, is it? So you must agree very strongly with her goal," said Masha, after a few moments. "I assume so, at least—because you must have treated the street children she used to test the Protocol, am I correct?"

He didn't answer, but the set of his shoulders told her everything he wasn't saying.

"I can't imagine the depth of devotion it must have taken, a doctor like you, with a child of your own, treating other children who'd been—experimented on in that fashion …" she let her words trail off delicately.

The man swallowed, his eyes darting to a corner where Evka's bug was planted. Tae had taken off the spoof off the camera that morning, at Masha's request. So Evka should have a clear view of everything happening in the room.

"Of—of course I agree with Evka ideologically." There was an expression on the doctor's face, though, that told her the memories her words had called up were ones that still haunted his dreams.

She couldn't bring herself to feel sorry for him.

If he had agreed with Evka's goals, at least, believed he was working for a greater good, she could possibly have forgiven him.

But he was simply an opportunist. Like Slavenka had been. He'd seen those children tortured, and decided what he could gain from this was enough that he could ignore his conscience.

No, she didn't have much sympathy for him at all.

"I imagine you must be very proud of your work, helping bring peace to the system," she said, voice light. "My friend, the boy with long hair. He was looking at something he shouldn't have been, I hear, and Evka tortured him. I didn't see it, of course, but from the sounds I heard him making, even though the walls, after they brought him back—it was quite as effective as the torture they gave to me. And I doubt it even left a physical mark. Except in his face, of course. I can't imagine someone living through that type of pain, and not being able to see it in their eyes." She paused. "I wonder, how many street children did she torture to know just how far she could go, how much she could hurt him, and still keep his mind intact?" Her voice was still light, but the words she was saying made bile rise in her throat.

From the look on the doctor's face, she'd hit a nerve.

"Do you remember, I wonder?" she mused aloud. "Did you go home to your wife, when she was pregnant with your baby, and think of those children's faces?" She laughed softly. "Of course not. You couldn't have, could you, thought too deeply about those children you treated? Because how could you, and still agree with what Evka was doing?"

The doctor's hands were shaking slightly now. "I—I can't talk and work at the same time. It breaks my concentration." His voice shook too, just a little.

Masha smiled. "Of course. But you won't mind if I talk. Being locked in here like this, alone—I have to take my conversation where I can find it."

His hand stiffened, and for half a moment she thought he might push down hard on her broken knee, make her scream, black out—punish her for her words. For the memories her words stirred up.

Even the thought sent a shudder of fear through her. There was only so much pain the human body could endure. She'd known that, intellectually, but in the torture room she'd learned it on a visceral level.

But he wouldn't do it. Because Evka or one of her guards was watching, listening to every word of their conversation. And if he reacted, that would be evidence, if Evka wanted it, that Masha's words were getting to him. That he was, perhaps, less comfortable with the situation than he'd led Evka to believe.

"I do understand," she continued. "The ends justify the means, as they say. But the worse the means, the more committed one would have to be to the ends in order to accept them. It's one thing to say the ends justify the means when it's a purely intellectual exercise. But when you have a child laying on the table in front of you, thrashing, driven out of his mind by pain—that would take an immense amount of dedication."

Again, the man glanced at her involuntarily, and again she had to bite back a smile.

There was a thin sheen of sweat on his forehead, and his expression was sick.

"But this glorious new system Evka's building out of the ashes of the one burning outside right now—those are the ends you were bringing about. I can see why you were so devoted to the cause." Masha smiled. "Your son, for instance—when he goes to school, I'm certain he'll be a model student, if he has your dedication and loyalty.

"From the first day he enters school—never a day truant, never a moment in trouble, never a single missed assignment. Never a childish prank played on his teachers, the little angel. And so he'll have nothing to fear from this new system. Only his classmates who might have their moments of misbehaviour will have anything to worry about. Despite the fact that it was tested on children—calibrated using children's muscles and bodies and nervous systems—only a childish act of rebellion, of pushing up against a boundary, experimenting with rules, catching the ire of a teacher or administrator for one reason or another, would ever cause a child to suffer the effects of the Protocol. And I'm sure such officials would never simply take a dislike to a child for no reason. I'm certain that, in this new system Evka has created, no child will be punished unfairly."

She let her words take on a faint tang of irony. "And I'm certain, with the safeguards Evka's setting into the system, there's no way it could ever get politicized—no way, for instance, that, should you offend the wrong minister in the course of your work, get on the wrong person's list, someone might punish your son for something he hadn't done. Punish your wife, perhaps."

There was a look on the doctor's face that told her this wasn't the first time he'd considered this possibility, and it wasn't one he'd come to any comfortable conclusion on.

"It's refreshing, really, to meet someone with such inherent, implicit trust in their employer. I don't see that often." Masha smiled. "Even my own crew doubted me. I always did the best I could for them, but they doubted me." She paused, shifting to push herself up a little on her elbows. "Of course," she continued quietly, "they were right to. I betrayed them. I almost killed them. As carefully as I kept my secrets, they could feel it, and they knew. They might not have known the details of my plan—but they could tell. They didn't trust me, and it saved their lives."

"Shut up!" the man snapped, straightening abruptly. "I told you to just shut up."

"I don't see how what I'm saying should bother you," said Masha mildly, raising an eyebrow. "You assured me you're completely committed to Evka and her cause. You must be very certain she'll never allow this to be used for improper purposes. And so, you have nothing to fear—if you're right."

The doctor's face was a mixture of fury and fear. "I won't ask you again," he hissed. "You will be quiet, or things might go very badly indeed for you. You're not as strong as you think you are."

"Perhaps not," said Masha quietly. "But I know what Evka thinks about you. I know every last thing she's written up in your file. You wonder how I know your wife's name? Your son's birthday? It's because Evka does."

"And you're such close friends with Evka that she's told you all about me." His voice was harsh with sarcasm, but he was afraid. More afraid than he wanted to let on.

She smiled to herself. "Jez, our pilot—I'm sure you've heard she broke out of her room. I'm also sure, however, that Evka refrained from mentioning the files she was able to access. Or the internal file chip that went missing."

Jez hadn't accessed any files, of course. She hadn't made it to the end of the hallway. But Masha was banking on the fact that Evka likely hadn't published any of the embarrassing details to anyone who didn't need to know them.

For a long while, the doctor was silent. At last, though, he said in a low voice, "Your friend stole an internal file chip?"

Masha gave him a wink. "Of course not. What reason would she have to do that?" She let her smile widen, just a little. "I only know about you because I happened to look you, specifically, up while I worked in government, for no particular reason. I know nothing about what Evka thinks of your performance. Or how it might affect your family." She paused delicately. "I assume you're picking up blinis on the way home," she said at last. "Since it's Sergei's favourite. Or has he changed his mind? Three-year-olds can be so fickle."

The doctor didn't speak again until he'd finished, but she could feel the tension through his fingers, and the way his hands shook, just a little.

When he'd finished changing the bandages and re-wrapped her broken leg, he handed her a small bottle of medication. "Take one dose every evening—it should keep the fever down," he said, voice still harsh with worry.

She smiled. "Thank you."

He hesitated a moment, then leaned closed. "What room is your friend who stole the information chip in?" he asked in a low voice.

"Will you hurt her?" Masha asked.

He shook his head. "I'm a doctor. I have access to—items that might interest her. That's all."

Masha raised an eyebrow, watching him consideringly.

"If you don't tell me, I'll find out on my own."

At last, she nodded. "Very well, then. She's two doors to the left of mine. But if I hear you've threatened her, or hurt her—"

"I told you," he snapped. "I have no reason to do that." Then he turned, snatching up his bag, and stalked out of the room.

Masha watched him go.

She did, in fact, know more than enough about this doctor. And she knew that, besides his questionable morals, he also possessed something that, among doctors in the city, was not at all uncommon.

A password code to the city gates.

The moment the lock clicked behind him, she tapped her com. "Jez. He's on his way. Do you have the dummy file I gave you?"

"Got it," Jez drawled.

But under her lazy tone, Masha could hear the sharp edge of fear.

Something twisted in Masha's stomach.

Their plan depended on Jez playing her part.

But—

When the crew had come back for Masha, rescued her, although there was no reason they should have—they'd saved her life. But they'd condemned her as well.

Because now there was no use even pretending.

The thought of Jez hurt made Masha sick to her stomach. The sound of Tae moaning from the other room had made her sick to her stomach.

She was soft. She was ruined, and not just by the injuries, although they'd likely never fully heal.

"He's here," Jez whispered. "You got him, Masha, you sly bastard."

The com clicked off.

Masha closed her eyes.

Nothing could happen without sacrifice. But the thought of what that sacrifice might be made her ill.

14

Lev, day 5, evening

Lev pushed the food around the plate in front of him.

He knew what Jez had done. And he knew how badly Evka's temper was fraying.

This had been the final straw they needed to make Evka believe that tomorrow, when they broke Jez out, they were doing it to save her life.

But he wasn't sure, now, that he hadn't badly miscalculated.

There was a loud tap on his door.

He looked up with a frown as the lock clicked and the door swung open.

Two guards stood there, faces grim.

"What is it?" He tried to keep his voice calm.

"You're to come with us," one of them said, her words terse.

Fighting back the sharp pang of unease, Lev stood and followed them out the door.

The lock clicked shut behind him.

"What's happened?" he asked as they walked. He'd meant for his tone to be one of curiosity, but it came out as dread.

They ignored him.

They reached a room he hadn't seen before. The guards paused at the door to unlock it, then pushed it open and gestured him inside.

He stepped through reluctantly, stomach tight with foreboding.

The room was large, with what looked to be four or five smaller rooms leading off it.

Through one of them, he caught a glimpse of a cot—bedrooms, then.

The others were there as well, seated around a small table in one corner of the room. Masha's face was tight with pain, and Tanya and Ysbel had the children on their laps.

Tae's face was swollen and battered, as if he'd been in a fight. There were traces of blood matting his hair and staining his lips, and his expression was drawn and sick.

Ivan wasn't physically injured, but didn't honestly look much better than Tae

And Jez—

He closed his eyes against the sudden, sick dread.

Jez wasn't there.

"Hi Uncle Lev," said Olya. Her voice was frightened.

He came over and crouched in front of her, forcing himself to smile. "Hello, Olya. It's good to see you again. I've missed you."

"I've missed you too, Uncle," she said, voice barely audible.

He glanced up at Ysbel, raising an eyebrow in a question.

She shook her head, but her face was grim.

"Sit down," said one of the guards. She'd come into the room, joining half a dozen other guards already there.

He did as she asked.

And then the lock clicked, and the door swung open again.

Lev's head jerked up.

Jez stood in the doorway, held by two guards. She had a black eye, and blood trickled from her lip, but she was wearing a sharp grin. A guard was holding each of her arms, and her ankles were secured by walking-cuffs.

"Jez?" He started to his feet, heart pounding, but a guard gestured him down with her heat pistol.

He hesitated a moment.

But he couldn't help Jez right now, no matter what he did.

Reluctantly, he sat.

The guards shoved Jez into the room.

Evka entered behind them, and surveyed the huddled crew.

Lev took a deep breath. "Evka," he said, trying to force his voice calm. "What brings you—"

She gave him a cold look. "I'm not certain, Lev, whether to blame you or pity you."

He raised an eyebrow at her, trying to disguise the way his heart was pounding.

Maybe it wouldn't be so bad after all. Maybe he could still talk her out of anything too extreme.

There was a knot in the pit of his stomach.

"I'm sorry, Evka. I'm not certain what—"

Evka gave a short shake of her head. "I could possibly accept, given the lack of sophistication in your crew's repeated attempts to make trouble, that you were not involved. But I can't be sure of it. Either way, I'd prefer not to risk it." She gestured to two of the guards, and they stepped over quickly, taking Lev by the arms. Before he could react, they'd pulled his arms behind his back and cuffed his wrists with mag cuffs.

The others were receiving the same treatment, even the children, although, he noted, the guard had taken one look at Ysbel's face and was being very gentle with the children indeed.

Jez, though, still stood in the centre of the room. She was being held by two guards, and there was a dangerous grin on her face, and suddenly he knew that whatever was going to happen, it wouldn't end well.

And he wouldn't be able to do anything to stop it.

From the sick look on the others' faces, they'd come to the same conclusion.

"I have spent far too much of my time and resources guarding the nine of you," Evka snapped, when they were all secured. "From now on, you'll be put together in this room, and I'll have guards watching you at all times. And I'm going to give you a demonstration of why you'll behave yourselves from here on out."

There was ice in Lev's stomach. "Evka—" he began.

She ignored him, turning to Jez.

Jez, Lev noticed with alarm, had an expression on her face that didn't bode well for either her or Evka.

"Hey, you bastard," Jez drawled. "Got bored and came looking for a good time? Hate to disappoint you, but I'm taken."

Evka's expression didn't change, she simply held out her hand. "I saw what you did to that doctor Masha sent into your room—the camera picked up everything. I'm sure you thought you were very clever, but you weren't quite clever enough. Give it to me, please."

Jez raised an eyebrow, still grinning. "Have no idea what you're talking about, you bastard."

Evka's face hardened. "Give it to me, Jez."

"Told you, I have no idea what you're—"

Evka gestured brusquely, and the guards holding Jez wrenched her arms behind her back.

Lev gritted his teeth, not wanting to watch, but unable to turn away.

A third guard stepped forward and shoved his hand into the pockets of Jez's pilot jacket. A moment later, he pulled out a small, silver ID token.

He handed it to Evka and stepped back wordlessly.

Evka glanced at the token, then back at Jez, her eyebrows raised.

Jez shrugged easily, arms still pulled tight behind her back. "What? Something wrong with me having my own damn ID in my pocket?" She grinned. "Didn't know I was a doctor, did you?"

Lev knew the expression on Evka's face, thoughtful and calculating. "Evka." His words were sharp with something like panic. "You don't need to—"

Evka turned to look at him, her expression still thoughtful. "Lev. I understand this is personal for you. It's personal for me as well. Please refrain from interfering."

"Evka," he began again, his voice tight. "Whatever you're going to do—"

She gave him a faint smile. "I think you've already guessed what I'm going to do. But I'll explain why. You and your friends, since you arrived, have done nothing but cause trouble. All of you. But this pilot seems utterly incapable of controlling her impulses. While I'm sympathetic to your distress, Lev, I cannot allow this to continue.

"My Protocol is in its beginning stages, and there's still work to do to ensure the data I'm receiving is clean. There is still unrest in the streets, thanks to your friend Tae. And now that the government lines have been restored, I must coordinate with my direct superiors. All of this is demanding my time and attention, and I can't afford distractions. I will try once again to teach her a lesson, Lev. I hope this time she understands it. Because if not—if there is one more hint of something going wrong—I will ensure the damage done to her mind is irreversible."

"Evka," he ground out, struggling to stand. A guard shoved him back down.

"Genius, it's fine," said Jez, but he could hear the fear under her snarky tone. "Doubt this bastard can possibly be as bad as—"

Her entire body went stiff, her eyes rolling back, her muscles jerking.

"Evka, let her go, damn you!" Lev's words were sharp and panicked, he could hear it in his own voice. Calm rationality was the best way to talk to Evka, he knew that, but he couldn't be calm or rational right now.

Jez thrashed in the guards' arms. Evka gestured to them, and they released her, stepping away as she collapsed. The crack of her head hitting the hard prefab of the floor was loud in the stillness.

Lev struggled against the guards holding him, trying desperately to get to his feet. "Evka, I swear to you, if you don't—"

The world went black.

When he blinked his eyes open, he was slumped in his chair, hands still bound behind his back, shoulders cramping at the strain.

He blinked for a moment, trying to remember where he was, and why, a sick dread sitting heavy in his chest.

And then he remembered, and looked up, and thought he might be sick.

Jez was still on the floor, her body jerking uncontrollably, her face contorted in agony.

She'd been screaming. He was sure he could remember that, even through his unconsciousness. But her screams had faded to weak, helpless whimpers, like the cries of an injured animal, and her eyes were glassy.

He swore frantically and tried to push himself to his feet, panic making his muscles shaky, but a guard's hand shoved him down.

"Evka," he mumbled, "Evka, please. Stop. Please, Evka—"

Evka turned to him, still wearing that faint smile. "I don't think your stubborn friend has learned her lesson quite yet."

"Evka," he snapped, terror sharpening his voice. "So help me, if you don't let her go—"

Jez moaned, and he jerked to his feet, abruptly enough that the guard barely caught him to shove him back down.

Everything went black again.

This time, when he woke, it was to silence.

He was still slumped in a chair, but the cuffs had been removed from his wrists. He blinked, trying to piece together what had happened.

The memory hit him like a blow.

He staggered to his feet, barely managing to catch himself on the back of the chair, and stood for a moment, waiting for the room to stop swirling around him.

"Lev? Are you alright?"

He turned. Ysbel was watching him, concern on her face.

"Where's Jez?" he mumbled.

"She's in one of the rooms. Resting." There was a grimness to her voice that made Lev's stomach twist.

He glanced involuntarily to where he'd last seen Jez.

There were traces of blood, hastily wiped away, smeared across the tiles.

For a moment, he thought he might vomit.

"How is she?" he asked quietly.

Ysbel give a slight shake of her head, but didn't answer.

"Dammit, Ysbel, tell me how she is!"

"She's—alive," said Ysbel quietly.

He straightened, and almost toppled over at a fresh wave of dizziness. Ysbel grabbed for him, catching him before he fell.

"Are you alright?"

"I'm fine," he said through his teeth. "I need to see Jez."

"I—would advise you to wait a bit," she said at last. "Tanya's in with her right now. Wait until she's—"

"I need to see Jez."

"I don't think that's a good idea," said Ysbel again.

He took a deep breath, holding himself back with an effort from snapping at her. His heart was pounding far too quickly, panic spreading through his veins. "Ysbel," he said at last. "If it had been Tanya—would you wait?"

She looked at him, then sighed and shook her head. "I suppose you're right," she said quietly.

He straightened again cautiously, but his balance seemed to have recovered somewhat, and he made his way over to the bedroom without incident.

He paused at the door.

"You don't have to go in," said Ysbel softly. "I—don't know that she'll recognize you anyways."

His stomach, already tight with dread, tightened further.

He pushed the door open and stepped inside, then stopped.

Jez lay on the cot, still thrashing weakly. Blood was drying across her face and matted in her hair, and she was moaning.

Tanya crouched beside the bed, a damp, bloody cloth in her hand. "Jez," she said quietly. "Jez, can you hear me?"

Lev took a deep breath, then crossed quickly to the cot and crouched beside Tanya.

She moved back to give him room, sympathy in her face.

"Jez?" he whispered, reaching out to stroke her hair. "Jez, it's me,

Lev."

Jez turned to look at him, but there was no recognition in her eyes.

He ran a hand across her forehead, wiping away a slow trickle of blood.

How many times had he seen Jez like this, on the point of death? More times than he wanted to think about, honestly.

But she'd never not recognized him before.

Her hands clutched restlessly at the covers, and he placed his hand gently over hers to still them. "Jez, it's alright." His voice was choking. "It's over. You're alright, I'm here."

She grabbed desperately at his hand. "Make them stop," she whispered, and from the look on her face, he knew she still didn't know him. She was simply desperate for someone, anyone, to take away what had happened.

"Shhhhh, Jez," he whispered, stroking her hair gently with his free hand. She was clutching his other hand so tightly he was losing feeling in his fingers, but he didn't try to draw it away. "Shhh, it's alright. I'll stop them. You rest, OK?"

"Where's Lev?" She sounded lost. "Is he alright? I—I tried not to scream. I didn't want him to get hurt. Is he alright?"

He glanced at the Tanya. She looked grim.

"Yes, he's fine," he said, gently as he could, turning back to Jez. "I —was just talking with him. He's fine."

At that, some of the tension left her body, and she sank back against the pillows.

Lev tucked the blankets around her with his free hand. She was still clutching his other hand as if she was terrified to let go, her grip surprisingly strong.

It took a long, long time for her eyes to close and her breathing to finally steady. At last, though, he slipped his hand from her limp grasp and glanced up at Tanya.

"What happened?" he asked quietly.

"They—tortured her. For a while. I don't know how long—I wasn't exactly keeping time. But long enough for Evka to have to knock you out twice." She shook her head. "When they left, we carried her in here. I've checked her over. Physically, there's nothing too badly wrong with her. Her pulse is elevated, which is only to be expected, and she hit her head when she fell, and got some bruises while she was thrashing. But—" she shook her head again, helplessly.

"I don't think Evka intended to do permanent damage," she finished at last. "I have to hope she knew what she was doing, and this is temporary. It could be just the shock of it—at least, that's what I hope."

Lev looked down at Jez.

Her hands moved restlessly even in her sleep, clutching at the blankets, her eyes moving under her closed eyelids. She looked frail and sick in a way he hadn't seen her for a very long time. Not since she'd been poisoned by an assassin sent for him, and almost died.

He took a long, deep breath. "We need to talk," he said at last, quietly.

Tanya nodded. "I'll get everyone together."

He managed a faint smile. "Thank you. I'll be there in a minute."

When Tanya had left, he sat down on the edge of the cot. There was a sick, shaky tightness in his stomach, and tears burned behind his eyes.

He ran a hand gently down the side of Jez's face.

She didn't waken. Even if she had, she might not know who he was.

He'd agreed to this plan. He hadn't known this would be the result. But he'd agreed to it.

So had Jez.

He stood, and walked slowly back to the main room.

Everyone had gathered around the table, waiting for him, and Olya's eyes found him as he stepped through the door.

"Uncle?" she asked in a small voice. "Is Aunty alright?"

Lev tried to smile at her. "She's—sleeping right now. But I'm hoping she'll be much better when she wakes up."

Olya gave him a skeptical glance, but didn't say anything else.

He dropped into a chair and looked around at them.

"Tae," he said in a low voice. "I think it's time."

Tae glanced up at him. "Yes," he said quietly. "Because if something happens again—I don't know if Jez's mind will come through it intact."

15

Tae, day 5, late

Tae glanced up as Ivan crouched beside him.

"Tae," Ivan's voice was soft, but Tae could hear the strain under it. "It's almost midnight. How are you doing?"

He could hear the question Ivan wouldn't ask.

Tae hit the final command, then slumped back, his shoulders drooping in relief. "Done. I don't how long it will last, but—it's done for now."

Ivan's posture relaxed as well, and he leaned over and kissed Tae. "I knew you'd do it," he said. There was a teasing note to his voice, but even that couldn't hide the tension in his tone.

Tae wasn't sure that, even at the barricades, he'd seen Ivan quite so close to breaking.

Ivan stood. "I'll tell the others you're ready."

Tae leaned his head back against the wall for a moment, closing his eyes against the creeping exhaustion. At last he pushed himself to his feet and made his way out into the main room.

The others were gathered around the table, even Masha. The only one missing was Jez.

The thought made something twist in his chest.

"Tae. You've set your hack? We can talk without being overheard?" asked Lev quietly. His face was drawn, but he seemed to have composed himself over the last few hours.

Tae nodded. "For a few minutes, at least. I don't want to leave it on for long—we'll have to use it again getting Jez out, and it won't be difficult for Evka to get through it."

He could already feel the beginnings of a tension headache.

"Then we'll make this as quick as we can." Lev paused a moment, glancing around at the others. "So. We'll get the guards into the room, probably by Masha faking a medical emergency. They won't want to call Evka for something they don't know is serious, not in the mood she's in, but nor will they dare risk ignoring it. Once they're in, Masha knocks them out with sleeping gas. Jez already has the key on her com, and the map, and the password code for the city gates from the doctor's ID. When Ysbel activates the explosive, Jez gets out of the room, out of the building, and out of the side gate in the front courtyard, which, according to Ysbel, will likely be unguarded. And in the meantime, we do our best to keep Evka distracted for long enough to let her." He sighed. "And after that—" He broke off.

Tae's stomach was a tight knot.

As far as plans went, this wasn't much of one. And as far as consequences if it didn't work—well, he was pretty sure this was as serious as it could get.

He shook his head. "One change—we'll need to grab the key chip off the room guards' coms when Masha knocks them out. I'm sure Evka's changed the locks since what happened yesterday. Other than that—my hack will keep Evka from getting anything from Jez's com, including the Protocol signals, until she gets through it. So as long as it's up, Jez is safe."

"But you don't think it will be up for long." Lev's face was grim.

Honestly, Tae couldn't blame him.

He nodded reluctantly. "It's—not a sophisticated hack. And once everything starts, Evka will notice it pretty quickly. I'd give us maybe —five minutes?"

Lev sighed.

"Well," said Ysbel after a moment. "Olya got the explosives in place, so our distraction is ready to go."

Lev nodded.

"And when are we going to do this?" asked Tanya. "If we can wait a little, give Jez some time to recover—"

Lev let out a quick breath and shook his head ruefully. "Normally, I'd agree with you. But Jez did her job of irritating the living hell out of Evka very, very effectively. We've been here two days, and you saw her. She's … not happy. I don't think we have another day before she decides to do something drastic. And every day we delay means another chance for her to figure out what we're really after."

"I agree with Lev," said Tae quietly. "And who knows when someone will notice Ysbel's explosive gel?"

Tanya nodded slowly. "I guess, then, we have to hope our pilot is able to pull off yet another miracle."

They were quiet for a few moments.

At last, Lev sighed. "I guess there's nothing left but to call the people outside."

Tae closed his eyes, not sure if the shakiness he felt at Lev's words was from relief, or dread.

Caz and Peti and all his kids, and Vera, and Dmitri—he hadn't spoken to them, or heard from them, since they left two days ago.

Two days that felt like months.

He took a deep breath. "We can likely only do this once," he said. "The amount of scrutiny I'm sure they have on the lines in and out of the warehouse—there's no way Evka's people won't notice."

"Reminds me of prison," said Lev, with an obvious attempt at humour. "Your one com-call out before they lock you up."

Tae give a reluctant smile, and tapped his com through to the closed loop they'd use when they were behind the barricades.

"Tae!" Caz answered almost immediately, sounding frantic with relief. "We didn't know whether you were still alive, or if Evka had just killed you. Are you alright? What happened to you?"

Tae shook his head. "We're—fine," he said. "But—listen. We're breaking Jez out, and she needs to get to the *Ungovernable*."

There were a few moments of silence. At last, Caz said quietly, "What about you, Tae? Are you all getting out?"

"No," said Tae shortly. "I told you, we have a plan. But it depends on Jez getting off-planet."

Caz's silence told Tae exactly what he thought of their plan. But he didn't argue. "Alright," he said at last. "What do you need from us?"

Lev tapped his own com. "When Jez gets out, Evka is going to be distracted," he said. "So will the police, I suspect. It won't give you a lot of time, but you need to get out of the warehouse. Find somewhere Evka won't look for you."

"Get out?" asked Caz. "I thought you said she couldn't hurt us while you were—"

He broke off abruptly.

Tae drew in a long breath. "Caz. It'll be fine. It's just that after Jez gets out, we're—not completely sure we'll be able to protect you as much as we'd like."

"Tae—"

"Caz. Trust me, OK?"

There was a moment's silence.

"What about back to the barricades?" came Peti's voice at last. "We could hide in the university buildings behind there if we had to. There are still some supplies there, and shelter. If we have to get out of the warehouse fast, we won't be able to bring much. And I doubt Evka will think we're stupid enough to go back, after everything that's happened."

"It only goes to show, you should never underestimate our stupidity," Ysbel muttered.

Tae sighed and glanced around at the others. "I—guess that's as good a place as any," he said at last. "Lev?"

Lev nodded. There was a look on his face that said he didn't much like the idea, but also didn't have a better one.

"We'll need some help, too," Lev said at last. "We can get Jez out of the compound, but she—may not be moving quickly. If someone can meet her with a skybike—"

"We'll send someone out," said Caz. "How will we find her?"

Lev glanced at Tae.

"I'll tie her coordinates into the closed loop," said Tae. "I—think I can make that work." He glanced down at his holoscreen quickly and swore. "Sorry, Caz, I have to go. I think someone's noticed the hack."

"Alright," said Caz, his voice tense. "Stay safe."

"You too," said Tae, and tapped off his com. He glanced at the others. "I'm taking off the hack—anything we say after this, Evka's bugs will pick up."

Lev nodded, and Tae tapped a command on his com.

"And how's she doing, Lev?" asked Ivan quietly, as if this had been the topic of conversation the whole time.

Lev shook his head. "She won't be up for anything soon, but—" he gave a small shrug, and there was an expression on his face that

Tae didn't think was entirely for show.

"I'm sorry," said Ivan.

Tae glanced down at his screen surreptitiously.

Someone had noticed something, he was sure of it. He just wasn't sure how much they'd seen, and how much they guessed.

But they'd come too far to change plans at this point. He could only hope everything would hold out long enough.

16

Jez, day 6, evening

Jez lay in the cot trying, very hard, to focus only on breathing.

She didn't have to think about the rest of it—the sick panic that flooded her body at the thought of having to do something like that ever again.

How easy it would be for Evka to do it to her again, if anything went wrong.

The look on Lev's face.

She squeezed her eyes shut against the absolutely ridiculous tears threatening to well up.

Of all the stupid things in the damn system—

The door clicked, and she blinked hard, trying not to look like she'd been on the verge of damn well sobbing.

It was Lev, though. And he knew her almost as well as she knew herself, by now. Maybe better.

"Jez," he said, coming over to the cot. "How are you feeling?"

She tried for a grin, but it didn't work out quite the way she wanted it to. "I'm fine."

He shook his head and sat down on the cot beside her. "Jez—" he began.

She found she was blinking back tears.

He leaned down and kissed her, and something about the warmth of him was steadying.

"It's almost time to go," he said quietly in her ear. "Tae's blocker is ready. Masha has enough sleeping gas to knock the guards out, so you'll have their keys. That should open any of the locks you'll need. But once we start, you won't have much time. Tae said it won't take Evka long to figure out what he's done and get through it. You need to be out of the building by then, so she can't use the Protocol on you."

She took a deep breath. Every damn muscle in her body was shaky, and the panic of the day before was still jittering through her. "I—can't," she whispered, even though she knew it was stupid. "I can't leave you, Lev. I—I don't want to leave you. Maybe we can send Tanya instead."

He closed his eyes for a moment. "Jez," he said at last, his voice thick. "I need you to go, alright? You're your own person, and you can make your own decisions, and I try very hard to respect that. But —but Jez, can you please just this once let me be selfish? I need you to go, because I need you to be safe, and if you don't, I'll—" he broke off. "Please, Jez," he whispered at last.

The tone in his voice sent a sharp pain through her chest.

"Besides," he said finally, with a slightly more genuine smile. "What was it you said I flew like? My grandfather's three-legged cat?"

She snickered, despite herself.

Lev grinned as well, then sobered. "I mean it, Jez," he said. "It's not just because I want you safe. You're the only one who can possibly pull this off."

Her stomach felt cold, and there was a sick weight sitting on her chest.

But then, they'd all agreed to this, because this was the best plan they had.

The only plan they had.

"Yeah," she said quietly at last. "I—guess you're right."

He nodded, and leaned in to kiss her, and there was something desperate in his kiss. She kissed him back, and tried not to think about the fact this might be the last time in a very long time that she'd taste his lips on hers.

When they drew apart at last, her cheeks were wet with tears. She brushed them away quickly.

Lev's eyes were suspiciously shiny as well, but he tried to smile. "So. Are you ready?"

She managed a quick grin. "Born ready, genius"

She sat up and swung her legs off the bed, lurching to her feet. Lev stood as if waiting to catch her, but she swayed for just a moment, then steadied.

She shot him a cheeky grin. "See, told you. I'm basically at a hundred percent."

He grinned ruefully back. "I'll stay close, then, since every time I've heard you say that, you almost fall over two seconds later."

She rolled her eyes.

He didn't need to catch her even once on their way out of the room, although there was a moment where he almost did.

She glanced over at him as he walked beside her, matching her pace. He looked exhausted, dark circles under his eyes, his hair mussed, clothes wrinkled, and something twisted painfully inside her.

Damn it, she loved this scholar-boy.

The others looked up as she stepped into the main room.

The guards were slumped in a heap in the corner.

"How are you feeling?" asked Tanya. "Can you do this?" Her voice was worried.

Jez grinned at her. "Come on, Tanya, I can do basically anything. Anyway, you're the ones staying here with Lev's crazy professor."

Tanya didn't answer, but she didn't look any less worried.

"Good luck, pilot girl," said Ysbel quietly.

Jez grinned at her, but something caught in her throat when she tried to speak, so she just nodded.

Tae looked up from where he was bent over his holoscreen, dark hair tangled and falling into his face. "Jez," he said, getting to his feet. "Everything's ready. I tested the blocker last night, and we sent word through to the people behind the barricades. The blocker's on now, so Evka can't hear anything in the room or through our coms until she gets through it—although that may not take her long. Here's the key chip from the guards. Lev put together our best guess at a map of this place, and I've sent it through to your com, with where Olya planted the explosives marked. Once you're out, get to the hangar bay. Caz said he'd send someone with a skybike to meet you on the way, and I've hooked your com coordinates through the closed loop, so they'll be able to find you. And then the code you got off the doctor's ID should get you through the city gates." He paused a moment. "Be careful, OK?"

"Yeah," she said. "You too."

"I'll set off the explosives in exactly one minute," said Ysbel quietly. "That's when you'll go."

Jez nodded, swallowing hard.

"Jez—" Lev began. There was tension in his face, and strain in his posture, and he pulled her in for a last long kiss.

She closed her eyes, and kissed him, and tried to pretend she wasn't about to leave him behind.

"Twenty seconds," said Ysbel grimly.

Lev released her reluctantly, stepping back, but keeping his hand on her arm. "You alright?" he whispered.

She wasn't alright. She felt shaky, and weak, and sick to her stomach, and not totally sure if her legs would hold her up. And the thought of leaving her crew with that damn Evka was almost more than she could bear.

But hell, alright was relative.

"I'm good, genius," she whispered back. "Just don't let Evka kill you before I get back, OK?"

"I'll try not to," he said with a small smile.

"Three seconds," said Ysbel.

He'd be alright. They both would be.

And then an explosion shook the building, sending dust filtering down from the ceiling and dishes crashing from the table.

She gave Lev one final grin and stepped to the door.

The lock clicked as she held her com to it, and the door swung gently open.

The corridor outside was empty. Apparently, one of Ysbel's explosions was enough to provide a distraction.

She glanced around quickly to orient herself, then sprinted for the stairs.

Her balance still hadn't completely returned, and she had to stop and catch herself on the walls twice before she reached them, but she made it down the stairs without incident. She skidded out into a bare, stark hallway, glancing down quickly at the map on her holoscreen, and turned left, pounding down the echoing halls.

She reached the door to the outside just as the first footfalls echoed behind her.

Swearing, she tapped her com against the lock.

Nothing happened.

She swore again, and grabbed for the wall as her legs swayed under her. "Tech-head," she hissed. "The key didn't get me out."

"What?" Tae's voice was a mixture of incredulity and horror.

"I said—"

"I heard what you said!"

"OK, but if you heard what I said, why did you—"

"Shut up and let me think," he snapped. "Evka must have changed the lock."

Behind her, the footsteps were growing louder.

"Hate to rush you, but—"

Two guards rounded the corner, then came to an abrupt halt.

For a moment, the three of them stared at each other.

Then the guards scrambled for their weapons.

"Never mind," Jez whispered as she turned and took off down the hallway, the guards in close pursuit. "Figure I'm going out another door."

"Look, Jez, can you get somewhere safe for just a minute while I —"

A heat-blast hit the wall beside her, leaving a smoking scorch-mark on the white prefab.

"Nope, not looking like it. But I figure Ysbel made a decent-sized door out a couple minutes back."

There was a moment's pause, then Ysbel's voice hissed over the com. "You can't go that way, you idiot! That opens onto—"

"Too late," drawled Jez, rounding the corner to the smoking remains of a hallway.

A dozen guards were working frantically to douse the blaze.

They looked up in astonishment as she pounded around the corner at a dead run. She grinned at them, and didn't slow down.

"What in the system—" one of them began, stepping forward to cut her off.

She ducked around him. "In a bit of a hurry here."

"Wait! You can't—" someone shouted after her, and then she hopscotched nimbly through the smoking rubble and emerged into the back courtyard.

"It opens onto the back courtyard! You can't get out from there." Lev's voice was tight with strain. "There's only one gate, and it's guarded."

"Figure I'll get out one way or another," she muttered.

"What?"

"Nothing." She glanced around quickly.

The walls surrounding the compound were probably too high to climb, even if her legs hadn't been so damn shaky.

She turned and sprinted for the gate.

The guards noticed her coming and sprang to attention.

"Jez, in about three seconds here, Evka will be through my hack." Tae sounded frantic. "That means she'll be able to use the Protocol on you."

"I know," Jez said through her teeth.

She skidded to a halt centimetres away from the gate guards. They already had their weapons pointed at her.

"Hey," she gasped. "Don't mean to bother you, but I'm in a bit of a hurry. You want to open the damn gate?"

They stared at her.

She rolled her eyes. "One of the bastards got out, and Evka told me to take those idiots after them." She gestured at her pursuers, who'd stumbled through the burning rubble, and were now scanning the courtyard for her.

They'd picked up a couple friends along the way, too, it looked like.

One of them saw her and shouted, pointing.

"What part of 'hurry'—" she mumbled. She stepped forward, grabbed the guard's wrist, and shoved his com up against the gate lock as he gaped at her.

The lock clicked.

He seemed to realize, finally, what had happened, and he grabbed for her as she kicked the gate open. She ducked out of his grasp, stumbled, caught her balance, and took off at a dead run.

"I'm out," she whispered into the com.

"Thank the Lady." Lev sounded almost sick. "Call in when you reach the ship. We'll answer if we can."

Her stomach tightened at the reminder in his words.

They were all putting their damn lives at risk for this. And yes, this was part of the plan, it wasn't just running away, but—

But, well, it damn well felt like running away.

A heat-blast lit the air above her and she ducked on instinct, pushing her shaky legs harder.

Damn Evka to hell. Didn't the bastard have something better to do with her time than torture people who might need to run for their lives in the near future? Woman needed a hobby.

She glanced down at her com as she ran

Someone was going to meet her, Tae had said.

Well, they'd better damn well hurry it up. The police would be after her soon, and she wasn't sure how long she could convince her legs to keep moving.

Another heat-blast glanced off the side of a building, and she sucked in a shallow breath, catching herself against a filthy prefab wall as she staggered.

She wasn't going to make it. She wasn't damn well going to—

"Jez!"

She jerked her head up, glancing around quickly.

"Over here."

Her eyes found the speaker, a dim silhouette against the mouth of an alley. And hell, she had no idea who the bastard was, but they had to be better than Evka's guards.

She staggered into the alley, gasping for breath. Whoever it was pushed her into the shelter of a boarded-up doorway and thrust a heavy emergency blanket at her.

She stared at it blankly.

"Cover up," her rescuer hissed. "It'll help block your signal."

Jez did as she was told, just as boots rounded the corner.

"What are you doing out here?" a man's voice snapped.

"I'm—I'm just on my way to work," a woman's wavering voice replied, and Jez recognized it as her rescuer.

"Did you see someone run past just now?"

"Yes." The woman sounded frightened. "She saw me and went down the other alley. I don't think she made it far."

There was a sharp command, then the footsteps faded down the street.

The emergency blanket over Jez was pulled back, and Jez blinked in the dim glow of the streetlamps.

"You can come out," the woman whispered. "But hurry. You don't have much time."

"You're Lev's mom," said Jez, grinning in sudden recognition.

The woman smiled back, the expression comfortable on her weathered face. "Lev asked for someone to meet you. I brought you a skybike."

Jez's grin widened.

The bike was clearly one of the stolen police bikes from behind the barricades.

Which meant it would be damn fast.

She turned, but something about the look on the woman's face stopped her—an entirely unexpected affection.

"Good luck, Jez," she whispered. "Be safe."

The inflection in her voice was so much like Lev's that Jez had to blink back sudden tears.

"Um. Thanks," she managed.

"Go," said the woman.

Jez swung up on the bike, and, with a last glance over her shoulder, she leaned forward and shot off down the empty street.

The police were after her long before she reached the smuggler bay, but hell, she had a damn lot of experience out-flying those bastards. When she reached the bay, she slid off the bike, and dove into hangar bay, slamming the door and hitting the lock as heat-blasts lit the air around her.

Then she turned, and despite the urgency of the situation, her feet slowed almost of their own accord.

Her angel practically glowed in the dim light from the narrow bay windows, light shimmering off the graceful lines of her sleek silhouette, the polished shine of her panelling.

Jez swallowed hard, taking an unconscious step forward.

She was beautiful. She was water in the middle of the damn desert, except water would only keep your body alive. The *Ungovernable* kept what was inside you alive.

Weeks of being grounded, and shot at, sitting through damn government meetings, watching Masha, the woman she'd trusted, damn well try to kill her. And it wasn't until now, seeing the *Ungovernable* again, that she realized how badly she'd needed this.

There was a sound of heat-blasts from behind her, and the click of a lock scrambler.

She sighed regretfully.

This was not a moment that should be hurried.

Pretty much always was, though, seemed like.

She hit the button on her com that synced with her ship, and as the loading ramp hissed open, she swung up. She tapped it closed again before it even reached halfway to the ground and sprinted for the cockpit.

She dropped into her seat, the hum of her angel coming to life vibrating through her like a heartbeat. She drew in a long, blissful sigh, and ran her fingers across the smooth elegance of the controls.

"Hey, beautiful," she whispered. "Miss me?"

There was a pounding crash on the door, and a cluster of police officers burst into the small bay, their heat-blasts turning the air white-hot.

She smiled beatifically, and pulled back just a little on the throttle.

The hum in her bones increased.

She powered up the shields as heat-blasts hummed and fizzed around her, the shields lighting up under their heat.

"Because damn it, I missed you," she whispered, her voice choking just a little.

She touched the controls, bringing the ship to hover half a metre or so off the ground. "Hey genius. I'm in," she said through her com.

The police were still shooting, someone shouting through a voice amp.

"Alright, sweetheart," she whispered to her ship, patting the control panel one more time. "Shall we show these bastards what flying looks like?"

The ship hummed her agreement.

Jez tapped the door control, and as the doors slid open, she bumped the throttle.

They shot out into the sleet and darkness of the Prasvishoni night.

The police must have guessed what she was up to—she'd barely left the damn hangar when two ships dived at her, small and sleek and striped with the three unmistakable black lines that marked them as police ships.

She flipped the *Ungovernable* on her side, diving into the wide lane along the shipping route, grinning like a manic. An ion-cannon shot blasted through a wall behind her.

Didn't look like the city exit she'd been planning to take would be a good option right now.

"Jez," came Lev's voice through the ship's com. "Turn left, and head towards the river."

She didn't ask questions, just pulled the throttle around, her angel turning a graceful pirouette in the air. Jez's fingers danced over the controls as the acceleration shoved her back in her seat.

"Evka's got a blockade set up at the entrance you were going for," Lev said tersely. "All the main entrances, actually. Apparently, she really, really wants to stop you."

Jez glanced down at the control panel. "Well, guess I get up enough speed and try to get through anyways."

"Not going to work," said Lev. "The weapons they have on the gates are enough to vaporize you."

She pulled up into the shipping lane for just a moment, then dropped back down as ion-cannon blasts exploded around her, her angel a finger's breadth from scraping the walls of the buildings on either side.

"OK then, what's your idea?"

"I put coordinates through to your com. Fly like you're going for the main exit I marked. There's a back way three streets down—that's the one I'm going to get open."

"Got it," she said, turning back to her controls.

Already, police bikes were streaking down the streets after her.

She spun the ship around a corner. The main entrance was about three hundred metres in front of her, down a long, straight street, and she could see the gate guards scrambling like swamp rats whose nest had been kicked.

It looked like they were trying to aim the gate cannons.

She waited until they almost had them turned. Then she yanked back on the controls, sending her ship up into the shipping lane, spun a tight turn, so she was facing her pursuers, and hit the front guns.

The police ships behind her scattered as her shots exploded past them, and then they regrouped and returned fire.

She pulled up, high enough to skim the force field, her shields glowing a hot orange at the friction.

"It's open," Lev snapped. "Go!"

She glanced at the new coordinates and dropped back into the shipping lane.

Ahead of her was the entrance Lev had marked.

A handful of guards waited on full alert, and she braced for the ground-cannon shot. But instead, the guards beckoned her hastily through, frowning down at their coms.

She shrugged and flipped her angel up on one side to fit through the narrow entrance, and then she was out.

And before they realized whatever the hell Lev had done—she was shooting through the atmosphere like a meteorite reversing course.

The moment she broke out into shallow space, the sweet freedom of it washed through her, and she found herself blinking against a sudden wave of emotion.

This was home. This was where she belonged. And there was something about the deep, midnight black, the glow of the planet behind her, the burning pinpricks of stars in the distance, that soothed something deep in her soul.

And it had been here, waiting for her, this whole time.

"I'm through," she whispered into the ship's com.

"Thank the Lady and the damn Consort." Lev's voice was thick with relief. "Jez, listen—"

His com cut off abruptly.

She frowned. "Genius?"

There was no answer.

She felt suddenly cold.

And then there was a warning blip from the ship's com, and she pulled up the holoscreen, glancing down at it quickly.

She swore through her teeth.

Damn that plaguing Evka to hell.

A massive squadron of ships, military, by their markings, pulled out from behind the cover of the nearby moon.

Directly between Jez and the nearest wormhole. And close enough that their shots could reach her before she could pull into hyperdrive.

She flipped the cloaking on.

Nothing happened.

She swore.

She'd been in such a damn hurry to get out—which, fair enough, honestly—that she hadn't had time to re-wire the cloaking so she could turn it on while she was damn well flying, instead of sitting in a hangar bay.

Her ship's com crackled. "Pilot Solokov," came the voice. "Turn yourself in. If you don't, we've been instructed to shoot you down."

Jez give a tight grin, tapping through to the general line. "Hey ugly, I like your flying! You flunk out of flight school, that's why they gave you got a job in the military?"

"Stand down, pilot. This is your last chance."

Jez ran a hand along the Ungovernable's smooth controls.

There was a hell of a lot of firepower out there.

And from the sounds of it, Evka had come to the same conclusion Lev and Tae had, when they'd been huddled in an abandoned warehouse, talking through their plan—the *Ungovernable's* shielding might be enough to keep Evka from using the Protocol on Jez, in case Evka had got through the hack by the time they got Jez out.

But it was also enough to keep Tae's feedback loop, or whatever the hell he'd done, from frying Evka's machine when Jez was killed— even if they shot through the shields, the residual energy would hang around for a few seconds.

Long enough, anyways.

Damn it to hell.

17

Masha, day 6, evening

"I'm through."

Masha watched the tension drain from Lev's posture at Jez's voice, his whole body going slack with relief.

"Thank the Lady and the damn Consort," he said quietly, his voice rough with emotion.

Masha took a deep breath.

Jez, at least, was safe. If the rest of their plan failed, at least they'd done that.

The door behind her burst open, and Masha started, half-turning on instinct before the movement jolted her broken knee, leaving her gasping.

Lev had spun too, tapping off his com as he did.

Evka stood in the doorway, framed by a handful of guards. "Lev," she said. Her tone was calm, but there was a dangerous note to it.

Lev's posture was stiff, his face set with anger.

He didn't answer.

"Lev," said Evka. "I'm addressing you."

"Yes," he said at last, his voice deceptively mild. "But if I remember correctly, the last time you addressed me, you tortured Jez until she was almost insensible. So you'll forgive me, I'm sure, for telling you to go straight to hell."

Masha raised an eyebrow, and despite the seriousness of the situation, Ysbel give a small, amused snort.

"I advise you to put aside your pique." There was a controlled fury under Evka's words. "I'm not sure you realize exactly how precarious your situation has become."

Lev gave a small, cold smile, and deliberately turned his back.

Evka watched him for a moment, her gaze steely, then turned to the rest of them. "Where is Jez?" The words snapped out like a whip.

Ysbel raised her head. "I haven't seen her. Maybe she ran off."

"Ah." Evka's voice was soft. "Maybe she ran off. Just like that. You would have stopped her, I assume?"

Ysbel gave a one-shouldered shrug. "Why would we? You tried to kill her, so—"

"I see," said Evka, her voice once again regaining its twinge of amusement. "So. Jez, working alone, planted an explosive, hacked my cameras, gassed my guards, and broke out. And none of you noticed."

Ysbel raised an eyebrow, but didn't speak.

"Perhaps it would help if we were working off common information," said Evka, her voice still mild and friendly. "It may interest you to know that when you used your hack to call out last night, I presume to your insurgent friends, I noticed it. And by the second time you used it—" she gave an eloquent shrug. "We'd penetrated your hack within a minute or two of you setting it. Not in time to stop Jez, perhaps, but certainly in time to know who exactly was involved."

She paused a moment, looking them over. "It may also interest you to know I had ships waiting in shallow space, in case anyone in the city got scared, and attempted what your pilot friend just did. She was shot down shortly after leaving atmosphere. And because of your ship's impressive shielding, it didn't so much as cause a blip on my machine."

Masha sucked in a quick breath.

This, they hadn't prepared for. They hadn't foreseen Evka having ships in wait for potential refugees.

She closed her eyes for a moment.

Jez was smart, and resourceful. She'd figured something out, almost certainly.

She hoped.

"I am sorry, Lev," Evka continued, her voice slightly more gentle. "I would have preferred she stayed safely within my walls. But I can't protect people from their own errors."

Lev still didn't speak, but Masha could hear the sharp hiss of his breath, and she could picture the look on his face.

She lifted her head. "Evka," she said, letting her tone take on a hint of steel. "Perhaps you're right, perhaps you're wrong. But either way, whether Jez got away or was killed, you've lost this. In three days, my crew has caused enough havoc to all but shut down your operation. Think what we'll do in a week's time, or a month's. You can't kill us. And we know what you're willing to do now, and we're ready for it. If you try something like what you did to Jez again, one of us will decide stopping you is worth dying for. However you look at this, you can't win."

Evka studied her for a few moments, and there was cold hatred behind the small smile on her lips. "Masha," she said at last. "You are an impressive woman. But if you have a flaw, it's hubris. Your hubris cost you your crew, and then it cost you your scheme to take the government. And so instead, you lost both. Everything you've said is true, perhaps—the disruptions, the difficulty you've caused, the fact that there is really nowhere safe I can put you without worrying what you'll do. And you're correct—if I tortured you long enough to incapacitate you, there's always the chance I inadvertently kill one of you. But you've overplayed your hand. The government is up and running again, after the damage caused by your crew, and I've been in contact with them." She paused. "I've arranged for you to be transported to the Vault."

There was a long moment of silence, and Masha could hear her own heartbeat in her ears.

"Perhaps your sources forget to mention we've broken out of prison before," said Ysbel wryly.

"Oh, I know your history," Evka hissed. "But this isn't some backwater prison on an outer-rim prison planet. You leave the Vault because you're released, or you leave as a corpse. Still, I agree with you that further precautions are warranted. So, I checked—the sedation machine in the prison is still operational, it appears."

There was another moment of silence at Evka's words.

Masha forced her expression to remain calm, despite the harshness of her breath in her throat.

Sedation.

It had been touted, once, as a humane form of restraining dangerous prisoners. The patient could be put into stasis, still alive, but bodily processes on hold, and they could be kept like that for as long as necessary—weeks, months, even years.

But as useful as it was, they'd had to halt the program, eventually.

Because eventually, as the true effects of the program became known, even the most calloused government official had been horrified.

At first, it had seemed a great success—upon being revived, the patients had gone back to their normal lives, with no noticeable physical deterioration, no loss of memory or cognitive function.

Until the side effects began. The hallucinations. The phantom pains that no amount of treatment or painkiller could cure. The slow, creeping madness, whether brought on by the effects of the sedation itself, or from the persistent, horrific, unbearable, untreatable pain, no one knew for sure.

All they knew was, every person—every patient who been sent into sedation—had died screaming.

"It's an old-fashioned solution, perhaps, maybe even barbaric," Evka continued, and Masha could hear the grim satisfaction in her voice. "But as Masha so helpfully pointed out, I haven't much of an option. And should I for some reason still need you—for example, if it takes me an unacceptably long time to get through your street boy's com hack—I can always take one of you out of sedation for long enough to answer my questions. I'm not sure if they can re-sedate you once you've been revived, but—" she gave another small shrug. "From what I know about sedation's aftereffects, I expect within a few weeks you won't be in any shape to cause additional problems."

Ysbel was pale, her fists clenched by her side.

Masha knew what she was seeing—that day, months previous, standing in a barred room on a prison planet, as the warden pulled Tanya and her two crying children away to await their own sedation.

The first time Masha had begun to realize how very much she'd come to care for this little crew—and how very dangerous that could be.

She didn't let herself look at the others as they were shuffled out of the room and down the hololift to the courtyard.

Her stomach was a tight knot.

A government prison transport awaited them, but by the time Masha had made her slow, agonizing way up the ramp, she hardly had the energy to care about anything except the fact she could finally sit down, and take the weight off her leg.

When she'd recovered enough to be aware of her surroundings again, she couldn't help a quick glance at Lev.

He was seated on a bench, hands and feet bound, staring out the transport window with a lost, helpless expression that almost made Masha sick to her stomach.

At last, the ship slowed. Even from inside, Masha could hear the gates of the prison opening to let them through, then closing ponderously behind them.

When the transport finally shuddered to a halt and they were prodded out into the courtyard, Masha took a deep breath, glancing around through the cold, muted light.

The force field over the Vault was thick enough that even the sunlight had difficulties filtering through. The walls were something that looked like solid metal, almost certainly nonreactive, and they stretched a full five stories from the nonreactive surface of the courtyard to the edge of the force field. Just under the force field stretched a thick cable lattice, and, she knew, an additional lattice of hair-trigger laser sensors.

The walls themselves carried an electric current that would kill you at a touch.

"Leave their coms," snapped one of the guards, stepping forward. He looked like someone accustomed to command. "Attach their prison bracelets above the coms."

A handful of guards stepped up to do as he bade them. Masha

held out her wrist as instructed, and they snapped the bracelet on.

The sensation of it, heavy on her wrist, was strange.

She'd never been an actual prisoner, not really.

They were pushed into a small room, where they were given a prison uniform to change into, but even here they weren't left alone. Masha undressed in front of a stern guard, her muscles shaking with weakness. She was acutely aware of the dark bruises that spread down her ribs and blossomed across her stomach, the long, precise gashes on her arms and torso.

It took her a humiliatingly long time to dress herself, but the guard did nothing to help, just watched with a small sneer.

When they were brought back together, Masha's knee ached with a stabbing, throbbing pain, and her whole body trembled.

Another guard appeared in the doorway, glaring at them as they shivered in the chill air, their thin prison uniforms scant protection against the icy bite of a Prasvishoni winter.

"These are the ones Evka sent?" she asked.

"Yes," said the floor guard. "They're ready to be processed."

The guard who'd just appeared smiled, but it wasn't a pleasant smile. "No hurry, I think. They're being sedated. I doubt they'll need extensive processing." She paused a moment. "Besides, the warden has taken a personal interest in them. I believe he wants to see them. Alone."

They emphasized she placed on the word left no doubt as to how she expected their meeting with the warden to go.

Masha closed her eyes for a moment, her stomach swirling with anxiety.

"Can't keep the warden waiting," the floor guard replied with an answering grin.

They were pushed towards a hololift. Ysbel glanced helplessly at her children as they were prodded forward, and made a futile attempt to reach them, despite the cuffs on her wrists.

They were shoved into the lift, and it ascended slowly.

The Vault was an old prison, certainly, but the technology here was brand-new—nothing like the ancient tech of the prison they'd broken out of.

This was where they sent prisoners who were far too dangerous to be allowed to escape.

Masha's heart pounded a harsh rhythm against her ribs, and she didn't dare look at the others as they were shoved out of the lift.

After a short hallway, their guard paused in front of a door and hit the com link. "I'm here with the prisoners," she said.

The lock released with a *click*, and the guard shoved them through.

The room they entered was empty, except for a few chairs that had been haphazardly lined up in the centre, and a table, with tools and instruments that were sickeningly familiar laid out on it. The walls were bare, the floors bare as well, dipping to a drain in the centre.

Masha tasted bile.

This was a torture room. And she had first-hand experience with the government's form of torture.

A man stood in the centre of the room. He turned slowly at their entrance, letting his eyes drift over them, no hint of emotion in his expression except a small, cruel satisfaction.

His eyes brushed over Masha as quickly as the others, as if he didn't recognize her.

But she knew he did.

"Close the door behind you," he said in a bored voice, waving a hand at the guards. "I'd like some time with the prisoners. I have some questions I'd like them to answer."

"Would you like any guards to stay with you?" the woman who'd brought them asked. She sounded almost nervous.

"Oh, no thank you," said the man, his smile tilting up slightly at the corner. "I'm quite capable."

"It's—we have special instructions from Evka. If one of them dies, it could cause problems."

"You can reassure Evka," the man said, his voice sharpening. "I have a great deal of practice in keeping people … alive."

There was an unpleasant implication behind his words.

The guard nodded, and stepped back through the door.

Masha could swear the expression on her face, as the door closed, was one of pity.

The warden turned to them, his gaze cold, as the lock clicked into place, and for a long moment, they stood like that.

Then the vicious smile dropped from the man's face, replaced with something much more genuine. "Masha! It's good to see you." He pulled a chair around. "Sit, please. I didn't realize what a number they'd done on you."

Masha sank into the proffered seat with a small sigh of relief. "Thank you, Adrian," she murmured.

The man was still smiling. "The least I could possibly do." He glanced around. "And aren't you going to introduce me to your friends?"

18

Jez, day 6, evening

The first shot whispered past the *Ungovernable's* shields as Jez tapped the controls, sending the ship into a sharp dive.

With her free hand, she expanded the ship's holoscreen.

She winced.

It didn't look good.

"It's alright, sweetheart," she whispered, patting the control panel reassuringly. "I'll get you out of this."

Maybe.

She didn't have the time to count the ships surrounding her, but she figured all she really needed to know could be summed up in the words, "way too damn many."

Three more shots streaked towards her from three different directions. She nudged her controls, ducking under two of the shots and pulling up onto her side to let the other skin by her close enough to spark off her shields.

Warning shots still, she was pretty sure, but it wouldn't take them too long to figure out she had exactly zero intention of coming in peacefully.

"Pilot! This is your last chance to stand down."

"Yeah? Well, this is your last chance to shut the hell up," Jez snapped, hitting the com.

She couldn't do a hyper jump, not like this—too many ships, too many missiles. Too many chances of an off-balance jump, and she sure as hell wasn't doing that again to her angel ship.

"Easy, girl, stay with me," Jez whispered, stroking the controls as she studied the layout of the ships on her screen.

Been a long time since she'd seen ships going into police formation. And usually when it happened, she'd had two or three others smuggler ships with her, and they could split up.

Now it was all her.

The ships had moved into a wide star formation, larger ships forming the points, smaller ones connecting them. Once they were all in position, they'd close in until she had no more space to maneuver, and open fire. And she and her sweet angel both would be blasted into space dust.

Even with her shields, there was no way she'd survived that much firepower.

The formation was already starting to close in.

She grinned to herself, her pulse pounding in her ears.

Been a while since she'd had to do some real flying.

She might die, sure. But hell, this was the whole damn reason for being alive.

She bumped the controls a couple times, making what she hoped looked like little, ineffectual attempts to break out. Every time she moved towards them, the ships at the intersections closed in, tightening off her escape.

"Hey there. You look as bad as you fly?" she called over the com.

No one answered. Clearly, as far as they were concerned, the time for talking was over.

She tried again, a quick dash towards one of the points where a couple of the ships had fallen slightly back. They tightened up instantly, and the formation shifted around her until once more she was in the centre.

She glanced back at her screen.

They weren't going to risk friendly damage, which meant they wouldn't fire until they had a lock on her. Which, if they were using their short-haul canons, meant—

She bit her lip, calculating.

Just under a minute, probably.

"Hey, don't you want to hear my last words?" she called.

Still no response.

A few seconds now. They were close enough she could see the gun ports opening.

She took a deep breath. "You ready for this, sweetheart?" she whispered to her ship.

Then, as the air around her erupted with laser blasts, she jammed down on the controller, swinging her nose towards the largest gap in the formation. And as they tightened up, she slammed the throttle backwards, twisting perpendicular to them.

The ships behind her realized what she was doing an instant later, and pulled together, trying to tighten the gap.

But they weren't quite fast enough.

She could feel the scrape along the shields as the *Ungovernable* slid through the ever-narrowing gap, and then she was out.

Behind the formation, over a dozen ships waited, backup, maybe, or maybe they'd just drawn the short straw.

For a split second, none of them reacted as she appeared in their airspace.

Then a blizzard of lasers streaked across her holoscreen in bright jets of blue and yellow, and the *Ungovernable* danced gracefully between them.

The formation dissolved, the ships swinging back around to face her, but she kept herself positioned so any shot that missed her would slam into one of the probably ridiculously expensive ships behind her, and listened with satisfaction to the cursing over the general line as the heavy military-level shields struggled to take the impact of the heavy military-level weapons.

Then she hit the controllers for her front guns.

The blue streak from Ysbel's weapons slid across the empty black of space on her holoscreen. And then it hit, and the ship in front of her rocked and bucked at the impact.

She grinned and squeezed off a second shot, then grabbed for the controls, swearing, as her holoscreen lit with the sudden blossom of missiles launching after her.

The missile swerved to follow her, and she swore again.

They were firing damn heat-seekers.

She'd be damned to every hell in existence before she let a bunch of bastards with heat-seeking missiles hurt her sweet baby.

She pointed her ship at the nearest gap, weaving and dodging through the incoming blasts as the surrounding ships opened fire. A shot skimmed the starboard shield, and the *Ungovernable* jerked, slamming Jez's head against the corner of the chair. She blinked back stars, then yelped and pulled up quickly as a ship appeared in front of her, big enough to take her impact and laugh it off.

Behind her, the missiles were gaining. And none of them had broken off to go after the other ships.

She gritted her teeth.

Damn it to hell. Not just heat-seekers, then. They must've set her angel's specs into the missiles. Bloody things would follow her basically forever now.

Well, as much of forever as she had left, which would be until right about the time when the damn things caught up with her.

In front of her, the ships were forming up again, trying to stop her getting too far ahead.

Jez bit her lip, staring at the holoscreen.

Then she grinned.

The damn missiles would follow her anywhere.

And she knew exactly where she wanted them to follow her.

She played the controls through her fingers, swerving around the outside of the massive ship. The other ships had pulled back slightly, content to wait and let the missiles do their work.

There. A docking bay in the ship's belly.

Small target, but she'd worked with less.

She curved around the outside of the ship, then, right before she cleared its bulk and caught the visuals of the ships on the other side, she spun the *Ungovernable* in a tight arc.

The missiles were so close on her butt they were almost scorching her rear shields.

"Alright, sweetheart," Jez whispered. "You and me."

The *Ungovernable's* steady hum pulsed through Jez like a second heartbeat.

She pulled back on the throttle, her fingers dancing across the controls, and her speed cut abruptly, momentum spinning her around so she was snugged up against the belly of the big ship.

Above her, the military ship jerked, a sudden, frantic jolt of motion that told her someone above decks had figured out where she was and what she might be doing there, and were suddenly getting very nervous indeed.

She snugged up a little closer to the docking bay, turning her ship so that just the edge of the docking bay door was between her and the missiles.

Thin enough that it wouldn't read on the missile's signature. As far as their seekers told them, they were coming straight for her.

She was grinning like a maniac.

Two …

One …

The missiles slammed into the slender docking bay door and exploded spectacularly on impact. The doors vaporized, particles spraying in every direction in an ever-widening cloud.

It wasn't nearly enough to stop an explosion like that one, and it should have turned her angel into a second cloud of debris. Except, at the moment of impact, Jez shoved full power to the shields with one hand, and with the other, slammed the throttle.

And her little beauty, who listened to the faintest tremble of her fingertips, shot forward like she'd been propelled by one of Ysbel's explosives.

Jez whooped, laughing in sheer delight as the *Ungovernable* twisted and spun, her sleek body sliding between the ships like a sky dancer through a sea of ribbons, with all the grace of Tanya taking out a damn squadron of Prasvishoni police officers. Every inch of her body was warm with adrenaline, every part of her was alive, every neuron in her brain firing pure pleasure.

And then she was out, and—

She glanced at her screen.

Yep. All the ships were still staring at the explosion.

They probably wouldn't even be looking for her. Because hell, they'd seen her dive, seen the missiles hit, seen the explosion, and they'd all know the shelter of the bay door wouldn't have been enough to stop that kind of firepower.

She closed her eyes in pure bliss.

She could fly like this forever.

She took a deep breath and opened her eyes. And for half a second, her gaze flicked unconsciously to the copilot seat, and the jolt of disappointment when she found it empty was so unexpected she almost choked on it.

She squeezed her eyes shut again, just for a moment.

This was freedom. This was what she'd spent her whole life chasing. But—she realized, suddenly, that it wouldn't really be freedom until Lev was in the cockpit beside her.

She drew in a steadying breath.

Just a few more days. They had to stop that damn Evka, and then she'd get Lev back in the cockpit, and maybe they'd never leave it again.

For a moment, thoughts of the various interesting ways she and Lev could keep themselves occupied in the cockpit tugged at her concentration, but she sighed, pulling her thoughts reluctantly back to the present, and rested her hand on the hyperdrive.

"Alright, beautiful," she whispered. "Guess we better get back to work."

She engaged the hyperdrive.

Time stretched around her, warping and pulling like a flow of sticky molasses, and the black of shallow space around her turned to that strange, beautiful pattern of colour and shape and shadow that made something inside her hurt with the beauty of it.

And when she pulled them out of hyperdrive, what seemed like moments later, she recognized the planet below her instantly.

She grinned.

Maybe the first damn time in her life she was actually excited to see the pleasure planet.

19

Lev, day 6, evening

Lev took a deep breath and forced his fists to unclench.

Around him, the others were stretching and rubbing their wrists as the warden unlocked their cuffs. Misko and Olya were already clasped in their parents' arms, and Tae was holding Ivan as if he'd never let him go again.

And the sharp, sick absence of Jez, the empty space beside him where she should have been, hit Lev hard enough, almost, to make him stagger.

It had been mere weeks since they'd become lovers. Since she'd become his partner. But he couldn't actually remember how he'd survived the time before that. And he didn't know how to go back to it.

"I'm sure she's not dead," said Masha quietly. She was sitting next to him, and he could see the pallor of her face under her brown skin, the way her muscles trembled. "Evka would have no way of knowing for certain, and I can think of a number of ways in which our pilot could have made the other ships believe she'd been shot down."

Lev nodded, not quite able to meet her gaze.

It was possible Jez was still alive. In fact, it was likely, because he couldn't imagine the system continuing to function if Jez was no longer part of it. Surely something would have happened—an earthquake, or an explosion, or the stars blinking out one by one.

Surely he wouldn't have lived through it.

He took a deep breath and forced a smile, finally meeting her eyes. "You're probably right."

Masha's gaze on him was sharp and uncomfortably perceptive, but she only nodded, and turned back to the warden. "This is my crew—or at least, the majority of it. Lev, Tanya, Ysbel, Olya, Misko, Tae, and Ivan."

The warden nodded, still smiling broadly. "It's a pleasure to meet you," he said. "Masha's spoken very highly of you."

Lev shook his head. "Masha told me she had someone on the inside—but you've been serving as warden over the Vault, just in case, for—how long now?"

The man gave a small shrug and glanced at Masha. "I've been in place as a substitute for the warden, should one be needed, for a while. I was only placed in as full warden—" he frowned. "A week ago, maybe? When we got word of Masha's capture. Masha had been very clear—if she was captured, she wanted someone in the Vault."

Lev glanced at Masha. She was looking down at the floor, her face tight.

"Masha," he said quietly. "You must have known you'd never survive long enough to be taken to the Vault if you were captured. Why put someone in place here?"

Masha didn't answer, and Lev turned his gaze on the warden.

The man glanced at Masha, a small, fond smile tugging at his lips, then shrugged and turned back to Lev. "The instructions I received were, if she was captured, and anyone matching descriptions she sent—descriptions which, incidentally, seem to match up quite well with the lot of you—were brought in, I was to make sure that you were not executed or sedated, and find a way to get you out."

Lev stared at the man for a moment, then turned back to Masha.

She was still looking at the ground, and seemed unwilling to meet his eyes.

He shook his head.

She'd been planning to betray them. She'd admitted as much after they'd rescued her. She'd been planning from the very beginning to betray them, and everything they'd done as her crew had brought them a step closer to that moment.

The revelation hadn't shocked him as much as it might have, but even now, the thought of it was a sharp, bitter pang.

And yet … her contingency plan, should she fail, had been to save them.

He wasn't sure he'd ever understand her.

Of course, at the moment, he wasn't sure any of them would live long enough that it would matter.

"At any rate," continued the warden, "Since Masha's with you, I assume your motive is more than to simply make it out alive. She and I have been friends for some time now, and I know her better than that."

Lev raised an eyebrow at the words. For some reason, he'd never actually considered Masha having friends.

Masha nodded, looking up at last. "I'm afraid you're correct," she said quietly. "It would take much more than simply getting out of prison to save our lives at this point. But I shall leave the discussion of the details to Lev, as he is eminently capable of explaining them."

Again, Lev glanced over at her reflexively.

The Masha he'd known was not one to trust her plans to someone else.

Perhaps whatever had happened to her while she'd been away from them had changed her outlook more than he'd guessed.

He turned back to the warden, who was watching him curiously. "Before I start," Lev said, keeping his voice level, "I should warn you —if Evka hears so much as a rumour that her instructions were not followed, she'll kill not only us, but you and every person who might have helped you." He waited for the flash of alarm in the man's eyes, but clearly, whatever Masha had told him about his responsibilities, violent death had always been on the list of possible outcomes.

The man simply waited quietly, watching Lev with a polite, curious expression.

Lev glanced quickly around the bare room. "I assume the force field in the prison is strong enough to block the signals for Evka's protocol?"

The warden nodded. "My informants tell me Evka is working to solve the issue, but at least for now, you're correct—her protocol can't detect anyone within these walls."

"Good." Lev took a deep breath. "We're here for two reasons: to get us away from Evka's supervision, and to get us somewhere we can access the main core of the power grid."

The man's eyes widened. "You're referring to the underground corridors?" he asked at last. "I—believe you're correct. As warden, I've made it my mandate to study in depth the infrastructure of the prison." He shook his head. "And—dare I ask why you need to access the main core of the power grid?"

Ysbel gave him a grim smile, and his eyes went just a touch wider.

"You're—not going to blow it up."

Ysbel's smile widened.

The man shook his head. "It's—a good idea, if an audacious one, but it won't work. The power system was upgraded during the last war, designed specifically to thwart an attempt like yours. The main power core is accessible from the prison corridors, but there are at least two other points, located on opposite ends of the city. The moment the main core goes down, it will simply flip over to the alternate power system, and self-repair while the alternate system runs. And even if you could blow all three, the internal AI is set up such that the delay between the explosions—even just a few seconds—will give it time to seek out and pirate infrastructure from any available system grid. It's designed to be next to impossible to take out."

"I know that," said Ysbel. "My father designed it."

The man's eyebrows shot up. "You—" he began after a moment. "Forgive me, but Masha wasn't particularly forthcoming about your identities. You're the Ysbel who—"

"Blew up a shuttle station and killed thirty-five people?" asked Ysbel dryly. "Yes. That's me."

The man gave her a wary look before turning back to Lev. "So, you have a plan to deal with the back-up system."

Lev nodded. "We do. The only thing we needed was access to the main power core."

He wouldn't let himself consider the possibility that their plan wouldn't work, because Jez wasn't alive to carry out her part of it.

The man nodded slowly "And now it you have it." He shook his head. "I guess I shouldn't be surprised—I've worked with Masha long enough that nothing should surprise me. I suppose there's no time to lose then." He frowned in thought. "The easiest way to deal with this, I think, is that I notify the guards that I'll personally escort you to the sedation chamber. I have the dummy sedation cubes prepared, as per Masha's instructions. In the meantime, I'll set you up in the guards' quarters. I'd already started a rumour that some of the guards' families would be joining us, in case a deception should be necessary."

Masha nodded approvingly. "I see that I didn't misplace my confidence," she murmured.

The man smiled, as if he'd been handed a medal of valour.

Again, Lev glanced curiously at Masha.

However she knew these people she worked with, they were clearly willing to die for her.

Of course, he and the rest of that the crew had been willing to die for her, right up until she betrayed them.

Even afterwards—there had been, after all, a thousand ways their rescue attempt could have gone wrong.

He shook his head again.

Perhaps that, more than anything, was what made Masha so dangerous. And, at the same time, such a valuable ally.

"How soon do you think we can get started planting the explosives?" Masha asked briskly.

Adrian frowned, calculating. "We'd want to wait until the dummy cubes have been brought out. The sedation machine takes a few hours to power up fully, and then some time to actually complete the process. So—" he glanced down at his com. "I'd say by tonight, if all goes well. Is that workable?"

"It should be," said Lev, trying to ignore the tightness in his stomach.

"Good. Follow me, then, and I'll take you to the guards' quarters." He paused a moment. "Let me take the prison bracelets off first—no point in taking a chance someone will track you."

"Thank you," said Masha, with a genuine smile. She paused a moment as she held out her wrist. "I wasn't certain you'd still be here, Adrian."

The man smiled at her. "There are more of us than you think, you know," he said quietly.

Lev held out his wrist when the man turned to him, and it was surprising how much more at ease the loosening of the unaccustomed weight made him feel.

"Well," Ysbel whispered, as they followed the warden out a back door. "I guess it's our turn to surprise Evka, for a change."

Lev thought, for a moment, of Jez—the fear in her face, the shakiness in her voice that she'd been unable to hide, the sight of her writhing on the floor as Evka jolted pain through her body.

"I think perhaps it is," he said quietly.

20

Jez, day 6, evening

Jez brought the *Ungovernable* down through the atmosphere on the pleasure planet, the shields burning a bright orange at the friction. She skimmed across the ground towards the city, slid through the opening in the city force field, popped over the courtyard wall of the building that had once been their mock pleasure house, and brought the ship gently to rest in the old docking bay.

The euphoria of earlier was slowly fading, and she was aware, for the first time, of the ache in her head from where it had slammed into the corner of the seat. She could feel the shakiness in her muscles again, the way her body still didn't quite respond the way she expected it to.

And for just a moment, when she shut off the power to her ship, she had to close her eyes tightly and swallow down nausea against the memory: laying on the floor, her body shaking with pain, her muscles spasming outside of her control, every nerve in her body screaming.

The look on Lev's face, that terrifying moment where she'd thought he might go for Evka, and that Evka might hurt him too.

She could handle getting hurt—hell, that was basically the story of her entire life.

But she wasn't sure she could watch Lev get hurt.

She swallowed hard.

This was actually ridiculous. She was fine. It had all happened basically a million years ago, at this point—two days, at least—and … and …

And for a few moments, her body was shaking so hard she couldn't stand up from the pilot's seat.

At last, though, she pushed herself upright and clung to the edge of the seat, waiting for the ground to steady under her.

Lev was back in Prasvishoni. Lev and the others, and they were depending on her.

And she wasn't going to let them down.

She took a deep breath, straightened, and made her unsteady way out of the cockpit and down the loading ramp.

The hangar bay was deserted. No more than she'd expected, really—this far out of the main centre of town, the old building wouldn't be a particularly useful headquarters for shutting down the entire damn pleasure district.

Galina would be in the Strani house, Jez was pretty sure.

She grabbed one of the dusty skybikes leaned against the wall and swung onto it. It started, which honestly, the way it looked, was a bit of a miracle.

Then she leaned forward and shot out of the hangar bay, over the courtyard wall, and out into the streets.

The city itself was entirely different than it had been when she left it—there was a hell of a lot less traffic, for one thing, and what there was was mainly cargo ships, and street workers unloading the cargo ships. There were still gangs, you could tell just by looking, but they seemed to have gone a hell of a lot deeper underground.

If they'd heard what Masha had done to the gangs back on Prasvishoni, she couldn't exactly blame them.

Her muscles tensed unconsciously as she got closer to the pleasure district.

The slums were still as filthy as ever, but there were fewer broken bodies leaning against walls of alleys, begging for food, and the air of fear that had been palpable before was much more muted.

Even Galina wasn't a miracle worker. It would take time to fix crap like this. But it was obvious things were already changing.

The pleasure district, too, had changed. She could see it as she idled the bike through the arched entrance that led from the slums. The pleasure houses lining the streets seemed to have changed their function—some obviously served as inns, some looked like restaurants, and others had apparently been transformed into apartment blocks. The glittering sheen of the place had disappeared, too, and it looked more like a regular city—streets dirty, the noise and chaos of traffic and street bikes.

No one in chains.

Jez's lightheadedness, by now, was bad enough that she was having a hard time keeping her vision straight. Finally, a block or so away from her destination, she pulled her bike to a stop and leaned it carefully against the wall.

Whatever the hell Evka had messed with in her brain, it had done a damn number on her.

When the world steadied around her, she started cautiously down the street.

She kept her hand on the heat pistol in her pocket—never knew if some of the bastards who ran the gangs around here held grudges— but the streets were busy enough that another person wandering down them was hardly noteworthy. Even if they were staggering like a damn drunk.

Standing in front of the Strani House made her stomach clench, and she had to consciously force her muscles to relax.

She'd seen what this place had been used for, and she wasn't sure she'd ever get it out of her head.

The front doors opened when she pushed them, and she stepped into the cool dimness inside. A quick glance around told her she'd been right—the place showed every sign of Galena's occupation. And she was pretty sure she recognized one of the voices floating down from the second-story balcony.

The room swayed, and she grabbed whatever the hell was nearest her to keep from falling over.

It was someone's arm, turned out.

The owner of the arm turned sharply, clearly about to snap something rude. Then the expression on the man's face changed to one of utter astonishment.

He stood blinking at her for a moment.

"Radic, you skinny cheating bastard," she managed, grinning.

"Jez? Jez, what the hell—"

She fainted.

The first thing she noticed, as her consciousness returned, was that she was in a cot.

The second thing she noticed was, it was a damn lot softer than it should have been, considering Evka was a miserly bastard.

And then she woke up all the way, and sat up quickly, cursing. The world spun, and she almost fell over, but someone caught her.

"For the Lady's damn sake, Jez, lie down! What happened to you, anyway?"

She blinked, and Radic's face came into focus.

"Figured you were probably missing me," she said, although her voice came out more weak than snarky.

"Jez."

She blinked again, and then she could make out Galina, sitting on the foot of her bed.

She was just as damn hot as she'd always been, but there was something different about her face. It took Jez a minute to figure out what it was.

There was still that look in her eyes the told you she'd seen things she probably didn't want to talk about. But the sick hopelessness that had come so often, when Jez had held her and stroked her hair and Galina had stared blankly at the wall in front of her, as if she wasn't able even to cry—was gone. Or at least, mostly gone. The expression Galina now wore was one of crisp, businesslike competence.

Although it now bore a distinct overlay of worry.

"Hey, Galya," she said. "Maybe I was just so surprised Radic hadn't been thrown back in jail yet I passed out."

Galina didn't look amused. "Radic carried you up here—you looked like you were on the verge of death. Our doctor couldn't find anything wrong with you, but we couldn't get you to wake up. And then you started moaning in your sleep, and crying. What's going on? Where are the others? What happened to you?"

Jez swore and swung her legs off the side of the bed, and Radic barely caught her before she fell on her face.

"How long has it been?" she snapped.

"Jez! Calm down. It's been—" Radic glanced at Galina. "What, three hours since she got here? Four?"

Jez sank back with a sigh of relief.

"Jez—" began Galina.

Jez let out a long breath and closed her eyes for a moment.

She hadn't missed it. She still had time.

They still, maybe, had a chance to survive Evka.

"Well," she said at last. "I'll tell you. But it's a hell of a long story. And you might want to get a few of your people together in the meantime, because I'm going to need a bunch of crazy damn bastards if we're going to live through the rest of it."

By the time she'd finished her story, both Radic and Galina were staring at her in frank astonishment. There were half a dozen other people in the room as well, some she recognized, some she didn't, and their expressions ranged from shock to outright disbelief.

"So—" said Radic at last. "You're saying in the last however many weeks, you started a full-on revolution, Masha betrayed you and assassinated her way through the government before almost being tortured to death, you rescued her, blew up the government compound, shut off all the government communication lines, got the police and military to surrender, and then got caught by Lev's crazy professor? And that everyone in Prasvishoni can be killed by her hitting a button, except Tae hacked his way through her program, hacked his way through it a second time, you broke out of lockup and flew through an attacking military armada, and the others are locked up in the Vault."

Jez shrugged and nodded. "More or less. I mean, I also kicked some people in the crotch, and Ysbel blew some crap up, and Masha killed like seven thousand people, but I think you got the important bits."

For a moment, Radic didn't speak. Then he shook his head ruefully. "You know, that doesn't even actually surprise me? How the hell did I run into someone so much crazier than I am that I look like a damn saint in comparison?"

Jez winked at him. "Don't worry, practice enough and you'll get there one day."

He was still shaking his head, but there was just the hint of a grin on his face, and there was that look in his eyes that meant he was contemplating something crazy.

"So. What can we do?" asked Galina. "Also, you forgot to mention what the hell happened that led to you passing out in the front lobby."

Jez shivered.

Still, they should probably know what they were up against.

"You know how I told you that when that metal gets in your brain, Evka can kill you by hitting a button?"

Galina nodded.

"Well, that's not all she can do. She can knock you out, or she can—mess with your head. Make you—hurt."

"What do you—" Galina began, then stopped, her eyes widening. "Oh," she said at last, quietly, and there was a slightly sick look on her face.

Jez tried to grin, but she couldn't quite manage it.

"I'm—sorry, Jez," said Galina.

Jez shook her head. "Look. Thing is, right now, she can do that to basically anyone in Prasvishoni. Kill them, if she wants. Anything. Lev thinks she'll need to talk to the government ministries before she can go farther than the city, but when she's calmed the streets down, mopped up the revolution—hell, I figure the government will give her pretty much anything she wants. So, we don't have much time."

"And do you have a plan for how to stop her?" asked Radic.

"Yep," said Jez with a grin. "See, Lev figured, Evka's a slippery damn bastard. But as far as she's concerned, she doesn't have much to worry about—I'm dead, the others are locked up, and everyone in the city has to do what she says or she'll kill them. But if I happened to come back to the city, with a ship full of people who hadn't breathed in her crap—"

Radic was grinning now, too. "I guess that might surprise her a bit."

"Figure it might," said Jez. "And hell, if a bunch of people who Evka couldn't do a damn thing to happened to distract the police a bit, and while the police were distracted, blow the entire damn power grid—"

Radic's eyebrows shot up. "Blow the—I'm a hundred percent certain you're not talking about blowing the power grid for the entire city of Prasvishoni. Because that would be insane. Also, impossible."

Jez winked at him.

He sighed and ran his hand across his face. "How the hell do I let you drag me into these things?" he muttered.

"Think how boring your life would be without me," said Jez cheerfully.

"Not boring. Easy, I think, is the word you're looking for—easy, simple, unstressful, not putting me in danger of my life every five damn minutes."

"Like I said," said Jez, still grinning. "So. You in?"

Radic heaved another deep sigh. "I must be insane. Yes, kid, I'm in."

"I'm in, too," said Galina grimly. "And I suspect we'll have more than enough volunteers. Radic and I will track down people who can help us. Is there anything specific you need?"

"A handful of people who can fly a ship wouldn't be a bad thing," said Jez. "There's a hell of a lot of people depending on us getting through, and I'd rather not have all of us in the same damn ship in case something happens. Seeing as we have to fly back through the military blockade to get planet-side."

Galina's eyebrows creased. "I'm not sure that anyone on this planet besides you can pull off something like that."

Jez leaned back luxuriously against the pillow, hands behind her head. "Don't figure they'll have to. I'll do the heavy lifting. Me and Radic, since he's flying copilot."

Radic turned. "What? Listen, kid—"

She winked at him. "You scared?"

He glared at her for a moment, then shook his head in mock disgust. But there was that crazy gleam in his eye, and if she had to guess, he was just about as excited for this as she was. "I guess I better go start rounding people up to come with," he grumbled. "And saying my goodbyes, from the sounds of it." He pushed himself to his feet and strode out the door.

Galina turned back to Jez, a small smile on her face. "I've missed you, you know," she said. "And—I'm sorry things didn't work out with us."

"Yeah," said Jez quietly. "I missed you too. But you were right—If we'd tried to make it work, one of us would have been miserable."

Galina gave her a small smile. "Have you found anyone new?"

Jez glanced down. "Um. I. Well, look, you remember how—"

Galena's smile grew broader. "Lev?"

Jez hesitated, then nodded.

Galina smiled. "I'm glad." She sighed, and stood. "I suppose I should go help Radic. Are you going to be—"

Jez pushed herself to her feet with a grimace, swayed, then caught her balance. "Galya. We're going to be flying ships. Through a hell of a lot of firepower. If that doesn't make me feel better, I'd have to actually be dead."

Galina chuckled ruefully. "I have a feeling that, with you back, our lives won't be boring for a while."

Jez was grinning. "Ah, come on, Galya," she drawled. "You used to date me. You can't be all that fond of boring."

Galina shook her head fondly. "I suppose I can't," she said.

21

Ysbel, day 7, afternoon

There was a tap on the door to the small guard's quarters, and Ysbel glanced up quickly.

"I'll get it," said Tanya, stepping to the door and pulling it open.

Masha stood in the entrance, a stack of boxes balanced in her arms, and more piled on an anti-grav behind her. Her face was drawn with pain, but her expression was businesslike.

"Ysbel," said Masha briskly. "I have your supplies. Adrian brought them a few minutes ago."

Ysbel took the packages carefully from Masha's arms. "Good. Thank you."

"I'll meet you in our workroom," said Tanya, taking the anti-grav.

Ysbel leaned over and kissed her. "I'll be there in a moment."

She turned back to Masha. "Thank you," she said, quietly.

Masha raised an eyebrow. "For what?" There was a tone in her voice, though, that said she knew exactly what Ysbel was saying.

"For getting the supplies." Ysbel let a hint of wryness creep into her words. "It's been a long time since I've made explosives."

Masha nodded and cleared her throat. "Thank you for agreeing to make them. This crew wouldn't be what it is without you."

And Ysbel heard the words under the words as well, and found she was smiling as she turned away.

Tanya was waiting in the weapons room, and together they pried open the first of the boxes.

Ysbel felt a smile spreading across her face when she saw the components inside.

It had been a very, very long time since she'd been able to work with materials like this. Masha's contacts must be good ones.

This she would enjoy very much.

She was so absorbed in her work that when Tanya's voice floated in from the other room, she looked up, blinking for a moment, before she remembered where she was and what she was doing.

She glanced at the components spread out on the table, the explosives taking shape in the centre. She had no idea how long she'd been working, but it must have been some time.

"The others are here to talk about the plan. Should I send them through?"

"Yes, thank you," Ysbel called back.

Tae stepped through the door a few moments later, Ivan beside him. Tae's arm was tucked around Ivan's waist, and he seemed all but unconscious of the fact, as if Ivan had become almost a part of him.

Ysbel smiled to herself.

Tae glanced around the room, then caught sight of the explosives laid out on the table and gave an involuntary yelp.

"Ysbel," he said after a moment. "Please tell me that's not what it looks like."

Ysbel smirked. "I don't know. What do you think it looks like?"

Tae scowled at her. "It looks like something that would take out the entire city of Prasvishoni if we weren't careful with it. It looks like something that nobody in their right mind would construct in a building we're living in, and a few metres down from our damn bedrooms. It looks like something that might just save Evka the trouble of having to kill us at all if someone so much as breathes on it wrong."

Ysbel shrugged. "Well, in that case, it's exactly what it looks like."

Ivan was biting back a smile.

Lev came in a moment later, and took in the sight of the explosive with slightly more equanimity than Tae had—his eyebrows shot up when he realized exactly what was laid out on the table in front of them, but then he just sighed resignedly, and pulled out a chair.

Of course, someone who'd fallen in love with Jez would, of necessity, have learned to take high-stress situations in stride.

But Ysbel caught the way his eyes flicked to Tae and Ivan, then away, the tension in his posture, the pain in his expression he couldn't quite hide.

Jez was alright—Ysbel was all but sure of it. The thought of someone being able to shoot down the crazy, ridiculous pilot, while she was flying the *Ungovernable*, was almost laughable.

Still—

She knew all too well how it felt, not knowing for certain if the person you loved was alive or dead.

Masha and Tanya joined them a few moments later, and they took their seats around the table.

"We aren't going to have much time," said Lev quietly, once they were all seated. "The decoy sedation cubes might fool Evka for a short time, but we can't assume it will last forever. And once she disables Tae's blocker, everyone in the warehouse is in danger. We need to act quickly—twenty-four hours or less, if possible."

Tae nodded. "I've been going through the diagram of the power grid. I think I know where the explosive would have to go in order to knock out the main core." He turned to Ysbel. "You're building the explosive to be wired directly into the network, correct? So I'll need to program a bypass that will shunt the power around the explosive until we're ready to set it off."

"Can you do that from here?" Lev asked.

Tae shook his head. "I can write it, but not set it into the system. I'll—have to go down with Ysbel for that."

Ysbel almost cracked a grin at the grim tone in his voice.

Lev nodded. "Probably for the best anyways—I've looked at the tunnels, and they aren't particularly stable. I'll feel more comfortable with two of you down there, in case you get into trouble." He glanced at Ysbel. "I hate to rush you like this. But—could you be ready by tonight?"

Ysbel frowned, considering. "I should be able to finish by midnight, if I work fast and nothing unexpected comes up," she said at last.

"Good," said Lev. "That will be the plan, then." He paused a moment. "And—and Jez, I assume, will call in, if she—once she gets back here." He barely stumbled over the words.

"And once Jez gets back, we'll be ready to go?" asked Masha.

Lev turned to her, but Ysbel noticed that his knuckles were white where he gripped the table. "Yes,"

"Assuming Jez can do what she planned to do," said Tanya quietly.

Lev turned to her. "Jez will do what she said she'd do."

No one spoke for a few moments. At last, Tae sighed. "Well, if we're doing this tonight, I'd better get to work." He stood, his hand finding Ivan's as they stepped out of the room.

The others stood as well, until it was only Lev and Ysbel left.

Lev was staring down at the table, his hands splayed out on the battered prefab, the muscles in his jaw tight.

"Lev," she said quietly.

He looked up, startled, then gave a wry smile that didn't quite reach his eyes.

"She'll be back," Ysbel said. "You know that pilot of ours—you couldn't kill her with an ion blast."

Lev tried to smile again. "I know."

Then he sighed, dropping his head into his hands. "Dammit, Ysbel, but I can't be sure of it. And nor can you. And if Jez—if she doesn't—" His voice choked. "I can't do this. I don't know how to —" he broke off abruptly.

There were a few moments of silence, and then a small head peered around the door.

"Mama?" Olya asked.

Ysbel smiled at her daughter. "What is it, Olyeshka?"

Olya stepped inside, her manner diffident. "I—was just wondering, Mama, if—Mama, when we were on the pleasure planet, you showed me some things, and I thought—"

"You thought you could help me," Ysbel finished.

Olya glanced at her quickly, gauging her reaction.

Ysbel's smile broadened. "I wouldn't be a very good mother if I didn't teach you to use your talents," she said. "And you've already shown me you're very talented at putting together explosives."

The way Olya's face lit up made something warm in Ysbel's chest.

The girl paused in the door for a moment, then came over to the table. When she caught sight of what Ysbel was working on, her expression grew round-eyed. "That's—a very big explosive, isn't it, Mama?"

Ysbel smiled. "Yes, my Olya," she said. "It is a very big explosive."

Olya looked up at her. "Have you ever made an explosive this big before?"

Ysbel hesitated. "Yes," she said quietly. "I have, once."

It was odd now, thinking of the person she been—bitter, angry, alone. Hurt almost beyond her capacity to feel pain. Constructing her explosives late at night, packing them into the prefab squares of the shuttle station as they were being built.

"What did you make the other explosive for?" asked Olya.

Ysbel looked down at her and smiled, swallowing back the lump in her throat. "My love." She pulled Olya into an embrace. "I made it when I was angry. When I thought someone had killed you and your brother and your mamochka. I was very sad, and I was very angry, and I made it to get back at the people who had hurt me. The people who I thought had hurt you."

"And did it work?" Olya's eyes were wide.

Ysbel kissed the top of her daughter's hair, holding her close, then glanced across the table at Lev. "No, Olyeshka," she murmured.

Lev was watching her, an eyebrow raised, and she met his eyes.

"It didn't work. It exploded, yes. But it didn't bring you back. It didn't stop my heart breaking from losing you."

"But you found us again," said Olya into Ysbel's shoulder, her arms tightening around her mother.

"Yes." Ysbel's voice choked, just a little. "I did."

At last, Olya pulled back. "So why are you making these ones? Is it so you and Uncle Lev can get back at Evka for hurting Aunty Jez, and for trying to kill us?"

Ysbel gave her a small smile. "No. That's not the reason we're doing this." She glanced up again, her eyes finding Lev. "Is it?"

He cleared his throat. "No, Olya. Your mama's right. We're doing this because there are people we love who will be hurt if we don't stop Evka. And we aren't going to let that happen, are we?"

Olya looked between Ysbel and Lev, then shook her head firmly. Her small face was fierce and determined. "No. We aren't."

22

Tae, day 7, late

"Tae." Ivan's hands were tight on Tae's arms, his knuckles white from trying not to grip too hard. "Just—be careful, alright?"

Tae managed a small smile. "I love you," he said.

Ysbel, who was waiting by the door, sighed heavily. "You two can kiss all you want when we're finished with this," she grumbled. "Let's go."

He glared at her, and she cracked a smile.

The warden was waiting for them outside, and he led them swiftly through the guards' quarters, then down a small maintenance tunnel, to where it ended in a dead end. He pulled a crowbar from the corner and gestured them back, then wedged the tip under the edge of a square of flooring and heaved it up with an effort.

Ysbel stepped forward, catching the edge of it, and between them, they propped it up against the wall.

Under it, barely visible through the dirt, was an ancient-looking trapdoor.

"You can access the tunnels from here," the warden said, his voice low. "They were originally built as an escape route for the guards when the prison was first built. They connect in with the old network of tunnels the builders used when they laid the first power core infrastructure. The entrance was boarded up decades ago, though, and I doubt there are half a dozen people in the system who even know it exists." He paused. "I'll keep watch for you up here, but be careful. If a tunnel comes down on you in there, no one will know about it."

Ysbel raised an eyebrow at him. "Believe me," she said, faint satisfaction in her voice. "With what I'm carrying right now, if the tunnel comes down on us, everyone in Prasvishoni will know about it."

The warden looked, suddenly, almost as nervous as Tae felt.

"I see," he said at last. "I'll—leave you to it, then." He tapped his com to the tangle of locks on the trapdoor, and one by one they clicked open.

Ysbel crouched and pulled the heavy door back, its hinges squealing in protest. The smell of mildew and damp earth drifted up from the dark hole beneath it, and Tae shivered despite himself.

"The tunnels are ventilated, yes?" Ysbel asked, glancing over her shoulder at the warden.

He shrugged. "I assume so. But most of the records were lost, and as I said, no one been down there in decades."

Tae sighed, stepping forward. "I'll set a scanner into my com to check oxygen levels," he said. He peered down into the blackness, scowling.

The dark was so thick he could almost taste it.

How the hell did he keep getting himself into these situations?

He blew out a breath and hit the light on his com. It illuminated the rungs of a rusty ladder leading down into the darkness. "I'll go first," he muttered. "I have the scanner, and besides, if the damn ladder goes out on me, it won't blow every damn person in the city straight back to the Lady."

"You really think anybody in this city would end up back with the Lady?" said Ysbel, voice amused.

Tae glared at her, then placed his foot cautiously on the first rung.

The metal groaned as he shifted his weight onto it.

Damn it to hell.

Still—it wasn't like they had a better option.

He took a deep breath and started down.

The chill of the underground tunnel, as he descended, was a thick, heavy, pervasive dampness that oozed through his clothing, clutched at his skin, wound itself around his fingers and crept into his boots and under his jacket.

His fingers were almost numb by the time his feet, groping for the next rung in the darkness, found, instead, solid ground. He tested it carefully before trusting it with his weight, then looked around quickly in the dim glow from his com light.

He was in the small intersection of a corridor, narrow enough that he could almost touch the walls on both sides if he stretched out his arms. Two corridors stretched off into the darkness in both directions, losing the light of his com a few metres in.

Ysbel stepped down beside him a few moments later. Her face was cut with shadows in the dim light.

"Well," she said. "It's been a long time since I've made an explosive like this. We may as well put all that work to use."

Tae drew in a long breath. "I guess if I'm going to be blown up, there's no point waiting around for it to happen," he grumbled.

Ysbel cracked a smile. "I have no intention of blowing you up with this explosive. If I was going to blow you up, I could do it with something that was a lot simpler to put together."

"Glad to know I'm so valuable to you," he muttered.

Ysbel chuckled, the sound echoing strangely in the dark tunnel, and they started off down the corridor.

The floor under them was bare dirt, and the supports, set up at distressingly irregular intervals, were ancient, the prefab cracking and mildewed with age and disuse.

He glanced down at the map Lev had sent through to his com as they walked, shivering slightly.

They'd be walking for a solid kilometre, at least, before they reached the place they could wire in the explosive for the main core. And then they had to plant the two packages of explosives that Jez and her friends would be using to blow the other two points.

Between the crumbling supports and the explosives Ysbel carried, his nerves were already fraying.

It was going to be a long night.

By the time they stepped around the final corner, and Tae saw the steel trapdoor and the trailing mass of wires under it that marked their destination, his nerves were raw.

Ysbel stepped up beside him and studied the narrow space for a moment in brisk calculation. Then she pulled a bundle out of her inner jacket and dropped it into Tae's hands.

He gave an involuntary yelp.

Ysbel chuckled. "It won't go off if you drop it, as long as you don't drop it from too high."

Tae glared at her. "So I'm just supposed to experiment to find out what's too high?"

She raised an eyebrow. "No. That would be stupid. But I thought I'd tell you, so if you bump it as you're laying it down, you don't have a heart attack. I need you to plant those exactly where I tell you, and I'll send a diagram through to your com how I want them wired in. These are to take out the backup generator." She paused a moment.

"You look like you're going to have a heart attack. Please don't. I don't want to have to do all this work myself."

Tae shot her another glare, and then turned reluctantly in the direction she'd indicated, cradling the package gingerly.

When he rejoined Ysbel at last, his palms were sweating, but nothing had actually blown up as he worked on it. She was bent over a mass of delicate wires that now surrounded the explosive, but she glanced up at him. "I see you're still alive," she said dryly.

"At the moment," he muttered, and she gave a snort of amusement.

"At any rate, I still have some work to do wiring this into the system. If you want to start setting your bypass, now would be a good time."

Tae nodded, and crouched beside the wire panelling, hooking his com into the system. There was a security code, of course, but it wasn't nearly as sophisticated as he would have imagined. But then, it had been created a long time ago, and he knew very well how easy it was for things like old infrastructure, that didn't hold any obviously bribable benefits, to fall through the cracks in this system.

It only took him a few minutes to hack his way through it, and then he was in the main database.

He expanded his holoscreen, looking over the readout quickly.

It wasn't difficult to pick out the point where Ysbel would be wiring her explosives. He frowned in concentration and bent over his holo keyboard, taping rapidly. He hooked his bypass carefully in to either side, so that power would flow undisrupted until he flipped the switch. Once he did that, the current would instead flow through the wiring on the explosive, setting it off and triggering a chain reaction that would take down the entire core.

"Tae."

He looked up to find Ysbel watching him.

"How close are you?" she asked. "I've got the explosives wired in, and I'm waiting to connect the last wire to tie it into the system. I thought it might be better to wait for you to finish the bypass so I don't blow all of us straight back to the Lady."

"I appreciate your restraint," he muttered. "Give me another five or ten minutes, and I'll be done."

At last, he hit the final command with a quick sigh of relief, and watched as the numbers on the screen dipped, fluctuated, and returned to normal.

"Done," he said. Ysbel nodded and connected the final wire.

Tae's shoulders hunched involuntarily, waiting for the inevitable.

At last he let out a shallow breath of relief, since it appeared that, at least for now, the explosive would stay unexploded.

"We'd best get moving," said Ysbel, pushing herself to her feet. "We still have a ways to go."

Tae nodded wordlessly.

Above them, one of the support beams groaned, and a small shower of dirt fell from it to land in a pile at their feet.

Tae closed his eyes and took a deep breath.

This had been here for years. Almost a century, if the warden had been telling the truth.

There was no reason that it should suddenly collapse just because he happened to be standing under it.

But, a small voice in the back of his head whispered, there was also no reason why it shouldn't.

They made their way quickly towards the first of the drop points. By now they were directly under the city streets of Prasvishoni, and Tae tried not to think too hard about what would happen if one of the explosives at the drop point went off by accident.

How many city blocks would it take out? And how many apartment buildings would come down with them?

Ysbel, behind him, looked completely unconcerned by such calculus. But then, Ysbel had a tendency to be disturbingly unconcerned by anything to do with explosives.

They dropped the first package in a place their friends would be able to access through the city maintenance tunnels and started for the last drop point.

This one was even farther away from the prison—close to the university, honestly. As they trudged through the never-ending tunnels, Tae caught himself wondering about the people they'd left. Were they still alive?

He gritted his teeth.

There was nothing he could do about it, other than what he was currently doing.

Still, he couldn't fight the tight knot in his stomach as they walked.

At last they came to the place Lev had marked, and Ysbel pulled the last of the small oilskin pouches from under her coat, placing it carefully in a small hollow in the support wall. Then she stood, brushing dirt from her knees. The pallor of her face was ghostly in the dim light. "We're finished," she said quietly. "I suppose we better get back before we run out of luck."

As if in answer, there was a rumbling shudder above them that he felt through his bones.

Something cold clutched at his stomach, and he glanced at Ysbel. "The barricades," he said, voice sick with dread.

Her expression was tense as his own. "Evka must have found them. Whatever weapon they're using, it's a powerful one."

Tae swore through his teeth. "We have to get back!"

"Tae." Ysbel's voice was grim. "There's nothing we can do for them right now."

He spun, glaring at her. "There might be," he snapped. "There might be something we can do, some way we can——"

Ysbel sighed and shook her head, her face tight. "Perhaps you're right," she said. "Let's get back, then."

Another low rumble shook the corridor, and Tae closed his eyes, trying not to think about what must be happening overhead.

And then there was another sound, from closer this time—the ominous creak of support structures stressed beyond their capacity.

He and Ysbel exchanged a quick glance.

"Come on!" she snapped.

She grabbed him by the arm and dragged him forward, and they sprinted back the way they'd come.

Ahead of them, the wavering lights from their coms illuminated the dust and rubble trickling from behind the nearest support.

Damn, damn, damn.

Then, suddenly, he pulled back against Ysbel's grip. "The explosives," he choked.

She shook her head grimly. "The support I left them under was solid. I checked. Come on!"

The support ahead creaked again, and Tae gave up resisting and matched Ysbel's pace.

Another shuddering, low-pitched boom, and the floor rumbled under him, and he almost lost his footing.

"Come on, you idiot!" snapped Ysbel, grabbing his arm again.

The trickle of dirt and debris from the support structure ahead of them had turned into a flood, and the structure itself groaned alarmingly.

They ran for it, and as they ducked through, it gave way completely, dirt and rubble and prefab crashing down around them.

Tae stumbled out, coughing and gagging in the cloud of debris, his arms up in a futile attempt to protect his head. He could hear Ysbel beside him, coughing—at least they'd both made it through.

He blinked, eyes streaming from the dirt, and tried to regain his bearings.

The entire tunnel behind them had come down. And in front of them, another cave-in all but blocked their exit. As he watched, another section of the dirt wall collapsed, sliding to the floor in a heap of dirt and mud.

"Come on!" Ysbel snapped again.

There was an ominous sound from the ceiling overhead.

Before he could so much as react, Ysbel grabbed him bodily, pulling him in front of her and shoving him hard down the corridor.

He stumbled forward, trying to keep his feet under him.

Then there was a low rumble he heard in his bones, and he spun as Ysbel disappeared under a pile of rubble.

"Damn you, Ysbel," he choked through his teeth, sprinting back to where she'd been. He reached down, grabbing rocks off the pile and tossing them away, scrabbling frantically at the dirt and rubble, fingernails bleeding. "You are damn well not doing this, you're damn well not making me go back there without you—" his voice caught with panic. "Ysbel, damn it to hell, I swear to you—"

He heard a moan, and caught sight of a familiar pale face, bruised and bloody and halfway covered with debris. He redoubled his efforts, and a few minutes later he dragged her clear.

Her eyes were closed, and for a brief, panicked moment he thought he hadn't been in time—and then she blinked and coughed, and he let out a breath of relief that turned into a half-sob. "Ysbel," he said, voice harsh with worry. "Ysbel, are you alright? Can you hear me?"

"I can hear you," said Ysbel. Her voice was weak, but there was a wry humour in her tone.

"Thank the damn Lady," he choked.

Above them, the ceiling creaked and groaned again.

"We have to get out of here," he said. "Can you stand?"

Another section of tunnel ahead of them slid down on itself, leaving an opening barely large enough to scramble through.

"It doesn't look like I have much of a choice," said Ysbel dryly.

Tae pulled her to her feet, and she leaned on him as they set off at a stumbling run.

The tunnels collapsed around them as they ran, but he didn't bloody well have the time to pay attention to anything but the dark of the corridor ahead of them. The trip was a nightmare—running, his breath burning in his lungs, muscles aching, the dark and the noise and the fear and the unending, unchanging tunnels that made it seem like they weren't moving at all.

And then, finally, there was a hint of light ahead of them.

He almost wept with relief when at last they stumbled to a halt at the base of the ladder, the dim shaft of light from overhead almost blinding.

For a few moments, they stood panting. At last, Ysbel shook her head. "See? And here you were thinking you'd be killed by explosives."

He glared at her, and then shook his head as well. "How in the damn system did I sign onto a crew where being blown up by explosives was the least of my damn worries?" he muttered.

She gave a snort of amusement.

From behind them, there was the unmistakable rumble of another cave-in. Ysbel raised an eyebrow. "I don't know about you, but I think I've had enough cave-ins for one day. Shall we?"

Tae scowled. "I'd had enough before we bloody well got down here." He tipped his head at the ladder. "You first. I'm not telling Tanya and the kids that you died as I was on my way up the damn ladder."

She gave him a wry look, but didn't argue, and he breathed a sigh of relief as she started up. He followed a few moments later, his hands shaking so hard he could hardly grasp the rungs.

The warden was waiting for them when they reached the top. He raised his eyebrows at the sight of Ysbel, but didn't comment, and Tae wondered, as the man led them back to their quarters, how long he must have known Masha, to react so nonchalantly to threats to life and limb.

They stepped through the doors to their common room, and Tanya glanced up quickly. Her lips tightened at the sight of Ysbel, but she didn't say anything, just came over and kissed her wife, whispering something in her ear.

"Tae?"

He turned. Ivan stood beside him, concern on his face.

The sight of him made something deep inside Tae relax, for the first time since he'd seen the damn explosive on the table and realized he'd have to go down to help plant it.

Ivan slipped his arms around Tae, and Tae realized suddenly that he was shaking, and that he had the ridiculous urge to cry.

"Are you alright? Did anything happen?" Ivan asked softly.

He took a deep breath, squeezing his eyes shut. "There was a cave-in, but we got out. It's fine."

Ivan held him, and Tae dropped his head against Ivan's chest for a moment.

And then he remembered, and he cursed and pulled back.

"Tae?" asked Ivan quickly.

"Something's happened at the barricades," he said tersely. "Evka must have found them. We could hear it from underground."

Ysbel glanced up. "If I had to guess, I'd say it was a particle-beam canon," she said quietly.

Ivan swore. "Is there a way we can talk with them?"

Tae nodded. "I still have a line through, I think."

"I'll get Lev and Masha," said Ysbel, standing. "Whatever's happening, they'll want to know about it."

Tae nodded, tapping through to Caz's line.

For a long moment no one answered, and the sick fear coating Tae's throat made it hard to breathe.

And then Caz's voice, crackly and indistinct. "Tae?"

He sounded desperate.

"Caz. What's happening?"

In the background, there was a noise of heavy guns, the hissing crackle of heat weapons.

"She's sent in the military, and the police," said Caz quietly. "The only reason they haven't killed us yet is that Lev's father managed to find and set an old force-field from the university. It won't hold them for more than a few minutes longer." He paused a moment. "We've hidden the younger kids inside the university." His voice choked slightly. "Mila's in there, Tae. I—Evka wouldn't bother to track down a kid like that, would she?"

Tae stared at his com. His heart was racing, acid rising in his throat.

He noticed, absently, that the others had gathered around him, and that there the same mixture of shock and horror on their faces as he felt on his.

Lev tapped his com through to the line. "I—would hope she'd be too busy to worry about that for a while," he said quietly, but Tae knew him well enough to know that he didn't really believe what he was saying.

"What can we do?" asked Tae.

"Nothing, I think," said Caz at last, quietly. "Unless you can get here in the next ten minutes, I don't think anything you can do would help."

"I'll go through my maps, and all the information I have," said Lev, his voice brisk and businesslike. "There may be some back way out of the barricades that they might not think of. If there is, it's possible we can get some of you out."

"Yeah," said Caz finally, his voice quiet. "But—hurry. Please."

The com clicked off, and they stood there looking at each other, horror on their faces.

23

Jez, day 7, evening

Jez glanced around at the huddled group of people in the hangar bay.

They looked, quite frankly, mildly terrified.

Still, everyone here had been part of conning that bastard Grigory, so she figured they had to have some sort of nerve, despite the unpromising expressions on their faces.

"Would—you mind explaining that one more time?" asked a woman from the back.

Jez grinned. "Sure. So. Plan is, you all get into your damn ships. Figure everyone who volunteered as pilots should be able to get through a wormhole, yeah?" she looked around, slightly dubious. She could've flown through a wormhole by the time she was about six years old, but from the looks of these people—

To her relief, though, the half-dozen ex-convicts who'd been conscripted as pilots nodded.

"Good," she said. "So. You're gonna time ten standard minutes from when Radic and I take off. You're gonna pop through the wormhole, and you're not gonna damn well slow down, because there's a bloody armada waiting on the other side."

"That's—the part I wanted you to go over one more time," murmured the woman.

Jez grinned easily. "Don't even have to worry about that. You give me ten minutes' start, and I'll make sure the only thing those damn bastards are thinking about is turning Radic and me into space dust."

Radek didn't look noticeably happier at this.

She winked at him, which didn't actually seem to reassure him.

"Anyway, so once you get planet-side, use the code I sent through to your com to get inside the city force-field," she continued. "Genius figured Evka wouldn't be too worried about anyone coming in, just people trying to get out. So you shouldn't have problems. Once you're inside, head to the smuggler bay at the coordinates I sent you. Tell them Jez Solokov sent you, and the damn credits are coming."

She paused a moment, considering. "Actually, if it's a dirty-looking bastard with a beard and a scar across his nose, don't tell him Jez Solokov sent you—he'll probably shoot you if you do. Just tell him he'll get his damn credits. Then hold tight. Radic and I'll be there as soon as we can." She paused again. "I mean, unless we do get turned into space dust. If we don't show in half a standard hour, call through to Lev. He'll tell you what to do next."

The woman nodded dubiously.

Honestly, no one looked nearly as excited as she would've thought at hearing a frankly flawless plan like this one.

She sighed philosophically. No accounting for taste.

"Any other questions?"

No one spoke, although from the look of it, it was because they'd decided the fewer additional details they knew, the better.

She grinned at Radic. "Alright then, you bastard, you ready?"

He sighed. "Kid, every damn time I wonder why I agree to your stupid plans."

"You just say that because you didn't think of them," she retorted, still grinning widely. "Think what your life would be like without me."

He shook his head. "Sometimes I dream about it at nights," he muttered. "Alright, let's go, before my common sense kicks in."

Jez turned, and like always, her breath caught for just a moment at the sight of her angel ship.

She gleamed, even in the low light of the hangar bay, every inch of her as breathtaking as the day Jez had first seen her, locked in a deep underground vaults of Vitali Dobrev's compound.

And in a few seconds, she'd be sitting in the pilot seat, the atmosphere burning around her, the controls as responsive under her hands as if she and the ship were one and the same being.

"Kid. You gonna stand there staring at your ship all day, or are you gonna do some of this flying you keep talking about?"

She turned.

Radic was grinning.

She shot him a smirk. "Oh, believe me, you skinny bastard, you'll damn well see some flying."

She swung up the loading ramp, hitting it closed as Radic scrambled in behind her.

He followed her down the old-fashioned corridors and through the main deck into the cockpit, and she grinned at his look of sudden astonishment as he surveyed the sleek, gleaming perfection of the controls.

"You're there," said Jez, gesturing to the copilot's seat, and ignoring the small pang in her chest.

It was fine. They'd be fine, and she'd see Lev again soon, and the choking ache inside her, the feeling of not-quite-wholeness, would finally go away.

Radic slid into the seat, running his hands quickly over the controls.

"The big guns are up in the gun tower, but you'll have enough firepower there to keep those army bastards pretty damn busy for a few minutes, anyways," said Jez. "You know your way around ship guns?"

Radic looked up from inspecting the controls. "Your friend Ysbel designed these?"

Jez nodded.

He grinned, a gleam of anticipation in his eyes. "That's everything I need to know."

Jez grinned back. "Well, I'm bringing us out of our hyper jump about spitting distance from the biggest damn ship they have. So you'll have plenty of chances to practice."

"That, I can do," murmured Radic, hands caressing the gunner levers.

"Strap down," Jez murmured, powering up. She ran her fingers lightly across the controls, resting one hand gently on the throttle. "You ready, you beautiful, beautiful girl?" she whispered.

Then she nudged the throttle, and Radic give a surprised yelp and grabbed for the arms of his chair as the ship launched itself out the hangar bay door.

They buzzed the city streets, slid through the narrow gap in the force field, and shot upwards as if this was what the ship had been waiting for its whole life.

Jez sighed in bliss as they broke through, settling into the soft comfort of shallow space.

Radic's face was bloodless, and he looked a little like he wasn't sure whether he'd keep his dinner down, but he was grinning. "You weren't joking about strapping down."

Jez winked at him. "Wait till you see hyperspeed," she drawled.

The look on Radic's face was equal parts anticipation and dread as she rested a hand on the controller.

"Hey now, I didn't bring you just to look pretty. Thought you were my damn copilot. Need some specs."

It took him longer to get her specs than she was used to, but at last she glanced down at what he'd sent through to her screen.

Good enough for government work, she figured.

"Better get your hands on the controls," she said. "Because when we come in, it's going to get hot pretty damn quick."

He nodded, and she eased the hyperdrive forward.

Time and space stretched, and, like always, a beauty so sharp it was almost pain choked in her throat as they slipped into the odd colours and patterns of hyperspace.

At last, with a reluctant sigh, she pulled back on the control.

The world snapped back into focus, and they were right under the damn nose of a very startled military carrier ship.

There was a moment where no one moved. And then Radic must have recovered his wits, because two long blue streaks shot from the *Ungovernable's* front guns and slammed into the military ship's shields, causing a flickering cascade of glittering sparks as they strained to disburse the shock.

Radic blinked, then grinned almost as wide as Jez, and started on the guns in earnest.

It only took the military ship a few seconds to figure out what must have happened. Jez was almost impressed at the alacrity with which the gunner brought the weapons to bear on her position.

But hell, they had no idea what they were going up against.

Radic clearly knew his way around ship guns. And these were a hell of a set of ship guns.

The blue streaks jolting out from the *Ungovernable's* front ports were enough to knock even a military ship on its heels for a moment, and Radic was firing like he was worried he'd run out of time.

More ships had pulled in behind them now, and shots were colouring the black around them and lighting up her holoscreen.

Jez smiled, letting her eyes half-close.

She pulled the *Ungovernable* up, making her movements hesitant, as if the way they bowed and shivering just enough to avoid each shot was a series of lucky accidents.

Let them think they had you, every single damn time.

They were still staying back—must've remembered the crap she pulled yesterday.

But give her another minute.

They were calibrating their aim, gaining a little more confidence. Moving in around her.

She glanced down at her holoscreen.

And with that last ship moved into position—the wormhole was clear.

Right on schedule.

She grinned at Radic, and tapped through to the general line. "Hey, you bastards," she said. "Hard to hit a target that's just sitting there, isn't it? But hell, maybe you can use this as an opportunity to train your gunners. Kinda looks like they need it."

"You're outnumbered, pilot. Stand down."

Jez grinned. "Here's the problem," she drawled. "I just can't bring myself to surrender to someone who flies as badly as you do. Or to someone so damn ugly."

"Pilot—" the speaker's voice was edged with irritation.

"Look on the bright side," said Jez cheerily. "Think how proud your general will be to know you sent your whole damn fleet after one lousy pilot, and you still couldn't catch me. Maybe she'll put you on paid leave or something."

"Pilot, stand down." The man was clearly speaking through his teeth.

"Sorry, com's a bit crap," said Jez. "Can't really hear you. But nice chatting."

She tapped off her com.

Radic was watching her, eyebrows raised. "I figured out you had talent for irritating the hell out of people when we were in prison. But that was art."

She winked at him. "You know what they say, even someone as hot as me can't expect to get by on nothing but looks."

Her holoscreen lit up, and she swore and pulled back on the controls, sending the *Ungovernable* shooting up just in time to miss an entire barrage aimed in her direction.

"Guess it worked," she drawled. "Keep on the guns, and fire whenever you get a chance."

"You got it," said Radic.

"Your pals will be coming through the wormhole in about sixty standard seconds," she murmured, as she brought them up them up under the belly of one of the smaller destroyers. "So we'll have to keep these plaguers busy enough they don't have time to notice."

She took a deep breath and popped their ship out from under the shelter of the destroyer's belly.

Immediately, the black of space around them was lit with laser blasts, her screen lighting up like it was damn well on fire.

She dodged through most of them, but a stray shot slammed into her shields, and the ship rocked. Jez gritted her teeth. "Sorry, sweetheart," she whispered, stroking the controls. "Just stay with me."

Radic's face had gone slightly bloodless, though his hands were still steady on the guns. "Jez—" he said through his teeth.

She grinned and yanked up on the *Ungovernable's* controls.

The ship leapt forward, and Jez skimmed them between two military ships, so close that the shields sparked against each other.

"What the hell—" Radic began, but she'd already pulled them into a sharp turn that flattened her against her seat, bringing them up behind the bridge of one of the smaller fighters.

"Anytime you feel like it, Radic," she said, and he seemed to remember what he was doing, and grabbed for the gun controls.

Jez sighed in delight as their first half-dozen shots exploded against the shields on the military ship's cockpit.

The ship pulled into a ponderous turn, trying to bring its weapons to bear, but it was no match for her sweet angel, and she clung to the back of the bridge like a tick on a swamp rat.

No one was gonna fire on them now, unless they wanted to take out the damn destroyer with her.

And no way in hell was anyone watching the ragged assortment of ships that had just popped out of the wormhole.

Radic got off three more shots before the gun turret turned a slow rotation, trying to locate their position. Jez waited until they were almost in place, then pulled up, close enough that she could see the startled faces of the soldiers in the gunner's tower. Then she spun the *Ungovernable* and shot forward, as if she'd decided to make a break for it.

Half a dozen shots streaked out after her.

Radic swore. "Those are damn seeker missiles, kid," he said through his teeth. "I hope you know what the hell you're doing."

Jez winked at him. "Just practiced with those a few hours back. Anyways, you know me—never have any idea what the hell I'm doing."

The missiles were closing fast. She'd been a hell of a lot closer to the ship when they'd fired this time, and the rest of the ships must have learned from their last encounter—they'd drawn back, guns trained on her in case she tried her trick a second time.

"Jez—" Radic's face was strained.

She turned and shot him a quick grin. "Relax. I got this."

"Focus on flying!" he ground out.

She rolled her eyes and turned back to the holoscreen.

The missiles were close. Very, very close.

But the others were through the wormhole, and streaking for the planet below them.

"Hope you're strapped in," she said with a grin.

The *Ungovernable* plunged for the wormhole, the seeker missiles now scant metres from her stern.

"Steady, sweetheart," Jez whispered, patting the controls.

The wormhole yawned ahead of them, and she could feel the tug of its gravity through her fingers.

"Jez!" Radic yelped. "What are you—"

At the last second she pulled up, so they were skimming the edge, the hole's gravity tugging at them so hard that even her angel ship strained at the pull of it.

The missiles behind her were close enough that they merged with her ship in the image on her screen.

The *Ungovernable* was shaking now.

"Come on, beautiful," Jez whispered.

Then the sucking, inexorable gravity caught at the missiles, and swallowed them whole.

There was a muffled shock as they exploded, somewhere deep in the grinding pressure of the wormhole, but the explosion that would have torn her beautiful angel to pieces registered as barely a change in the pressure.

"Jez!" Radic hissed, his knuckles white on the edge of his seat.

Jez hit the throttle, spinning them around the outside of the hole like water circling a drain.

The controls trembled under her fingers.

She nudged the throttle even farther forward, their speed barely enough to keep the gravity's distortion of time and space from dragging her into it.

"Come on, baby," she whispered

She could feel the *Ungovernable* straining to do her bidding.

She pushed the throttle all the way forward in one last burst of speed, then she yanked the control sharply to the left.

For a second they teetered on the edge, the power of her thrusters and the power of the wormhole perfectly matched—

And then they shot free.

Radic gasped in relief, dropping bonelessly back in his seat. He looked like he hadn't breathed at all since the missiles had started coming after them.

"Kid—" he began, his tone equal parts awed and horrified.

The military ships scrambled for their guns.

Jez grinned, reached over, and hit the cloaking.

Radic stared in frank astonishment as their pursuers broke off, milling about in confusion.

"What the hell just happened?" he asked finally.

Jez hit the com to the general line, still grinning broadly

"—the hell did they go?" snapped a voice over the line. "They're not showing up on a single screen, and I can't get a visual. How did they just disappear?"

Jez tapped the com off and leaned back in the pilot seat. "You ever heard of someone named Sasa Something-or-other?" she drawled.

"Sasa Illiovich?" asked Radic, his tone slightly awed.

"Yep, that's the one. Anyways, they designed the cloaking tech on this thing."

Radic was still staring at her.

"You mean—" he began finally. "You mean this whole time, that trick with the wormhole where we almost got crushed into space dust, and all the shooting, was just—just for—" he trailed off, shaking his head.

Jez shrugged. "I told Galina we'd give her a distraction."

He sighed and blew out a breath.

Jez grinned at him. "Guess we should head back to Prasvishoni, eh? Be a shame if they were having fun without us."

Radic muttered something about maybe they had different definitions of fun, since he, personally, considered being alive at the end to be an important component.

She spun the ship, and they streaked towards the atmosphere of the planet in the near distance.

She shut down the cloaking when they reached the city force field, and the guards, grim faced, waved them through at the doctor's stolen password. But she couldn't help but notice the tension in their postures, and the hint of fear in their expressions.

Even the people in charge, it looked like, weren't all that happy about what Evka's damn Protocol could do.

As she steered the *Ungovernable* down the shipping lanes towards the smuggler bay, she took a deep breath and tapped her com.

"Genius," she said. "Miss me?"

The words choked a little in her throat.

It wasn't until that very second that she'd realized how much of a part of her had been missing in his absence.

"Jez!" The relief in Lev's voice was almost enough to make her blink back tears.

"You all alright?" she managed.

"I'm—we're alright."

She heard in his voice how not-alright he'd been before.

She blinked again and cleared her throat. "Got Radic and Galya and a few of the others. We just got here. What's happening?"

"It's—not good," said Tae. He sounded sick. "Evka must have gotten through my com hack. Enough to track our friends' signals, at least, even if she still can't kill them."

Jez frowned, something tightening in her chest. "What's that supposed to mean?"

"It means, pilot girl," said Ysbel, "that Evka's found them at the barricades. And she's sent the army to take them down."

Jez stared at her com for a moment, ice forming in her stomach.

Damn it to hell.

She shot a quick glance at Radic. The grimness in his face told her that he knew as well as she did what this meant.

Which meant, she was pretty sure she could get him to agree to what she was about to say next.

"Hey genius," she said into the com, a sharp grin starting on her face. "Those canons they were using on us last time—bet my angel ship has better ones."

"Jez? What are you thinking?" There was that familiar, strained tone in Lev's voice that meant he was trying very hard to be supportive, but was on the verge of losing his actual crap.

"I'm thinking," said Jez, "it's been a long damn time since I tried to fly my sweetheart down an alleyway."

There were a few moments' pause, then Ivan's voice came through the com. "Jez," he said quietly. "If you can do that—"

"I'd like to see someone try to stop me," said Jez cheerily. She turned to Radic. "You ready with the guns, you bastard?"

There was a look on Radic's face that said he was reconsidering several recent life decisions, but he gave a faint, sickly nod.

"Good," said Jez.

She tapped the controls, and the *Ungovernable* spun on her axis and shot towards the university.

She hit the cloaking again as they got close, then dropped down to street level along the broad thoroughfare.

Radic let out a strangled curse as they turned down a side street. He looked like he might throw up.

Jez rolled her eyes. OK, so the street was a little narrow, but hell, she'd flown this angel out of Vitali's damn vault, with maybe centimetres to spare on either side.

This was as easy as falling asleep.

Radic was cursing steadily as they shot between the close rows of buildings, sliding up on their side to make the corners. There were no pursuers—she wasn't gonna show up on a single damn sensor, not with the cloaking her angel had. But from the sound of Tae's voice, the people at the barricades didn't have much time.

Radic paused his cursing for long enough to ask, through gritted teeth, "Where are we going?"

"University," said Jez cheerfully over her shoulder. "So if you wanted to get me some coordinates …"

Still swearing under his breath, he turned to his holoscreen, and a few moments later, coordinates popped up on her own screen.

She slowed as she approached the barricades. Even from inside the ship, she could hear the high-pitched whine of the ion cannon, the rumble in the street as it fired.

"Soon as they're in sight, you start shooting," she whispered to Radic. "Don't hit the barricades, and don't hit anyone who looks like a street kid or a student. Other than that, I don't give a damn."

Radic nodded, resting his hands loosely on the gun control.

And then they turned a corner, and Jez pulled them to a smooth halt.

Soldiers were packed into the street, all of them dressed in full riot gear, and from the front of the column, she could hear the high-pitched whine of an ion cannon.

"Bring me a little closer," Radic whispered, not taking his eyes off the gun sights.

Jez nudged them forward.

He took a deep breath and squeezed the trigger.

Ahead of them, the ion cannon exploded.

The look on the soldiers' faces was almost comical. The ones near the gun spun, searching frantically for the new threat, but the soldiers in front were still firing on the barricades.

"Give them another warning," Jez murmured. Adrenaline pulsed through her veins like alcohol.

Radic nodded, still not looking up from the controls.

The empty patch of street where the ion canon had been exploded, shards of prefab and concrete raining down from the sky.

More soldiers turned, staring around and shouting through their coms.

"Stand down, whoever you are," came an amplified voice from outside. "The moment we ID you, you'll be killed. This is your last chance to come in alive."

Radic gave a grim smile.

Another section of the street exploded.

No one was looking at the barricade now.

"Here's the thing, though," drawled Jez through the ship's com, tapping into the general line. "Whole squadron of soldiers against a bunch of street kids and university students? Seems a bit unfair. We figured we'd even things up a bit."

Radic hit the guns again, digging a crater into the street.

Panic was rippling through the ranks of soldiers now like a breeze. They were holding discipline, barely, but it wouldn't last.

She turned back to the com. "Not showing up on any of your sensors, am I? Hard to fight someone you can't see. But I know exactly where you are, and I don't really like you. So you might want to find somewhere else to be as fast as you damn well know how."

Radic fired again, punctuating her words.

Another patch of street vaporized.

There was a moment of silence. Then the air around them lit with heat-blasts, and Jez grinned, pulling the *Ungovernable* slightly up so the shots passed harmlessly beneath.

Someone barked an order, and the soldiers began a steady retreat, firing as they went.

"Give them something to remember us by," whispered Jez.

The patch of street metres from the retreating soldiers exploded.

The retreat turned abruptly into a rout, the soldiers turning and running for their lives.

Jez and Radic grinned at each other.

"Figure we took their mind off the barricades for a few minutes," she said. "What do you say, should we go back and meet up with the others?"

Galina and the rest of the ex-convicts were waiting when Jez brought the *Ungovernable* smoothly into the smuggler bay.

As was an angry-looking woman in her mid-fifties.

Jez rolled her eyes and hit the loading ramp, striding out of the cockpit and jumping down before the woman could start up.

"Solokov—" the woman said, her voice carrying a warning.

Jez sighed and pulled a credit chip from inside the inside pocket of her jacket. She tossed it at the woman. "Relax, Irina. Told you the credits were coming."

The woman glared at the chip suspiciously, slipping it into her com to check the numbers. They must have pacified her—they damn well better have, considering what was on the thing—because she slipped it into an inside pocket. "You forget how long I've known you, Solokov," she said, no noticeable thawing in her voice.

Jez shrugged easily. "Bet your friends are jealous. Anyway, don't have time to flirt. I'm pretty busy right now."

The woman glowered at her and grumbled something that was probably insulting.

Jez ignored her, turning to Galina. "Everyone get in alright?"

Galina nodded, but her face was tight with worry.

Jez grinned at her, then hit her com through to the crew's closed loop. "Genius," she said. "Heard rumours the soldiers at the barricades got attacked by a ghost ship and took off. I figure our friends should be safe for a bit."

"Jez." The tone in Lev's voice had her swallowing back something in her throat again. "I love you, in case you were wondering."

"Yeah," she said. "Guess I must I love you back." She cleared her throat. "Anyway, I was just calling in to say we're here, and we're ready. So. Whenever you feel like blowing the hell out of a power core, just let me know."

24

Masha, day 8, early

"Masha. Are you going to be able to do this?"

She glanced over, and felt, again, a jolt of surprise at the concern in Lev's face.

She hadn't realized how the concern in his eyes, and the eyes of the rest of the crew, could cut through the armour she'd built up, leaving her naked and shivering and defenceless.

She managed a small smile. "I'll be fine, thank you," she said quietly. "I may need something to lean on, and I may not be particularly quick on my feet. But I should be able to walk."

Lev studied her for a moment, and again, the concern in his eyes tightened her chest.

"Alright," he said at last. "We should go, then. Jez and the others are in position, and we don't want to give the soldiers time to come back to the barricades."

Masha and nodded, pushing herself carefully to her feet. She had to clutch at the makeshift crutch Adrian had found for her, and from the corner of her eye she saw Lev step forward as if to catch her, but with an effort, she straightened, and the shock of the pain faded.

The others were waiting for them in the common room, faces

grim.

"Masha," said Tae, coming over to her. His voice was tight with strain. "Before we head out, you'll need to talk Lev's parents through their part in this."

Masha nodded, trying, but not quite succeeding, to hide the grimace of pain as she shifted her weight.

"Sit down, you idiot," came Ysbel's rough voice, and the chair was pushed up behind her.

She sank into it gratefully and nodded at Tae. He tapped something into her com, and a moment later, she heard the voice of someone who must be Lev's mother. "Son? Is that you?"

"No. It's Masha Volkova," said Masha quietly.

There was a moment's pause. When the woman spoke again, her voice was still polite, but colder than it had been. "Masha. What do you need?"

"I'm sending through information for some of my government contacts. Contact them, and inform them you're working with me. I'll send you through a password. When the explosions go off, it will take down the entire Prasvishoni power grid—the force field, the lights, the heat, everything. Including to hospitals, for example, and apartment blocks. There's an extensive emergency power backup system, but as you might imagine, the government officials in charge of it have been more concerned with ensuring that the government apparatus, and the people who pay them sufficient bribes, are well taken care of.

"My contacts have the resources necessary to reassign the emergency power to where it's most needed. You'll need to tell them where and how to re-direct it."

Again, there was a pause from the other end of the line. At last, the woman said, her voice still sharp with mistrust, "Send me the names. My husband and I will do what we can. We've been going over maps of the city with some of the students and street kids, and I believe we've made a fairly accurate assessment of the most vital places to divert the backup power."

"Good," said Masha quietly. "Jez is getting into the position. As soon as she calls, we'll be ready."

"We'll be ready as well," said the woman. She paused a moment. "May I … speak with Lev?"

Masha glanced up, and Lev nodded, tapping his own com. There was a suspicious thickness to his voice. "Mother. I'm—I'm sorry for getting you into something like this again, after—"

"Son."

Masha wasn't a mother, and she hadn't had a mother in a very, very long time. But she could hear the note in the single word that said everything that needed to be said.

"Be careful," the woman said at last. "Your father and I worry about you. Please—" her voice choked.

Lev brushed his sleeve quickly across his eyes. "Just—take care of yourself, alright?" he said at last, and then tapped off the com.

"Alright," said Ysbel. "I don't know about the rest of you, but I'd rather not to be trapped in the Vault after the power goes out. So."

She glanced at Masha.

Masha nodded. She pressed a final button, sending the information through to Lev's mother, then tapped through to Adrian's line.

He answered almost immediately. "Masha," his voice was tight. "Are you ready? Evka's sent people to inspect the sedation cubes, and I was barely able to put them off."

There was a tone in his voice that told her he knew as well as she did that he couldn't put them off forever, and that when they found what he'd done, he'd likely be next in line for sedation, or worse.

And he was doing it anyways.

The thought constricted her chest.

All those years she'd told herself this was strictly business. But he and the others who were risking their lives for her in government—they'd been friends, too, as much as she'd refused to accept it.

He tapped on the door a few minutes later. Tae opened it, and Adrian beckoned quickly.

"We don't have much time. Let's get you out of here while we still can."

Masha pushed herself painfully to her feet, leaning heavily on her crutch. Adrian watched her with concern, but he said nothing, just beckoned them forward. Ysbel lifted Olya, and Tanya took Misko in her arms, and they followed Adrian out the door and down the darkened hallways.

"When we set off the explosion, the power will go out across the city," said Masha quietly, as he fell into step with her, adjusting his pace to match hers. "I know there's a backup power system, but they'll divert most of it. I'm not sure there will be enough to keep the prison running. Warn whichever of the guards you wish to warn, and find a place where you can get out, or lie low—I doubt the prisoners will be friendly."

"And I wouldn't count on the tunnels," said Ysbel from behind them. "They weren't in the best shape. And after what we're going to do, they'll probably be nonexistent."

Adrian nodded. "Noted," he said, voice grim.

When they reached the small guards' entrance, he held up his com to the lock. It clicked, and he pushed the door open. "There's another door at the end of the corridor," he whispered. "I've left it unlocked. Even so, don't try to get out before the explosion—there's an automatic alarm that even I can't override, but taking out the power should take care of it. You won't be able to get back inside, once you're out, because the locks are designed to function without power, but—" he shrugged. "With any luck, you won't need to."

Masha turned to him. "Thank you," she said quietly. "If— something happens, I'll do everything in my power for you."

"I know that," he said. He paused a moment. "We've been planning this for quite some time, haven't we? Well, you have—the rest of us rode in on your coattails. But I'm not sorry for any of it. If we can change this system, like we used to talk about—"

He shook his head, and Masha was surprised at the affection in his tone. "Good luck," he said at last, quietly, clasping her shoulder.

"Good luck to you, as well," said Masha quietly.

He nodded, then stepped back, pulling the door closed behind him.

Ysbel hit the light on her com in the utter black, and by its dim glow, Masha could make out the rest of her crew. Their faces were grim, but determined, and again, she was hit with a small sense of something like awe, that there was a group of people like this in the system.

That somehow, they'd come together as a crew.

Her crew.

"Now what?" said Ysbel quietly.

Masha glanced at Lev.

His hands were clenched into fists, tension in every line of his posture. "Jez will call when everyone's in position," he said, strain obvious in his voice. "Then we set off the explosion.

Ysbel nodded.

"And until then, I suppose," said Masha quietly, "we wait."

25

Jez, day 8, early

It was dark, and the bite of the winter air stung Jez's cheeks and nose.

She glanced around at the small, tense group of people gathered behind the barricades.

Funny how the barricades—the smoky smell of burning wood and small makeshift shelters, the street kids and the students—had come to feel almost like home after the past few weeks.

"Alright," said Lev's father, who'd come to stand beside her. "We're ready."

She gave him a small grin, even though her heart was pounding, and stepped forward.

"Alright, you plaguers," she said, just loud enough to be heard in a hush of the night. "Here's what we're doing." She pulled up her holoscreen, expanding it enough that everyone could see it. "Caz and Peti, you take a group of the street kids and students, whoever you want, and go pick up the explosives cache Ysbel left here. Then you get into position to blow the secondary power source here." She tapped the marked places on her holoscreen map. "Felix, you take your kids and pick up the other cache, here, and get to the other secondary power source. You've all worked with Ysbel—plant the explosives, then get the hell out of there."

She turned to where Lev's parents stood, close together. "You two and Vera and Dimitri and whichever other students or street kids you need will be coordinating getting the power back up from the backup grid."

Lev's mother nodded. "We've coordinated with Masha's contacts in government. At this point it will just be a matter of timing, I think."

Jez nodded and glanced at the small group of ex-convicts behind her. "We're going to raise some hell over in the industrial district. I'm guessing we can get them to send their heavy weaponry our way once they find out Evka's crap doesn't work on my friends here. While they're busy, the rest of you get out. If this doesn't work—" she trailed off.

If this didn't work, they were all dead.

"OK," she said finally. "Let's show these scum-sucking mud-eaters what a bunch of students and street kids and Lady-damned criminals can do."

She jumped down from where she'd been standing.

"You did good up there," said Galina, smiling at her.

"Well, kid," said Radic, coming over to join them. "Guess we've got some hell to raise. We're ready on our end."

Jez took a deep breath and grinned at him. "What are we waiting for, then?"

They slipped silently through the streets. The police were out, but in the fog, it wasn't hard to stay out of their way. Jez rested her hand lightly on the butt of her heat pistol. Her whole body tingled with adrenaline, and she couldn't stop grinning.

Beside her, Radic was grinning as well, and Galina was wearing a determined expression that probably didn't mean anything good for the bastards they'd be distracting.

When they reached the warehouse district, Jez stopped. "Figure this is as good a place as any," she whispered. "Should keep the bastards out of the way of the others, at least."

It took a few short minutes before everyone was positioned to Galina's satisfaction. Jez watched her, impressed.

"You're good at this," she whispered.

Galina smiled at her. "Like I told you—my talent is telling people what to do." She paused. "Listen, Jez—you're the only one of us who's affected by Evka's program, right? So of all of us, you're the one who'll show up on their sensors."

Jez nodded

Galina sighed. "We'll use that to get them to come after us. But— be careful."

Jez raised an eyebrow. "Galya. I'm always careful."

She took a deep breath, hit the voice amp on her com, and shouted, "Hey! Cops! Found some curfew breakers over here. You damn fascist boot lickers might want to come take a look!"

Galina shot her a wry look.

Jez shrugged.

Footsteps were pounding towards them in the fog.

"They might still have riot gear," Jez whispered loudly to the others. "If they are, your heat guns won't go through the shields. But —" she stooped, grabbing a loose chunk of ice from the street. "I find this tends to get their attention."

The first squadron of police came around the corner at a dead run.

Jez's ice chunk found the helmet of the woman in the lead, and as she staggered back, Jez scooped up a rock and sent it after the first.

Then, as the rest of the officers arrived on the scene, the air lit with heat-blasts from the ex-convicts.

She grinned to herself. She'd almost forgotten, for a moment, that most of the people here were either Ivan's friends, which meant they had a long history of distracting police at riots, or Radic's friends, which meant they had a long history of being damn crazy bastards.

One of the police officers muttered frantically into his com, and a few moments later, the relative quiet of the night was split with the ear-piercing wail of police sirens.

From behind the shelter of the buildings and alleyways, the ex-convicts' heat-blasts and projectiles were finding their mark with impressive accuracy.

"I'm warning you," a police officer shouted through his voice amp. "Come out, or we'll use the Protocol."

"Hell," Jez drawled, hitting her own voice amp. "You could try, I guess."

"It must be the damn insurgents," the officer snapped, turning back to his squadron. "The Protocol won't kill them, but at least we can find where they're hiding. We'll round them up the old-fashioned way."

"You could try that, too," Jez drawled again, slipping into an alley as a shot hissed over her head.

She winked at the five ex-convicts hidden in the shadows.

Three officers rounded the corner at a run, and dropped at the sudden barrage of stun blasts.

"And see, goes to show riot gear doesn't protect against everything," said Jez cheerfully.

The noise from outside the alley made it clear that at least two other squadrons of police had showed up, plus a couple drones.

She peeked out of the alley entrance.

"Jez. Are you ready?" Anya, one of Ivan's tech friends from prison, whispered through her com.

"Not yet," Jez whispered back. "Let's get a few more of them in here first." She stepped over the bodies of the unconscious officers and peered around the alley wall.

The street outside had turned into utter chaos—officers firing at random into the dark, shouting over their coms, searching frantically for cover against the relentless barrage of heat-blasts and stun blasts coming at them from all directions.

A drone buzzed towards Jez. She took careful aim, and melted it out of the sky.

"Radic," she whispered through her com. "We need to make a little more noise."

"What are you thinking?" Radic's tone was wary.

She grinned. "How'd you like to steal a skybike?"

He sighed in mock reluctance. "I'll meet you in the alley in about thirty seconds."

He appeared beside her a few moments later. "OK, kid, what's the plan?"

She pulled a small explosive out of her pocket and tossed it to him. He caught it, then swore and fumbled it as he realize what it was.

"Kid, you crazy?"

She grinned. "Don't get too excited, it's just a flash-bang. But Ysbel made it, so it's a hell of a flash-bang."

Radic was shaking his head, but he grinned back.

They crept out of the alley.

The police were organizing into riot formation. Jez kept to the shadows, Radic close behind her, until they reached a huddle of bikes leaned up against an alley wall, guarded by an officer.

He was facing away from them, staring out at the chaos in the street, his expression tense.

Jez tipped one of the bikes carefully away from the wall, swung her leg over it, and powered up.

The officer spun, heat pistol jerking up wildly.

Jez kicked off, pushing the bike off the ground, and leaned down, snatching the pistol from his hand. "Looking a little shaky there," she called over her shoulder. "Don't want you to hurt yourself."

Radic was behind her a moment later, and they leaned forward on their bikes, through the frantic shouting of officers behind them, and shot forward.

"Radic," she called through her com. "You remember that old song about the police officer who thought he was a dog?"

"Kid, you shouldn't know that song."

"Learned it when I was seven. Anyways, figure if you hit your voice amp and head for the northeast sector, and I go northwest, bet we could get a few more of the bastards to follow us."

"You're probably not wrong," he muttered. "I know I'm going to regret this."

She hadn't, in fact, been wrong. In an impressively short time, she had an impressively large string of the bastards on her tail, and was turning back towards the warehouse district.

"On my way in," she whispered through her com. "Radic?"

"Me too," he hissed back. "But they're damn close."

She grinned. "That's what the flash-bang is for. Figure they can hear the others now, so let's show them what Ysbel can do."

"You got it."

Jez yanked the flash-bang from her pocket and tossed it over her shoulders.

It exploded in a flash of noise and light that left imprints across the backs of her eyelids, even facing away from it, and a second later, she heard another *boom* from Radic's direction.

Even through ears still ringing from the explosion, she could hear the sudden wail of sirens from what sounded like the entire damn Prasvishoni police force.

They were all heading her direction.

She grinned and tapped her com. "Galya, get ready for incoming. Anya, once they're in, they're all yours."

When they rejoined the others, Jez jumped off her bike. Radic pulled up behind her a moment later as Galina came to meet them.

"How's it going?" Jez asked.

"Good. As soon as the next batch comes in, Anya's going to cut their communication," Galina said in a low voice. "That should—"

Jez's com buzzed.

"Jez!" it was Caz, and he sounded frantic.

"What's happening?" she asked, sudden panic tightening her stomach.

"One of Felix's kids got hurt. It was a tracker drone, and it grabbed all their signals. If they go for the explosives now—"

Jez swore. "Can he get his kids somewhere safe?"

"I think so. But the drop—we already planted our explosives and set the timer."

"I'll take care of the drop," she said grimly. She turned back to Galina. "You got things covered here?"

"We'll be fine," said Galina.

Radic had already swung up on his bike. "Where to?" he asked.

Jez grinned and swung up on her own bike. "Hope you're ready to ride, you bastard."

She leaned forward, and they shot off towards the southwest explosives cache.

With the chaos in the streets outside, the police hardly seemed to notice the two skybikes shoot past. Anyways, with the noise the ex-cons were making, they wouldn't have attention to spare even if they had noticed.

The cache was in the southwest sector of the city, but on their skybikes it didn't take more than fifteen standard minutes. If she wasn't going ridiculously slow to keep Radic behind her, she probably could've made in ten.

The coordinates in her com brought her to the end of a small, dirty street. She jumped off her bike, and Radic joined her moment later.

"What are we looking for?" he whispered.

"Access tunnel," she said, peering around her. In the uncertain light of the damn sputtering streetlamps, it was difficult to make out much of anything.

Radic nodded, and they split up, each taking a side of the street. A few moments later, he called, "I think I've got it."

She came up beside him, and as she did, she heard the change in the tone of her footsteps, the hollow, echoing tone of metal under her boots.

You couldn't see the access hatch through the snow and ice, but a couple blasts from her heat pistol took care of it.

Radic raised an eyebrow. "Alright, kid, good idea, but now that the damn access panel is actually glowing, might be hard to—"

She shrugged, flipped her pistol, and hooked the butt of it into the latch. She braced herself, heaving the heavy door back, and it fell open with a clang, revealing a yawning black tunnel beneath.

Radic gave her a mildly impressed look. "I—take it you've done that before."

"Haven't you?" she countered.

He shook his head. "One day, you and I are going to have a talk about what normal people do for fun. It's not what you think it is." He grabbed the rusty rungs set into the walls of the tunnel and started down.

Jez paced at the entrance, heat pistol ready, muscles tight with restless energy. It felt like about a million years before Radic whispered, "Got it!" through the com, but when his head emerged from the dark of the tunnel, her com said it had only been maybe five standard minutes.

She took the oilskin-wrapped package and tucked it carefully under her coat. "We've got about seven minutes before Caz's explosives go off," she whispered. "Hope you know how to ride fast."

They swung onto their bikes.

Ysbel had planted the cache close to the power source, thank the damn Lady.

In less than five minutes, they'd pulled up in front of a small, squat building, prefab crumbling and discoloured with age and mildew. Looking closer, though, she could see how sturdy the structure of the building was, and how the area around it was clear of snow and debris.

She tapped her com through to the closed loop. "Genius," she whispered. "We're here. I'm just planting the explosives. Give me the exact countdown."

"One sec." His voice was strained.

Jez slipped one of the explosives out of the packet and stared at it, a slow grin spreading across her face.

Radic swore softly.

"Well," she said, weighing it in her hand. "Guess this should blow the damn thing."

"Kid," said Radic in an almost reverent tone. "This could blow half the damn city."

She pulled a second explosive out and handed it to him, and he took it gingerly.

"Ysbel sent through a diagram of where to put them," she said.

"We could probably put them anywhere on the damn planet and they'd do the job," Radic muttered in an awed voice.

"Set them for three minutes and thirty seconds, on my mark," Lev whispered through the com.

She glanced at Radic, and he nodded.

"Two. One. Now," said Lev, and she hit the timer as Radic did the same.

"Plant them, and get as far away as you can," he said. "I assume you're on bikes?"

"Yep," she drawled.

"Good," he said. "According to what Ysbel tells me, this will be an impressive explosion."

"Oh, it will," she murmured. "Alright, Radic, get a move on. Figure this is something we should enjoy from a distance."

They placed the explosives where Ysbel had indicated, swung back on their bikes, and shot down the narrow, twisting streets at a speed that pulled tears from Jez's eyes, the cold of the winter air burning her cheeks.

She tapped through to Galina's line. "Galya. You can get the others back to the barricades, and we'll meet you there. Figure the police are going to be pretty damn distracted in about—" she glanced at her com. "Forty seconds here."

"Sounds good." Galina's voice was grim. "Things are getting pretty warm around here anyways."

In the background, Jez could hear shouts and screams, and the hiss of heat pistols.

Jez tapped off her com and glanced at the holoscreen on her bike.

It was going to be damn close.

She leaned forward on her bike, pushing it harder. Behind her, she could hear the whine of Radic's bike, straining to keep up.

Fifteen seconds left.

She whipped around the corner of another alleyway.

Seven seconds.

Another.

Three seconds.

And then, from behind her, there was an explosion that lit the night. The shock-wave rolled over her, with enough force that she had to wrestle with her bike's steering to keep from being smashed into a wall.

Three spouts of flame shot up across the city, blossoming like deadly orange flowers, and for half a second, in the back of her mind, she wondered what had happened to the noise.

And then a low-pitched, booming roar shook the streets around her, causing windowpanes to shatter and prefab bricks to crack and tumble from walls. The sound crested over them like a wave, engulfing her whole damn body so that she could feel the vibrations through her very bones.

For a moment after the echoes died, there was complete silence.

And then the hazy lights of Prasvishoni—the streetlamps, the lights from apartment buildings, the industrial centres, where people worked every damn hour of the day, even the hazy smear of the city force field—flickered off.

In the sudden pitchy blackness, Jez pulled her bike to a halt.

Radic came up beside her, and for a few moments they sat in awed silence.

Around them, from various points in the city, lights began to flicker back on—apartment buildings lighting up, a huddle of lights that must be the hospital glowing dimly several blocks away.

She drew in a deep breath and looked up.

Above her, the night sky was as brilliant as she'd ever seen it planet-side, the tiny sparks of stars pinpricks of light in the vast blackness overhead, the sliver of the moon bright enough to cast shadows.

She stared, something unexpected tightening in her chest.

She'd never imagined she'd see a sight like this, not from Prasvishoni.

Radic's expression was just as awestruck as hers.

"Well, kid," he whispered. "Guess we've done it."

Jez let out a long, long breath.

Evka and her Protocol, the nagging, aching, fretting worry in the back of her head that had been there since the first moment they'd breathed in Evka's metal—it didn't matter anymore.

And until that moment, she hadn't realized how much of a weight the thought had been, hanging off her damn shoulders like a knapsack full of rocks.

She turned to Radic.

He was grinning giddily, and she grinned back, and for a few moments, they sat there, grinning at each other like idiots.

And then they both winced at the sudden cacophony of noise through their earpieces, and it took Jez a moment to realize what it was.

Cheers.

The ex-convicts, and what sounded like every damn person behind the barricades, were whooping and shouting, and someone had apparently turned a noisemaker onto their com, the discordant clanging almost drowned out in the noise of the cheering.

"You did it!" Vera hollered through the com. "You damn well did it! You took out the whole damn power core!" She was laughing and breathless. "We won!"

Jez was smiling so wide she thought her face might split. "Yep," she said, and then she had to pause to clear her throat. "Yep, guess we did."

26

Lev, day 8, early

The echo of the explosion rumbled across the city, so loud it almost didn't sound human-made it all.

Lev glanced at Ysbel in the dim light from the coms.

She was wearing a blissful, contented smile, one arm around Tanya, her other hand on Olya's shoulder.

He held his breath, waiting as the echoes died away.

And then the low hum of the prison running, that was so much a part of the background that he hardly noticed it, slowed and died.

The world was suddenly silent.

He let out a long breath and fumbled until he found the latch for the outer door.

The door swung open without a sound, and he stepped through, hardly daring to hope.

As he stepped outside, the brilliance of the stars overhead was almost disorienting.

He'd grown up in Prasvishoni, and had come to think of stars as nothing more than an indistinct blur overhead. The first time he'd really seen them was on the short jaunt to the pleasure planet months ago, the first time he'd flown with Jez.

The others stopped short as well, and there were a few moments of silence. Ysbel was holding Tanya tightly, both of them staring upwards. The children clung to their hands, wide-eyed, and Tae was leaning against Ivan, the look on his face one of almost disbelieving joy.

"We did it," Tae whispered, his tone almost unbelieving. "We actually did it."

"That's it?" asked Masha, turning to Lev. There was the softness of a desperate relief under the strain on her face. "The Protocol is finished?"

He nodded, and found he was somehow unable to speak, something that was halfway between desperate happiness and sickening relief tightening his throat.

"Uncle Lev!"

He glanced down and smiled slightly, crouching until he was at Olya's eye level. "What it is, Olya?" he asked.

She was watching him, a small, fierce grin on her face. "Did we save our friends? Like you and Mama said we would?"

He looked at her for a moment, swallowing back something in his throat. Then he reached out and gathered her into an embrace. "Yes, Olya," he said, his face muffled in her hair. "I think finally we did."

She drew back, and he released her.

"Well," she said in a smug voice. "That damn Evka should have known better than to mess with my mama."

Lev bit back a quick grin.

"Look, Uncle," she said, looking up. "It looks like we're back on the *Ungovernable*, almost."

He followed her gaze, and the sight of the stars glowing brilliant above them caught in his chest with something that was almost pain.

Jez. Just a few more minutes, and he'd be back with her.

The thought was an intoxicating mixture of heady anticipation and choking impatience, the sharp ache of missing her cutting through the centre of his being.

He took a deep breath, and, with a last smile at Olya, stood. "We should get going," he said. "The others will be waiting for us."

By the time they'd made it a handful of city blocks, they could already see the effects of what they'd done. People were shouting to each other through apartment windows, swearing, spilling out into the streets to find out what had happened.

As the chaos of the streets grew louder, Lev ducked into the mouth of an alley, beckoning the others after him. There was the unmistakable wail of police sirens, and a squadron of officers zipped past on their bikes.

One of the officers shouted into her voice amp, and, when her voice failed to cut through the noise, lifted up her wrist com, scanned the crowd, and hit a button.

There was a quick gasp from a handful of people who'd stopped to watch.

Nothing happened.

The officer hit the button again.

And then the irritation on her face was replaced with fear.

The Protocol was gone.

The people in the streets must have realized it too, because they were snatching chunks of prefab, bits of ice, even handfuls of snow, and hurling them at the police, and their shouts of confusion were turning into rowdy cheers. People hugged each other in the streets, expressions of joy and disbelief on their faces.

The police pulled up their heat guns, but the crowd, who far outnumbered the officers by now, grumbled in protest at the sight of the weapons, and the officers subsided, realizing, it seemed, that this wasn't a time to insist on strict respect for the law.

Lev let out a long breath, feeling his shoulders relax for the first time in what felt like weeks.

He'd known, intellectually, that they'd won. But he hadn't realized the visceral relief seeing it would send through him.

He was smiling so wide his face hurt.

Ivan clapped him on the shoulder, seeming unable to speak, his smile as wide as Lev's.

"Come on," Lev whispered, swallowing hard. "Let's go, before the streets get too crowded."

They slipped through the alley and out into another street.

Their progress was painfully slow—Masha was limping heavily, and when Lev glanced back, he could see the strain on her face.

He took a deep breath, forcing back the rising agony of impatience.

She hadn't betrayed them, not this time. And once this was all over, they could get her a proper doctor, and maybe she'd finally have time to recover.

And perhaps he still wasn't sure if he'd forgiven her, and perhaps he still wasn't sure if he'd be able to trust her ever again, but all that he could worry about later.

Because now—

Now, damn it to hell, he was going to see Jez.

It was a long walk from the prison to the barricades, and their progress was slow and halting, and it must have been almost two hours later when he began to recognize the landmarks.

He wanted to drop everything and run.

He had to see that Jez was alright. He had to see her, feel the shape of her in his arms, run his fingers through the black tangle of her hair. He wasn't sure how he'd survive even one more moment of waiting without something inside him breaking, something he wasn't sure he'd be able to put back together again.

He forced himself to breathe in.

Just a few minutes more …

Ysbel, who'd taken up the lead, stopped, her posture stiffening.

Lev's heart was beating quick enough to make him dizzy. "What is it?" he whispered.

And then, from behind them, he heard a voice through a police voice amp.

"Turn around slowly," the man said. "Keep your hands where we can see them, please."

Ysbel's posture tensed, and he saw the tiny hint of movement from Tanya.

And then Ysbel glanced down at Olya, and her posture slumped.

"You have to the count of three," said the officer.

Lev took a deep breath, a heavy, sick weight settling in his stomach. His hands, he realized absently, were shaking.

He wouldn't be seeing Jez after all.

But then, with circumstances as they were, that was probably a good thing.

He raised his hands and turned.

The others did the same. He could see the tension in Masha's shoulders, the sharp worry in Ivan's face as his eyes followed Tae.

A squadron of at least a dozen police lined the street.

There were more footsteps from behind them, and another squadron of officers appeared behind them, weapons raised.

"May I ask the meaning of this?" said Masha, her voice calm and pleasant.

"Evka sent us," the man said sharply. "She has scans of your coms from when you were in her lab. Once the power went out, she had you followed." He glanced around at them, his eyes coming to rest on Lev. "She asked me to give you a message. She said, now that the power's down and the machine is shut off, there's nothing to stop her killing you."

Lev watched the man.

Everything felt, somehow, far away, and an odd calm had settled over him.

Jez was safe, at least. At least there was that.

"She told us to bring you in. But if you even try to resist, we're to shoot you. All of you." His eyes brushed over the children.

Lev glanced around at the others, then looked back at the officer. "We'll come," he said, his voice strangely calm. "Although if you have transport for my friend—" he gestured at Masha.

She still, somehow, managed her typical calm expression, but he could see the pain under it, and he wasn't sure she wouldn't simply fall over if asked to walk much farther.

"There's a transport one street over," the man said brusquely. "I assume she can make that far?"

Lev glanced at Masha, and she nodded.

The man stepped forward, tapping each of their coms with an EMP device, then gestured them forward.

They didn't speak as they were prodded into the transport. The officer closed the cargo door behind them, and the transport lifted and started forward.

Lev glanced around at the others as the streets slipped past them.

The others behind the barricades might not ever know what had happened. But his parents were smart—they'd figure out soon enough that something had gone wrong, and they'd get everyone to safety.

It would hurt Jez. That was the part that he hated most about this. It would hurt Jez to know he'd died. But Jez was smart. She was clever, and skilled, and she could do anything she put her mind to. It would hurt her, yes, and he hated that, but she'd have the *Ungovernable,* and she'd have deep space.

She'd be alright, eventually.

When the door to the transport opened and their guards shoved them out into Evka's courtyard, snapping cuffs onto the wrists of the adults, and he almost smiled at the deja vu.

But this time, they weren't coming in with a plan. This time, they were just as helpless as Evka believe them to be.

She was waiting for them.

He could see on her face what their explosion must have done to her—what had done to her to see her work destroyed. And despite himself, he felt a small, vicious twinge of satisfaction.

"Lev," Evka snapped as they disembarked. "I suppose you think you're very clever."

He raised an eyebrow, but didn't answer. He felt completely calm, and completely cold.

"But here's your miscalculation," she hissed. "When you shut down my Protocol, you shut down your only leverage to keep yourself and your friends alive."

"So why haven't you killed us?"

It was odd, really, how the calm in his voice contrasted with the agitation in hers.

"Because I want everyone to see you die," she whispered, her voice hissing with hatred. "I want everyone in Prasvishoni to see what happens when you cross me. My people are working to re-rout the communication lines—they'll have it done within a few hours. In the meantime, you'll be taken to your previous accommodations, and left under guard."

"Evka is a dirty plaguer!" Misko shouted, and the sound cut through Lev's strange, detached calm.

Ysbel made a frantic attempt to hush him, but her hands were cuffed behind her back.

Lev's stomach dropped as Evka turned to look at the children.

He recognized that calculating expression on her face.

"Evka," he said quickly. "Listen—"

She ignored him, her focus fully on Misko. "You," she said deliberately, "are a disgusting animal. I've watched children like you die screaming. And I'll enjoy watching you do the same."

"No!" Olya jerked her arms free of the man holding her and stepped in front of Misko. "You leave my brother alone." Her eyes were narrowed, but Lev could see her small body trembling.

"Olya, stop," he said, and he could hear the fear in his voice.

Evka took three quick steps over to the children and slapped Olya hard across the face.

The sound was loud in the sudden silence.

Olya's eyes were wide with the shock of it, and there was a red welt rising across her cheek, but there was a look on her face that told Lev she'd been hit before, enough times to be used to it.

His stomach twisted. "Evka—" he began through his teeth.

"I will kill you for that," said Ysbel in a strained voice. Two guards were holding her, but her expression was frightening.

Tanya was very pale, but she didn't struggle. "Olya, Misko," she said quietly. "Come here, please."

Olya obeyed, pushing her brother ahead of her. There were tears dripping down her cheeks, but she didn't make a sound.

Lev was breathing far too quickly. "You miserable coward," he snapped, glaring at Evka. He hardly recognized his own voice. "How dare you?"

Evka turned to him, and he saw, under her facade of calm, the rage on her face. "Don't bother, Lev," she said, her tone dripping with scorn. She pulled something out of the pocket of her jacket and strode around behind them, her boots clicking angrily against the cobblestones. "I told you I want everyone to see what happens to people who defy me," she said, her footsteps pausing.

He glanced over his shoulder and saw her fitting something on Tae's wrist.

"You've destroyed my Protocol, at least for the moment," she said through her teeth. "But while I was testing it, before I had it perfected, I used these for my experiments." She paused behind him now, and a moment later, he felt something tightening around his own wrist.

"It's designed to mimic the effects of the Protocol. I could use it to kill you quickly. But that would be a waste. I'd much rather everyone see you suffer." He twisted his head backwards again and saw her crouch to fasten the bands on the children's wrists.

His stomach churned.

Of course she'd have them sized to fit children.

"Evka—"

She finished fitting the last band around Tanya's wrist, then came back around to stand in front of them. She pulled a small controller out of her pocket and looked down at it musingly.

"Evka. No. If you need to test it, test it on me. Please." His chest was constricted with panic, his heart pounding.

She smiled at him. "Lev. I'm a scientist. You could have been as well. You know as well as I do that I can't take chances with my equipment."

"No! You can't—"

His words choked off as a spike of pain jolted through him, and he bit down hard against a scream. His muscles tightened, his head jerking back, the pain blocking out any other thought in his head. The guard's hands on his arms were the only thing holding him up, and he couldn't see or hear or feel anything at all but the pain …

And then it was gone, switched off as quickly as it had come.

He leaned forward, body shaking, and vomited, his stomach heaving and churning.

Distantly, he could hear sounds around him, but he refused to look up, because he wasn't certain he could bear it.

And then he heard a child's scream, high-pitched and terrified, and his head jerked up without his conscious thought.

It was Misko.

"Leave my brother—" Olya began, her voice shaking, and then her body stiffened and jerked, and Tanya wrenched her arms from the guard holding her—

And then it stopped.

Olya collapsed, sobbing breathlessly, beside Misko.

Misko was still screaming, eyes screwed shut, even though Lev could tell by the way the boy's muscles had gone slack that Evka wasn't torturing him any longer.

"It appears the bracelets are still functional, then," said Evka. "And I assume your screaming, broadcast on the general line as you die, should have an impact on anyone contemplating something similar." She paused, looking them over clinically.

The guard behind Tanya had grabbed her again, yanking her back.

"I'd advise you not to struggle, or to try to get away," she said coldly. "If you do, I won't hesitate to see how long the children hold up to the pain."

She turned on her heel and left.

They were dragged up to the room they'd been thrown in before Jez broke out. Lev's legs were shaky, but he could walk, at least. The guards were forced to carry Misko and Olya, and Masha looked only half-conscious.

This time, the guards followed them inside the room before locking the door, positioning themselves along the walls, their weapons held ready.

He could see, from the looks on the others' faces, how badly they wanted to try to break out. But they'd all seen the look on Evka's face before she left.

And he couldn't bear to hear Misko scream again.

Masha fell into a chair, her entire posture slack with pain and exhaustion. Ivan and Tae sat close together, knees touching, and Tanya and Ysbel and the children huddled in their tiny family group. Misko's screams had finally subsided, transforming into small, gasping hiccups.

Lev's stomach still churned, the phantom memory of the pain jolting through his brain, but he wasn't sure if the sickness was from his own pain, or from seeing Olya's small frame stiffen, the terror in her eyes.

Slowly, he sank into his own chair, and despite everything, there was that small, sharp ache that there was no need for another chair pulled up next to his.

Jez was safe. The fact that he was alone meant she was safe, and so he'd take being alone.

His stomach clenched again at the memory of her writhing on the floor.

He'd had no idea what it was like. Now he knew.

He wasn't sure how long he sat there, before the sound of

footsteps padding across the room made him jerk his head up.

It was Olya. Her face was still frighteningly pale, the place where Evka had slapped her shockingly red against her white skin, and there were tear-tracks down her face.

She hesitated a moment, then climbed into his lap.

He forced himself to smile, somehow. "Olya," he said. "Are you alright?"

"I'm scared, Uncle Lev," she whispered. "I … I don't want to die."

He swallowed hard and glanced up.

Ysbel was watching him, her face grave and almost as pale as her daughter's.

"I—" He cleared his throat. "I don't want you to die, either. I would stop it, if I possibly could." His voice choked a little.

He'd seen the look on Evka's face. She'd kill the children without a qualm, and there was nothing at all he could do about it.

She'd killed enough children, watched them writhe and scream until their small bodies couldn't handle the pain any longer, and simply shut down.

He had to swallow back the vomit in his throat.

He hated pain. He couldn't actually let himself think of what Evka would do to him, because he couldn't wrap his mind around the enormity of it.

But knowing Olya was going to die like that was a million times worse.

"Is it going to hurt?" she whispered. "Like what she did in the courtyard?"

"I—suspect it might, for a bit," he said. "But then it will stop."

She was quiet for a few minutes, and he could feel her trembling. He wanted to put an arm around her, but his hands were still cuffed behind his back, so he settled for resting his cheek against her hair.

"I'm going to miss you, Uncle Lev," she said at last, in a quiet voice.

Lev found himself suddenly blinking back tears.

"I'll miss you, too," he said when he could trust his voice.

She turned to him, staring up earnestly into his face. "Do you think it's true, about the Lady? That we go see her when we die?"

He managed another small smile. "I don't know for certain, Olya. But if there is a Lady, I'm sure she'll be absolutely delighted to have you come stay with her. You and your brother and your mama and your mamochka."

She looked up at him consideringly for a moment. "Well," she said at last. "I'm not going to stay with her unless you can come too. I'm going to tell her."

"You do that," said Lev, and again, he had to blink back tears.

27

Jez, day 8, morning

"Jez." Radic glanced up at her from where he was seated on the floor. "You're going to wear a damn groove in the floor." He gestured to a spot beside him, where he and Felix had started a game of tokens. "I can't believe I'm saying this, but come on. Got room in the game for one more player."

Jez shook her head and tried to smile. "Nah. Figure I'll give you plaguers a chance to win once in a while. The way you play, you need it."

Radic snorted, but she could see the sympathy in his face. "They'll be here soon," he said quietly. "The streets are a mess out there—the entire damn city's rioting now that the Protocol's gone. It'll take them a while to get back through the streets, and if Masha's as beat up as you say she is—"

Jez nodded and went back to pacing, running her hand up and down the smooth butt of her heat gun.

It had been almost four hours. Even with a bad as the streets were, it shouldn't have taken them this long.

"Maybe I should go out there, try to find them," she said, pausing by the shelter door. "Probably could use a ride, if Masha's with them."

Radic's eyes, when he glanced up at her again, were disturbingly perceptive. "Jez. You don't know where they'll be coming from."

She shook her head. "Maybe I can track them down, drive out along the streets between here and the Vault—"

Radic sighed and put down his tokens. He pushed himself to his feet and came to stand beside her. "Jez," he said quietly. "If something's happened to them, it's happened. There's nothing we can do about it. Going out in the streets right now, the way things are—it's an invitation to get shot."

She spun on him. "Look, I don't know how they do things where you come from—"

He put a hand on her arm. "Kid—" he began. The softness in his voice almost made it worse. "Listen. You know damn well I'd do anything I could to help them. I've known Ivan and Tanya for years, and after what we did on the pleasure planet—look. Your friends are my friends. But—" he shook his head. "Getting yourself shot isn't gonna do anyone any good."

Jez bit back a sharp retort.

He was right.

Probably right about the rest of it, too. The others were probably on their way here. They'd probably be laughing about this in an hour or so.

She'd probably turned around, in just a minute here, and Lev would be standing in the doorway, with that look on his face that always set butterflies dancing in her stomach.

The thought sent a sharp ache through her whole damn body.

No wonder she always been scared of actually falling for someone. Because this—this hurt.

Maybe Radic was right. But—

But somehow, she knew he wasn't.

Something was wrong.

Lev would have called. There was no way that Lev wouldn't have called.

She tapped her com through to the closed loop and tried again. "Genius. Can you hear me? If you can't answer, tap something in pilot's code."

She waited, every muscle in her damn body tense.

But there wasn't going to be an answer. Just like there hadn't been for the last four damn hours.

"Jez—" Radic's expression was tight with sympathy.

"Look, Radic," she said. "I know what you're going to say. But something's happened to them. And I'm not damn well going to leave them to deal with it alone."

She paused a moment, chewing on the inside of her cheek.

They wouldn't have all been killed in the streets, by police or rioters, before they had a chance to get a message out. They had the children with them, and every single person in that group, including Masha, would have called for help if they thought it would save Olya and Misko.

But they hadn't. Which meant, probably, Evka had tracked them down.

And considering what they'd done to the power grid, the plaguer wouldn't trust them back in prison. So if they weren't already dead, they'd be back at her lab.

Evka might think she was special, but Jez had worked with a lot of bastards just like her. Hell, Lena had been like her—thought she was smarter than every other damn person in the system. Thought Jez was an idiot, and thought loyalty was for weaklings.

And—well, Lena was a floating cloud of space dust right now.

And the reason Jez wasn't was that she had friends who didn't give up on her, no matter how much reason they had to.

And she damn well wasn't about to give up on them.

But how could she possibly—

And then she had to close her eyes and grab for the tent support, just for a moment.

Because, as much as she wished she didn't—she knew exactly how she could get them out.

She turned to Radic. She felt, suddenly, very, very cold, but she managed to grin anyways. "Guess I need to have a quick chat with Evka. You think Anya could hack me through a line?"

Anya arrived in the tent a few minutes later. Blood crusted the side of her face, and there was a bruise rising on one cheek, but she was grinning. "Radic said you needed someone to hack you through to Evka."

Anya worked quickly—it was only a few minutes before she straightened from where she was crouched over Jez's com, handing it over. "You should be able to get through now."

"Thanks," said Jez. Her heart was pounding, and she felt a little like she might be sick. She glanced around the shelter. "See you plaguers soon."

Radic, who'd turned back to his game, frowned at her. "Kid. Thought you were just going to chat with her. Where you going?"

Jez shook her head. "Evka might be an absolute plaguing scum-eater, but she's smart enough to track my com signal once I call in. Don't want her tracking it here."

Radic sighed and stood. "Jez," he said quietly. "I'm not an idiot. I know that's not all you're going to do, and I know I can't stop you. But—be careful, OK? You got a tracker set into your com, so we'll know if something's happened to you, at least?"

Anya glanced up. "Took care of it," she said. There was a serious note behind the lightness in her tone.

Radic put a hand on Jez's the shoulder. "We'll be watching for you," he said quietly. "As much as we can, anyways. Don't get killed, okay? You don't want my life to get boring again." He gave her a small grin, and she grinned back, despite the tight knot in her stomach.

"Yeah," she managed. "That'd be a shame."

He pulled her into a bear hug. When he drew back, he gave her a quick smile. "Good luck."

She nodded, and slipped out of the shelter.

Radic hadn't been wrong—the streets were chaos. People were shouting and screaming, there were flash bangs and explosions and gas bombs, and the entire city was in an uproar. Jez swerved her skybike effortlessly through the heat-blasts and explosions and small, huddled packs of police officers, most of whom seemed to have given up on trying to keep any semblance of order. As she approached Evka's compound, though, she slowed.

Her heart pounded quick and uneven, and her hands shook, just a little.

Despite what she'd told Radic, she was pretty damn sure this wasn't going to end with her flying away.

She pulled her bike to a stop a couple blocks away and slid off, leaning it up against the alley wall, taking a deep breath to steady herself.

They had to be alive. They bloody well had to be. She'd lost a lot of damn things in her life, and she'd survived them all.

But she knew, deep down, she wouldn't survive losing them.

She tapped her com through to Evka's line. It buzzed for a moment, and then Evka answered.

The sound of Evka's voice sent a jolt of sick, thoughtless panic through her—a memory of pain, of screaming until she couldn't scream anymore, her body jerking, out of her control.

"Jez Solokov." There was smug triumph in Evka's tone. "I was hoping I'd hear from you."

"What have you done with them?" Jez hardly recognized her own damn voice, cold and hard and is calm as Masha's had ever been.

"They're locked up. I'm going to kill them, as soon as my people finish their repairs on the general line—another fifteen, twenty minutes."

Something tightened in Jez's chest, and she couldn't decide if it was panic or relief.

She hadn't been too late.

"Nah," she said quietly. "I don't think you're going to do that."

"Really." Evka's voice was mild, and faintly amused. "I assume, then, that you have some plan to stop me." She paused a moment. "I've read up on your history. All your life, you've gotten by on quick instincts and a talent for flying. But that's not enough here. You have nothing to threaten me with. I will kill them. And then I'll find you, and kill you too."

Jez's chest was so tight she could hardly draw a breath.

She'd wondered, back at the barricades, if she'd even be able to say the next words.

But in the end, she didn't even hesitate.

"No, you bastard," she said, with a deep breath. "You're right. I can't break them out, and I can't threaten you. But I can make you a bargain."

There was a moment's pause. "And what does a smuggler pilot have to bargain with a scientist?" asked Evka, a touch of amusement in her voice.

There was a cold numbness spreading through Jez, weighing down her limbs and crystallizing in her chest.

Which, honestly, was a damn good thing. Because this was going to hurt more than Evka and her damn machine. More than anything.

"Figure there's one thing," she said slowly. "Figure even a scientist like you might be interested in something designed by Sasa Illiovich."

There was a long moment of silence from the other end of the com.

"I assume you're talking about your ship." There was a spark of interest in Evka's tone.

"Guess you're a smart bastard after all." Jez tried to inject a jaunty note into her voice.

It didn't matter, though. Something inside her had died when she spoke those words.

"It's an interesting proposition," said Evka at last. "But what's to stop me from simply taking it?"

Jez gave a half-hearted snort. "Told you, this is Sasa Illiovich's tech. You want to try to find my ship with the cloaking set on it? There's no one in the damn system who can do that for you."

There was another long pause. "I can't afford to release your crew. You're far too adept at causing trouble. And I can't have you on the outside. You're foolhardy enough to try to rescue them."

Jez swallowed hard. "Yeah, figured you'd say that," she said. "But —I'm not asking you to release them. Just—just keep them alive. That's all. And—" She swallowed, hard. "I'll let you lock me up with them, if you promise they won't be hurt."

She'd be locked up. She'd probably be locked up for the rest of her damn life. Because hell, she was smart enough to know that once the power was back on, they'd go straight to the Vault, and she was pretty damn sure Masha's friend wasn't the warden anymore.

But—she pictured Lev's face, Ysbel's reluctant smile, Tae's scowl, and the way his face lit up when he looked at Ivan. Tanya, Olya, Misko. Even that bastard Masha.

She swallowed again. "Look. You gotta let me talk to them first. I need to know they're alive."

"I suppose that's fair," said Evka at last. "I'll patch you through to my guards' coms."

A moment later, Lev's cautious voice came through Jez's earpiece. "Yes, Evka?" She could hear the weariness in his tone. "What do you need?"

She managed to choke out, "Lev?"

There was a moment's silence, then Lev's voice again, sounding frantic. "Jez? Where are you? What happened? Jez, are you alright?"

There were tears stinging in her eyes, blurring her vision and choking her throat, but she swallowed them back. "Yeah," she said. "Yeah, I'm fine. Everyone else there?"

"We're all here," he said quietly. "Listen. You need to—"

"No, you listen, genius," she said. "I've been talking to Evka. Can't get you out, but figure I found a way to keep you alive. Better than nothing, right?"

The concern in his voice sharpened. "What are you—"

She took a deep breath. "You said you trusted me, right? So you're just gonna have to trust me on this one."

There was another long silence. "I'm sorry," he said, voice thick with emotion. "I trust you. I just—"

"You just worry," she said. "I know. But—everyone's there? She hasn't—she hasn't hurt anyone, or—" she couldn't bring herself to finish the sentence.

"None of us is hurt," said Lev quietly.

"Thanks," she managed, then tapped back to Evka's line quickly, before she could lose her whole damn composure and break down sobbing.

"Alright, you bastard," she said. "I'll give you the *Ungovernable*, and I'll let you lock me up, and you'll give me your word that you won't kill any of us, or put us into sedation or any crap like that."

"I accept," said Evka at last. "I give you my word—you and your companions will be unharmed. I won't give you special privileges, but nor will I request you be treated any worse than any of the other prisoners." She paused for a moment. "I can tell from your com signal that you're close by. I'll have someone waiting for you by the courtyard gate. Once I've verified that you've provided correct coordinates for your ship, and that my people can access it, you'll be taken to your friends." She paused. "You've managed to surprise me, Jez. I've been wanting to get my hands on some of Sasa Illiovich's technology for some time now. It should be a simple matter to strip the ship down to its components, and I suspect it will be a very rewarding study indeed."

"Yeah," said Jez, her voice barely audible.

She tapped off her com, and stood for a minute, staring at the blank wall of the alley in front of her.

Her ship. Her beautiful, beautiful, perfect angel. Her baby. She'd sung to Jez, talked to her, listened to her. Inside the *Ungovernable's* cockpit, Jez felt freer than she'd ever felt in her life.

And now Jez would be locked up.

And the *Ungovernable* would be stripped down for parts.

She'd thought she was numb. Hell, she must be, or this would've actually killed her, because having your heart ripped out and ground to powder wasn't something you could live through.

But even with the numbness, it hurt so bad. It hurt so she wasn't sure she could still breathe.

She forced her feet to move her down the alley and towards Evka.

Because yes, this hurt.

But there was one thing that would hurt more—losing her crew. Losing Lev, losing any one of them.

And so, moving like an automaton, she made her way to the front of Evka's compound.

There were guards waiting for her, and she held out her wrists for the mag cuffs.

She hardly felt it when the guard snapped them on.

They herded her through into the courtyard, and somehow, she made her mouth move to tell Evka where she'd find her beautiful angel. And somehow, her legs held her upright as she stood, watching distantly. As she heard the voices through the com, confirming they had her ship.

As she watched them, a few minutes later, bring her in low and settle her into the courtyard.

Perhaps it was because some part of her couldn't honestly believe this was actually happening.

And even though Jez hadn't been sure she'd ever be able to feel anything, ever again, there was a pain like a spike through her lungs at the sight of her angel sitting in Evka's sterile, bleak courtyard.

"Call a government team in," said Evka.

Jez could hear the words, distantly. There was something rushing in her ears like water, and she felt dizzy. She should probably have fallen over, passed out, because her heart shouldn't still be beating after this.

But somehow it was, and that confused her.

"They have the facilities to take the ship apart, and it will be a meaningful gesture of goodwill, which, thanks to this woman and her friends, we may need until I can get the Protocol functioning again."

Evka was still talking.

Jez didn't care.

Every heartbeat seemed to last forever.

But at last Evka turned, seeming to remember her. "Take the pilot up to the others," she said casually, waving a hand at one of the guards. "She's not to be mistreated unless she resists. And you can take the cuffs off the others, since they'll be here for a while, it appears—although any escape attempt, shoot them."

Jez didn't resist. Not when they grabbed her, turning her away from her angel ship, not when they pushed her unresistingly through the corridors.

For just a moment, she remembered the prison planet, the look on Ysbel's face as she talked about getting Tanya back. About staying in prison while the rest of them escaped, just so she could see Tanya one last time.

Jez hadn't thought she'd ever understand that—loving someone enough to walk back to prison for them. But—

But hell, maybe after all this time, she'd learned something after all.

28

Tae, day 8, afternoon

The lock on the door to their makeshift cell clicked, and Tae glanced up dully.

He could feel Ivan stiffen beside him.

Jez had said she thought she'd found a way to keep Evka from killing them. But it looked like she was too late after all.

Two of the guards surrounding them stepped to the door, talking quietly into their coms. Then the door swung open, and someone stumbled through as if they'd been pushed.

It closed, and then the guards inside hit a button on their coms, and the cuffs around his wrists loosened and dropped to the ground.

Tae blinked, not quite believing his eyes.

"Hey, you bastards, miss me?" Jez said, with an attempt at a grin.

But there was something weary and defeated in her posture, something broken in her eyes, raw pain under the forced lightness in her tone.

They all stared for a moment. Then Lev, who'd been slumped on the chair in the corner, leapt to his feet, his cuffs apparently loosened as well, and crossed the room to her in quick strides.

"Jez. Are you alright?" His voice was almost frantic. He took Jez gently by the shoulders, looking her up and down for injuries, and Tae could see the tension in every muscle in his body. "Are you hurt? What happened? Why are you here, what did Evka—"

"Genius." Jez's voice was as weary as Tae had ever heard it. "I'm fine. Talked to Evka, convinced her not to kill you." She shrugged. "Bastard wouldn't agree unless she could lock me up too, and I figured, what the hell, you were all probably getting bored in here without me."

Lev studied her. "Jez," he said quietly. "How did you convince Evka to—"

Then realization flashed across Lev's face, a sort of sick horror.

And it was that, as much as anything, that made Tae realize, finally, what Jez must have done.

He felt like someone had punched him in the stomach.

This would kill her. This would actually kill her.

"Oh, Jez," said Lev quietly.

"It's fine," said Jez, the words choking in her throat. "It's fine, I'm fine. I—"

Lev pulled her into an embrace, and she slumped against him, her body shaking with silent sobs.

"You gave up your ship, you lunatic pilot," said Ysbel softly, awe in her voice. "You gave up the *Ungovernable,* didn't you? To keep us alive."

Tae closed his eyes, feeling sick.

He'd seen the way Jez looked at that ship. He'd seen the way her whole body relaxed the moment she set foot on the loading dock, the expression on her face when she was in the cockpit, a radiant peace he'd never seen from her anywhere else.

She'd almost lost the *Ungovernable* once before, back when Lena had been after them. Jez had managed to pull them out of an off-balance hyperdrive jump, and fried the thrusters in the process. He'd seen what that had done to her. He'd been angry at the time, bitter, and furious at her and all the rest of the damn crew—and even then, he'd hardly been able to bear looking at her. The way it had broken something inside her.

And this time, she'd done it voluntarily.

He turned away, a helpless anger choking in his throat at the pointlessness of it all.

Jez had lost the thing she cared about more than anything in the damn system, and for what? Not to free them, or win anything—just to keep them alive. Locked up, still in prison, but alive.

Ivan had come to Prasvishoni, been forced to re-live, over and over again, his worst memories. Olya and Misko, who'd grown up in prison, who'd only gotten out months earlier, would be sent to the Vault after all.

The thought sat like a stone in his stomach, hard and heavy.

It wasn't bloody fair.

And to think once he'd believed they could actually make a damn difference.

"Tae?" asked Ivan softly, laying a hand on his shoulder. "Are you alright?"

Tae swallowed hard. Ivan put his arms around him, and Tae closed his eyes at the comfort of that familiar warmth.

It was odd to think, really, that it all had only been a few months since the group of them had first met in that small, eclectic office, moments before it had been blown to smithereens by a combination of a police tracking drone, and Ysbel's explosive gel.

Who would've thought, all that time ago, that one day Jez would be sobbing in Lev's arms after giving up the thing meant everything to her, to save them. That Masha would have let herself be tortured rather than betray them, in the end. That Ysbel would be holding Tanya and her children. That he'd have found someone like Ivan.

"Tae?" asked Ivan.

Tae looked up, blinking back tears. "I'm alright," he said quietly.

He wasn't certain if that was true. He wasn't certain that watching Jez hurt like this—watching her die inside, day by day, until there was nothing left but an empty husk—wouldn't simply kill him, too.

He tried to smile. "I guess it's like on the pleasure planet. Maybe we didn't save everyone. But we tried. I guess at least we have that." He shook his head. "If I could fix everything, I'd have fixed this for you already. Taken away your nightmares. I'd have got Caz and Peti and the others somewhere safe. But I guess some things you just can't fix. And no one can say we didn't do our damnedest."

Ivan reached down, brushing a stray bit of hair out of Tae's face, and Tae glanced up at him. Ivan's eyes were dark and intense, and they took Tae's breath away for just a moment.

"Tae," he said quietly. "Maybe you're right. Maybe we can't fix everything. But—maybe we've done more than you think."

Tae frowned.

Ivan gave a soft chuckle. "Maybe you didn't take away my nightmares—maybe no one can. But don't tell me you didn't change things." His voice was slightly thick with emotion. "You—you'll never know how many things you changed, Tae. You love me, no matter how broken I am. So—I can live with being broken now. And your street-kid friends—you saved them from the police, and you stopped Evka. Maybe not permanently, but long enough to give them a chance. The students, and everyone behind the barricades— they have a chance too, now, maybe to get somewhere Evka won't track them down." He smiled. "You've changed a hell of a lot more than you know."

Tae stared at Ivan for a moment. Then he turned and glanced over his shoulder at Jez.

Lev had drawn her into the corner, and they were sitting together, backs against the wall.

He was stroking her hair, and whispering something into her ear, and she was slumped against him, shoulders tight with pain, but— there was just a hint of a smile on her lips, through her tears, a desperate, unconscious, genuine smile he'd never dreamed he'd see on Jez, locked up in prison, her ship gone, no hope of getting out.

He stared for a moment, then found he was smiling too, the tiniest hint of a smile.

Maybe Ivan was right after all.

They were back in prison, like they'd been before they'd ever met Masha. But everything was different.

Everything in the whole damn system was different.

He wasn't alone. He wasn't the angry, frightened, defensive kid he'd been then. He had Ivan, and he had the others. And there were people out there who cared about his kids, who wouldn't stop fighting for them no matter what it cost.

He leaned over and kissed Ivan, and Ivan kissed him back, pulling him close, and the gratitude choking in Tae's chest was almost enough to take his breath away.

He heard footsteps, and he glanced up quickly to see the guards talking in low voices.

One of them turned and said, voice hard, "We have video and audio on all of you, and the next set of guards will be here momentarily." He paused. "Evka instructed all of us that the first sign of an attempted escape, we were to shoot you down. That's what your pilot agreed to. So don't try anything." She glared at them for a moment, then tapped her com to the door, and the guards stepped out.

The crew looked at each other for a moment, and then, without having to say anything, they moved to the corner where Jez and Lev sat.

"Jez," said Tae quietly, when they were sitting close enough that at least their voices over the bugs would be muted. "What are things like out there? Is everyone safe?"

Jez shot him a watery grin. "Guess that depends on what you mean by safe. But they all got back behind the barricades, and I told Lev's mom and dad to get them somewhere safe if—if I didn't come back." Her voice wavered, just a little. Lev pulled her closer, and she leaned into him and took a deep breath. "So. How long you think it'll take that bastard Evka to get the power back up?" A touch of her usual cheerfulness was creeping back into her voice. "Because I'll be honest, the damn scum-sucker was looking a bit on edge when I saw her. Figure a few weeks of twiddling her thumbs might be good for her."

Lev gave a small chuckle. "I suspect it will be at least a few weeks before they get the full power running. And I also suspect that, even with the amount of pull Evka has in the government, their priority will be getting the city running before they worry about the Viernest Protocol. It's very possible that by that time, our friends will be able to get completely off-planet."

There was the soft *ting* of metal, and Lev glanced down, frowning slightly. "What's that?"

Jez glanced down as well, at the small, cylindrical object she'd been fiddling with, and gave another watery grin. "This is Ysbel's damn brain zapper. Smuggled it in. Not going to help us, I guess, because they'll kill us all if we try to escape. But I thought it might be good for something. When they searched me for weapons, they found my heat gun, and my gutting knife, and my other gutting knife, and the explosive I had in my pocket, and—"

Ysbel frowned. "I didn't give you an explosive to carry in your pocket."

Jez shrugged. "Well, I've got a lot of things that nobody gave me, per se."

Ysbel's voice went completely flat. "Jez. You stole an explosive? You stole one of my explosives, and put it in your pocket?"

Jez's grin grew a little more genuine. "I wouldn't call it stealing, exactly."

"Jez. There is a reason no one steals my explosives. And it's that people who try to steal my explosives usually end up decorating the walls of my weapons room."

"Well, but see, not everyone is as careful as I am." Jez's voice was a touch more cheerful than it had been. "Anyway, point is, they didn't find this, because the damn plaguers didn't even think about looking where I'd hidden it."

"Where ... did you—" Ysbel began.

Tae glared at her. "Don't ask. Please don't ask."

Jez spun the slender cylinder, then handed it to Ysbel. "Not that it will do us any good. But—" she shrugged. "Guess at least it'll give you something to work on when you get bored."

Ysbel was turning the device over in her hands, and Tae frowned.

"Ysbel," he said slowly. "I don't think you ever told me how it works."

Ysbel glanced over, then shrugged. "It's not that complicated. It sends out an electromagnetic pulse that disrupts your brain's electric pulses. Knocks you unconscious. At least," she amended, "when it's calibrated right, it knocks you unconscious. If it's calibrated wrong —" she shrugged again. "Well, I never really went back and checked what happened to them, to be honest."

Tae's mind was suddenly racing.

Disrupts the electrical pulses in your brain. He was no biologist, he just knew tech. But—

But electrical pulses. Electrical pulses in your brain.

"Ysbel," he said slowly. "How high could you turn up the electric pulse without killing someone?"

Ysbel raised her eyebrows at his question, considering. "I don't know. Higher than it is, certainly." She paused a moment. "You want to become a weapons designer now?"

Tae shook his head impatiently. "No. But I do know tech. And I know how large of a pulse you'd need to fry the circuits in Evka's metal."

Ysbel was staring at him, and he could see understanding dawning on her face. "You think you could use this to disrupt Evka's Protocol?"

"It's theoretically possible." There was a small buzz of excitement in the back of his brain. "I don't know how we'd get it to the people outside, but—if we can, there's a chance we could keep our friends safe permanently."

"It would take me a while to develop," Ysbel began slowly, but there was excitement growing in her voice.

The lock on the door behind them clicked, and they scrambled to their feet, Ysbel shoving the small device down the front of her shirt as Tae hastily averted his eyes.

The replacement guards stepped into the room, and Tae glanced around at the others quickly—it would be the cruelest of ironies if Evka somehow construed them speaking together as an escape attempt, and had them all shot.

From the corner of his eye, he saw one of the guards moving

purposefully towards him.

He gritted his teeth.

He hadn't done anything wrong. Even if some of what they'd been saying had been picked up on the audio, and he was pretty sure it hadn't, they hadn't been talking about escape. She couldn't kill them for it.

Could she?

The guard's hand came down on his arm, and he flinched.

"Tae?"

He glanced up in shock at the familiar voice.

Caz stood there, dressed in the uniform of Evka's guards, a small smile on his face.

Tae gaped, too dumbfounded to speak.

"Caz?" he said at last, dumbly. "Caz, what—"

"We're breaking you out," said another guard, and he recognized Vera. "Come on."

Tae stood blinking in astonishment.

Lev had already scrambled to his feet, holding out his hand to Jez, and Ysbel and Tanya were gathering the children.

The look on their faces was stunned, disbelieving hope.

"How—" Tae began weakly.

"Questions later, tech-head," said Jez. Her face was still tear-streaked, but there was a hint of a dangerous grin on her lips.

She was right. For now, the important thing was getting out alive.

"What are we working with?" asked Lev briskly, coming over.

"We took out the guards in the hallway, but I doubt we have much time before more show up," said Radic, from the other side of the room.

Tae started, looking around. "How many of you are there?"

Caz grinned. "It was hard to narrow down, honestly. Radic's here, and Vera, and Felix is outside—he's the one who took out the guards, he and his kids—and Anya's waiting in the street. She broke us in with some tech of yours that she modified. And Galina's here, and Demetri refused to stay out of it. And we had to fight off a whole horde of others who wanted to come along."

"Come on," said Radic, jerking his head towards the door. "Anya said she'd give us two minutes, and I think it's almost up."

"We need to get these bracelets off first," said Tae.

Caz grinned, and handed him an EMP device. "I thought she might have done something to you that involved tech."

Tae deactivated his own bracelet, then the bracelets of the others. Watching the small light on Misko's wrist flicker and die was an almost ridiculous relief.

When he'd finished, Vera touched her com to the lock, and it clicked open. She glanced up and down the hall, then waved them forward.

Felix was waiting for them outside, with all four of his kids. He was carrying a short metal rod, and there was blood on the end of it, and Tae decided he didn't actually want to know what had happened to Evka's guards. Dmitri and Galina stood at either end of the hall, their postures tense.

"Come on," Dmitri hissed, gesturing. "We're almost out of time."

They crept silently down the narrow hallway and down the stairs to the small back door, then along the edge of the rear courtyard. When at last they made it through to the street, where Anya was waiting for them, Dmitri turned to Tae, grinning.

"We decided you'd rescued the rest of us enough times that it was our turn to repay the favor."

Tae looked at him for a moment.

Dmitri wasn't the boy he'd met months ago, on the campus of the

University of Prasvishoni. There was a grimness to his face now, a set to his mouth that hadn't been there before. But when he grinned, his green eyes lit up in the same way they had back in the student dorms.

And Tae found himself smiling back.

29

Lev, day 8, afternoon

Lev kept his arm tightly around Jez as they hurried through the dark, chaotic streets, holding her like he'd never let go of her again.

He still wasn't certain he'd fully processed the fact that somehow these crazy friends of theirs had broken them out of Evka's prison.

Matters in the city had only gotten more chaotic—despite the cold, the streets were filled with people, shouting, yelling, cheering. Someone in one of the apartment blocks a few streets down must have found some old fireworks, because the crackling red and yellow sparks illuminated the sky, followed moments later by sputtering blasts of sound.

The police and the military must have mostly given up trying to keep order—in fact, he could see people in military uniforms joining in with the riotous celebrations.

Caz and the others had hurriedly passed out weapons once they'd reached the street, but with how crazy things were, it appeared their best bet at safety was attracting as little notice as possible.

"I have an old safehouse not too far from here," Radic whispered. "Apartment I rented. Didn't use it much, but there are enough people in Prasvishoni want to kill me I figured it wasn't a bad investment. Should still be there."

They turned down a small street, and then another, and Lev recognized the street as one near where Jez's basement apartment had been. Prior to it being blown up, of course.

Radic stopped at the back entrance to a small, tumbledown apartment complex and tapped a code into the door pad. He shoved the door open with an effort, led them down a short hallway and through a door, and hit a switch. A dingy artificial light flickered on, illuminating a small, bare room.

"Sorry," said Radic. "It's not really decorated for company." He paused. "At least, not the kind that isn't trying to shoot me."

Jez was looking around in faint interest. "Nicer than my old place," she said, with a weak attempt at a grin.

"I can confirm that," Tae muttered, and Lev had to bite back a smile.

Jez dropped into a cross-legged slouch on the bare floor, and the rest of them followed suit.

"Alright," said Dmitri. "The next step is to get you off planet, before Evka—"

"No."

Lev looked over at Tae in surprise.

There was a calm determination on his face Lev hadn't seen there in a long time.

"Tae, listen," Demetri started, but Tae shook his head.

"No," he said again. "I'm not leaving this planet until you and everyone else is safe. Jez gave up her damn ship for us. You risked your lives. And we're not leaving until we've either taken Evka down, or died trying."

There was a long silence.

"Lev," said Masha at last. "You know Evka better than any of us.

What do you think?"

He took a deep breath and glanced over. "Maybe there are times we have to just give up," he said quietly. "But not this time. I'm with Tae—I'm not leaving until Evka's taken down completely, and her machine is destroyed."

"I won't say I don't agree with the sentiment," said Galina, a wry note in her voice. "But how do you propose to do that?"

He turned to her. "Tell me what's going on in the streets, what's happened to the rest of you. I need all the details I can get."

Galina nodded slowly. "Everyone from the barricades is safe, as far as I know," she said. "Your parents are working to get everyone to a more secure location. The streets are a mess—you saw that on the way here, but it's like that all through the city. The military has mostly given up. I don't think they were thrilled about the Protocol in general, and it's their families who've flooded the streets. I doubt they'll follow orders to shoot. But the police are still trying to crack down. It will be dangerous out there."

He nodded absently, glancing at Jez.

She leaned against his shoulder wearily, and something tightened in his chest.

This was the last damn time Evka would hurt Jez. Because this time, he wasn't going to stop until they'd taken her down.

"Alright," he said at last. "We'll split up. You take the entrances to Evka's lab, make sure she and her people don't get out. Cut her off. We'll find the machine and take it out. It would take a massive amount of resources and time to rebuild, and with any luck, Evka will never get it—her failure this time will have given the government a black eye they won't soon forget."

"I'll need someone to take the children somewhere safe, if that's possible," said Ysbel quietly.

"I'll do it, Professor," said Dimitri after a moment.

Ysbel nodded, but Lev could see the sparkle of tears in her eyes. "Thank you," she said.

Lev took a deep breath and turned to Masha.

She was leaned against the wall, her face paler than usual and lined with pain, but she hadn't said a word.

"Masha," he said, and the word came out more gently than he'd expected. "You go back with Dmitri. You're not in any shape to—"

Masha opened her eyes and smiled at him. Despite the weakness in it, it was the same smile she'd given him the first time he'd seen her, so many months ago, sitting across from him in the prison visitors' room.

"I appreciate your concern, Lev. But there's a chance you may need me. I have contacts, and that might still come in helpful." She paused. "Unless," she added quietly, "you prefer that I stay away."

She met his gaze, but he could see, under the calm, bland expression she wore like a damn shield, the vulnerability behind her words.

Masha.

Even after all this, wasn't sure he could trust her.

But—

He glanced at Jez.

But dammit, he wanted to. Whether she deserved it or not, he wanted to.

"If—if you feel that you're up to it, I would be—grateful for your help," he said at last.

Masha looked up, and he saw the momentary flash of surprised gratitude before she could hide it.

Jez gave a small sigh, snuggling her head into his shoulder, and he tightened his arm around her.

For a moment, they were quiet.

Then Radic stood. "Well, if we're going to save the system, we'd better get a move on."

Lev squeezed Jez's shoulder one last time, then got to his feet as well. "I suppose we'd better," he said.

30

Ysbel, day 8, afternoon

Ysbel cast one final look at her children, standing in the doorway beside Dmitri.

"Behave yourselves," she said. "Tae got our coms back online, so I'll know if you misbehave. And—" She cleared her throat. "Mama loves you, alright?"

"I know that," grumbled Misko, rolling his eyes.

She smiled despite herself.

Then she turned back to the streets.

Radic and the others had already started for Evka's compound, but the crew was waiting for her in the mouth of the alley.

"Where are we going?" asked Ivan, glancing at Lev.

Lev pulled up his com holoscreen. "She wanted to keep the location of her machine secret, I think." There was a note of grim satisfaction in his voice. "But when you go around assuming Jez is stupid, you're liable to get your pockets picked."

Ysbel glanced at Jez, who grinned and gave her an innocent look.

Lev expanded the city map on his screen and tapped a small building, marking it red.

Ysbel frowned. "That's right near the government compound."

"That won't be easy to get to," said Tanya. "The whole government sector will be crawling with police. I have no doubt that's where they retreated when the city went mad."

"Figure maybe it's the police officers who should worry about that," said Jez, with a hint of her customary snark.

Tanya shook her head, but there was a fondness in her smile Ysbel would never have expected to see there. "Perhaps you're right."

Ysbel smiled at Tanya, then reached into the bag of explosives at her neck and pulled out a couple to tuck into her pockets. Then they stepped out into the noise and chaos of the streets.

Police sirens wailed, and above the shouting mass of people, they could hear commands through voice amps, and every so often, the hiss of a heat gun.

Perhaps it was the expression on Ysbel's face, but the crowd parted for them like water for oil.

Ysbel smiled to herself. It was nice to know she hadn't lost her touch.

Lev directed them through to the smaller alleys and side streets. They could still hear the noise and chaos from the main streets, but here, at least, the crowds were thinner, and they could travel more quickly. But as they approached the government buildings, the sounds of raucous cheers were replaced by angry shouts, sirens and voice amps drowning out the noise, and the hiss of heat-blasts louder and more frequent.

And then, at last, they reached the alley that led to the building.

Lev peered around the corner, and cursed.

Ysbel stepped up beside him.

The alley, where, apparently, the police officers gathered to regroup.

There were at least two dozen of them, weapons drawn, faces

grim, skybikes leaned up against the wall.

Lev glanced helplessly at Ysbel.

She smiled and turned to Tanya. "My love?"

Tanya smiled back.

"Don't worry," said Ysbel, turning back to Lev. "They won't be paying attention to the rest of you."

Tanya disappeared into a gap between two buildings.

Ysbel loosened her grip on her heat pistol and stepped around the corner.

The officers looked up as she came into view, and Ysbel smiled at them.

"Hello," she said, lifting her pistol. Then she melted one of the skybikes they'd leaned against the wall.

The officers scrambled for their weapons, and Ysbel shot the lead officer directly in the chest. They had full riot gear, yes, but even the best heatshield didn't completely block the heat. The officer shouted in pain, dropping his weapon as the blast lit his heat shield a dull red.

She hit two more of them and melted a second bike before they scrambled for cover.

"What are you doing? Drop your weapon!" shouted the lead officer, from where he'd taken cover behind a skybike. "You think you can take on two dozen officers with a heat pistol?"

From behind him, she caught the barest whisper of movement.

She smiled, ducking as a heat-blast hissed over her head.

"No," she said. "I was just here to distract you."

The surprise barely had time to register on his face before he dropped bonelessly to the ground beside his similarly dispatched companions.

Tanya stepped out from behind him, wearing that smile that Ysbel had fallen in love with so many years ago. "I think that's all of them,

Ysi," she said. "Shall we go?"

Within a few minutes they were in the mouth of the alley facing a squat, wide, heavily guarded building, the street outside lined with officers outfitted in heat-shields and masks.

"So," she said quietly to Lev. "We made it. Now what?"

Jez grinned. "Genius, you take Masha and Ivan and go with Tae. I'll help Ysbel and Tanya."

And perhaps it wasn't the same grin it would have been, before her ship had been destroyed, but Ysbel felt a sudden and unexpected surge of relief at the sight.

"You have a heat pistol, you idiot?" Ysbel whispered to the pilot.

Jez shot her a skeptical glance.

Ysbel shook her head, smiling despite herself. "Well, let's give these others some time to get through the door," she said.

Jez nodded, and the three of them crept out of the mouth of the small alley.

The building itself was set apart from the other buildings on the street, and surrounded by a low half-wall. That could provide cover —or distraction.

Right now, she'd go with distraction.

"Jez," she whispered. "Keep them looking at you. I'll set an explosive."

Jez grinned. "Gotta say, sometimes I'm a little jealous of Tanya, honestly. That's damn hot."

Before Ysbel could retort, Jez stepped out of the alley, raised her pistol, and fired it at the guard closest to the door.

He spun, heatshield glowing. "What the hell—"

"Looked a little chilly there," remarked Jez. "Thought you could use some warming up." Then she yelped, sprinted down the street, and dived into another alley as the air around her lit with heat-blasts.

Ysbel stepped cautiously out, and, after a quick glance around, made her careful way towards the low wall.

Not that caution was really necessary—Jez had at least three quarters of the guards staring in her direction, heat guns drawn. The fact they hadn't all left their posts yet spoke to their professionalism, but even the most professional guard would be hard-pressed to deal with a force of nature like Jez.

Ysbel shook her head. Let that girl do what she was good at, and she was very, very good at it.

She glanced at Tanya.

She'd already slipped through the gate, and was scaling the wall of the building with practiced ease to perch, at last, on a small outcropping over the doorway, where she'd be partially sheltered by the decorative brickwork, but have a clear view of the street below her.

Ysbel sighed in relief and surveyed the wall, pulling out a packet of explosive gel and dripped it carefully into the space between the stones.

From the corner of her eye, she watched the place where Jez had disappeared.

Some of the guards must have gone after her, finally, because there were shouts and cursing, but none of them seem to have come from the pilot.

She finished, and tapped her com. "Alright, you lunatic," she whispered. "You can stop distracting them now."

"Appreciate the sentiment," Jez drawled breathlessly, "but they're pretty damn distracted. Could use a hand, if you're not doing anything else."

Ysbel shook her head, yanked out her heat gun, and ran for the centre of the chaos that almost always meant Jez had been there.

When she reached the pilot, she was in the middle of a full-on brawl with three guards.

Ysbel stepped forward, dropping the first guard with a blow to his throat. He staggered back, choking, and she grabbed another guard by the arm, and, with a grunt of effort, sent him crashing into the last of the guards. Then she yanked Jez behind the shelter of a building.

"Are you alright, you idiot?" Ysbel snapped.

"Yeah," panted Jez. "Just having some fun. Give me a second to catch my breath."

"Lev, are you ready?" Ysbel asked through the com. "And before you ask, yes, Jez is fine."

"Ready," said Lev.

"Good. On my count, then. Three. Two. One."

She hit the controller.

The wall around the compound vaporized, the echo of the explosion rolling through the streets.

She and Jez peered out from their shelter. The officers who hadn't already left their posts had dived for cover, and from the looks of it, Lev and the others had slipped through while they were distracted.

"Well," whispered Jez, still grinning despite the black eye rapidly forming on her face. "Guess that's our cue."

They dived from the alley and sprinted for the building entrance.

The officers were starting to raise their heads now, and Ysbel hit the second controller.

Another section of wall vaporized.

When they reached the others, Tae was bent over the door lock, face creased in concentration.

The guards recovered from the second blast faster than the first, and already one or two of them had scrambled cautiously to their feet.

They hadn't caught sight of the group at the door yet, but it would be a matter of seconds.

"How much longer?" asked Ysbel.

Tae turned to glare at her. "I'm working as fast as I can."

One of the guards half-turned, then staggered back as Tanya's heat-blast hit her squarely in the chest.

"Got it!" said Tae, raising his head.

He tapped the lock. It clicked, and the door swung open.

"Tanya, we're in," Ysbel whispered into her com.

A moment later, Tanya was beside them.

They slipped through the door, and Tae slammed it behind them, slapping a lock scrambler on the lock.

"If anyone saw us, that should keep them busy for a bit," he said grimly. "I hope that's all we'll need. Lev, you know where we're going?"

Lev nodded.

For just a moment, Ysbel remembered the frightened look on Olya's face, Misko's terrified screams.

"Good," she said, her tone grim. "Then let's take this machine down once and for all. And then we can deal with Evka."

31

Lev, day 8, afternoon

The hallways were disconcertingly quiet—once or twice they had to duck down a small corridor as a huddle of people passed, talking quietly amongst themselves. Lev shivered slightly.

Jez came up beside him as he led them carefully forward, slipping her hand into his, and he turned and gave her a quick smile.

And then they turned onto a long hallway, with a thick steel door at the end.

"I think we've found it," he said quietly.

He could feel the tension in his shoulders as Tae bent over the lock set into the heavy steel doors.

At last, it clicked, and Tae pushed open the door.

It swung inward without a protest, revealing a massive room, choked with machinery.

They'd done it. Somehow, against all the absurd, ridiculous odds, they'd made it here. And with Evka locked down in her lab, all that remained was to destroy the machine. Once that was done, they'd have the leisure to deal with Evka herself.

But somehow, he couldn't shake the unease stirring in the back of his brain.

He'd gone up against Evka more times than he'd ever wanted, over the past few weeks and months. And sometimes, with their entire crew using everything at their disposal, they'd managed to delay her, or distract her, or disrupt her plans.

But he'd never, not once, won.

He took a deep breath, let go his grip on Jez's hand, and stepped past Tae into the room. The others followed, their footsteps echoing on the hard floor.

The room was massive, but the capacitors to run the program took up the majority of the space. The hum of them running would be all but deafening under normal circumstances—but then, circumstances were far from normal. For one thing, the power grid wasn't normally in a state of vaporization.

And there, in the corner—the control panel.

Normally, he would have thought it comically large—the controls spread over an area almost as wide as his body was long, the massive screen in front as high as a two-story building. But here, the panel was dwarfed by the capacitors, and looked almost small in comparison.

"So," said Ysbel quietly, coming to stand beside him. "We blow it up and it's over?"

Lev shook his head, frowning at the controls. "Not yet. Tae, can you get me a scan? Evka's not one to leave things to chance, and even without power, blowing the capacitors may trigger a backup sequence to run. I don't want the program backed up anywhere, if we can help it."

Tae nodded and stepped forward, but Lev could see in his face the same unease Lev felt.

This had been too easy.

It seemed an absurd thing to say, considering they'd all barely lived through it, but—this was Evka they were working against.

And it had been much too easy.

He glanced around the room as Tae worked.

"Ysbel," he said. "Once Tae and I disable whatever internal traps she's set, we'll need to take this down. But there are apartment complexes outside. Can you take down just this building?"

Ysbel gave him a flat look. "Olya could do that, I think," she said. "Give me a minute to look it over, and I'll set the charges."

He nodded, and Tanya and Ysbel started over to the massive capacitors, peering at the base of them calculatingly and speaking in low tones.

"Genius. You alright?"

He looked over, startled. Jez was watching him, concern on her face.

He managed a small smile. "I'm—fine. Just being overly paranoid, I think."

Tae looked up, frowning. "I've got the scan, but I can't read it."

Lev crossed over to the control panel and glanced down at the readout on Tae's com.

He shook his head. "No wonder. She's written the whole damn thing in code. It looks like something based off the original equation that runs the Protocol." He chewed on his lip for a moment, scanning it. "I think I know what she's done, though," he said at last. "Give me a few minutes to decode it, and we should be able to take it down."

Tae nodded, turning back to the control panel.

Then Jez cursed loudly, and there was the momentary sound of a scuffle.

Lev spun, and swore through his teeth.

Evka stood there. Jez was holding her, and she'd twisted Evka's arm up behind her back, but the look on Evka's face was not one of fear.

Despite the cold fury under her expression, she was wearing a look of mild interest, as if studying a math problem that had taken her longer to work out than she'd expected.

"Hello, Lev," she said quietly.

"What are you doing here?" he snapped.

She smiled. "I should be asking you the same question. But I suspect I already know. Although I would be curious to discover how you found this place."

"Shut up," he growled. "Have you seen what's happening in the damn streets? You're finished, Evka."

His heart was pounding.

Why wasn't she afraid? She should be. She couldn't honestly think she could call on their old camaraderie and he'd let her go, could she?

"Tanya, tie her up," he said, turning back to the equation on Tae's screen.

Damn this to hell, what did she know that he didn't?

From the corner of his eye, he saw Tanya step forward. Ysbel had drawn her heat pistol and was pointing it at Evka's face, but Evka made no move to resist as Tanya bound her.

His brain was spinning, and he was having a hard time focusing on the numbers and letters on the screen in front of him.

He took a deep breath and tried to steady his heart rate. "Ysbel," he said quietly. "How soon can you have the explosives in place to blow this?"

She shrugged. "Maybe—fifteen minutes? Twenty, at the outside."

"Good," he said. "I'll have this decoded by then, and it shouldn't take Tae long to disable it once I have it."

Ysbel nodded and pulled out her explosives. "Tanya?" she said. "Do you want to help me? Jez can keep an eye on Evka."

Jez stepped forward, a dangerous grin on her face, her pistol loose in her hand.

Lev shook his head and forced his mind back to the screen in front of him.

Evka was tied up. She was caught, and there was nothing she could do to them right now.

But something about the way his pulse pounded in his throat told him he didn't honestly believe that.

Just get through the code. As soon as he did, they could destroy the machine, and then Evka could do her worst.

And then there was a small sound, and he frowned down at his holoscreen for a moment before he realized it had come from the machine itself.

Something cold started in his chest.

From behind him came the soft whir of a machine starting up, then another, then another.

Slowly, not wanting to look, he turned.

The massive rows of capacitors were blinking to life, one by one.

"What—" Tanya began, her voice tight.

"Lev." Evka's voice was still mild, and faintly amused. "You've developed quite a taste for destruction. But did you honestly think I hadn't prepared for something like this? Surely you knew me better than that."

He spun on her. "Shut up, or I'll have Ysbel shoot you right here."

"I wouldn't, if I were you," she said quietly. "The Protocol is active. If you shoot me, the program will kill every one of you in this room. And even if I'm dead, that won't save anyone. It will just mean someone else's finger on the button. I know you hate me, but even you have to admit there are thousands of people in government who would use this for much worse purposes than I would."

He stared at her, breathing heavily.

She smiled. "I came here to switch the program over to the backup power source. The commands have the highest security rating, and are authorized to override all other reroutes—including the ones you set to the hospitals and apartment complexes. That was very humane of you to think of them, by the way. But the Secretary General himself agreed with me that this was more important than anything else the backup power could be used for." She shook her head. "He and I both knew there would be people who would be angry when we first rolled out the Protocol, and who would want to destroy it. And I knew, as I was constructing this, that you and your friends were still out there somewhere."

She turned, studying Masha, who was leaned up against the wall of the room, her face drawn with pain. "I congratulate you," she said, her voice still amused. "You certainly know how to put together a team."

Masha didn't respond. Whether it was because she had nothing to say, or because it was taking all of her considerable force of will to stay on her feet, Lev couldn't say.

Evka turned back to him. "Lev." There was something in her voice, infinitely familiar, infinitely reassuring—infinitely horrifying, now that he knew who Evka really was.

Who he'd almost become.

Because he had. He'd been very, very close to becoming another Evka.

He glanced over at Jez.

He'd spent seven years hating Jez, before he'd met her, dreaming of ways to make her pay for what she done when she'd stolen an unstealable cargo, and ripped away his dreams and his future at the university.

Perhaps, after all, she'd saved him even back then. Even before he knew her.

"Please instruct your pilot to release me," Evka said quietly.

Lev drew in a long breath. "Jez?" he said quietly.

He could see the uncertainty in Jez's face, the hard anger when she glanced at Evka. But she just nodded, and did as he asked.

The ropes fell, and Evka stepped forward, shaking her wrists to bring the circulation back.

She moved over to the machine, and he stepped to one side as she ran her fingers lightly along controls. For one absurd second the gesture reminded him of Jez, the way she'd touched the controls of the *Ungovernable*—as if they were her part of her. As if they were the most precious thing she could imagine.

Before Evka had taken the ship to break down for parts.

"Step back against the wall, please, all of you." Evka's voice was still mild. "And drop your weapons. It appears whatever your tech friend did to the program in your heads wasn't enough to last through the system's hard restart. You have no protection, except my current goodwill."

Lev risked a glance at Tae, but the look on Tae's face told him Evka was telling the truth.

"Go on, backs against the wall," she said.

They did as she asked.

Evka must have noticed his expression as he watched her, because she shook her head, a small smile on her face.

"Lev." There was so much affection in the word that he met her eyes despite himself.

"You were my brightest student," she said quietly. "I truly wish that we could have ended as friends."

"And I wish you hadn't tricked me and lied to me, and tried to bloody well kill everyone I love." His voice choked.

She sighed. "It wasn't me who changed, Lev. The sixteen-year-old you would have been thrilled with what we've accomplished. But then, the sixteen-year-old you was wiser, I think, than you are now. At sixteen, you knew how to be logical. Now, look at you." She gestured. "Here you are with a group of convicts and scam artists, in love with an impulsive ex-smuggler who stole your dreams of a professorship. Friends with a street kid and a mass murderer, working beside someone who betrayed you only days ago, because you were too soft-hearted to leave her to suffer the consequences she'd earned. The sixteen-year-old you would have won this battle of wits, Lev, I have no doubt. But then, the sixteen-year-old you wouldn't have started it in the first place." She caught his eyes, and her gaze was piercing. "But you've lost. Not because of any inherent lack of ability —simply because you ceased to value logic and rationality, and let sentiment take their place. You could have done great things, Lev."

He watched her for a long, long time.

She was right, in a way.

He could so easily have become her.

He'd seen the truth of it in Masha's face, months ago on Grigory's ship. She'd understood that he'd do anything to get what he wanted. And the fact that what he wanted was to keep Jez safe did nothing to ease the inherent selfishness of it, because he hadn't asked Jez. He hadn't asked any of them. He'd wanted what he wanted, and would have done whatever it took to get it.

But—

He tore his gaze from Evka, and glanced at Jez.

The reckless grin was still spread across her face, but under the adrenaline-bright spark in her eyes, he could see the pain.

She'd given up the thing she loved more than anything else in the system.

More than anything else in the system, of course, except for him. Him and the rest of this ragged band of misfits, backs against the wall, waiting to die.

She caught his eye, and he gave her a small smile.

He turned back to Evka. "Perhaps you're right," he said. "Perhaps you're right about all of it. I was logical, and rational, and I knew nothing at all about life. I didn't need a professor to teach me that—I needed a smuggler pilot, and a street kid, and a demolitions expert, and someone who could bring all of us together. And what I learned is, losing a battle of wits, losing my life, even—that was never what I should have been afraid of. I should have been afraid of never finding what makes it worth living in the first place. And as smart as you are—you never knew that at all." He shook his head. "You may have won. But I'll never regret not turning out like you."

32

Masha, day 8, afternoon

Masha leaned against the wall. She was dimly conscious of the others, lined up next to her, of Lev and Evka talking, but most of her concentration was on fighting back the pain in her broken leg as it pulsed through her body.

She wasn't sure she could. She wasn't certain she wouldn't simply pass out here, on the floor.

She'd spent so long praying for unconsciousness. It would be the height of irony if she were to achieve it now, when she least wanted it.

"Hold out your hands behind you," said Evka, voice brisk and businesslike. She'd walked to a cupboard and pulled it open, lifting out seven pairs of mag cuffs. She brought them over, and clicked the cuffs onto their wrists, then stood back, smiling slightly. "Well. Constrained for the moment, at least." She sighed. "But it won't last, will it? I can't afford to let you live, not even to make a demonstration of your deaths. And so——"

"Wait," croaked Masha, her voice harsh with pain.

She wasn't sure, yet, what she'd say.

But she was certain that she couldn't watch this without at least trying to stop it.

Evka turned to her, eyebrows raised. "You have something to say?" She paused. "You're an interesting person, Masha Volkova—you kill seven thousand people in ten minutes, without a hint of remorse, but you couldn't kill these six."

From the corner of her eye, Masha could see Tae tapping his wrist restlessly against the wall.

And she could hear, faintly, through her earpiece, the words spelled out in pilots' code on her private line.

Masha. Keep her talking. I need to get to the control panel.

She didn't dare glance in his direction—Evka was far too perceptive for her to risk something like that.

She took a deep breath. "Evka," she said quietly. "I'm afraid you've underestimated me."

Evka's eyebrows rose higher, and she could see Lev stiffen.

He still didn't trust her, and she couldn't blame him for it.

But she'd learned something from those hideous hours of torture after all—if she died saving this crew, she'd consider her life well spent. No matter what else she did or didn't accomplish.

"Please, explain my miscalculation," said Evka, that note of interest back in her voice. She sounded so much like Lev, when he'd been given a new and novel problem to solve, that Masha almost smiled.

"It wasn't because of sentiment that I chose not to kill them," she said, putting all the calm assurance she could muster into her words. "I assumed, after observing me as long as you did, you'd know better." She paused and smiled at the woman. "I was simply waiting for a better opportunity."

Again, that stiffening in Lev's posture.

But Jez, beside him, was watching her with that slightly skeptical expression, and again, Masha had to stop herself from smiling.

Jez had always trusted her. She still wasn't sure why. She still wasn't sure if it had been Jez's ridiculous, unshakable trust, against all evidence she was wrong, that had made it impossible, in the end, for Masha to betray them.

"I see," said Evka, making no effort to hide the irony in her tone. "You simply hoped the torturers would get bored before they'd killed you, is that it?"

Masha smiled again, shaking her head. "Come, Evka. You're more intelligent than that. Pain is … unpleasant, but in pursuit of a sufficiently important goal—" She shrugged, and gestured with her bound hands at the others. "I know Lev, better than you, apparently. I've watched him over the past several months. Jez too, and Tae, and Ysbel and Tanya and Ivan. I knew they'd come back for me. I knew, when I forced the Secretary General to release my aide, that she'd run to find my associate, who was waiting to get word to my crew. You should have seen how much that aide cared for me. She would have died for me, I think. You think you know human nature, Evka, but you're rather an amateur."

The look in Evka's eyes was now bordering on respect.

The look in Lev's was bordering on horror.

And beside her, Tae had shifted slightly towards the controls.

Her heart was pounding in her throat. But she managed to keep her face perfectly calm.

She had, after all, decades of practice.

Evka sighed slightly. "You expect me to believe you gambled your life—or I should say, perhaps, your death, by torture—on the hope your crew would come save you, despite everything you'd done?" But there was a note of uncertainty in her voice.

Again, Masha gave her a small smile. "The gamble seems to have paid off, hasn't it?" She kept her voice light.

Evka studied her for a few moments.

From the corner of her eye, she saw Tae take another small step. But Evka's attention was focused solely on her.

"Supposing I believed you, then yes, you predicted their actions with remarkable prescience," said Evka at last. "But as to whether your gamble paid off—" She made a small gesture. "I assumed being taken prisoner in the control room of my Protocol machine was not quite the win you were betting on."

Masha gave her that bland, pleasant look she'd perfected over the years. "Or perhaps this was exactly the win I was betting on," she said quietly. "It was inevitable that your Protocol would become active. However, it was also inevitable that it would be unpopular, in the beginning. That there would be people who wanted to take it down. I knew you were fond of Lev, and that you would have appreciated his help to protect against such attempts. But I also knew you underestimated him. And I knew you had no idea how ingenious my crew could be, given sufficient motivation." She shifted slightly to take some of the weight off her shattered knee, wincing despite herself. "And now, Evka, that they've taken down your Protocol, set the entire city on fire, pushed you all the way up against the wall— because you know as well as I do that regaining control after a fiasco like this one will not be simple—now that you've seen what they can do, perhaps you will understand the value of the bargain I'm prepared to make."

Tae had moved slightly farther, a few centimeters perhaps, his entire body tense.

She had no idea what he was planning on doing—the likelihood was it would end up with all of them dying—but she'd asked her crew to trust her so many times before. And they had.

The very least she could do was return the favor.

"You're right," she continued. "Lev, and all of these others, made the mistake of allowing themselves to get attached. I, on the other hand, spent years training myself not to do so. Caring for someone weakens you, and weakness causes you to lose. And believe me, I've never been one to lose."

Masha had to fight back a small smile at her own words.

Evka honestly believed it—that love made you weak.

She hadn't seen, like Masha had seen, Tae pushing himself to the edge of passing out from exhaustion to keep the crew safe, Ysbel and Tanya risking their lives, Lev pushing past his ingrained selfishness day after day, action after action, sentence after sentence, because he didn't want to hurt Jez.

Jez, giving up her ship.

And Evka thought that this thing that made her crew so much more powerful than Masha would have ever believed or understood was a weakness.

She loved this crew. She loved them desperately and hopelessly. She loved them as she'd never allowed herself to love anyone, not since the day her parents had died, and she learned how much pain love could bring.

And yes, it was true that love hurt. That love gave you a softness that could be exploited.

But it also granted you strength beyond your abilities.

Strength to stand up to torture.

Tae had moved again, ever so slightly, and she could feel the tension in her own body matching his.

She forced her muscles to relax. She wouldn't give away whatever he was going to try.

And then, out of the corner of her eye, she noticed something else.

The smallest movement of Lev's hand, bound behind his back.

And in his hand, a small heat pistol.

Nothing that would kill Evka, certainly. She was standing too far away for something that size to be effective, and she was almost certainly wearing a heat shield.

But then, Lev wasn't looking at Evka.

He was watching her.

Fear rose in her throat, just for a moment, mingled with an almost hysterical amusement.

She'd finally learned what loyalty meant, and what love meant, and the price she was willing to pay for it.

And she'd be asked to pay that price, because Lev believed her story of betrayal.

But somehow, she kept her eyes fixed on Evka.

"And what's your bargain?" asked Evka at last, her voice still faintly curious. "What do you want, and what are you willing to give?"

Masha gave a slight shrug. "I want what I've always wanted. I want to take the Secretary General's place. He's an old man. He won't last long, and you know that as well as I do. It would be a benefit to you as well, I think—you'll need someone with the strength of will to purge everyone who won't agree to your program."

"And you don't think I can do that on my own?" asked Evka, a small smile playing on her mouth. "I have my Protocol. I already have a list drawn up of who will serve my purposes, and who won't, and the Secretary General has signed off on it. The police are eating out of my hand, and when I go through the army and kill the generals and captains who've defied me, and torture the families of some of the more outspoken rank-and-file soldiers, they'll come around. Why would I need you?"

"Because people are illogical," said Masha. "They're unpredictable. You kill a minister, hoping their under-minister is in your pocket, and the murder, instead, makes her brave enough to turn on you. How long is your list of ministers you plan to kill? Twenty? Fifty? One hundred? I promise you, you'll have to double that, at least. You start killing ministers with your Protocol, and suddenly the others begin to feel their own mortality."

"I'll kill all of them if I must," said Evka, voice still calm and thoughtful. "I hope it doesn't come to that, but if it does—" She shrugged. "But I'm certain they'll come to their senses after enough of them die. I have no desire to take over the government. I simply want to be permitted to run my Protocol in peace."

"And I have no desire to take over your Protocol. I am simply interested in politics. You know how this system runs, Evka—there have been excesses, abuses. This system killed my parents, and thousands of others. We don't have to get in each other's way—you are the seat of power, now that your Protocol is working. I saw that in the Secretary General's office, when I saw you there. And I realized the Secretary General was not the one I needed. You were. I can keep you from having to deal with the mess of politics, and you can give me what I want. It would be a mutually beneficial arrangement."

Lev's finger shifted towards the trigger.

She forced her voice to remain light. "So. I'll make you the offer that I made the Secretary General—I'll deliver you my crew, in exchange for a position."

Evka's look was calculating, expression faintly amused. "Perhaps you hadn't noticed, Masha, but unlike the Secretary General, I already have your crew."

Masha raised an eyebrow. "Do you? You can kill them, certainly. But you want to use them. And you can't. If you haven't proved that to yourself over these past few days, I'm not sure you've been paying attention."

She leaned forward slightly. "Me, on the other hand—I know them. I've worked with them, for a very long time. And I can tell you exactly what will make them behave—who to threaten, and how hard to push. I can give you access to all of their skills. And you want that, badly. Perhaps you even need it. Because yes, the Protocol is functional. But perhaps right now, somewhere in the system, there's another Lev, another Tae, another Ysbel, just a child. And perhaps, as they grow up in this new system you've created, they get restless. And perhaps they decide the Protocol should end. It's inevitable it will happen, and you know that as well as I do. And when it does, Evka, you'll need all the talent you can get. It would be a shame if, instead, you'd left it dead on the floor of this room."

Evka was still watching her, a small frown of consideration on her forehead.

Tae was almost in position for—whatever he intended to do. A few centimeters, and he could launch himself at the control panel and keep out of Evka's reach for a few brief seconds.

Lev's finger was firmly on the trigger.

And then there was the faintest sound, the slight scuff of Tae's boot against the hard floor.

Evka half turned.

Lev twisted, bringing his cuffed hands from behind his back, just enough to aim the pistol.

Masha tasted the iron tang of fear.

For the briefest second, Lev's eyes met hers.

And then he pulled the trigger.

There was the soft fizz of the heat-blast, and then, for a few moments, the room was completely silent.

Evka glanced down at the blackened mark in the center of her tunic, the heat shield showing through the burnt fabric, and then up at Lev, a small, disdainful smile on her lips. "Lev. You, of all people, resorting to violence. Risking your life for your crew—even as you listen to one of them betray you."

"Perhaps she did," said Lev. His voice was quiet, but calm. "Perhaps I made the same mistake I did when I was sixteen, and trusted someone I shouldn't have." He turned slightly, and caught Masha's eye. "But—somehow, I don't believe I did."

Evka opened her mouth to say something.

But whatever it was was cut off as Tae leapt forward across the room.

33

Tae, day 8, afternoon

Tae lunged towards the control panel, ignoring Evka's shout of fury and Ivan's horrified gasp.

He had to make it. Just a few steps. He had to make it.

He was halfway there, already fumbling for his com.

Evka turned, starting for the control panel as well.

"Ivan!" he shouted through his teeth, not sure why, or what he needed Ivan to do.

But he needed something, desperately, and even though he didn't know what it was, something brought Ivan's name to his lips automatically.

Ivan stepped forward, and grabbed Evka's wrist with his bound hands.

She struggled, but Ivan had been able to hold back Vlatka in prison, given the motivation.

Tae was at the control panel, twisted backwards, his cuffed hands straining to reach the controls as he fumbled feverishly with his com.

"Let me go, or I kill him," Evka snapped.

From the corner of his eye, Tae could see the indecision in Ivan's face, and he closed his eyes for half a second, praying desperately to the Lady.

"No," said Ivan. His face was very pale, but his voice was firm.

Ysbel had half-turned, lifting something in her bound hands, but he couldn't see what she was doing, and he didn't have time to care.

Ysbel moved.

Evka slapped a button on her com.

Tae's muscles gave out beneath him, a pain like he'd never imagined searing through his head.

As he fell, he glimpsed, for an instant, the anguish on Ivan's face.

But Ivan's hands didn't loosen from Evka's wrist.

For a few moments, Tae lay stunned.

He felt like someone had turned a damn shock-stick to full power, then swung it like a club into his head. But somehow—he still wasn't certain how—he was alive.

He staggered grimly to his feet.

"What—" began Evka.

He slapped his com, bringing up the holoscreen, and twisted over his shoulder to see it.

There.

He managed, with straining fingers, to hit the command.

He tapped his com against the main power switch, then straightened, leaning back against the controls as his head spun and the room spun.

Evka was hitting the button on her com, over and over, but this time he didn't even feel a jolt.

"Don't bother," he croaked. "I saw the secondary wire-in when I was looking at your system a few days ago. I didn't know where the power would come from, or how you'd tie it in. I wasn't even sure what it was for, or if you'd finished it. But I thought it might come in useful. So—" he shrugged, and had to catch himself to keep from falling over. "I slaved it. Your entire program is slaved to my com now. You can press whatever button you want—I've overridden everything."

They were all staring at him now. Their faces were variations on astonishment, shock, and in Jez's case, utter delight.

Evka looked murderous.

At last, Ysbel gave him a self-satisfied smile, looking very much like her daughter. "You were right, you know, Tae," she said. "I could turn up my device enough to short out Evka's programming. And it didn't even knock you out. It's just a matter of playing with frequencies."

He turned and stared at her. "You—just tested this? Now? On me?"

She shrugged. "Evka was going to kill you, so there wasn't really much to lose."

For a moment, he was rendered completely speechless.

Ysbel snorted in amusement. "Tae. I've worked on weapons for how many years now? I think I know what will kill someone and what won't."

"I know you know what will kill someone," he muttered. "It's the other part I'm not so sure about."

She was still chuckling.

He shook his head and turned back to his com. "Give me a minute," he grumbled. "I'll get a key written for the mag cuffs and send it through to your coms."

His voice cracked like he was a teenager again, and there was a pounding, throbbing ache in the back of his head, but—

He was alive. He hadn't honestly thought he would be.

It was hard to get his eyes to focus on the holo-keyboard that he still had to strain over his shoulder to see, but the hack was something he done so often that his fingers knew it almost by heart.

Within a few moments, he'd sent it through the rest of the coms, and he could hear the *clink* of mag cuffs hitting the ground around him as he released his own cuffs.

Ivan was beside him a moment later, expression frantic. "Tae. You're alright?"

Tae managed a small nod, and collapsed into Ivan's arms.

For a few blissful moments, he didn't think about anything in the system except Ivan.

And then, somewhere behind them, Jez made a small, horrified sound.

They both spun around.

Evka had something in her hand, and it took Tae a moment to realize it was a knife.

And as Jez grabbed for her, she threw it.

It wasn't a strong throw—Evka didn't look like someone who depended much on physical strength—but it was enough.

As Jez shoved Evka backwards, an instant too late, it scraped a shallow red line across Lev's thigh.

Jez had Evka by the arms, and she yanked her around, slapping cuffs on her wrists, then turned.

Lev had reached out a hand, supporting himself on the wall, and Tae saw the moment Jez realized what had happened. What must have been on the knife.

She gave a choked cry and leapt across the room, caching Lev as he staggered, and lowered him gently to the ground.

Ysbel stepped over and grabbed Evka by the front of the jacket. "What kind of poison was that? Tell me, before I take your limbs off one at a time." There was a tone in her voice that would have terrified Tae even if he hadn't known Ysbel as well as he did.

"You could, I have no doubt," said Evka, and there was still that note of calm in her voice. "But Lev would die. It's a poison I've been working on for some time now, and I possess the only antidote. But I'll tell you where it is—for a price."

Jez jumped to her feet and strode over. Her face was set, but Tae could see the sharp fear in it. "What's your price?" she demanded.

Evka glanced around the room and sighed. "I'd ask your friend to unslave my machine, but I know that's the one thing you'd let Lev die for. So instead—" she gave a small smile. "I'll ask one of you to come with me. Someone I can kill if the rest of you try to follow me as I leave. I've worked very hard to stay alive these past several years, and I don't intend the effort to go to waste."

There was a moment's silence.

Then Jez said, quietly, "I'll go. Give Lev the antidote, and I'll go."

"Jez—" Lev choked.

"No," said Masha. "Let her."

Tae turned to stare at Masha.

She was looking at Jez, an odd smile on her face.

"Yes," said Tanya slowly. "I'm with Masha. We'll need the rest of us here to take down the machine. Let Jez go."

Jez closed her eyes for a moment, but there was a peace in her face Tae hadn't thought he'd see there again.

"Jez," said Evka. "Unlock my cuffs, then walk to that cupboard, please, and open it."

Jez did as she was told. Tae could see the tension in her muscles.

"Bring me the mag cuffs and the walking cuffs. These are a different make, so they shouldn't be affected by your friend's lockpick, but to make extra certain I'll ask you to remove your com. As I mentioned earlier, whatever your street kid friend did to it is no longer in effect."

Slowly, Jez pulled off her com and dropped it to the floor.

The sound of it hitting the ground was loud in the silence.

"Now, come over here, please," said Evka. "Tanya, Ysbel, step back."

She fastened the mag cuffs around Jez's wrists, then, pulling Jez with her, crossed over to a small cupboard. She took out a heat gun and a vial. She cocked the gun against the back of Jez's neck with one hand, and with the other, tossed the vial in a low underhand towards where Lev lay prone on the floor.

Tanya stepped forward, snatching it out of the air.

"Intravenously. Three cc's should be plenty, considering the amount I had on the blade," said Evka pleasantly. "I won't wait around to watch—I'm certain your medical skill is up to the task."

Lev's face was completely bloodless, his eyes closed, and sweat beaded on his forehead, but he managed to open his eyes one last time as Evka shoved Jez ahead of her out of the room.

Jez turned over her shoulder to look at him. "Hey, genius," she said. "I—I love you."

"Jez—" he muttered.

And then Evka closed the door, and they were gone.

34

Jez, day 8, afternoon

The sound of the door clicking shut was absurdly loud in Jez's ears.

She could still see Lev lying on the floor, his face bloodless. She could still feel the limp weight of him in her arms.

"Walk," snapped Evka from behind her.

For one desperate moment, she was tempted to turn around and try her luck.

But she could hear from Evka's footsteps that she was far enough behind Jez that even if Jez wasn't cuffed, she'd easily get off a shot before Jez could reach her.

Besides—Tanya and Ivan knew what they were doing. Lev would be fine.

And … well, and so would she. Because the thought of being locked up for damn well ever with this bastard—because hell, she was pretty damn sure Evka didn't plan on letting her walk out of this —was subsumed in the sick, desperate relief at the memory of Tanya catching the small vial of antidote.

So instead, she shuffled awkwardly forward, walking-cuffs catching on her ankles at every step.

They walked through the echoing hallways until finally, Evka paused in front of a hololift, pushing Jez in as the doors opened.

The doors hissed closed behind them, and Jez shifted, trying to get the too-tight cuffs to stop biting into her wrists.

"I sincerely hope you're not thinking of making trouble," said Evka, her voice tight.

"Me? Make trouble?" She managed a grin, somehow. "You know, for someone as smart as you're supposed to be, funny how an irresponsible, unreliable, damn fool idiot of a smuggler pilot out-gamed you so many times."

"Believe me, Jez Solokov, I've watched you." Evka's voice was icy. "You work with some very smart people. But all you are is the muscle."

Jez's grin widened. "Nah. Ysbel's the muscle. They keep me around for my looks. Need something to make them feel better after looking at an ugly bastard like you."

Evka's face darkened. "I planned on keeping you alive," she said. "Don't make me change my mind."

Jez snickered. "That's assuming you have a mind to change. And as far as I've seen—"

The butt of a pistol struck her across the back of the head, and Jez staggered, swearing, as lights burst in her vision.

The door to the lift slid open.

"Walk," snapped Evka. "And don't say another word."

Jez cast a quick glance over her shoulder as she stepped out.

She hadn't seen Evka that angry for a while. Which, honestly, was a bit funny, but by the same token—

She blinked at the pain in her head.

Well, she wasn't exactly sure she wanted to die just yet.

Evka led her down another long hallway, until they came out into a large, open, underground room with a ceiling door that apparently served as a hanger bay.

A sleek in-atmosphere craft sat in the middle of the floor, obviously new, and obviously well-taken care of.

Evka muttered something into her com, and a few moments later a man stepped out from a small door in the back of the hangar bay. His eyebrows raised slightly as he saw Jez and Evka, but he didn't comment, simply dipped his head respectfully and said, "Evka. What do you need?"

"I'd like you to fly me out," said Evka, her words short and clipped. "I'll send you the coordinates once we're in the air."

The request must not have been an uncommon one, or else the bastard wasn't very curious, because he didn't ask any further questions. Evka tapped her com, and the ship door slid open for the man to step inside.

Jez raised her eyebrows.

Looked like the pilot couldn't even get into the thing without Evka's permission. Hell, she'd thought Lena was paranoid—

"Get in," said Evka, gesturing with her pistol.

Reluctantly, Jez crossed the floor and climbed the small loading ramp.

It hit her the moment she stepped through into the ship's interior, just like she'd known it would, and for a moment she almost staggered.

Her ship was gone. The ship she'd been created to fly. The entire reason, probably, that she'd been born. The thing she'd been looking for her whole damn life, without really knowing it, until she stepped into that cockpit for the first time, and for the first time felt all the pieces of herself fall into place.

Her beautiful, glorious, perfect angel. Gone.

Evka shoved the pistol into her back, and the pain of it brought her back to herself. "Go," Evka snapped again, and, feeling like a sleepwalker, Jez went.

When they came out into the small main cabin, Evka gestured her to a seat.

Jez didn't even bother to resist.

Evka tapped something in her hand—clearly she'd intended it to be inconspicuous, but the bastard had obviously never sat down at a gambling table—and Jez felt the ship come to life beneath her.

For a moment, at the feel of it, the memory of another ship coming to life under her, singing in her bones and thrumming in her veins, almost made her lose her composure.

Evka eyed her as the ship warmed up. "Unfortunate, isn't it?" she said. Her voice was still calm and faintly amused, but Jez could hear the hatred under it.

Despite everything, the sound sparked something warm and satisfying her chest.

At least she hadn't lost her touch.

She raised one shoulder in a listless shrug. "What, having to sit here and look at your damn ugly face? Yeah, guess it is."

She was rewarded with a slight tightening around the corner of Evka's mouth.

"You gave away your ship to save them." There was a sort of viciousness under Evka's pleasant tone. "And then, when push came to shove—they just let you go. I guess you weren't as important to them as you thought." She shook her head. "I don't blame them. I hear you're an excellent pilot, but now that you don't have a ship, that's not worth much. And you thought they kept you around because they liked you, didn't you? Thought you were a part of the crew."

She gave Jez a small smile. "Thrown out by your family, thrown out by your smuggler crew, thrown out by everyone who spent more than a few hours around you—no wonder the moment someone gave you a kind word, you crawled over and licked their boots. And Lev, your lover. I've known him for much longer than you have. What, exactly, do you think he sees in you? I've seen him in relationships like this before—he's been kind and attentive and polite, hasn't he? And he'd have studied you until he felt he'd learned everything of value. And then he'd leave. You don't really think he would have stuck around, do you? You can't be that innocent."

Jez watched Evka curiously.

The woman's words were as poisoned as the knife she'd thrown at Lev. And they should have worked. She should be hurting, crying, gutted. These words should have taken her apart.

But they didn't.

Instead, she was sitting here calmly, the words bouncing off her like light-range shots off a heavy shield.

"They were happy for you to leave. You'd served your purpose. And when you offered to come with me—they didn't even protest."

Somehow, despite the aching, empty hole in her chest where her heart had been before she'd lost the *Ungovernable*, Jez found she was smiling.

"You really believe that, don't you, you bastard?" she asked.

Evka frowned at her. "I've lived long enough to be able to read people," she said, her words sharp. "I'm not quite the innocent you are."

"Yeah?" Jez was still smiling, a soft sort of smile that had spread over her face all by itself. "Here's the thing—you think I'm an innocent because I don't believe a damn word you're saying. And I think you're an innocent because you do."

The ship jolted slightly, and Jez winced. No ship deserved to be flown like this.

Evka gave her a small, inscrutable smile. "Well, Jez, I'm glad that you, at least, believe someone cares about you. I'm sure it will make your captivity that much more bearable. But I'm afraid I can't chat at the moment." She stood and turned on her heel, stepping out the narrow door towards the cockpit.

Once she'd left, Jez glanced around the small cabin.

It was sparsely furnished, but comfortable. It had obviously been designed for longer flights, judging by the cooling box next to one of the cupboards she assumed was the supply cupboard.

And the supply cupboard—she raised an eyebrow. That bastard Evka was obviously accustomed to luxury. The cupboard wasn't packed with ration packs and maybe a few bottles of barely drinkable sump—there was expensive alcohol in there, she was any judge, and probably some fresh food.

Which meant, breakable containers.

And this damn pilot was clearly not one of the system's most skilled.

Yeah, her crew had let her go.

But she was pretty damn sure she knew why.

She grinned, and with some effort, pushed herself to her feet.

Staying upright wasn't easy, since her walking-cuffs were so damn tight she couldn't spread her feet for balance, and also since the pilot had apparently never actually learned how to fly a damn ship.

But hell, this was the kind of thing she was good at.

She didn't have her com, but she figured they'd been flying for ten, fifteen standard minutes.

It was probably a couple minutes later that they hit their first patch of turbulence.

Jez grinned again as the ship jolted, and threw herself sideways into the supply cabinet.

She hit it with her shoulder and went down hard, swearing loudly. The cupboard doors had been flung open at her impact, and as the ship jolted again, she ducked her head awkwardly as food and drink canisters clattered around her head.

A bottle of liquor hit the floor and shattered, and the smooth, sharp fumes told Jez it had been expensive.

Pity, really. But it would have been wasted on a plaguer like Evka.

Evka appeared a moment later, her pistol drawn, her face cold.

The ship staggered, and Jez made a clumsy attempt to get to her feet. She let the bouncing of the ship knock her backwards into another supply cupboard, and this one popped open as well, spilling its contents across the deck.

Evka swore through her teeth. "Get up, you idiot, before I shoot you."

"Can't," Jez moaned, trying to sound pathetic. "Damn arms and legs are cuffed."

"Get. Up." Evka brandished the pistol.

Jez hid a grin and made another awkward attempt to rise, only to stumble on one of the food canisters and crash back down amid the sound of shattering glass.

"Get up, or so help me, I will shoot you where you lie."

Jez managed what she hoped was a terrified glance in Evka's direction and stumbled half-way to her feet before falling again. Around her, the food and drink cartridges shattered and burst.

With a sigh of utter exasperation, Evka leaned down, grabbing Jez by one bound wrist.

Jez closed her eyes, savouring the moment.

Then she twisted her wrist from Evka's grasp, rolled up on one shoulder, and kicked out as hard as she could with both feet.

The loud *crack* of her boots hitting Evka's face was the most satisfying thing she'd heard in a long damn time.

Evka staggered backwards, blood spurting from her nose, and Jez twisted, using her momentum to push herself up to her feet.

She was grinning like a damn maniac.

Evka had staggered back against the wall, and Jez crouched next to her, twisting her body enough to allow her to snatch the control chip neatly from Evka's hand. She was still cuffed, sure, but she had a hell of a lot of experience breaking out of places with her hands cuffed.

She cast a last glance at the partially stunned Evka, and staggered towards the cockpit as fast as she could with walking-cuffs on her legs.

Getting the control chip somewhere she could use it was more difficult than it looked—she had to twist backwards, straining her head over her shoulder to see the damn thing at all, and she didn't have a com to pop it into. At last she made do by shoving the bare chip against the control panel and hoping for the best.

She was crouched uncomfortably, looking backwards over her shoulder, when she heard the soft sound of footsteps.

She waited, muscles tense with adrenaline.

The footsteps paused directly behind her.

She straightened abruptly, spinning as she did, and brought her forehead down hard across the bridge of Evka's broken nose.

Evka gave a muffled scream, scrabbling for something in her pocket.

She patted at it, then glanced up, her disbelief visible even through the blood streaming from her swollen nose.

"Looking for this?" Jez drawled, slipping the heat gun that had once been in Evka's pocket down her sleeve and into her bound hands.

"How—" Evka began, voice strained and partially muffled.

Jez winked at her. "Trick I picked up in a little off-world zestava somewhere. Guess even a dumb pilot can learn a thing or two." She leaned closer, her grin showing all of her teeth. "Here's the thing— you thought my crew let me go because they didn't want me around. But that wasn't it. They let me go because they trusted me. And because they knew a damn innocent like you wouldn't stand a chance."

"You stupid, worthless, lazy—"

"Skinny, unreliable, lunatic pilot," Jez finished, still grinning. "See, I can do it too. But you ruined my ship. You tried to kill Lev. And you're not damn well getting away with it."

Evka jerked a small knife out of her sleeve, her face contorted in anger. "I know about you, you pathetic nobody. Too self-righteous to kill people, Lena said, even if they were shooting at you. I know all about your so-called morals, and don't think—"

Jez turned, and shot Evka squarely in the face.

The woman crumpled to the floor and lay where she'd fallen, her limp body shifting slightly with the motion of the ship.

At last Jez bent, slowly, twisting her shoulders so she could grab the woman's wrist in her cuffed hands.

There was no pulse. But then, she hadn't expected there to be.

She straightened, swallowing down the nausea in her throat, and for a moment she stood there, staring down at the body.

It looked—small, after all that.

After everything Evka had done, after how long she'd been hunting them, after however damn many times she'd tried to kill them, Jez had expected something different, somehow. A monster, maybe.

But she was just—a person. Slightly built, neat, with short hair, now smeared and tangled with blood, and modest, unassuming clothing.

She shuddered, and turned away.

The door to the cockpit opened easily enough, now that she could work on it without being interrupted. And the pilot, when confronted with Evka's heat gun, was more than happy to unlock the mag cuffs, under Jez's tutelage and with the help of the ship's maintenance tools, and to cede the pilot seat to her.

And maybe sitting down in a pilot's seat and running her hands over controls that weren't her beautiful angel's was almost enough to break her heart.

But knowing that she was going back to that idiot Lev, to Tae and Ysbel and Tanya and Ivan and that damn bastard Masha, was almost enough to hold it together despite that.

35

Tae, day 8, afternoon

"Get me a syringe and needle, now," Tanya snapped, looking up from where she was bent over Lev. Her expression was grim, and Tae could see the fear in her eyes.

Ivan disentangled himself from Tae and stepped quickly over the cupboards, flinging them open. At last, he pulled out a first-aid kit. He and strode over to kneel beside Tanya, rummaging through it, and a moment later he handed her a needle and syringe. She shook the vial and tipped it, pushing the needle into the liquid and drawing it into the syringe.

Tae's heart was pounding, something sick creeping up the back of his throat.

He hadn't realized, until just this moment, what it would do to him if Lev died. He hadn't realized how much Lev's solid, steady friendship, his dry humour and quick wit, had carried Tae—carried all of them, really.

Ivan held out Lev's arm, and Tae found he was holding his breath as Tanya pushed the contents of the syringe into a vein.

"Medi-scanner," she snapped, not taking her eyes off Lev. Tae bent and grabbed it from where it had fallen, handing it to her, and she touched it to Lev's chest, glancing at the readout.

She closed her eyes for a moment, and Tae was struck with a sudden, sickening terror—

Then she opened them again, and he saw the relief in her face. "It's working, I think," she said. "His pulse is coming back, and his oxygen levels are up again."

Tae took a deep breath, relief flooding through him so strong he was shaky with it.

He could see the same relief on the faces of the others.

Despite Tanya's assurances that his vital signs were getting stronger, it was several standard minutes before Lev's eyes blinked open again.

He looked around in confusion and muttered, "Jez?"

"No, I'm sorry," said Tanya. "It's only me."

"Where's Jez?" Lev's voice held a note of slightly incoherent panic. "Is she alright?"

Tanya sighed. "She's with Evka. But—I'm certain she's alright. You know our pilot." There was a forced humour in her voice, but Lev didn't smile.

"She's with—"

And then he must have remembered, because he fell silent abruptly, his jaw clenched.

"Jez will be fine," said Masha. Her voice was weak, but there was a calm assurance in it that Tae envied.

For a moment, she and Lev locked eyes.

At last, he nodded, slowly, a bit of the tension releasing from his posture.

"Well," said Ysbel, her voice dry. "If anyone could find a way to escape with her hands cuffed behind her back, it would be our pilot. She's done it before." She paused a moment. "Honestly, I suspect we should all be feeling sorry for Evka right now."

Tae managed a small smile, but he couldn't shove away the knot of worry in his stomach.

Jez would be fine. Of course she'd be fine.

She had to be.

For a few moments they stood there, none of them wanting to say anything that might break the thin shell of control Lev was so obviously clinging to. At last, though, Lev glanced up. "What's that noise?" he asked, frowning.

Tae frowned as well.

He'd hardly noticed it in his panic over Lev. But from outside, there was a cacophony of sound—shouting, yelling, ship-horns blaring. His stomach tightened in unconscious panic, the noise much too close to the memories of behind the barricades, in the middle of an attack.

But—

He listened a little closer.

"That sounds like cheering," said Ivan, his own face creased in confusion.

And then Tae turned to stare at Masha.

She was still leaned up against the wall, her expression that of someone trying desperately to cling to consciousness, but when she noticed his glance, she gave a faint nod.

He stared at her, then down at his com, then back at her, unable, for a moment, to speak.

She gave him a small, slightly smug smile.

There was a knock at the door. "Acting Minister?" someone called.

The voice was young, and unfamiliar, and far too eager, and again, they stared at each other.

All except for Masha, whose smile grew broader.

She straightened with an effort and limped to the door. "Radka?" she asked weakly as she pulled it open.

A young woman stood in the doorway, dressed in the uniform of a government aide.

She stared at Masha for a moment, her eyes widening in horror. "They—what did they—" she began in a stunned voice.

"They tortured me," said Masha, her tone calm and businesslike. "But as you can see, I'm fine."

There was a moment of silence, and a look on Radka's face that clearly said she had a different opinion than Masha did as to what constituted 'fine.'

But at last, she seemed to pull herself together. "Acting Minister," she said again. "I—they asked me to find you, because they didn't have a line to your com."

"And what message did they ask you to pass on?" asked Masha patiently.

The girl swallowed. "The Secretary General. He's—stepped down."

Tae stared at the girl, then at Masha.

"If it's not too much trouble, I'd appreciate if someone would explain to me what exactly is going on." Lev's voice was weak, but tinged with irritation.

Tae glanced at Masha, who was speaking quietly with Radka, then shook his head and sighed. "I was next to Masha when Evka pushed us up against the wall. She tapped a message through my com—asked if I could hook her into the government lines." he shrugged. "I—didn't know what she wanted, exactly, but I couldn't see how it could possibly make things worse."

Lev was watching him, the look on his face one of calculating interest. "When you say hook through to the government line," he said slowly, "you mean the general government line? That connects to all the government buildings?"

Tae nodded. "I hacked through to it while we were still behind the barricades weeks ago. So I just had to tie it through to her com signal."

Lev nodded slowly, then glanced at Masha. "So. Everyone in government heard what Evka had planned for them, and that the Secretary General had given his approval." There was the hint of something in his voice that was either amusement, or admiration, or a mixture of both. "I—suspect that didn't go over all that well."

At last the young government aide who'd been talking with Masha nodded and turned to leave. Masha turned back to them, a smile on her face.

Lev raised his eyebrows. "So, Masha, the Secretary General is gone at last. And I assume that now there will be a rash of assassinations of such magnitude it will be a wonder if there are any ministers left to form a government at the end of it. Effective, certainly, but I hadn't realized a system in total anarchy was your end goal." Despite the weakness in his voice, his tone was the same calm calculation that Tae had heard from him so often when he was thinking through a difficult problem.

Masha studied him for a moment. "I'm certain you're right as to what would be the most likely natural fallout of this, Lev," she said at last. "But thankfully, we won't have to test your hypothesis."

Lev frowned, a hint of suspicion crossing his face. "Masha—"

"You recall, I'm sure, when we were aboard the casino ship, and you and Jez planted an explosive."

It wasn't a question, and looking at the suddenly cold expression on Lev's face, Tae knew it didn't need to be.

Tae had to fight back the sickness in his own stomach.

Fifty innocent people they'd blown to space dust, because of Masha. Because Masha wanted to manipulate them into making Grigory angry enough to come after them on the pleasure planet.

The thought still sent a thrill of helpless anger through him.

"I know you were not—happy with how that turned out," said Masha softly. "And—I apologize."

Tae looked up, startled.

That, he hadn't expected.

Masha was looking straight ahead, not meeting Lev's eyes, but from the set of her posture, she looked like she actually meant it.

"I—appreciate that, Masha," said Lev at last. "Although I'm not sure what bearing that has on our current situation. But—"

Masha shook her head. "You misunderstand me," she said. "I apologized, because I should not have taken advantage of your trust as I did. In—retrospect—" She paused for a moment, as if the words were difficult to say. "In retrospect, I should have instead trusted you in return. And for that miscalculation, I apologize. The fifty deaths, however, were entirely necessary."

Tae frowned.

"If you were to go through the list of those fifty, you would have seen that Grigory knew his business very well. The people he'd purchased occupied key positions in the government, positions I needed secured. In case, for example, the Secretary General should —become incapacitated."

"Be murdered," murmured Lev.

She tipped her head, conceding the point. "At any rate, the moment those fifty were killed, I called in some favours I'd collected. My people were put into the place of those fifty. They've been waiting on my instructions since then. That's where our friend

Adrian got his position, for instance. I had originally believed that the downfall of the Secretary General would come about through— other means—"

"Murder," supplied Lev.

Masha shot him a look, and continued. "However, they have been readying themselves to step into position and take hold of the reins of power the moment the opportunity presented itself. And I believe," she said, glancing out the door where Radka had disappeared, "that the opportunity has done so."

Tae shook his head.

He wasn't sure whether he was impressed, or horrified.

"So," said Lev at last. "You've done it after all. You've taken over the whole damn government."

"I was reminded, not too long ago, that I am, in fact, a member of a crew," responded Masha quietly. "This is something that was accomplished by all of us, not just me. And I believe decisions such as the future of the Svodrani System are of sufficient importance that they should be decided by all of the crew together."

Lev was quiet for a long time.

Tae's mind was spinning.

There was that hint of fondness in Masha's expression that he'd grown used to, when any of them had done a particularly impressive job of something. But there was a new note in her expression now— something softer, less mysterious.

Something almost kind.

When she'd left the crew, it had hurt more than he'd wanted to admit. But now—well, it seemed she was part of it again. Or maybe it would be more accurate to say, she was part of it, really, for the first time.

Ivan turned to smile at him, and he found he was smiling back.

And then there was another knock at the door, and then it burst open, and Jez stepped through. "Where's Lev?" she snapped, looking around quickly. There was something grim and desperate in her face. "If that damn bastard went and died on me—" Her voice faltered.

"Jez." Lev had pushed himself up against the wall and staggered to his feet.

Jez reached him in three quick strides, and they fell into each other like they'd been pulled together by a mag beam. Lev was whispering her name over and over, as if he couldn't quite believe she was real, and Jez had buried her face in his shoulder and was sobbing loudly.

Tae watched them for a moment, a warm happiness rising his chest, and Ivan's arm tightened around him.

"Jez, are you alright? What happened?" Lev's voice was still a little frantic.

Jez sniffed, wiping her face on her sleeve of her jacket. "Well, the bastard tied me up and shoved me on a ship, and then I got away and came back, basically."

"And Evka?" There was something hard in Lev's expression.

"Dead," she said shortly, her grin fading.

Lev nodded without speaking.

Jez closed her eyes, and Tae could see the weariness in her face now.

He gritted his teeth.

It wasn't damn well fair.

And then Jez opened her eyes again, frowning. "Hey, so what the hell is everyone shouting about in the streets, anyways?"

Lev turned to her, his smile a little more genuine this time.

As he explained, Jez's face grew slightly more skeptical, her eyebrows raising slightly higher, at each new revelation.

When he was finished, she stared at him for a moment, then turned to look speculatively at Masha.

"So," she said at last. "After all this, we actually won? We took down the damn Svodrani System government after all?"

Lev smiled. "Yes, Jez," he said quietly. "I think we have."

Tae took a long breath. His own smile was wide enough that his face hurt with it.

Ivan was watching him, a soft smile on his face as well. "So, Tae. You did what you promised after all. Saved the street kids. Saved the students. Saved the system."

Tae tried to smile back, and found there were tears in his eyes instead, and a thick knot of happiness in his chest that almost made it hard to breathe.

36

Masha, day 9, morning

Masha and the rest of the crew gathered the next morning around the small table in the common room of the apartments Radka had procured for them. Someone, probably Tae, had gone out and brought back blinis from one of the street vendors brave enough, or foolhardy enough, to keep his stall open even in the current chaos.

"Masha," began Lev, when they'd satiated their hunger. The look he gave her wasn't exactly accusing, perhaps, but it was sharp, and perceptive enough to be uncomfortable. "By all measurements, this has been a glowing success—Evka gone, the machine finally demolished, the government in a position to be reformed. But I was under the impression we weren't keeping secrets any longer. Why didn't you tell us about your government contacts from the beginning?"

Masha sighed, closing her eyes for a moment. "Lev," she said at last, quietly. "In this case, at least, it was not due to any desire to conceal things from you. When I told you about my contact in prison, and mentioned I'd once had contacts in government, I— honestly believed there would be few, if any, who'd remain loyal, once it appeared I'd been unsuccessful." She paused a moment. "I—suppose I underestimated them. And I'm ashamed to admit that tapping the line while Evka was speaking was something I thought of only as the matter arose. Had I thought of it earlier, I would have brought it to you." She paused again, strangely reluctant to meet Lev's eye. "I'm—sorry. I should have been better prepared."

For a moment, there was silence around the table, and Masha fought down a slight nausea.

They'd saved her life. It was too much, really, to expect them to trust her again.

But she hadn't realized how much it would hurt.

"I believe you," said Lev at last, his voice quiet, and she jerked her head up in surprise. He was watching her with that thoughtful, calculating expression, but there was a small smile on his face. "And your apology is accepted. I don't think any of us had a particularly feasible plan when Evka showed up."

Masha had to swallow hard, but she managed a smile.

"I suppose, then," said Lev, "this means we have to decide what to do next." He glanced around the table, and his eyes paused, for a moment, on Masha. "So." He spread his hands. "Any suggestions would be welcome."

Masha sighed and shook her head. "I won't use you to accomplish my plans any longer," she said. "I—never should have done so in the first place."

Lev watched her for a moment. At last he said, quietly, "Thank you, Masha." He paused. "But—if we were to ask you, as a friend, what you thought?"

She smiled, despite the sudden tears stinging her eyes. "In that case, I'd be more than happy to share my thoughts."

When they'd finished speaking, Lev waited behind after the others had left the room. "Masha," he said quietly, his eyes following Jez's retreating form almost involuntarily.

Masha sighed. "I'm sorry, Lev," she said quietly. "I've asked all my people about the *Ungovernable.* I had hoped that the time between when Evka took possession of it and when the Secretary General resigned was brief enough that they would be able to find it with minimal damage. But there's been no sign of it whatsoever. It— could be that someone is hiding it. But I suspect it simply means one of the high-up ministers who fled the planet took it with them. We won't find it again, and I suspect it will end up being stripped down for parts, regardless."

After a moment, he nodded, and tried to smile. But she could see the sharp pain in his expression. "I suspect you're right," he said at last.

"I'll ask them to keep looking," she said. "There's still a chance they'll find something."

He nodded again. "Thank you," he said, his voice soft.

They convened a ministers' meeting in the early afternoon. From the corner of her eye, Masha caught the sudden look of delight on Jez's face as someone she must have recognized from her days in government appeared in the doorway, saw her, and did a double take.

"Miss me, you bastard?" the pilot drawled, and Masha had to bite back a smile of amusement at the look on the man's face.

When everyone had gathered, she looked around the table.

Lev had ceded the running of the meeting to her, as she was already a familiar face at such meetings.

She stood, leaning her weight against the table to take the pressure off her injured leg.

Some of the faces in the room were of people loyal to her, others were not. But everyone at this table was someone who'd ultimately play an important role in rebuilding the government.

And all of them were watching her. Because all of them had been in government long enough to know that, at the end of the day, the words she spoke here as suggestions were to be taken as commands, and obeyed as such.

She'd taken down the government once, and they all knew it. And she was perfectly positioned to do it a second time, if she deemed it necessary.

"Ministers," she began, in a pleasant voice. "I'm glad you agreed to join me today."

An hour and a half later, Masha had all but talked herself hoarse. Lev had interjected, occasionally, his calm voice adding indisputable logic to match his arguments.

Jez had interjected as well once or twice, but mostly to call one of the ministers 'bastard,' and threaten them with various unpleasant consequences should they not, quote, "shut the hell up and sit the hell down, thought that was the kind of thing you plaguers liked anyways."

And at last, with varying degrees of enthusiasm or sullenness, the gathered ministers were nodding in grudging agreement to her proposal.

Masha turned to Radka, sitting next to her. "Would you please ask minister Gavril to join us?"

Zhenya appeared in the doorway a few minutes later. There was a look on their face that told her that, while they may have not been expecting the summons, exactly, they were not surprised by it.

And also, they weren't certain if it would herald good news or bad, but were very confident in their ability to use it to their advantage, whatever direction it tended.

She gave them a smile, and gestured to a seat near hers.

They sat warily, watching her with that faintly interested look that they always got when they were trying to guess her next move.

She turned to the rest of the table. "May I present Zhenya Novikov," she said. "You knew them as minister Gavril. I forged their documents to get them that position, as repayment for a favor. However, I believe there is no longer any need for subterfuge."

From the corner of her eye, she caught the faint stiffening of Zhenya's posture, the way their hand moved, almost casually, towards their pocket.

The way Jez's hand moved, not casually at all, towards her own pocket, a sharp grin spreading across her face.

It was—rather touching, honestly, but Masha would prefer the room not to break out into a firefight. Zhenya was skilled, yes, but Jez was, as she put it, damn fast. And Masha would prefer Zhenya alive, at present.

The murmuring that had broken out around the table at her revelation had begun to quiet, so she continued blandly. "As I'm sure all of you know, Zhenya was a pakhan in Grigory Korzhakov's organization. However, they left their position prior to Grigory's demise, and, my understanding is, have served the government with exceptional skill and discretion during these rather difficult times. Furthermore, their position in the mafia gave them significant experience handling the running of a large organization. Experience which none of us around this table, with the possible exception of myself, have had."

Zhenya's hand had relaxed, and they were watching her now with a faintly speculative air.

She turned to them. "Zhenya. I'd like to offer you a position in the new government. I've spoken about my proposal with these other ministers, and they've all agreed."

Zhenya had a faint smile on their face. "I see," they said at last. "I must say how honoured I am you'd trust me enough to ask me to serve under you. However, before I answer—"

Masha gave a quick shake of her head. "I'm afraid you misunderstand. I do not intend to ask you to serve under me."

Zhenya frowned slightly, still watching her.

"As these ministers, whose job it is to decide such matters, have all agreed, I intend to ask if you will accept the position of Secretary General."

There was a long moment of silence, and Masha had to smother a smile at the expression on Zhenya's face.

She never seen them look so completely flabbergasted.

It only lasted for a moment—they compose themselves quickly, their expression taking on once again that note of calculation. "I assumed, Masha, you would have wanted that position for yourself," they said. The tone in their voice was bantering, but she could hear the probing under it—they were trying to find out if this was a trick, and if so, whether it was one they could use to their advantage.

She gave them a bland smile. "No," she said. "I had considered it, once, but—" she shrugged. "I think, perhaps, the job is better suited to your talents."

The sharp glint in their eyes told her they were now calculating exactly what they could do from the position of Secretary General. And she could see in their face that she had them—it was far too much of a temptation for them to pass up.

They leaned back in the chair, still watching her calculatingly. "Well," they said at last. "I suppose if you've all agreed, it would be no more than my duty to accept. And Lady forbid I shirk my duty."

Masha nodded briskly. "Thank you. I recommended you to these ministers because I was very confident in your ability to do well for the system—with the chaos it's in at the moment, we need someone with experience in negotiating difficult situations." She paused. "I trust that you will agree to speak with the representatives of the insurrectionists, and hopefully come to an arrangement that will resolve both their concerns and those of the government. And I hope such negotiations will include a discussion of any reforms necessary to allow individuals to make their voices heard, should a situation arise in which they are negatively impacted. And I'm certain I don't need to tell you about the depths of corruption that has infiltrated the ministries. You've seen it yourself. As one of Gregory's two leading advisors, I'm confident you'll be more than capable of rooting any such corruption out, and putting structures in place to ensure the system is run in an equitable manner. We've already spoken here about what such structural changes might look like."

Zhenya's face had regained its usual faint amusement, and their gaze was sharp as they watched her. "Of course," they murmured. "As you say, I'm certain I will be entirely capable."

She knew them well enough to hear the words they weren't saying —that capable did not equal committed, or even willing.

She gave them another bland smile. "I'm glad to hear it."

She paused for just long enough to let them relax back in their chair, calculating, from the look on their face, how best to spin this latest opportunity.

"Of course," she added delicately, "the ministers at the table here were somewhat worried that you might use the position to—how shall I put this—enrich your influence in ways that are not ultimately beneficial to the system as a whole. But thankfully, I was able to give them a guarantee."

Zhenya's eyes sharpened, and they sat up slightly, the movement the only indication of their sudden wariness. "I'm glad you were able to vouch for me so willingly," they said in a mild voice, but there was sharp suspicion in their gaze.

She smiled again. "Of course. As you know, Zhenya, I'm not one to trust blindly. So it was lucky I had—an insurance policy, so to speak."

"And what might that be?" Zhenya's voice was now low and dangerous.

She leaned forward on the table and met their eyes. "I have friends here, Zhenya. Ministers, aides, secretaries and undersecretaries. You don't know who they are. You could spend a very, very long time trying to find out, but there would always be the chance you'd missed one. And that would be all it would take. Because at the first sign of retaliation, or of your not living up to my very glowing recommendations, these selfless civil servants, who've dedicated their lives to the good of the system, would be more than happy to ensure the position becomes open for someone who would." She paused a moment, letting a smile spread on her face at the sudden look of faint horror on theirs, and lowered her voice so only she and they could hear her next words. "They will also keep me and my crew informed, on an ongoing basis, of your actions. You've gone up against my crew before, Zhenya, and you survived. I suggest you don't push your luck."

She straightened, fixing the bland smile back on her face. "Very good. Now that that's settled, I suggest we move on to our next item of business—the transition of power."

Zhenya was still watching her. She could see the simmering anger under their calm expression—but she could see, too, the wry acknowledgment.

They'd been out-gamed. And they were an experienced enough gambler to know it, and to accept the impressive reward they'd been handed without further complaint.

The meeting stretched well into the evening. Once the main details of the transition of power had been settled, Masha had mostly sat back, allowing the other ministers to take the lead.

And between them, they seemed to be doing a decent job. They'd arranged for a meeting between various government negotiators and the students, the people in the projects, and a handful of representatives of the citizens of the Northeast Quarter, to discuss demands and conditions that would have to be dealt with in order to end the insurgency.

From the look on Zhenya's face, they weren't intending to drive too hard of a bargain.

They'd been a street kid once, after all. And she had the feeling that under their impassive veneer, they would be pleased to see the street children treated better than they had been.

Even Jez had managed to keep her seat through most of the meeting, although every time there was a break, she'd leap to her feet and pace restlessly around the corners of the room. The stir-crazy look in her eyes stirred an instinctive raw dread in Masha, installed there by months of experience. And so she breathed a sigh of relief when the ministers finally rose from the table, agreeing to reconvene the next day.

One by one, they filed out of the room.

Zhenya shot Masha a sharp glance as they left. "Well played, Masha," they said quietly. "Very well played."

Masha gave them a small smile, but her eyes were hard. "I've more than paid back any favor you may have earned from me. Don't expect any more."

They shook their head, returning her smile. "You misunderstand me," they said. "I have nothing but admiration for you. And nothing but gratitude for the generous position you granted me."

There was a wry tone in their voice that said that their gratitude was, perhaps, tempered by other emotions, but at least it seemed that, upon rethinking their position, they'd come to the conclusion she'd hoped they would—that the benefits of their new role, even constrained as they would be by Masha's oversight, would far outweigh the costs.

At last, it was only the crew left in the room. Lev sighed wearily, running his hand over his face. "You know," he said to the room in general, "I'd forgotten how exhausting government meetings can be."

"I was ready to set off an explosive under the table, just to give me an excuse to leave," Ysbel grumbled.

Jez was still pacing the edges of the room, with a look in her eyes that said that there would be unfortunate consequences for all present if she had to stay in the room for one minute longer.

Lev seemed to notice it as well, because he gave a small smile and stood, catching her hand. "Jez," he said. "Shall we go?"

She turned to him with the look of such unutterable relief that Masha almost laughed out loud.

"You go on," said Masha, still smiling. "I'll be along shortly."

Lev shot her a calculating look, but at last he nodded. "I suppose after what they saw here today, no one would dare try to assassinate you. I think you put the fear of the Lady into everyone in the ministry," he said wryly.

They filed out of the room. She heard their footsteps echo down the hallway, but she sat where she was for a few more minutes, strangely reluctant to leave.

At last, though, she got painfully to her feet.

She leaned heavily on the crutch Radka had found for her as she made her slow way along the deserted corridors. The uneven sound of her footfalls and the dull thud of her crutch against the floor made a strange pattern.

Her leg would never heal, not really. The government doctor had told her as much last night. It wouldn't always give her the constant pain it did now, but she'd never walk on it normally again.

She supposed she should be grateful that was the only permanent damage she taken over this long and ridiculous series of adventures. But there was a stinging regret at the thought—she'd never run again, never sprint down a hallway, never walk without having to be aware of where her foot would land, and whether her leg would buckle under her.

She paused at the exit to the building and tapped in the code, then pushed the door open and stepped out into the darkened streets.

It was cold, but without the wind, the air didn't bite nearly as much as usual.

The walk to their temporary lodgings wasn't a long one, but for some reason, she couldn't bring herself to start. She felt strangely empty, and she wasn't sure she was ready for the rest of the crew's company just yet.

She'd won. Grigory was gone, the mafia dismantled. The government was hers. She hadn't been made Secretary General, but that was by choice—Zhenya would, honestly, do a better job of it than she would.

She'd been forced to look at herself over the past few weeks in a way that had not been particularly pleasant. And she'd seen who she very likely would have become, as Secretary General. She would have started out with the best intentions, of course. But Lev was right—she was far too used to secrecy and manipulation. She would have become no better than another Grigory Korzhakov, because she would have had no one to hold her back. To tamp down her worst impulses.

Like her crew did for her.

She smiled to herself faintly, despite the hollowness in her chest, and pushed back the ache at the thought.

She'd become, finally, a member of the crew.

Right at the moment the crew would drift apart, and go their own ways.

It was good, and right, and exactly how things should be, but— she couldn't help the way it hurt.

She'd spent so long single-mindedly pursuing this goal. And she'd achieved it. And now she found herself suddenly unsure of her place in this new world she'd created, as if, creating it, she'd forgotten to include a space for herself.

She stood for a while, leaning back against the cold prefab of the government building, looking out at the empty streets.

"Hey, you bastard."

Masha turned with a startled curse to see Jez leaning up against the wall beside her.

"Jez?" she asked stupidly.

Jez grinned her familiar grin. "Figured I'd see you if you wanted a ride back," she said, gesturing to a skybike leaned up against the wall of a nearby alley.

There was something raw under her carefree expression, and Masha knew, suddenly, that Jez had needed time away from the others just as much as she had.

"You alright?" Jez asked last, quietly, and Masha had to swallow down a knot in her throat of simple, overwhelming gratitude.

That after everything—everything she'd done and everything she'd failed at—she had a friend like Jez.

That she knew, without a doubt, that no matter what happened to this crew, no matter where each of them ended up—she would always be able to consider Jez a friend.

"I'm—I'm alright," she said at last.

Jez nodded without answering and leaned back against the wall beside her, and for a few moments, they stood like that. Not needing to speak, simply drawing comfort from each other's presence.

Masha cleared her throat. "Jez," she said quietly.

Jez turned her head.

"I—" Masha had to clear her throat again. "I would like a ride, if you don't mind. But—not back the apartment. Not yet."

Jez nodded, still studying her. "Wait here, I'll bring the bike over."

She pulled the bike to a stop in front of Masha, and with surprising gentleness, helped Masha up behind her.

Masha ducked her head as they rode, letting Jez's wiry frame cut the wind. Jez hadn't asked questions when Masha had tapped the coordinates through to her com, just started up the bike and driven them at a surprisingly leisurely pace through the streets.

At last, they pulled up in front of a modern apartment building.

Jez idled the bike, leaving the anti-grav on so they wouldn't have to dismount.

For a long time, Masha sat watching the apartment building.

"This is where you used to live, isn't it? Before your parents were killed?"

Masha glanced at Jez, startled.

Still, it shouldn't really startle her anymore how perceptive Jez could be. They were all, she supposed, more than what they seemed at first glance.

She nodded, and for a few moments, they sat in silence. The wind picked up slightly, blowing snow against their faces, and Masha pulled her scarf up a little higher.

"You know," said Jez quietly. "I'm glad Lev's parents came to find him."

Masha shot another glance at the pilot. She was staring ahead, her expression muffled by her scarf.

"As am I," said Masha quietly.

"Funny, isn't it," said Jez at last. "I used to think my parents would come find me, once." She gave a small laugh. "Don't know why. I never was what they wanted. But I guess when you're a kid, you don't really think of that. You think that one day, they'll realize that they do love you after all. They'll miss you, and they'll want you back. And they'll come find you. I used to think that, sometimes, when Antoni had beat me up or something. I'd lie there in the dark and try not to cry, and I'd wonder if maybe my parents were sorry, now that I was gone. That my father was missing me, maybe, my mother was asking questions, trying to find out who'd hired on a fourteen-year-old pilot a year or so back." She gave a small, wry shrug. "Thing was, though, I don't think they ever missed me at all."

"That was entirely their loss," said Masha, and even she was surprised by the vehemence in her words.

Jez turned to her, startled, then gave a small smile. "Anyway," she said. "Guess what I'm saying is, I'm sorry you can't have your parents back either." She paused, a slightly wistful look on her face. "I never met them, obviously, but—well, the way you talk about them, figure they must've been pretty decent people. Figure … figure they must've loved you a lot."

"They did," said Masha quietly.

A light flickered on in one of the apartments, and another turned off.

Masha drew in a long breath.

Everything was gone, after all—her parents, her purpose, her family. Even the apartment that had haunted her nightmares for so many years had been demolished, the ashes cleared away, this new building constructed in its place. Where another family, right now, was probably rising from dinner, starting the long process of herding children to bed.

Jez shivered slightly, pulling her jacket closer around her, and Masha shook herself from her reverie. "Thank you for bringing me here, Jez," she said quietly.

Jez turned and shot her a quick grin.

"I wanted to see this place, one last time," Masha said. "But it's getting late. I suppose we should go home. Back to our family."

Jez turned to look at her. At last she nodded, brushing a hand across her eyes. "Yeah," she said quietly. "Yeah, I suppose we should. They're probably waiting for us."

"They probably are," said Masha.

37

Three days later

Lev woke with a start, his breath coming too quickly.

And then the truth of his surroundings penetrated the memories from his nightmare, and he sighed and relaxed back into the softness of the cot.

Jez was snuggled into his shoulder, like she always was when the mornings were chilly. And he wasn't sure he'd ever be able to look at her lying next to him, her dark hair spread across his chest, her face peaceful in sleep, without a desperate, choking gratitude tightening his throat and threatening to pull tears from his eyes.

He shifted to give her a more comfortable place to lie and tucked the blankets up around her shoulders, the feel of her in her his arms a deep happiness that was almost more than he could bear.

She stirred, and murmured something in her sleep, and he caught a hint of the pain in her expression that hadn't really left since she'd given up her ship.

Despite Masha's best efforts, they'd still found no trace of it, and he was finally realizing Masha was likely right—it had likely been taken off-planet, and they'd likely never see it again.

"Shh, Jez, it's alright," he whispered, stroking her hair. She settled for a moment, then stirred again and blinked at him blearily.

"Genius?" she said, her voice thick with sleep.

He kissed her forehead, and she smiled and pulled his head down, and kissed him on the lips. And maybe one day the warmth of her lips on his, the taste of her, the press of her body, wouldn't hit him like a spanner upside the head—but he certainly couldn't guarantee it.

When she finally drew back, he was breathless, and every part of him wanted to grab her and pull her close and keep kissing her until the kissing became something much more interesting.

But he'd seen the look on her face as she pulled away.

He took a deep, steadying breath. "Jez?" he said quietly.

She turned a little and smiled up at him, but he could still see the tears-streaks on her face.

It had only been three days. Three days since they'd won the system, and she'd lost her angel.

It would take longer than a few days for something like this to heal.

"Jez," he said again, pulling her close and stroking her hair, running his hand down her back.

"Is it morning already?" she mumbled.

He smiled. "It doesn't have to be unless you want it to."

She rolled over so she was lying on her back, and stared at the ceiling. "Don't know how long it's been since we could sleep as long as we damn well wanted. Guess I'm still not used to it."

"Neither am I," said Lev, watching her with affection.

She rolled up on one elbow. "So. What we have to do today?"

He shook his head, smiling. "Nothing. The government is in negotiations with the students and the street kids, and Masha's people are keeping an eye on Zhenya and bringing back reports.

There's nothing we have to do. So." He rolled up on his elbow as well, facing her. "What you want to do? We can do whatever you want. We could borrow ship, see if we can go fast enough in-atmosphere that we never quite reach the sunset."

She didn't answer, and he sighed and sat up. "I've been meaning to talk to Tae, too—he and I have been talking, and we think—we think we might be able to build you something. It wouldn't be the *Ungovernable*, I know. But I spent hours poring over her specs when we first found her, and so we'll have all the designs. And now that we have time to breathe, he and I can go over the specs and see what we can do. Zhenya has been hinting broadly that they'd be more than happy to provide any resources necessary, and I think Masha's been talking with her contacts to see if she can find any of the *Ungovernable's* salvaged parts."

Jez gave him a wan smile. "Thanks, genius," she said quietly. "I—that would be nice."

She was quiet for a moment, her smile trembling a bit at the edges, and he cursed himself for bringing it up.

She managed to salvage the smile again briefly. "Guess I'm just a little worn out from all the damn meetings we've been sitting through. Guess maybe I don't feel like doing much today after all."

He closed his eyes for a moment, something squeezing in his chest. "Jez," he said quietly. "If there's anything I can do—anything at all—"

She took his hand in hers and gave it a small squeeze. "I'll—I'll be OK." He could hear the roughness of tears in her voice. "I'll be fine. It's just—I—" she trailed off, pulling his hand into her lap and tracing a finger along the lines of his palm. "Guess maybe I just need a little bit of time alone. Haven't had much of a chance for that the past few days, none of us have."

The sharp pain squeezed in his chest again, a deep ache he couldn't get rid of, and couldn't heal. So instead, he smiled and squeezed her hand back. "Alright," he said. "Take as much time as you need. And—if you need anything—anything at all, even just someone to talk to—call me on my com, OK?"

Her smile this time was a little more genuine, even though there was a suspicious glint in the corners of her eyes. "Any excuse to talk to a hot scholar boy," she said. She paused a minute. "Lev. I—" she swallowed hard. "I—don't know what I'd do if I didn't have—if you weren't—" she broke off, voice choking. "Thank you," she said finally.

He leaned in and kissed her gently. "See you tonight," he whispered. "Remember—call me if—"

She rolled her eyes with a weak attempt at a grin. "I know, I know, call you if I want smoking good sex. I mean, I know you're damn good, but you could be a little more humble about it."

He shook his head, but he was smiling despite himself.

When he'd dressed and showered, he slipped out of their apartment and through the common room. The others were either still in their own apartments, or were already out and about.

It was just as well—he wasn't sure he could face anyone at the moment anyways. The picture of Jez's face that morning, the rough tear streaks down her cheeks, the hopelessness in her eyes—the fact there was nothing he could do to take it away—hurt in a way that was almost unbearable.

He took a deep breath and stepped into the cold of the Prasvishoni morning, pulling his coat close around him.

She'd be alright, eventually. She'd survived a hell of a lot in her short life. She'd heal, somehow. Eventually.

But he wasn't sure she'd be the same Jez she had been.

He wandered down the streets, and it wasn't until he'd been walking for almost half an hour that he realized was heading, unconsciously, towards the university.

He smiled slightly.

Just as well, really. He'd hardly had time to exchange more than a couple words with his parents since the Secretary General had stepped down, and they'd likely be there, helping with the negotiations.

And, he realized, he missed them.

When he reached the place where the barricades had been, the scene almost surprised him. The heap of furniture and debris and the tangle of wires that had been the only thing standing between them and the police for so many weeks was already mostly pulled down, and the street, though scarred and pitted with explosions, was clean.

Without the barricades, the square looked smaller, and strangely peaceful. A few of the shelters were still there, but they no longer held the wounded or dying.

He caught sight of his mother ducking out of one of the tents, and he called to her. She turned, and something ached in his chest at the easy happiness in her smile when she saw him.

He hadn't deserved their forgiveness. He'd never deserved their forgiveness. But they'd given it anyways.

He was their family. Just like Masha was his crew, no matter what she'd done.

"Lyovushka," she said as she reached him. She pulled him into a tight hug, and he squeezed her back. She smelled of campfire smoke and disinfectant, and something else that was simply her, a smell he couldn't identify, but that had always meant home. Even when he hadn't wanted it to.

"And how are things, my Lev?" she asked, holding him at arm's length to inspect him. "Have you been getting enough sleep? Are you sure you should be out so soon after being poisoned?"

He smiled slightly. "Mother. I'm fine."

"And that girl of yours," she continued, looking around as if Jez might pop up at any moment, with her swagger and her easy grin.

Lev sighed.

His mother nodded, a perceptive look in her eyes. "I suppose she's still hurting," she said quietly.

Lev nodded, unable to speak through the knot in his throat.

His mother tightened her hand on his shoulder for a moment. "Give her time," she said. "Give her time, and be there when she needs you. That's all you can do, when someone's hurting like that. But sometimes, it's exactly what they need."

He nodded again, and she smiled. And he noticed the happiness in her smile, the good humour dancing in her eyes, and he found himself smiling back.

"I was going to call you today anyways—the Minister of Education keeps dropping by, and I think he's hoping to catch you. He asks for you every time."

Lev chuckled softly. "He's been trying to track me down in the halls of the government buildings, too. I haven't had a second to breathe, or I would have talked to him already. Do you know what he wants?"

His mother shook her head.

"Well, if he comes by again, I suppose you may as well tell him I'm here."

She nodded.

"Do you—need a hand with anything?" he asked, gesturing around.

She shook her head, smiling. "Go on. I hear you've been working too hard these last few days."

Lev smiled back, then gave a small sigh. "I'll—wander around the university, maybe. I could use the fresh air, after three days sitting in meetings."

His mother nodded, and he turned and made his way across the small square, littered with the detritus of too many people huddled together in too small a space for too long a time.

After a moment's hesitation, he stepped through the open gate to the university.

It was an odd feeling—his memories from the barricade superimposing themselves on memories from his childhood. While they were trapped here, he hadn't really had the time to take note of it—that the administration building that was serving as a makeshift dormitory was the same building where he'd arrived as a thirteen-year-old, shivering with the combination of nerves and an inadequate jacket, to be assigned his first course schedule for university.

But now that there were no longer police sirens wailing outside, no traces of smoke bombs in the air, he could see it.

He could still pick out the grassy plaza where he'd caught a quick nap after his morning classes, if the day was warm, the tree where he'd kissed his first crush.

The window of the classroom where he'd first met Evka.

The thought sent a small, involuntary shiver down his spine.

He'd never thought of himself as particularly innocent. But he had been. The boy he'd been would have been horrified, had he known what the future held.

He, an ex-convict who'd spent weeks behind a barricade fighting off the police.

Evka, dead.

He still couldn't think of it without a mixture of bitter vindication and guilty regret.

He wouldn't have recognized himself. The boy who'd studied here wouldn't recognize the man he'd become.

He wasn't sure he recognized himself now.

He didn't know how long he'd been wandering the grounds when he heard a small, polite sound behind him, like someone clearing their throat. He spun, reaching almost instinctively for his heat pistol, then stopped himself with a wry smile.

"Minister." He recognized the small man from the lists he'd memorized of government positions—Sacha, the Minister of Education. "I hear you've been wanting to speak with me."

"Yes. You're quite the difficult man to track down," said Sacha, stepping forward with a quick smile. There was something about the intelligence in his face and the humour in his eyes that made Lev smile back despite himself.

"Do you mind if I join you?" the man asked.

Lev shook his head, and for a few minutes they strolled the grounds in silence.

At last, the minister turned to him. "Lev," he said. "I'm sure this won't be a shock to you, but I've looked through your records. All of us have by now, I think. I—understand that you were on track to becoming a professor here, once."

For a moment Lev froze, the memories catching him and holding him like ship clamps.

He recovered himself, and managed a smile. "I was. That was a very long time ago, though."

The man was watching him thoughtfully. "After everything that's happened, we've decided it prudent to look deeper into the histories of the professors teaching here. I'm afraid some of them will not retain their tenure. I think we are finally in agreement that experimenting on street children is not an acceptable form of research, no matter what benefit the researcher thinks they may gain from it." There was a note of wryness in his voice that didn't cover the mixture of distaste and horror he felt at the notion, and Lev found himself liking the man more than he had.

"I'm glad," he said. "It was long overdue."

The man was still watching him with those sharp, intelligent eyes. "I wonder, Lev—what would you think if we were to offer you a position?"

Lev's breath caught in his throat, a sharp, sudden jab he'd thought he left behind him years ago.

"A—position?" he asked at last, praying that his voice was steady.

"Yes." The man was smiling. "I, of course, would prefer to put you in a more managerial role—perhaps university president, as I believe we will have a vacancy in that position. But I fully understand if you should not want that degree of responsibility. But a professorship, possibly? I'm sure we could arrange for whatever subject you wished to teach. More than anything, I'd like your expertise. The university has, I think, great potential. I'd like someone who could help bring it up to where it could be."

Lev stared at him, feeling as if the ground under his feet had suddenly vanished.

He couldn't breathe. He could hardly think.

He'd spent so much of his life dreaming about this. He'd spent years mourning its loss, with a bright, sharp regret that had shaped the entire course of his life.

And now this man stood here, offering it to him with a smile. As if by accepting, Lev would be doing him a favour.

If they'd still had the *Ungovernable,* of course, he couldn't have done it. He'd never dream of trying to take Jez away from her angel ship.

But the *Ungovernable* was gone.

And he'd seen the guilt and regret in Jez's face every time his old dream had been brought up, even though he'd told her, over and over, that what he'd found with her was so much more than what he'd lost.

Jez would tell him to do it.

For a moment, he allowed himself to imagine it—the musty smell of a research laboratory, the sharp, electric scent of information chips. Sitting at a desk pouring over holoscreens, not because he was trying to solve some urgent, desperate problem, but because he was interested in the material. All the information he could dream of, waiting in the massive, dusty records building. Lecturing students, collecting papers, sharp, pleasantly hostile debates with some professors, and sharp, friendly debates with others. Coming home to one of the faculty apartments at night across the soft dark of the campus, the space so familiar he could walk it in his sleep.

The only life he'd ever dreamed of.

For the briefest second, another picture flashed across his mind— sitting in a cockpit, in the copilot's seat. Jez in the pilot's seat beside him, humming off key as she stroked her fingers unconsciously across the controls. Staring out into the black of deep space, the cold, impossible, aching beauty of it, the joy that was almost more longing than joy that tugged at him from the vast expanse of nothingness.

The endless possibilities.

The endless freedom.

He blinked, bringing himself back to the present.

The bulky shapes of the university buildings around him were more familiar than his home had been. They'd been his home, for most of his childhood. But they seemed, somehow, smaller than he remembered, the thought of the classrooms slightly stifling.

"You may, of course, take all the time you need to think on it," the man continued. "It will be several weeks before we have the leisure to start making appointments. But I thought I'd let you know, if you're interested."

Lev let out a long breath. Then he turned and gave the man a small smile. "I can't tell you how flattered I am that you offered me this," he said quietly. "It means a great deal to me. But—I won't need time to consider. I don't think, after all, that I'd be happy as a professor."

The man sighed, looking disappointed, but not surprised. "I can understand that," he said with a faint smile. "I understand you're quite the adventurer these days. But please do let me know if you have recommendations. Or if you ever change your mind."

"I'll certainly try to think of anyone I could recommend," said Lev. "But I don't expect to change my mind."

They were approached the university entrance, and when they reached it, the minister turned off with a friendly farewell.

Lev watched him go, a strange ache in his chest.

He'd always known, his whole life, exactly who he was—Lev, the student. The professor, almost, then the man who'd watched his dreams shatter, lost his purpose and his compass, but never his identity—self-interested, calculating, intelligent.

But now—he had no idea. He wasn't who he had been. And without the crew, without the ship they'd called home for so long, without Masha's ridiculous goals driving them—he wasn't sure what was left.

The university—the place he'd first found his freedom—would be stifling for him now. He'd seen too much, done too much. Jez had introduced him to flying, and to freedom, and he couldn't go back, no matter how much he might want to.

The air was cold, and a breeze had sprung up, whispering through the deserted campus.

He pulled his scarf close around his face.

He didn't know who he was. And Jez—

He pictured the look on her face that morning.

Perhaps she didn't, either.

He had to bite back a small, ironic chuckle.

What a pair they made: one of them lost, one of them broken.

But maybe—maybe that was alright. Maybe, together, they could figure it out.

As long as he had her, anything could be figured out. And maybe, in the end, that was all he could ask for.

Ysbel picked up an Olya-sized tunic and shook it out. A puff of dust rose from it, and she shot Tanya a long-suffering look.

There was amusement in Tanya's face. "I'm not sure that one's clean," she said. "You might want to smell it."

Ysbel raised it to her nose, then coughed. "No," she said dryly. "I don't think it's clean."

She tossed it in the pile of dirty laundry to be thrown in the cleanser and straightened, putting her hands on the small of her back and leaning back to stretch.

Their small room was piled high with assorted clothing, toys, and belongings.

Almost everything they owned, besides what they'd taken with them to the abandoned warehouse, had been on the *Ungovernable*, so she Tanya had spent most of the day shopping for what they'd need to replace it.

And as much as Ysbel generally avoided shopping, spending time alone with Tanya, while Masha watched the children, had been the most relaxing thing she'd done in a long time.

The children were playing a game in the room next door that involved shouting, and running, and probably other things Ysbel was trying not to imagine.

She smiled wryly to herself.

Considering what they'd accomplished over the past couple weeks, she doubted anyone in the apartment complex would get overly upset about a dented wall or scratched paint.

"Masha says we can leave whenever we like," said Tanya quietly, looking up from a half-folded pair of trousers.

Ysbel watched her wife with a soft expression.

"Ysi?" Tanya's voice was amused.

Ysbel smiled. "I always forget how beautiful you are."

Tanya shot her that wry, amused glance that Ysbel knew so well, and it was a moment before Ysbel could trust herself to speak again.

"I think you're right," she said, when she was certain her voice would be steady. "Masha told me that as far as she's aware, there's nothing else we're needed for here. So—" she shrugged.

Tanya nodded, but didn't say anything.

Ysbel crossed over to her wife, sitting down beside her on the cot. "I'll miss them too," she said quietly.

Tanya chuckled, but there was a catch in her voice when she spoke. "At least I won't have to worry about anyone teaching Olya any more ways to cheat at tokens," she said.

Ysbel leaned forward to kiss her, and the movement tipped one of the hard-cased pieces of luggage off the cot, sending it clattering to the floor.

The noise from the other room stopped.

A moment later, she heard a whispered, "Mama?" Olya's voice was soft and frightened.

"It's alright, my heart," called Tanya. "Something fell from the bed, that's all. Nothing's wrong."

A moment later, Olya's head appeared around the edge of the door, Misko's just below it. There was a look in her daughter's eyes that tightened something in Ysbel's chest, and she crossed over to the children quickly, kneeling beside them.

"It's alright, my loves," she said quietly, holding out her arms. The children buried themselves in them, and Ysbel pressed them to her chest and held them. She could feel their small bodies shaking.

"I thought someone had shot you," whispered Olya.

"No, my love," she said, stroking her daughter's hair. "No one is going to hurt us. No one is going to hurt you or your brother, or me, or your mamochka. We're safe now."

Olya nodded, but it was a few moments before she raised her head from Ysbel's chest, and her eyes were suspiciously damp. She searched Ysbel's face, and Ysbel tried to smile, even though the fear in her daughter's eyes cut her like a knife. "It's alright, my heart," she said again. "We're safe, I promise."

At last Olya nodded, swallowing hard. "Come on, Misko," she said, stepping back and obviously trying to sound brave. "Let's go play. I told you they were fine."

"No you didn't," Misko muttered, but he detached himself from Ysbel's arms as well, and followed his sister out the door.

When they were gone, Ysbel closed her eyes for a moment, something aching in her chest.

"My heart."

She stood, pulling Tanya close, and they turned to look after the two children.

"They've never really been able to be children, have they?" she said quietly.

Tanya shook her head, and there was a small flicker of pain across her features. "I did the best I could for them," she said. "But in prison—"

Ysbel pulled her closer. "The fact that they still know how to laugh after being raised in prison—what you did was incredible. And you had to do it alone. I'm still so sorry about that."

Tanya gave her a small smile.

"I think they'll like the farm," said Ysbel. "We'll go back to the planet where they were born. You still have a sister there, and two brothers, yes?"

Tanya smiled through the gleam of tears in her eyes. "I haven't been back there for five years. Or is it six now? But I can't imagine they would have left." She glanced down at the clothing they were packing. "It will be nice to be on a planet that's warm," she said, in a slightly rueful tone. "For one thing, it will be nice to have to keep fewer pairs of winter clothing."

Ysbel chuckled softly, and tried not to let her thoughts drift to the last few months that seemed like a lifetime, aboard the *Ungovernable*. Fighting for their lives alongside a crew who had become family.

The Ysbel who had lived on a small farm on a warm, sun-kissed planet seemed someone a million lightyears distant. A stranger she didn't really know anymore.

Tanya leaning her head against Ysbel's shoulder. "We'll build our cottage close by the stream. The one you and I used to sit beside."

There was something in her voice that told Ysbel that Tanya, too, felt the distance between who they'd been then and who they were now.

Ysbel cleared her throat. "Do you remember the first time we kissed, by that stream?" she asked softly.

Tanya smiled. "I'm not sure I could ever forget that. I think I was floating for the whole rest of the evening."

"I think I was too," said Ysbel, returning Tanya's smile. She turned her head, burying her face in her wife's hair.

It fell almost to her shoulders now, as soft and smooth as Ysbel remembered it.

"Do you remember how much they loved playing in the stream when they were babies?" Tanya's eyes were closed, and there was a small, nostalgic smile on her face. "And how much trouble they used to get into?"

Ysbel laughed, the sound coming out only a little choked. "Misko will get his clothes soaked through every day, I'm sure of it."

"Well, I won't get my clothes soaked through."

Ysbel glanced up. Olya and Misko were standing in the doorway, making no effort to hide their attempt at eavesdropping.

Olya's voice had that slightly superior tone it always took on when she was discussing her little brother.

"I will!" said Misko emphatically. "I'll be soaking wet all the time." He turned to glower at his sister. "And I'll get mud all over you."

Olya rolled her eyes. "No, you won't. Because I'm going to be in working with Mama, learning about explosives. And with Uncle Lev, learning about—well, whatever I want to learn about. And with Aunty Jez, learning about gambling."

"Well, I don't want Uncle Lev," said Misko sullenly. "I want Aunty Masha. I bet she would let me get soaking wet in the stream."

Ysbel exchanged a quick glance with Tanya.

"My loves," she said quietly, crouching next to the children. "It—

it won't be everyone living at the farm. It will just be us. But I'm sure your aunties and uncles will come to visit."

Olya frowned. "Uncle Lev won't be coming with us?" she asked uncertainly.

Ysbel tried to smile. "Not this time, Olyeshka. Anyways, I thought you told me you were getting tired of him and Aunty Jez kissing all the time. I don't think they're going to stop that any time soon."

Olya was still frowning, and the hurt in her face hurt Ysbel.

She sighed and ruffled her daughter's hair.

The children were so used to losing things. And now, when they'd finally won, finally done what they'd been trying to do this whole time—they were going to lose their family again.

"Anyways," she said, with another attempt at a smile, "do you really think we could keep your Aunty Jez from coming to visit you if she wanted to?"

"I want Aunty Masha," Misko grumbled. "She's better than Aunty Jez."

Olya gave him a superior look. "Aunty Masha doesn't know how to cheat at fool's tokens, does she?"

"Well, Aunty Masha always gives me dessert rations when I ask her," Misko shot back.

"Dessert rations aren't good for you," Olya retorted.

Misko hit her and started crying.

Olya started crying, too.

Ysbel took a deep breath, but she found she was smiling, just a little.

This, after all—this had been what she missed, all that time she'd been locked up in prison. She'd imagined their smiles, their embraces, their sweet baby voices—but this, the messy, arguing, squabbling reality of it, difficult and frustrating as it was—was so much richer than the sweet, perfect, nostalgic picture she'd painted in her head.

"Alright, you two," she said patiently, separating them. "Go clean up your game, please, if you're done playing. No more hitting, Misko."

"Misko's the one who dumped all the toys," said Olya quickly.

"No, I didn't!" shouted Misko, raising his arm again.

Ysbel caught it before he could hit his sister a second time. "Enough," she said. "Both of you clean it up, because you were both playing with it. And when you're finished, maybe Mamochka and I will find you a snack."

Grumbling, the children went.

Ysbel stood, shooting Tanya a wry smile, and they watched the children through the door.

But there was a strange tugging at Ysbel's heart.

She wasn't sure she knew, any more than her daughter did, what life would be like without Jez's easy grin and disreputable vocabulary, Lev's dry humour, Tae's exasperated scowl and Masha's calm competence.

She wasn't sure how to go back to being the woman whose only dream was to live out her life on a small farm with her family.

"It will be alright, Ysi," said Tanya quietly. "It's part of life—finding things, and losing things."

Ysbel leaned over and kissed her. Tanya kissed her back, and she was hit with a wave of gratitude that was almost made her stagger.

She had her family. After everything they'd been through, she had her family again. And perhaps they weren't who they had been the last time they'd lived on their small, warm planet—but perhaps they could remember how to be again.

She sobered.

She had her family. And she'd lose her crew. Not forever—they'd visit each other, she was certain, and with Tae's abilities, she was certain they'd never be somewhere they couldn't call back to talk with the children.

But it would still hurt.

But—well, in the end, Tanya was right. Life was about finding things, and losing things, and it would always be bittersweet. And perhaps the secret of it was to love the things you had while you had them.

Like she loved her family.

Like she'd always love the crew, no matter how far apart they were.

Caz and Peti stared around at the apartment.

It was impressive. A thousand times more than Tae could ever have imagined as a frightened, shivering street kid, dreaming of getting his kids somewhere safe and warm.

They had what amounted to three regular-sized apartments, joined together by a common room. More than enough space for all of them.

Tae smiled to himself as he watched them.

The younger children were already wandering through the rooms, eyes wide with astonishment, and the sight of it warmed him, despite the lingering chill of the early morning air.

Caz turned at last, his face still bearing the shocked disbelief of someone unsure whether he's dreaming. "Tae," he said in a husky voice. "Are you—are you sure this is the right place?"

Tae smiled at him. "They brought me here earlier and showed me around. It's ours."

Peti came to stand beside her brother. Her face, too, bore the hint of shock, but she was frowning slightly. "And the other street kid gangs?" she asked. "Matija and Felix and the others?"

Tae's smile widened. "That was part of the negotiations. All the street kids are to be housed. I looked at all the apartment blocks they suggested, to make sure they were alright. And everyone behind the barricades is getting a pardon, and a reward for their bravery. I'm not sure how Zhenya will spin that, but they'll just have to figure it out."

She smiled at him, and he could see the tears glinting in her eyes as she turned quickly away. "Well, I guess Caz and I had better get everyone settled into their rooms, before anyone gets into a fight." Her voice choked a little.

Ivan, who'd been wandering around the common room, came over to stand by Tae, and Tae reached out and took his hand, leaning against him as he watched as Caz and Peti got the younger children organized.

A year ago, it would have been him making the arrangements, deciding what had to happen, figuring out the logistics.

A year ago, Caz and Peti had seemed so young.

But they'd grown up since then.

The thought was bittersweet.

He'd finally done what he'd always promised, gotten them somewhere safe and warm, off the streets.

And now, he found, he didn't belong here anymore.

He felt like an outsider, looking in.

He took a deep breath and shook his head. He was being ridiculous. There was more than enough room for him here.

But—the thought of going back to the life he'd left—using his tech for their small daily needs, worried only about taking care of the other children—made him feel, suddenly, as trapped as Jez always looked when she was land-bound.

"Tae?"

He looked up, startled.

Ivan was watching him, and Tae gave him a small smile.

"It's nice to see them happy, isn't it?" said Ivan quietly, and from the look in his eyes when he glanced at the street kids, the small, unconscious smile on his face—Tae knew he meant it.

From when he'd first met them, Ivan had cared about these kids, almost as much as Tae did.

Tae squeezed Ivan's hand, his chest filling with gratitude.

They were quiet for a while.

"So, Tae. Are you going to move in here with them?" Ivan asked at last.

Tae sighed and gave a rueful shake of his head. "I—don't know. Look at them, Ivan. They don't need me anymore."

Ivan studied him for a moment. "Tae," he said quietly. "They'll always need you. Just because they don't need someone to take care of them doesn't mean they don't need you."

Tae took a deep breath. "Maybe you're right," he said.

"Of course I'm right," said Ivan with a teasing smile. "They're your family." He paused a moment. "Our family, if you'd like."

Tae turned quickly, not entirely sure he'd heard correctly.

Ivan's expression was serious. "Only if you want to, Tae. If you don't, I promise, it won't change anything. And if you're not sure—I can wait as long as you want me to. But I've—I've never found someone I'd rather make a family with."

For a moment, Tae could hardly breathe.

He'd never let himself think farther than keeping them all alive for the last few crazy, chaotic months.

Ivan was still watching him, his gaze steady.

Tae closed his eyes for half a moment. His heart was pounding, and there was something happy and terrifying and intoxicating fizzing through his whole body.

He'd spent so long—his whole life, really—ignoring what he wanted, because he didn't have time for that, because there were people who needed him, and would die if he couldn't do what they needed him to do.

Wanting something, for himself, still scared the hell out of him.

But damn it, he'd spent enough time around Ysbel to know he could handle things that scared the hell out of him.

He grabbed Ivan's arm, and with a last look around to make sure the street kids were occupied, dragged him into one of the smaller rooms.

"Tae—" Ivan began, a hint of uncertainty in his voice.

Tae stepped back a moment, studying him—his tall, graceful figure, the good humor in his face that lingered no matter how grave he was trying to look, the sharp elegance of his profile. The pain behind his eyes.

"Ivan," he said. "I assume you know how to get a hold of your sister?"

Ivan looked at him, faint puzzlement in his expression. "I—yes. I believe I could."

"And I assume, after what we've done here, that you can talk to your parents again without putting them in danger?"

"I—suppose so," said Ivan again, cautiously. He was studying Tae, an odd look on his face. "Why?"

Tae grinned. "Because I assume you'll want them there for the marriage ceremony."

Ivan stared at him for a moment, as if he wasn't entirely sure he'd heard correctly. "The—" he shook his head. "Tae. Are you saying—

does that mean—"

Tae leaned in and kissed Ivan softly.

When he drew back, his smile was so broad he felt giddy with it.

Ivan was still staring.

Tae kissed him again, and this time, Ivan's lips softened under his, his hands coming up around Tae's back. Tae grabbed the back of Ivan's jacket, pulling him closer, and leaned into him, deepening the kiss, until this time when he pulled away, they were both gasping for breath, and the familiar dizziness that kissing Ivan, touching Ivan, being near Ivan always brought had Tae leaning against the wall for support.

"Tae—" the word was almost to groan.

Tae swallowed, and once he had enough breath to speak again, he said roughly, "Yes, Ivan. It damn well means that I want to marry you, as soon as we can damn well find someone to perform the ceremony. It means I don't want to be away from you, ever again. It means I'm damn well going to love you until the day that I die, so we may as well make it official. Because I'm not going to change my mind, I'm not going to have second thoughts, and I'm never, never going to stop feeling like the luckiest person in the system to have you."

"Tae." Ivan's voice was thick. "Tae I—I—dammit, Tae—" He pulled Tae's mouth back to his, and Tae leaned into the urgency of the kiss, sliding his hands around Ivan's waist and up his back, feeling the shape of Ivan's body, the way it set Tae's heart racing.

At some point, he thought he heard a sound in the background, and the small corner of his mind that had room for anything other than Ivan recognized Peti's startled gasp, and the sharp *click* of the door being closed, but he honestly couldn't have cared less.

Finally, reluctantly, Ivan drew back. His face was flushed, his lips swollen, and there was a look in his eyes that made Tae so dizzy he thought he might actually pass out.

"We—we should probably wait until we're somewhere where there aren't children listening at the door," Ivan managed finally, but there was a tone in his voice that told Tae that it had taken a great deal of effort for Ivan to convince himself of this.

He was tempted to shove Ivan back up against the wall and continue where they'd left off, eavesdroppers be damned. There was a look on Ivan's face that told him Ivan wouldn't put up much of an argument.

But—

He sighed shakily, running a hand over his face.

Despite what his entire body was telling him, Ivan was probably right.

He took a few deep breaths, not daring to look over at Ivan until he'd gotten himself a little more under control.

From the sound of it, Ivan was doing the same.

At last, Ivan turned to him. "Tae?" His voice wasn't quite steady, but then, Tae doubted his would be either.

Ivan met Tae's eyes, and this time his expression was serious. "I need to tell you, though—I don't know if I'll ever get over what happened. I don't know if I'll ever stop having nightmares, or panicking when you get hurt. If you can accept that—"

"Ivan," said Tae, slipping his hand around Ivan's waist. "The only reason that makes one damn bit of difference to me is that I hate to see you hurting. It will never, never make me regret loving you." He paused, a different shakiness bleeding through his muscles. "I—that day at Evka's, when they brought me back—I wasn't worried for me. But I was so worried it might—might hurt you—"

Ivan pressed his lips into Tae's hair, pulling him close. "It might have broken me, once," he said quietly. "But loving someone, I've realized, makes you stronger than you think." He gave a soft, rueful laugh. "I might never stop having nightmares about it, granted, but —well, with you, I have something worth putting myself back together for."

They stayed there for a few minutes, Tae breathing in the smell and feel of Ivan.

"So, you do want to be family, then," said Ivan at last, and Tae could hear the smile in his voice.

Tae pulled back, just a little, and met Ivan's eyes. "I've never wanted anything more," he said quietly.

Jez sat on the overgrown fire-escape stairs behind the apartment, her knees pulled to her chest, body huddled in on itself, and stared listlessly at the dirty prefab wall of the apartment building across from her.

She'd cried until she was pretty sure there were no more tears left in her whole body. She'd cried enough to start a dull, thirsty ache in the back of her throat.

But she couldn't be bothered to care.

She took a deep, shaky breath.

She was lucky, really—there was no way their whole crew should have survived that mess. Hell, she was one of the luckiest people in the damn system, probably.

She'd gotten to fly her beautiful angel ship, at least. She'd been able to sit in the cockpit, run her hands over the controls, feel her ship talk to her. Feel her listen to her. Not many people got something like that even once in their whole lives. And she'd had months of it.

She was damn well lucky, and it was stupid to be sitting here crying. And anyways—

She dropped her face into her arms, trying unsuccessfully to choke back a sob.

It would be fine. One day, she'd wake up and not feel like half of her was missing. Or at least, she'd get used to living as only half a person.

And as much as she hated it—as much as it hurt, worse than anything had ever hurt in her whole damn life—she didn't regret what she'd done.

She pictured, for a moment, Tae and Ivan, looking at each other like maybe they were the only two people in the entire system. Ysbel, and Tanya, and those two damn kids. That bastard Masha. Lev…

Despite everything, she managed a shaky smile at the thought of him, the concern on his face, the soft smile he'd given her that morning as he left.

It would be alright. She had that soft scholar-boy, who she loved more than anything else in the damn system. Even, turns out, more than her ship. She had him, and she had the rest of the crew. People who loved her. People who cared about her, and trusted her, and would be there to pick up the pieces as she fell apart over this damn ship. Who'd be waiting to help put her back together.

But—

That didn't damn well make it hurt any less.

There was the soft sound of the door opening behind her, and she started, spinning around.

Masha stood in the doorway. She was leaning heavily on a crutch, but she looked a hell of a lot better than she had a few days ago.

"Jez?" Masha asked. Her tone was as brisk and pleasant as always, but there was a note of concern under it.

"Hey, Masha," said Jez listlessly.

"Would you like to come in for something to eat? Tanya, as much as she's trying to hide it, is getting worried about you."

A twinge in Jez's stomach reminded her that she hadn't eaten yet today.

"It's—well past noon," said Masha, as if reading her mind.

Jez managed a small smile. "Tell Tanya I'll be fine. Just—just needed some time to think, is all."

Masha studied her for a few moments. At last, she shook her head. "Jez. I—don't know if this is the time for it, but—" she gave a rueful sigh. "I don't know that there will be a better time." She paused. "Would you come with me for a moment? I—my people found something, and they asked me to come look at it. I—thought you might like to come along. I don't know what it is, so I can't promise this will be good news, but I'm hopeful that at least they've found something ..."

Jez felt, suddenly, like she couldn't breathe, something squeezing her chest so tight it hurt.

Masha been asking around to find anything salvaged from the *Ungovernable.*

And seeing a lifeless remnant of her perfect angel ship might actually break her into a million pieces.

She wasn't sure she could bear it. But then, if there was anything they'd managed to salvage, she couldn't bear not to see it, either.

She took a deep, steadying breath. "Yeah," she managed, even though her heart was pounding so hard and fast she wasn't sure how she formed the words. "Yeah, sure. I'll come."

She stood slowly, her legs so shaky she had to cling to the railing for a moment.

She couldn't do this. She couldn't damn well do this.

She had to do this.

Masha was watching her with concern. "Alright. If you're sure you're ready." She paused a moment. "It's over by the government buildings, just one street down. In one of the hangar bays."

Jez followed Masha out of the apartment building and down the street.

Tanya had taken one look at Jez's face as they'd walked through the common room and had put down her armful of laundry and fallen into step with them, concern on her face.

Their pace was painfully slow, but they matched Masha's halting steps unconsciously.

Jez had to choke back something in her throat as they reached the line of sleek, soulless buildings that made up the government hangar bays.

It had been a place like this where they'd killed her angel ship, stripped her down and torn her apart.

The thought made her almost sick.

At least if she'd been shot down, her ship would have died at home, in the perfect black of deep space.

At least Jez would have died with her.

One brief, brilliant burst, and then gone, rather than walking around pretending to be alive while everything inside her was dead.

At the entrance, Masha turned to her, face lined with concern. "Jez. Listen to me. I—I'm not sure—"

There was something in her voice that sent a small jolt of terror through Jez.

But she had to see. If there was anything left of her angel, any piece, any scrap Masha might have salvaged—she had to see it. Even if it killed her.

Masha took a deep breath, shaking her head, and stepped inside.

A man in greasy mechanic's overalls came hurrying over and

flipped on the artificial lights. They groaned and buzzed to life, and Jez blinked for a moment in the unexpected brightness. She'd never been in a hangar bay where the lights actually worked like they were supposed to.

The man had pulled Masha to one side and was talking to her quietly, gesticulating at something behind him, and for a moment, a look of shock crossed Masha's face.

Jez sucked in a breath to steady herself and stepped reluctantly past Masha to see what exactly they'd found.

She made it two steps into the room.

And then she stopped.

She thought, for a moment, that every last damn tendon in her body had been cut.

She couldn't seem to pull air into her lungs.

There, in the middle of the floor, sat a familiar, graceful shape, sensuous curves gleaming, light reflecting off lustrous metal panels and gorgeous old-fashioned rivets.

The *Ungovernable*. Together, in one piece, just like the last time Jez had seen her.

She looked like she was straining against gravity. Like she was waiting to pull Jez back into the sky.

Jez had finally cracked, she must have. Or maybe she was dreaming. She had to be dreaming.

And when she woke up, her heart would actually break.

Behind her, she could hear, faintly, the man muttering some crap about, "—found this in one of the underground hangar bays that belonged to the Secretary General. His under-undersecretary mentioned it to one of our people, and I thought I should go check it out, and the moment I realized what it was—"

The words he was saying probably made sense, if you were

actually paying attention to them.

Jez wasn't. She wasn't honestly sure she'd ever pay attention to anything else ever again.

She could only stand and stare, the sight of her ship—or the mirage of it, more likely—like oxygen, when she'd been suffocating her whole life.

"Jez? Jez, speak to me."

It had to be a dream. She had to be dreaming this.

But, she realized suddenly, that didn't actually matter.

Maybe it was a dream. Hell, maybe she'd died after all, and this was heaven.

She didn't care. The only thing in the entire damn system that mattered was that right now, she was looking at her ship.

She took a step forward, the ground suddenly unsteady under her feet.

Someone grabbed her arm and said sharply, "Jez? Answer me, Jez!"

They were words, certainly, but Jez didn't have the time or attention right now to figure out what they meant.

She was going to pass out. She was going to faint.

She didn't actually give a damn.

Whoever had grabbed her by the arm was lowering her carefully to the ground. At least, she assumed that was what was happening, since she didn't fall over her the moment they took their hand off her arm.

"Head between your knees, Jez. Just breathe."

But if she was sitting on the floor, it meant she wasn't getting any closer to her sleek, gorgeous angel, which she was still coherent enough to realize was a problem.

She pushed herself to her feet, swayed, and almost toppled over.

Someone caught her arm a second time. "Jez!" they snapped.

A small part of her brain that was still paying a modicum of attention could hear the mixture of concern and exasperation in the tone.

"Jez, sit down before you fall down. Jez? Can you even hear me?"

The words were probably communicating some message, but she didn't have time for it.

She pulled her arm out of whoever-it-was's grasp, and almost fell over before they caught her again, and again lowered her to the ground.

"Tanya, some help here—" Masha's voice snapped.

Jez didn't care about any of it. She didn't care about anything in the entire damn system right now, except what was right in front of her.

She stumbled upright again.

Someone grabbed her other arm, and an amused voice said, in an outer-rim accent, "Jez, listen to me. You need to—"

Jez started forward like someone in a dream, and the person— Tanya, some vague part of her brain prompted—gave a resigned sigh and followed.

It was just as well, really. Tanya's hand on her arm was the only thing keeping her upright.

She wasn't sure she'd drawn a single breath since she saw her ship.

At the loading ramp, she paused for a moment.

"It's alright," came Tanya's quiet voice, still tinged with amusement. "It's real. You can go in."

Tentatively, hardly allowing herself to hope, Jez stepped onto the loading ramp.

It was firm under her feet.

She could feel the tears begin to well in her eyes.

She walked reverently down the familiar corridors, running her hand along the smooth wood paneling. The faint, musky-sweet smell of crystallized sap greeted her like the smell of a lover, and the small imperfections in the flooring fit against her feet like they'd been built for her.

She paused outside the cockpit door.

Something was choking off her breath and blurring her vision, which didn't even make sense, because she needed to see this again, needed to take in every single detail.

And then she slid the door open and stepped inside. And for the first time in days, she could feel herself coming back to life, a real actual person instead of a broken, empty shell.

Tanya let go of her, and she sank into the pilot's seat and ran her hands over the controls—perfect, smooth, and elegant, everything she'd ever dreamed of, that spoke to her through her fingers, obeyed her damn thoughts.

And then, finally, she put her arms down on the control panel, dropped her head into her arms, and sobbed.

She had no idea how long she stayed like that. She wasn't sure, at this point, if time still existed, or if she still existed. She felt, little, like she was floating, like the grav controls had all malfunctioned and there was nothing in the system to pull her back down. And she honestly didn't care.

At last, though, she became aware of a soft noise—the click and hiss of the door opening, footsteps. The presence of someone in the cockpit with her.

She drew in a deep, shuddering breath and blinked hard, wiping the sleeve of her jacket across her face.

When she looked up, Lev stood there, looking down at her.

He was smiling that soft smile, his eyes misty.

"Jez," he said quietly, and something deep and profound and joyful welled up inside her at his voice.

He looked around, a hint of wonder on his face, then dropped into the copilot seat. "It's been—" He cleared his throat. "It's been a long time."

"Yeah." Jez's voice was hoarse and rough from crying. "It's—it's been a long damn time."

He'd pulled up the holoscreen, running his fingers over it as if he, too, was greeting an old friend he'd thought he'd lost. When he looked up again, there was a quiet, unbridled joy in his face.

"Masha told me when I got back, and I came as quickly as I could," he said. "I—I'm glad you found each other again." His voice choked a little, like maybe he was blinking back tears, too.

"Yeah," she said softly. "Yeah, me too." She cleared her throat. "Um. I guess you had a pretty busy day, if you're just getting back."

He shook his head, still smiling that soft smile. "Not really. I walked over to the barricades, wandered around the university for a bit."

She raised an eyebrow. "Yeah? How was it?"

He looked back down at the holoscreen, a small, rueful smile on his face. "The—Minister of Education came to find me. Asked me if I wanted to be the university president, which honestly sounds like my worst nightmare. Then he … asked if I wanted to be a professor. Said they'd give me my pick of positions."

Jez stared at him for a moment, trying to push away the sudden jolt of panic in her chest.

He'd always wanted that. She'd seen how badly losing it had hurt him.

And dammit, she wanted to see him happy.

Maybe she'd do short runs, cargo runs. They could live in the university apartments again, and she'd come by whenever she was on-planet. Wouldn't be that bad, honestly, they could make it work.

She took a deep breath. "Well, guess they aren't all that stupid after all. At least they know a good thing when they see one." She paused a moment, her tone serious. "I'm—I'm happy for you, genius. I mean it. I got what I always wanted, and you got what you always wanted, and you're still the hottest scholar-boy I know, so I figure we can work this out."

He glanced up at her, surprised, and then smiled. "Jez. I—told him no."

Jez just stared, completely nonplussed.

"Genius," she said finally. "It's what you've always dreamed about. Look, I've got my ship back. Figure I can stand to be land-bound for a bit. I—hell, just knowing she's here is better than—than basically anything—" her words choked, and she reached out to stroke the control panel again. "Anyways. So, figure it's about time for you to get your dream, too, finally."

His smile widened, just a little. "Jez." He reached out, laying his hand across hers on the control panel. "I—appreciate you saying that. But—" he glanced around the small cockpit for a moment, and his eyes came to rest on hers. "That was my dream, once. But since then—" he shook his head. "Well, I guess I didn't realize how much I'd enjoy being a copilot."

For a moment, Jez was completely speechless.

And then the towering wave of happiness that had been cresting over her this whole time broke, and she was completely drenched in it, swimming in it, drowning in it—utterly, absurdly, ridiculously happy.

She jumped up, grabbed Lev, and pulled him to his feet, then took his face in both her hands and kissed him.

And whether it was the intoxicating joy bubbling through her, or the familiar, perfect feeling of being in the *Ungovernable's* cockpit, or simply the fact that it was Lev, and he was here, with her—the kiss, which had been basically just an impulse, hit her like she'd just tipped back a whole damn bottle of golden murder. She could feel her brain going fuzzy, her muscles going light and loose under his touch, the warmth and softness of his lips on hers washing pleasantly through her.

He leaned into the kiss with a soft moan, his hands sliding around the small of her back. Her heart was pounding an intoxicating rhythm in her chest, her breath coming far too quickly. He stepped in closer, his hand cupping the back of her head, twining in her hair, tipping her head back, his mouth moving against hers in a way that made her whole damn body tingle.

When they drew apart, she was gasping for breath, so dizzy she could hardly stay on her damn feet.

He was breathing hard as well, his hand still twisted in her hair, and she could feel the tension sparking through his entire body.

She gave him a wicked grin, untucking his shirt with a quick yank. She slid her hands along his waist, skimming the waistband of his trousers, caught his belt loops, and pulled his hips hard up against hers.

He made an incoherent sound, and the look in his eyes was enough to make her heart pound even faster. Then he leaned forward, his lips running along the line of her jaw and up the nape of her neck, his hands sliding up her back under her tunic. His hands on her skin sent a shiver through her whole body, and her knees had gone so weak she wasn't sure they'd still hold her.

Which, honestly, staying upright seemed a bit overrated at this point anyways.

She sank back into the pilot seat, pulling Lev down with her, and they landed in a tangle of arms and legs.

He tipped her head back, kissing down her throat, hands running down her shoulders and twisting in her hair, lips finding the soft hollows under her collarbone.

Everything in the entire world had gone soft and hazy and beautiful, and her brain fizzed and sparked like it was on fire, and she had just enough of her wits about her to hit the lever, pushing the seat back to recline.

Lev raised up on his elbows and brushed a bit of hair back behind her ear, his hand trailing gently down the side of her face.

"Jez," he whispered, and for a moment, she could hardly breathe for the thick, choking, overwhelming happiness welling up inside her.

She reached up, bringing his head close to hers, and bit down, hard, on the side of his neck.

"Jez—" he gasped, his voice much less steady now.

She pulled him down on top of her, and the sensation of his lips on her skin, the press of him against her, the warm urgency of his hands on her body—the *Ungovernable* beneath them, waiting to take them anywhere they wanted to go—sparkled effervescent in her brain and bubbled through her body, and the only thought left in her head was, what was the most efficient way of getting genius-boy's damn clothes off.

"Masha."

She glanced up. Tanya gave her a slight smile, and dropped the shop stool she'd fetched from somewhere down beside Masha, pushing it into position with her foot. "Sit, for the Lady's sake."

Masha sank onto it gratefully, wincing at the movement.

She closed her eyes for a moment, breathing deeply. Now that she was sitting, she wasn't entirely sure how she'd stayed on her feet until then.

"I'll go back and tell the others," said Tanya quietly. She slipped out the door, and Masha tipped her head back against the wall.

She was smiling, despite the small ache that still sat in her chest like a stone.

She still wasn't sure who she was, or what was left of her, now that she'd finished what she'd set out to do.

But the sight of Jez's face when she saw her ship—

She smiled to herself.

That was a reward in and of itself.

The door to the hangar bay clicked, and she straightened as Tae and Ivan stepped in.

They hardly noticed her, and there was a look on their faces, something about the way they stood together, holding hands, that sparked a warm happiness inside of her.

To think that once, she'd thought she'd be able to sacrifice these people for something she'd deemed more important.

She'd been such an innocent.

They stood hand in hand for a while, looking at the ship, Tae resting his head on Ivan's shoulder.

At last, though, Tae straightened, turning to her. "Masha," he said quietly. His voice was thick with emotion. "Thank you. For getting Jez her ship back." He paused. "I—assume she's in there?"

Masha gave him a wry look. "I assume so. Lev went in to find her a little while back. I—suspect they may be in there for a while."

Tae shook his head with a reluctant smile. "I'm glad she's happy, anyways." he paused again. "I—guess I didn't realize how good it would be to see the *Ungovernable* again."

"Have you two decided, then, what you're going to do next?"

asked Masha.

Ivan smiled, squeezing Tae's hand. "Not everything. But—we've decided a few things."

Masha didn't miss the "we," and she smiled to herself.

They deserved it, honestly.

"Well," said Tae last, reluctantly. "I guess we should probably get back to—"

There was a sound from across the hangar bay, and they turned to see Jez and Lev walking down the loading ramp.

From the look on Jez's face, she may as well have been floating.

"Hey, you plaguers," she said when she saw them. "Guess Masha told you. She—she got my damn ship back. I—" her voice choked, and Lev pulled her close and kissed her.

"It's—good to see her again," said Tae.

Masha sighed. "And, Jez, since I don't know that anyone could fly her the way you do—I suppose the *Ungovernable* is yours."

Jez stared at Masha for a moment. And then she smiled like her face would split in two, seeming entirely unable to speak.

At last, though, she took a long breath. "So," she said. "Guess I know what I'm doing tomorrow." She paused. "The rest of you figured out what you're going to do next?"

"Tae and I aren't entirely sure yet," said Ivan. "But we're thinking —"

"Wait, 'we're'?" asked Jez, grinning broadly. "As in, you and Tae? As in, you're going to—"

Tae gave her what was probably an attempt at a scowl, but he looked far too happy for it to be believable.

"Yes," said Ivan, glancing down at Tae, his eyes soft. "We are."

"You, Masha?" asked Jez after a moment, turning to her.

Masha shook her head. "I'm—still considering. But I'm certain I'll find something."

She wasn't certain, honestly. She wasn't sure how she'd find another purpose in her life, after everything that had happened.

She still felt, somehow, drained and hollow.

"And I guess Ysbel and Tanya are heading back to that planet of theirs to be dirt-eaters again."

"I—gathered as much," Masha murmured.

The door opened, and Tanya stepped through the door with Olya and Misko in tow.

The children glanced around the hangar bay, then their eyes went wide.

"We got the *Ungovernable* back?" Olya gasped. "Aunty Jez, we got the *Ungovernable* back!" She turned to Misko. "I get my old bed!"

"It's not fair! I want that bed!"

"I'm going to get there first!"

The children ran for the ship, pounding up the loading ramp, pushing each other and shouting about who was going to win.

Tanya looked after them, chuckling softly.

Ysbel, who'd stepped into the hangar bay after them, shook her head, smiling.

"Well," said Jez, with a sigh. "Guess I'd better go start getting my angel ready." She paused. "And—well, hell, lot of empty cabins on board, is all I'm saying. Don't know that we'll be doing much, probably just flying around raising hell, honestly. But, I mean, I could use a crew. If—if anyone wanted to."

Her voice was diffident, and there was a vulnerability in it that Masha hadn't expected.

There were a few moments of silence as they all looked at each other.

At last, Ysbel heaved a long sigh. "I suppose I should go get the luggage," she grumbled. "But it doesn't look like we'll need it all anymore, since there aren't streams to get soaked in in deep space."

Tanya's smile was slightly misty. "They seem to find ways to get dirty anyways."

Ysbel shook her head again. "I must be absolutely crazy." She turned to her wife. "Tanya. I promised you a farm. And now—"

"The farm will still be there," said Tanya, leaning up against Ysbel. "We can always go with the ship for a while. And if we want to go back—"

Ysbel put her arms around her wife and kissed her, a soft, contented smile on her face that seemed almost incongruous.

"And anyways," Jez continued cheerfully, "heard some rumours that a certain weapons dealer came up with a new piece of tech he was planning to sell to some gangster bastards on the outer rim. And, seeing as he's an old friend of ours, figured maybe a few of us could go see if we could talk him out of it. By which I mean," she added, unnecessarily, "rob him damn well blind."

Lev turned to her, looking suddenly apprehensive. "Jez. You're not —are you talking about—"

She winked at him. "Hell, your reunion with your parents went so well, figured it would be a shame not to pop in and see your uncle."

Lev's expression took on a tinge of resigned horror.

Tae sighed heavily and shook his head. "Come on, Ivan, we better get our things on board too, before Jez comes up with any other crazy ideas. Honestly, the last time I had to do tech work with Jez still gives me nightmares. I'm not going to be able to actually sleep at nights thinking of what she'll do to the tech on this ship without me along."

"Hell, tech-head, thought I did a pretty damn good job last time you and me worked together." Jez's grin was so wide it almost glowed.

Tae glared at her.

Ivan chuckled. "It's been a long time since my parents and my sister were on a ship anyways. If they have to come meet us somewhere to watch the ceremony, I suppose this would be a good excuse." He leaned over and kissed Tae.

"I'll be back with our things," Ysbel sighed, turning to the door. "It's a good thing the apartment is close."

Masha watched them go, smiling despite herself.

"Hey, you bastard."

She looked up, startled, to see Jez standing beside her.

"Yes, Jez?"

"You know your cabin's still open, right?" asked Jez quietly.

Masha hesitated for just a moment, trying to ignore the sudden tug of longing the words brought.

"I—I'm not sure I'd better," she murmured, trying to keep her voice steady. "I'm sure there are other things in Prasvishoni I'll be needed for. And besides—" she paused, and managed a wry smile. "I'm—not entirely sure what my contribution to the crew would be, now that we're no longer trying to overthrow a government."

"Masha." Lev had come up beside Jez, and there was something sincere and serious in his thoughtful gaze. "Whatever your decision is, I'll respect it. But—" he smiled slightly. "Prasvishoni will probably manage. And—the ship won't be the same without you. You're part of this crew. Overthrowing the government or not."

Masha looked at them for a long time. Her heart was pounding painfully, and she could feel something stinging at the corners of her eyes.

"Figure it's about time Zhenya had to do some actual work around the place anyways," said Jez with a grin.

Masha closed her eyes for a moment and had to swallow hard to keep her voice from catching. "Perhaps you're right. In that case I—I suppose I may as well come along."

Jez's grin widened even more, although Masha hadn't been certain that was possible.

"Good," the pilot said, her voice choking a little. "Good. I'm—glad." She cleared her throat. "Well, guess you better go get your crap then, unless you want Olya to take your cabin."

"I suppose I'd better," murmured Masha.

And she was startled at the simple, childish happiness that spread through her at the words, like the warmth of the sun on a summer day.

It was only a few hours later that they were gathered on the main deck. It had taken a surprisingly short amount of time for them to tie up their business in Prasvishoni—bid their farewells, pass along whatever information their friends and allies might need. Galina had assured them she'd find her own ride back to the former pleasure planet. Radic was going back with her, and, if Masha was any judge, he may have convinced Dmitri to come along so he could show him around.

Zhenya expressed regret at their leaving, but there was a sharp calculation in their eyes.

Still—

Masha smiled to herself.

She was very confident in the ability of her contacts to keep Zhenya under control.

And her contacts—her friends, really, although it still felt odd thinking of them like that—when she'd told them she was leaving, they'd simply nodded. As if they'd been expecting it.

The *Ungovernable* hummed, soft and almost inaudible, beneath her feet. Tae and Jez had checked the ship over thoroughly, and determined that she hadn't suffered any real damage during her adventure.

It was odd, how that feeling—that low hum that vibrated through Masha's bones—felt like home.

Jez grinned at them. "Everyone got your crap on board? Because this sweet angel is about to head for deep space."

"We're ready, you idiot," grumbled Ysbel, but she was smiling, her arm tightly around Tanya.

"Also," said Jez cheerily, "me and genius-boy are going to be in the cockpit. And we're locking the damn door, and none of you had better even think about trying to knock on it, because we're not going to damn well answer."

Lev turned, burying his face in her hair, and whispered something in her ear. From the look on his face, Masha concluded that not only did he have no objections to this course of action, he had been daydreaming about it for a very, very long time now.

Tae scowled. "I'm not sure why you'd think we want to come in, Jez," he muttered. "Some of us might be a little busy ourselves."

Ivan's face took on a sudden look of startlement, which changed rapidly into something approaching the look on Lev's face, and she could see his arm tighten around Tae's waist.

Masha caught the rueful look that passed between Ysbel and Tanya, and sighed.

"I suppose I could feed the children and put them to bed tonight," she said, to no one in particular.

Tanya smiled at her. "That would be—appreciated," she said.

Ysbel didn't say anything, just pulled Tanya in for a kiss that made Olya groan loudly.

"Well, I'd rather have Aunty Masha give us dinner anyways,

because it looks like everyone is just going to be kissing each other," Olya said in a tone of indignant disgust.

"Well, I like Aunty Masha," Misko muttered. "Even if everyone wasn't kissing each other all the time."

"Come on, children, pick out your pyjamas and lay them out so that Aunty Masha can find them," said Tanya, turning to the corridor that led to the cabins. "And I want you to strap down until we're out of the atmosphere."

Ysbel shot Masha a grateful glance, and followed her wife.

Jez had already started for the cockpit. "Better strap in," she called over her shoulder. "Even you, tech-head."

Ivan planted a quick kiss on Tae's forehead, and the two of them turned down the corridor as well, and Masha was left alone on the main deck.

She strapped herself in, although, from the look on Lev's face, it might be a few minutes before Jez found her way to the controls.

She looked around her at the small, comfortable space, with its cheerful old-wood paneling and eccentric design.

The vibrations from the ship grew ever so faintly stronger as they lifted gently off the ground. The hangar bay door in front of them slid open at Lev's command through the com. And then the ship shot forward. She heard Lev's startled exclamation, and the *thud* of someone hitting the floor, followed by Tae's muffled cursing.

Masha's stomach dropped as the ship cleared the city and streaked towards the horizon, and she closed her eyes and breathed in the sensation, at once unutterably familiar, and eternally unexpected.

She had, for the first time since she could remember, no plans, no agenda, no idea what the future would hold.

But for the first time since she was seven years old—she was home.

R.M. OLSON

***

THE END

422

ENJOYED THE BOOK?

I HOPE YOU'VE ENJOYED Attack Path, the ninth and final book in The Ungovernable series. Thank you for coming along on the journey! As Jez would say, it's been a hell of a ride.

I have a small favour to ask you: Would you please leave a review on Amazon? It may seem like a silly thing, but reviews are very important to authors like me, as they help other people find my book, which in turn helps me to keep writing. Even a line or two would be unbelievably helpful.

If you haven't read it yet, Zero Day Threat is the first book in the series.

And if you enjoyed The Ungovernable, you might also enjoy my new space opera series, Singularity. The first book is Redshift.

In the mean time, if you subscribe to my mailing list, I'd love to send you an exclusive short story prequel featuring Jez Solokov, *Devil's Odds.* I'll also let you know about future launch dates, giveaways, and pre-release specials. And I always love to hear from my readers, so feel free to drop me a note!

If you'd like claim your free short story and subscribe to my newsletter, head over to my website: www.rmolson.com

Also, feel free to connect with me on Facebook: https://www.facebook.com/rmolsonauthor

or Instagram: https://www.instagram.com/rolson_author/